WHAT YOU DON'T KNOW CAN KILL YOU

"What my husband does is a mystery to me," Marla said. "Don't you think that's odd?"

Marla chuckled humorlessly. "My whole life is odd, Nick. A husband who doesn't confide in me, a daughter who rejects me, a father who despises me and a brother-in-law who . . . who . . ."

"Who what?"

She couldn't admit it. Couldn't say the damning words— that she was attracted to him, that at his touch her knees went weak and her blood ran hot. "Who . . . bothers me. And yes, I do think it's all strange. Real strange. I just hope that I can figure it out soon before I go out of my mind."

"Or before you get killed," he said solemnly.

A chill ran through her blood. "Killed?" she repeated. She'd considered the fact that someone might be trying to murder her, but she'd always tossed off the idea, condemned it as her own brand of paranoia. To hear it from someone else made it so much more real.

Marla sighed and shook her head. "No way. This is too far-fetched. I was in an accident. Period. There wasn't anything sinister about it," she said, trying to convince herself. No one was really trying to kill her.

Or were they?

"Why would someone want me dead?" she asked.

"Because someone's afraid of you, of what you'll remember. . . ."

Books by Lisa Jackson

Stand-Alones

SEE HOW SHE DIES
FINAL SCREAM
RUNNING SCARED
WHISPERS
TWICE KISSED
UNSPOKEN
DEEP FREEZE
FATAL BURN
MOST LIKELY TO DIE
WICKED GAME
WICKED LIES
WITHOUT MERCY
YOU DON'T WANT TO KNOW

Anthony Paterno/Cahill Family Novels
IF SHE ONLY KNEW
ALMOST DEAD

Rick Bentz/Reuben Montoya Novels
HOT BLOODED
COLD BLOODED
SHIVER
ABSOLUTE FEAR
LOST SOULS
MALICE
DEVIOUS

Pierce Reed/Nikki Gillette Novels
THE NIGHT BEFORE
THE MORNING AFTER
TELL ME

Selena Alvarez/Regan Pescoli Novels
LEFT TO DIE
CHOSEN TO DIE
BORN TO DIE
AFRAID TO DIE
READY TO DIE

Published by Kensington Publishing Corporation

IF SHE
ONLY
KNEW

Lisa Jackson

ZEBRA BOOKS
KENSINGTON PUBLISHING CORP.

http://www.zebrabooks.com

ZEBRA BOOKS are published by

Kensington Publishing Corp.
119 West 40th Street
New York, NY 10018

Zebra and the Z logo Reg. U.S. Pat. & TM Off.

ISBN-13: 978-1-4201-3241-0
ISBN-10: 1-4201-3241-5

First Printing: October, 2000
30 29 28 27 26 25 24 23 22 21

Printed in the United States of America

ACKNOWLEDGMENTS

I would like to express my thanks and appreciation to all those people who helped me with the research and structuring of this book. Without their help it would not have been possible. Thanks to all my friends and family and special thanks to: Nancy Bush, Ken Bush, Matthew Crose, Michael Crose, Mary Clare Kersten, Nancy O'Callaghan, Michael O'Callaghan, Ari Okano, Kathy Okano, Betty Pederson, Jack Pederson, Sally Peters, Robin Rue, John Scognamiglio, Larry Sparks, Linda Sparks, Celia Stinson and Mark Stinson, who is dying to be a villain in one of my books. You're the best!

Prologue

Northern California, Highway 17

"It's the next car . . . she's coming in the next car, a black Mercedes coupe, an S500, traveling south, just as we planned."

Crouching low in the underbrush, with fog creeping over the wet earth, he strained to hear the anxious voice crackling through the static of his two-way radio. "I thought she drove a Porsche."

"She's driving a Mercedes," the voice snapped angrily. "You've got about ninety seconds."

"Got it." Eyes narrowed, he focused all his attention on the twisting road that cut through the canyons and hills in this part of California. Sure enough, through the mist and darkness, he heard the soft purr of a finely tuned engine. The car was, indeed, climbing. Getting nearer.

She was getting nearer.

His heart hammered. He remembered the scent of her skin. The look in her eyes. The depth of her betrayal.

She deserved this, the self-righteous bitch. He only wished she could know that he was the instrument of her death.

Adrenalin surged through his blood.

"Don't blow this. It's our only chance," he was instructed.

"I know. I know."

"It's worth a hundred grand."

A lot more than that, he thought but didn't say it. *A helluva lot more.* "I'll take care of it." He snapped the walkie-talkie off, slammed down the antenna and stuffed the headset into a deep pocket of his jacket. Sweat prickled his scalp and ran down his neck, though it was barely forty degrees in this stretch of woods. Slipping his ski mask over a face already painted black, he jogged through a carpet of wet leaves, his old army boots still sturdy, his camouflage suit a perfect cover in the mist-shrouded night.

Branches slapped his face. The air was dank and thick with the smell of wet earth and something else: His own fear. That he would fail. That somehow she would survive. That she would end up laughing at him.

No way. No fucking way.

Somewhere nearby an owl hooted, barely distinct over the pounding of his heart. And a rumble of low gears and a heavy engine . . . not that of the Mercedes. Coming from the other direction. The saliva dried in his mouth.

Steady, he reminded himself as he emerged from the woods at the designated bend in the road. He hoped to God that the truck was a few miles away and hurried across the wet pavement with the stealth of a SWAT team member. He checked his watch. Thirty seconds. The damned car sounded close. He gritted his teeth; saw a flash of headlights through the fog and trees.

Come on, bitch, just come on.

Louder, from the south, the truck—a semi from the sound of it—was gaining speed. *Shit.*

Crouching low on the narrow road, he positioned himself between the sharp S curves. Concentrating hard, he heard the whine of the coupe's tires singing on the wet pavement. *Hurry,* he silently urged, his eyes narrowing. *You can beat the truck. You have to.*

The car sounded closer.

Good.

He glanced at his watch again, the illuminated dial counting off his heartbeats. Everything was going as planned except for the truck. A few more seconds . . . He licked his lips in anticipation.

Brakes whined in the night. Too close. Too damned close. He swung his head southward, toward the oncoming roar. There was a catch in the eighteen-wheeler's engine as the driver shifted into a lower gear.

Every muscle tightened as he listened. He couldn't risk a witness. Sweat ran down his spine.

He could abort. There was still time.

But when would he get another chance?

A hundred grand. And just the beginning.

Besides, she deserves this . . . and it fucking fell into your lap.

The truck's engine growled loudly, reverberating through the forest of sequoia and oak. An eighteen-wheeler hurtling down the steep grade.

In the opposite direction, the Mercedes, if his information was right, was purring ever-upward, the driver innocently unaware that she was about to die.

His breath came in short gasps. *Slow down. Think of it as an exercise—just as you did years ago when you were with the special unit. You can do this. A few more seconds and you're home free.* His heart was a drum; his hands soaked in sweat beneath his tight-fitting gloves.

Twin beams rounded the curve from downhill. The truck's brakes squealed from uphill.

Now! He sprang, stood in the middle of the southbound lane. The sleek car accelerated, caught him in its headlights and swiftly he lifted the cover on his belt, exposing the mirrors he'd fastened to his torso.

The driver slammed on her brakes.

With a squeal, the Mercedes' tires locked. The car swerved to the right, hit the gravel on the shoulder and spun. He caught a glimpse of the driver, a horrified expression on her beautiful face as she screamed and desperately cranked on the wheel. There was another person—someone in the passenger seat beside her. *Shit!* She was supposed to be alone. He'd been assured she would be alone!

He jumped into the northbound lane. Avoided being hit by a speeding German-crafted fender by inches. Stumbled. Fell. The mirrors on his belt cracked. Glass splintered. Glittered in the headlights' glare. Hell. No time to do anything about it. Gasping, he was on his feet. Running. Toward the timberland.

Get out of here.

The semi rounded the corner, pinned him in its huge head-lights, flooding the wet pavement with near blinding light. He jumped and caught sight of the driver's panicked face. He was bearded, a big bear of a man, yelling over the scream of brakes. Eighteen thick tires screeched, burning rubber. The cab twisted, the truck jackknifed.

Oh, shit, oh, shit, oh shit! Run, you bastard!

Rolling over the guardrail, he launched his body into the protective cover of oak and redwood. He landed hard, his ankle twisted, the joint popping painfully, but he couldn't stop. Not now. His heart pumped furiously. Sweat poured down his face beneath the mask. From the corner of his eye he saw the Mercedes scraping along the guardrail on the far side of the road. Sparks flew. With an agonizing shriek, polished steel sheared.

He catapulted down the hill and heard the groan of metal rending as the car hit the weakened spot in the guard rail, then broke through, barreling through the trees.

As planned.

But the truck, the damned truck was out of control, careening down the hillside.

He was running now, his ankle screaming in pain, his lungs

on fire. The semi blasted down the hill. Tires locked. Metal shrieked. The entire forest shook as the big truck slashed through the guardrail, following his path, an angry metal behemoth chasing after him, tons of twisted metal chewing through the brush. His heart thundered, his legs pumped faster. The semi roared.

Run, run! His ankle hurt like hell, his lungs were about to burst.

He rolled, raced, ignored the agony of shredding tendons, while zigzagging through the trees. *Where the hell was it? His Jeep.* Where? Desperately he tried to avoid the path of the jackknifed death trap. He dived headfirst over a fallen log, then scrambled to his feet as berry vines clawed at his clothing. He hoped to hell he could get to the Jeep in time, start the damn thing and put some distance between himself and the wreckage.

The ground shuddered.

His feet flew out from under him, and he landed facedown on the ground.

In a blinding flash, a fireball shot upward from the trees, billowing bright red and orange. Night was suddenly day.

Tortured screams, horrid, agonizing sounds that would haunt him forever, pierced the night as the truck exploded and sparks showered the forest, raining down to singe his hair, ski mask and jacket. Smoke, smelling of diesel and charred rubber, spewed through the forest. For a second he thought he'd die.

God knew he deserved it.

Then he saw it. As if delivered from hell. In the fiery illumination he caught sight of his Jeep, blood-red flames reflected in its tinted windows. Parked just where he'd left it on the abandoned logging road.

Lurching to his feet, he unzipped his pocket, fumbled for his keys. He reached the rig and yanked open the door. He'd made it. Almost. Smoke clogged his throat as he threw himself into the Jeep's interior. He was shaking, his ankle throbbing as he twisted on the ignition and the engine caught. The forest was bathed in eerie light. He kept the ski mask on as a precaution and slammed the door shut.

Ramming the Jeep into first, he gunned the engine. Tires spun in the muddy tracks. "Come on, come *on!*" The Jeep lurched forward. Shimmied. Mud flew.

Shit, he needed a cigarette. Bad.

Finally the damned tires caught. He glanced into the rearview mirror and glimpsed the aftermath, fire and smoke billowing upward in the misty night.

She's dead. You killed her. Sent her black soul straight to hell.

And she fucking deserved it!

He snapped on the radio. Through the speakers, throbbing over the whine of the Jeep's engine, Jim Morrison's voice rocked out familiar lyrics.

"Come on baby, light my fire . . ."

Yeah, well, never again. The bitch wasn't ever going to light anyone's fire again.

Chapter One

She couldn't see, couldn't speak, couldn't . . . oh, God, she couldn't move her hand. She tried to open her eyes, but her eyelids wouldn't budge. They weighed a ton and seemed glued shut over eyes that burned with a blinding, hideous pain.

"Mrs. Cahill?"

Mrs. Cahill? There was a touch, someone's cool fingers on the back of her hand. "Mrs. Cahill, can you hear me?" The voice, kind and female, sounded as if it was carried from a great distance . . . far away, from a spot on the other side of the pain. *Me? I'm Mrs. Cahill?* That sounded wrong, but she didn't know why.

"Your husband's here to see you."

My husband? But I don't have . . . oh, God, what's happening to me? Am I going crazy?

The fingers were removed and there was a heavy feminine sigh. "I'm sorry, she's still not responding."

"She's been in this hospital nearly six weeks." A man's voice. Clipped. Hard. Demanding. "Six weeks for Christ's sake, and she's shown no signs of recovery."

"Of course she has. She's breathing on her own, I've noticed eye movement behind her lids, she's coughed and attempted to yawn, all goods signs, indications that the brain stem isn't damaged—"

Oh, God, they were talking about brain damage!

"Then why won't she wake up?" he demanded.

"I don't know."

"Shit." His voice was lower.

"Give her time," the woman said softly. "We can't be certain, of course, but there's even a chance that she can hear us now."

Yes, yes, I can hear you, but my name isn't Mrs. Cahill, I'm not married and I'm dying from this pain. For God's sake, someone help me! If this is a hospital, surely you have codeine or morphine or . . . or even an aspirin. The fog closed in around her and she wanted to give in to it, to feel nothing again.

"Marla? It's Alex." His deep baritone voice was much closer. Louder. As if he were standing only inches from her. She felt a new pressure on her arm as he touched her, and she wanted to let him know she could hear him, but she couldn't move, not at all. The smell of cologne assailed her, and she instinctively sensed it was expensive. But how would she know? The fingertips on her skin were smooth, soft . . . Alex's hands. Her husband's hands.

Oh, God, why couldn't she remember?

She tried to recall his face, the color of his hair, the width of his shoulders, the size of his shoes, *any* little trait, but failed. His voice brought back no images. There was a faint smell of smoke that clung to him as his sleeve brushed her wrist and she felt the scratch of wool from his jacket, but that was it.

"Honey, please wake up. I miss you, the children—" His voice cracked, emotion strangling him.

Children?

No! There was just no way she had kids and didn't know it. Or was there? That was the kind of thing a woman, even a woman lying drugged and half-comatose in a hospital bed would immediately realize. Certainly her intuition, the female animal in her would sense that she was a mother. Trapped motionless in this blackness she knew nothing. If only she could open her eyes . . . and yet the cozying warmth of unconsciousness was so seductive . . . Soon she would remember . . . It was just a matter of time . . .

Cold horror crept up her spine as she realized she couldn't conjure up one single instant in the years that were her life. It was as if she had never existed.

This is a nightmare. That's the only explanation.

"Marla, please, come back to me. To us," Alex whispered gruffly, and deep in her heart she wished she felt something, one smidgen of emotion for this faceless stranger claiming to be her life partner. His smooth fingers linked through hers and she felt pressure on the back of her hand, the pull of an IV needle stuck into her arm. Dear God, this was pathetic, a scene from a schmaltzy World War II movie. "Cissy misses you and little James . . ." Again his voice cracked, and she tried to drag up some tiny thread of tenderness from her subconscious, a tiny bit of love for this man she couldn't see and didn't remember. The void that was her past gave her no hint as to what Alex Cahill looked like, what he did for a living, or how he made love to her . . . surely she would remember that. And what about her children? Cissy? James? No images of cherubic toddlers with runny noses and flushed cheeks or gangly adolescents fighting the ravages of acne flashed through her mind, but then she was sinking. Maybe they'd finally put something in her IV as she felt herself detaching from her body . . . floating away . . . She had to focus.

"How long?" he asked, dragging his hand away from hers. "How long is this going to last?"

"No one can tell you that. These things take time," the nurse replied and her voice sounded far away, as if through a tunnel. "Comas sometimes last only a few hours or . . . well, sometimes a lot longer. Days. Weeks. No one can predict. It could be even longer—"

"Don't even go there," he said, cutting her off. "That's not going to happen. She *will* come around." His voice was like steel. He was a man used to giving orders. "Marla?" He must've turned to face the bed again as his voice was louder once more. Impatient. "For Christ's sake, can't you hear me?"

With every ounce of effort, she tried to move. Couldn't. It was as if she were strapped down, weighted to the mattress with its crisp, uncomfortable sheets. She could not even raise one finger, and yet it didn't matter . . .

"I want to talk to the doctor." Alex was forceful. His words clipped. "I don't see any reason why she can't be taken home and cared for there. I'll hire all the people she needs. Nurses. Aides. Attendants. Whatever. We've got more than enough room for round the clock, live-in help in the house."

There was a long pause and she sensed unspoken disapproval on the nurse's part . . . well, she assumed the woman was a nurse . . . as she struggled to force her eyes open, to move a part of her body to indicate that she could hear through the pain.

"I'll let Dr. Robertson know that you want to see him," the nurse said, her voice no longer coddling and patient. Now she was firm. Professional. "I'm not sure he's in the hospital now, but I'll see that he gets the message."

"Do that."

Marla drifted off again, lost seconds, maybe minutes. Her sluggish consciousness discerned voices again, voices that interrupted her sleep.

"I think Mrs. Cahill should rest now," the nurse was saying.

"We'll leave in just a minute." Another voice. Elderly. Refined. It floated in on footsteps that were clipped and solid, at odds with the age of the woman's voice. "We're family and I'd like a few moments alone with my son and daughter-in-law."

"Fine. But please, for Mrs. Cahill's sake, make it brief."

"We will, dear," the older woman agreed and Marla felt the touch of cool, dry skin on the back of her hand. "Come on, Marla, wake up. Cissy and little James, they miss you, they need you.'' A deep chuckle. ''Though I hate to admit it, Nana isn't quite the same as their mother.''

Nana? Grandma? Mother-in-law?

There was a rustle of clothing, the sound of soft soles padding across the floor and a door opening as, presumably, the nurse left.

''Sometimes I wonder if she'll ever wake up,'' Alex grumbled. ''God, I need a cigarette.''

''Just be patient, son. Marla was in a horrible accident, and then suffered through the surgeries. She's healing.'' God, why couldn't she remember? There was another long, serious sigh and a kindly pat of fingers on the back of her hand. A waft of perfume . . . a scent she recognized but couldn't name.

Why was she in the hospital? What kind of accident were they talking about? Marla tried to concentrate, to think, but the effort brought only an ache that throbbed through her head.

''I just hope there won't be much disfigurement,'' the old woman said again.

What? *Disfigurement?* Oh, please, no. *Disfigurement?* For a second she was jolted out of her haze. Her throat, already parched, nearly closed in fear and her stomach felt as if it had been twisted and tied with rubber bands. She tried to remember what she looked like, but it didn't matter . . . Her heart was racing with dread. Certainly someone somewhere watching her monitors could see that she was aware, that she was responding, but no loud footsteps pounded outside the door, no urgent voice yelled, ''She's stirring. Look, she's waking up!''

''She has the best doctors in the state. She . . . she might not look like what we expect, but she'll be fine, beautiful.'' Alex sounded as if he was trying to convince himself.

''She always was. You know, Alexander,'' the woman who called herself Nana said, ''sometimes a woman's beauty can be a curse.''

An uncomfortable laugh from this man who was her husband. ''I don't think she'd agree.''

"No, of course not. But she hasn't lived long enough to understand."

"I just wonder what she'll remember when she wakes up."

"Hopefully, everything," the woman said, but there was an underlying tension to her words, a pronounced trepidation.

"Yes, well, time will tell."

"We're just lucky she wasn't killed in the accident."

There was the tiniest bit of hesitation before her husband replied, "Damned lucky. She should never have been driving in the first place. Hell, she'd just been released from the hospital."

Another hospital? It was all getting fuzzy again, the words garbled. Had she heard it right?

"There are so many questions," her mother-in-law whispered.

Yes, so many, but I'm too tired to think of them right now . . . so very tired.

Whistling sharply to his three-legged dog, Nick Cahill cut the engine of the *Notorious* and threw a line around a blackened post on the dock where he moored his fishing boat. "Come on, Tough Guy, let's go home," he called over his shoulder as the boat undulated with the tide of this backwater Oregon bay. Rain drizzled from a leaden sky and the wind picked up, lashing at his face. Whitecaps swirled and danced in counterpoint to the seagulls wheeling and crying overhead. The distinctive odors of diesel, rotting wood and brine mingled in the wintry air of Oregon in November.

Hiking the collar of his jacket around his neck, Nick grabbed his bucket of live crabs and stepped onto the pier just as his dog shot past in a black-and-white streak. A shepherd mix of indecipherable lineage, Tough Guy hurled his body onto the slippery planks and, paws clicking, scrambled up the stairs to the parking lot on the bluff. Nick followed more slowly, past sagging posts covered with barnacles and strangled by seaweed.

"There's somebody here ta see ya," grunted Ole Olsen, the

old coot in the window of the bait shop located at the landing. He jerked his chin toward the top of the stairs but didn't meet Nick's eyes, just kept working at tying a fly, as he always did.

"To see me?" Nick asked. No one, in all the five years he'd been in these parts, had ever dropped by the marina looking for him.

"Ye-up. That's what he said." Seated on his stool, surrounded by lures and coolers holding bait and Royal Crown Cola, Ole was a fixture at the marina. A burned-out stub of a cigar was forever plugged into one corner of his mouth, a ring of red hair turning gray surrounded his bald pate, and folds of skin hid his eyes more effectively than the magnifying glasses perched on the end of his nose. "Told him you'd be out awhile, but he wanted to wait." He clipped off a piece of thread with his teeth, turned over a bit of orange fuzz covering a hook that looked suspiciously as if it would soon resemble a salmon fly. "Figured if he wanted to, I couldn't stop him."

"Who?"

"Never gave his name. But you'll spot him." Ole finally looked up, focusing over the half glasses. Through the open window, his face framed by racks of cigarettes, tide tables and dozens of the colorful flies he'd tied himself, he added, "He ain't from around here. I could tell that right off."

Nick's shoulders tightened. "Thanks."

"Enny time," Ole said, nodding curtly just as Tough Guy gave a sharp bark.

Nick mounted the stairs and walked across a gravel lot where trucks and trailers and campers were parked with haphazard abandon. In the midst of them, looking like the proverbial diamond sparkling in a pail of gravel, a silver Jaguar was parked, engine purring, California plates announcing an intruder from the south. The motor died suddenly. The driver's door swung open and a tall man in a business suit, polished wingtips and raincoat emerged.

Alex Cahill in the flesh.

Great. Just . . . great.

He picked one helluva day to show up.

"About time," Alex said as if he'd been waiting for hours. "I thought maybe you'd died out there." He hitched his jaw west toward the sea.

"Not so lucky this time."

"Maybe next."

"Maybe."

Alex's intense eyes, more gray than blue, flashed. "So you're still an irreverent bastard."

"I keep workin' at it." Nick didn't bother to smile. "I wouldn't want to disappoint."

"Shit, Nick, that's all you've ever done."

"Probably."

In a heartbeat Nick decided his mother must've died. For no other reason would Alex be inconvenienced enough to wear out some of the tread on his three-hundred-dollar tires. But the thought was hard to believe. Eugenia Haversmith Cahill was the toughest woman who'd ever trod across this planet on four-inch heels. Nope. He changed his mind. His mother couldn't be dead. Eugenia would outlive both her sons.

He kept walking to his truck and slung his bucket into the bed with his toolbox and spare tire. Around the parking lot, a once-painted fence and fir trees contorted by years of battering wind and rain formed a frail barricade that separated the marina from a boarded-up antiques shop that hadn't been in business in the five years Nick had lived in Devil's Cove.

Alex jammed his hands deep into the pockets of a coat that probably sported a fancy designer label, not that Nick would know. Or care. But something was up.

"Look, Nick, I came here because I need your help."

"You need *my* help?" he repeated with a skeptical grin. "Maybe I should be flattered."

"This is serious."

"I suspect."

"It's Marla."

Son of a bitch. Beneath the rawhide of his jacket, Nick's

shoulders hunched. No matter what, he wasn't going to be sucked in.

Not by Marla.

Not ever again.

"She's been in an accident."

His gut clenched. "What kind of accident?" Nick's jaw was so tight it ached. He'd never trusted his older brother. And for good reason. For as long as Nick could remember, Alex Cahill had bowed at the altar of the dollar, genuflected whenever he heard a NASDAQ quote and paid fervent homage to the patron saints of San Francisco, the elite who were so often referred to as "old money." That went double for his beautiful, social-climbing wife, Marla.

His brother was nothing but a bitter reminder of Nick's own dalliance with the Almighty Buck. And with Marla.

"It's bad, Nick—" Alex said, kicking at a pebble with the toe of his polished wingtip.

"But she's alive." He needed to know that much.

"Barely. In a coma. She . . . well, she might not make it."

Nick's stomach clenched even harder. "Then why are you here? Shouldn't you be with her?"

"Yes. I have been. But . . . I didn't know how else to reach you. You don't return my calls and . . . well . . ."

"I'm not all that into e-mail."

"That's one of the problems."

"Just one." Nick leaned against the Dodge's muddy fender, telling himself not to be taken in. His brother was nothing if not a smooth-talking bastard, a man who could with a seemingly sincere and even smile, firm handshake and just the right amount of eye contact, talk a life jacket off a drowning man. Older than Nick by three years, Alex was polished, refined and Stanford educated. His graduate work, where he'd learned the ins and outs of the law, had been accomplished at Harvard.

Nick hadn't bothered. "What happened?" he asked, trying to remain calm.

"Car accident." To Alex's credit he paled beneath his tan.

Reaching into his jacket, he found a pack of cigarettes and offered one to Nick, who shook his head, though he'd love to feel smoke curl through his lungs, could use the buzz of nicotine.

Alex flicked his lighter and drew deep. "Marla was driving another woman's car. Over six weeks ago now. In the mountains near Santa Cruz, a miserable stretch of road. The woman who owned the Mercedes, Pamela Delacroix, was with her." There was a long pause. A heavy, smoky sigh. Just the right amount of hesitation to indicate more bad news. Nick steeled himself as a Jeep with a dirty ragtop sped into the parking lot, bouncing through the puddles before sliding to a stop near the railing. Two loud men in their twenties climbed out and opened the back to haul out rods, reels and a cooler. They clomped noisily down the stairs.

"Go on," Nick said to his brother.

"Unfortunately Pam didn't make it."

A coldness swept over Nick. "Jesus."

"Killed instantly. There was another vehicle involved, a semi going the opposite direction. Long-haul truck driver. Charles Biggs. He'd been at the wheel sixteen hours and there's talk that he might have been on speed, meth or something. Who knows? The police aren't talking. The trucker might've fallen asleep at the wheel. No one knows for certain. Except Biggs and he's in the burn ward. Burns over sixty percent of his body, internal damage as well. It's a miracle he's holding on, but no one expects him to make it."

Nick wiped the rain from his face and looked out to sea. "But Marla survived."

"If you can call it that."

"Son of a bitch." Now Nick wanted a smoke. He shoved his hands deep into his jacket pockets and warned himself not to believe his brother. Being older and smarter, Alex had taken delight when they were children to play him for a naive fool. There had always been a price to pay. Today, he suspected, was no different. "So the guy fell asleep and the truck wandered into Marla's lane?"

"That's just one theory." Alex took a drag on his Marlboro. "The police and insurance companies are looking into it. Had the highway shut down. The vehicles never hit each other, at least that's what they think. The Mercedes ended up off one side of the road, the semi further down the hill on the opposite side. Both vehicles broke through the guardrails, both ended up smashed into trees, but the truck exploded before the driver could bail out of the cab."

"Damn," Nick muttered under his breath. "Poor bastard."

Alex snorted his agreement. "There've been detectives all over the place, asking questions of everybody, waiting for Marla to wake up and tell her side of the story." He scowled darkly at the waters lapping in the bay. "She could be charged with negligent homicide, I suppose, if she was the one who crossed the center line. I . . . I haven't gotten into the legalities of it all. Not yet. This . . . it's . . . well, it's been a nightmare. Hard on everyone."

That, Nick believed. If the situation hadn't been grim, Alex would never have made the trip. Hell. Rainwater ran down his face as he opened the cab door and reached inside, found the remains of a six pack of Henry's, ripped one from its plastic collar and tossed it to Alex, then popped the tab of a second for himself.

"If Marla does pull through—"

"If, Alex? If? She's the strongest, most determined woman I know. She'll make it. For Chrissakes, don't put her in the grave yet. She's your damned wife!"

A beat. Unspoken accusations. Memories that had no right to be recalled—seductive, erotic and searing with hot intensity. Nick's throat turned to dust. The wind slapped his face. He drank a long gulp while Tough Guy whined at his feet. But his thoughts had already turned the dark corner he'd avoided for years, the narrow path that led straight to his brother's wife. Forbidden images came into play, taboo pictures of a gorgeous woman with a lilting laugh and mischief in her eyes. He heard the gentle lap of the water against the dock below and the traffic on the highway, the dull roar of the sea pounding the coast on the other side of the jetty, the call of the seagulls, yet nothing was as loud as the thudding of his own heart.

Nick nodded to his brother, encouraging Alex to continue. Taking another pull from his can as he tried and failed to push Marla from his head. Rain dripped off his nose. He thought about suggesting they sit in the pickup's cab but didn't.

"*If* she makes it, there's a chance she won't remember anything or that portions of memory will be lost. I don't really understand the whole amnesia thing, but it's weird. Eerie." Alex smoked in the rain and seemed unaware that he was getting drenched. His brown hair was plastered to his head, his Italian leather shoes soaking up Oregon rainwater from the puddle collecting at his feet. "God, Nick, you should see her. Or maybe not." Alex's voice actually quavered and he hesitated for a second, sucking so hard on his Marlboro that the tip glowed red in the gloom. "You wouldn't recognize her. I didn't and I've lived with her for nearly fifteen years. Jesus." He shot a plume of smoke from one side of his mouth, popped the can of his beer and took a long swallow. "She was so beautiful . . . well, you remember . . ." Alex's voice cracked as if in deep pain.

Nick didn't believe him and, sipping his beer, tried to push aside the image of a woman who had nearly destroyed his life. He stared toward the suspension bridge that spanned the narrow neck of the bay and allowed traffic to rush along the rugged Oregon coastline, compliments of Highway 101, but in his mind's eye, he saw Marla . . . gorgeous, full of fun and laughter Marla. "Aside from the memory loss, will she be okay?"

"You mean other than the fact that she won't look the same?"

"Doesn't matter."

"It will to her."

Nick snorted. "You can afford plastic surgery. I'm talking about damage that would make it so that she couldn't function."

"We don't know."

"And she will regain her memory eventually?"

Alex lifted a shoulder and glanced toward the sea. "I hope so."

For a split second, a mere heartbeat, Nick felt a tiny prick of pity for his brother's wife.

"Time will tell."

"So they say."

"But she'll be changed."

"Too bad," he said sarcastically as he studied the water-saturated gravel and the muddy pools beginning to run in rivulets toward the cliff.

"It is."

Nick took one last swallow from his beer, crushed the can in his fist and tossed the crumpled empty into the back of his truck. Marla's image slipped on illicit wings into his mind again. Alex wasn't exaggerating. Marla Amhurst Cahill was a gorgeous woman. Seductive. Naughty. Sexy as hell. With silky skin that was hot beneath a man's fingers and a come-hither smile that put Marilyn Monroe to shame. She had a way of getting into a man's blood and lingering. For years. Maybe forever.

Nick turned sharply. "Cut to the chase, Alex. Why are you telling me all of this?"

"Because you're family. My only brother—"

"Bullshit."

"I thought you'd want to know."

"There's more to it." Nick was certain of it. "Otherwise you wouldn't have driven all this way and taken six damned weeks to do it."

Alex nodded slowly, the corners of his mouth pulled into a thoughtful frown. "She's . . . she can't talk, her jaw's wired shut and she hasn't woken, but she has moaned and tried to say a few words." He took in a deep, bracing breath. "The only one we understood was 'Nicholas.' "

"Give me a break." The breeze slapped Nick's face and he was angry.

"She needs you."

"She's never needed anyone."

"We thought—"

"*We?*"

"Mother and I and well, we ran it past the doctors, too. We thought you might break through to her."

"You and Mother," Nick growled. "Hell."

"It's worth a try."

Nick glanced to the waterfront where vessels clustered near the docks looked dismal, small sailboats with skeletal masts stretching upward like dozens of bony fingers in stiff supplication to an unheeding heaven. The thought of seeing Marla again stuck in his craw.

And burrowed deep in his mind.

Alex tossed his cigarette onto the gravel, where it sizzled and smoldered near an ancient Buick's balding tire. "There's something else."

"More?" *Here it comes,* Nick thought uneasily, and felt as if he'd been duped into allowing the family noose to slip over his head.

"I need a favor."

"Another one? Besides visiting Marla?"

"That's not a favor. That's obligation."

Nick shrugged. Wasn't about to argue. "Shoot."

"It's the business . . . what with the accident, I'm having trouble concentrating, spending all of my time at the hospital with Marla. When I'm not there, I have to deal with the kids."

"Kids? Plural?" Nick repeated.

"Oh, maybe you didn't know. Marla had a baby a few days before the accident. In fact, it happened the day she was released from the hospital." Alex paused, reached into his coat pocket for a handkerchief and mopped his face. "The baby's fine, thank God. Little James is doing as well as can be expected without his mother." Alex's voice held a touch of pride and something else . . . *trepidation?* What was that all about?

Nick scratched the stubble covering his chin, the tip of a

finger sliding over his scar, a war wound that he'd received at the age of eleven, compliments of Alex, and he sensed that there was a lot more to this story—stark omissions over which his brother had so easily slid. ''The baby wasn't with her?''

''No, thank God. Now he's home, with a nanny. As for Cissy, she's a teenager now and oh, well, you know how they are. She's pretty wrapped up in herself these days.'' Alex added quickly, ''She's upset that her mother's still in the hospital, of course, worried, but . . .'' He shrugged, and an expression of calm acceptance shrouded his patrician features. ''Sometimes I think she's more concerned over whether she'll be asked to the winter dance than whether her mother will survive. It's all an act, I know. Cissy's worried in her own way, but it's the same way she's always dealt with Marla.''

''This just gets better and better,'' Nick muttered.

''Doesn't it?'' Alex snorted, then sniffed and swiped his hair from his face.

''I'm surprised Marla had another baby—I didn't think she was too into kids.''

''She did grow up,'' Alex said, casting him a look.

But Nick found it odd that she would have another child so many years after the first. She was just too damned self-centered. Stubborn. Egocentric. A goddamned princess. He sniffed, looked down at his boat and thought that half an hour ago his only problem had been dealing with a lingering headache, the result of becoming too friendly with a bottle of Cutty Sark the night before. But this . . . shit. Nick squinted at the clouds rolling on the horizon.

Alex cleared his throat. ''So, look, Nick, the deal is that right now I need your help.''

''What kind of help?'' Nick asked suspiciously. The rough hemp of the Cahill family noose tightened around his neck as rain drizzled from the sky.

''You're a troubleshooter for corporations.''

''I was, once upon a time.''

''You still are.''

"No more. That was a while back, Alex. I've done a lot of things since. Now, I fish. Or try to."

Scowling, Alex swept a glance around the weathered marina, then to the bucket in the bed of Nick's truck. Alex didn't seem convinced. "A few years ago you brought several corporations back from the brink of failure and now, well, believe it or not, I could use that kind of expertise. Cherise and Monty aren't happy that they've been cut out of the corporation. They seem to think that since they're Cahills they should have a piece of the pie."

"Cherise and Monty. Great." Things had a way of going from bad to worse. It seemed to go with being a Cahill. He leaned against the truck and Tough Guy sat at his feet, looking up, expecting a pat on the head. Nick obliged.

"Yeah, well, all that mess with Uncle Fenton and his kids was supposed to have been cleared up long before I came on board," Alex said. "Dad dealt with his brother, but Fenton's kids seem to have forgotten that. At least Cherise has. She's the one squawking. Probably because of that damned husband of hers. A preacher. Christ. This is all ancient history. Ancient *fucking* history. Or it should be."

"Dad handled Fenton the way he dealt with everyone," Nick said, remembering the tyrant who had been their father. Samuel Jonathan Cahill had been a blue-nosed bastard if ever there had been one. "His way. Period."

"It doesn't matter. The point is Fenton was paid for his share of the corporation years ago. End of story. Cherise and Monty can bloody well take care of themselves. I've got enough problems of my own."

Nick had heard this argument all his life. He was tired of it, but couldn't help playing devil's advocate, especially where his brother was concerned. "You really can't blame them for being ticked off. They both thought they'd become millionaires, but their damned father pissed everything away."

"I don't *blame* them for anything. In fact, I don't give a shit about either one of them. Monty hasn't worked a day in his life and Cherise hasn't done much more except collect ex-husbands and turn into a religious nutcase. I've tried with her, even found this last one—a preacher, no less—a job. Shit, what a disaster that became.'' Alex swatted the air. ''Doesn't matter. I wish Cherise and Montgomery would both just pull a disappearing act. Permanently.'' He finished his beer in one disgusted swallow, then wiped his mouth. ''Christ, what a couple of leeches. Blood-sucking leeches.'' Alex stepped out of the puddle and leaned against the Dodge's dented fender. ''And if they feel slighted, well, as they say, 'them's the breaks.' '' There wasn't a smidgen of pity in Alex's voice. ''But it's too damned cold and wet to stand out here discussing them. They're just minor irritations.''

''They probably don't think so.''

''Tough. Besides, they're not the reason I came up here.''

''Marla is.''

''Partly.'' He met Nick's gaze.

''So now we're down to it, aren't we?'' Nick said as the wind shifted, whistling across the parking lot.

''Yeah, that's right. We are.'' Alex's voice was dead-earnest. All business. ''Cahill Limited needs a shot in the arm.''

''Or the head.''

''I'm not joking.'' Tiny white grooves bracketed Alex's mouth, and for a split second he actually looked desperate. ''And it wouldn't hurt you to show a little family solidarity. We could use it. Mother. Me. The kids. Marla.''

Nick hesitated.

''Especially Marla.''

The noose was suddenly so tight he couldn't breathe. Tough Guy scratched at the running board of the pickup and Nick threw open the door so that the wet shepherd could hop inside. But the decision had already been made. Both he and Alex knew it. ''I'd have to find someone to take care of the dog and my cabin.''

''I'll pay for any inconvenience—''

''Forget it.''

"But—"

"This isn't about money, okay?" Nick climbed into the cab, shoved Tough Guy to his spot near the passenger door and jabbed his keys into the ignition. Knowing he was making a mistake he'd regret for the rest of his days, he said, "I'll be there, okay?" Angry with himself and his fierce, misguided sense of loyalty, Nick added, "I'll look over your damned books, make nice-nice with Mother and I'll visit Marla, but you don't owe me a dime. Got it? I'm coming to San Francisco out of the goodness of my heart, and I'll leave when I want to. This isn't an open-ended deal where I stay on indefinitely."

"The goodness of your heart, now there's an interesting concept," Alex said, skipping over Nick's concerns.

"Isn't it?" Nick grabbed the door handle. Wind and rain lashed the cab. "That's my best offer, Alex. My only offer. I'll be there within the week. Take it or leave it." Pumping the accelerator, Nick turned on the ignition and didn't wait for an answer. The Dodge's engine coughed, sputtered, then caught.

Cross with the world in general and himself in particular, Nick slammed the door shut and flipped on the wipers. Nothing his brother could say would make any difference one way or another.

Like it or not, he was on his way to San Francisco.

"Hell," he ground out as the wipers slapped away the rain and he threw his pickup into reverse. Gravel sprayed and, on the bench seat beside him, Tough Guy nearly lost his balance.

"Sorry," Nick growled as he jerked the truck into first and glowered through the foggy windshield. Alex stood in the puddle-strewn lot, his wool coat catching in the breeze, his expression as dour as an undertaker's. Nick snapped on the wheezing defroster, then flipped the stations of the radio, but he heard only static.

He thought of Marla, and his gut tightened. He still wanted her. After fifteen years. *Fifteen damned years.* There had been more than a dozen women in his life since then, but none of them, not one woman had left the deep impressions, the scars upon his soul that she had. His gaze narrowed on his reflection in the rearview mirror. Harsh blue eyes glared back at him. "You're a fool, Cahill," he growled under his breath. "A goddamned fool."

Chapter Two

"Will Mom remember me?" an impertinent girl's voice demanded, and Marla strained to open her eyes. The pain had abated, probably due to some kind of medication, but she couldn't move her mouth. Her tongue felt thick and tasted awful, her eyelids were too heavy to open and she had no sense of time. She knew only that she'd floated in and out of this state of semiconsciousness, her mind a jumbled blur. But she wanted to see her daughter. Marla fought to lift a lid but couldn't.

"Of course your mother will remember you," her mother-in-law said softly, her sharp, staccato footsteps snapping loudly as she approached the bed, the soft chink of jewelry accompanying the scent of that same elusive perfume. "Don't worry."

"But she looks terrible." The girl again—her daughter. "I thought she'd be better by now."

"She is, but it just takes time, Cissy. We're all going to have to be patient." There was a tiny hint of reproach in the older woman's voice, almost a warning.

"I know, I know," Cissy said with a theatrical sigh.

In the past few days floating in and out of semiconsciousness, Marla had come to recognize the nursing staff, Dr. Robertson and her family members by their colognes, their footsteps, and their voices, though often she was confused, in that nether state between waking and sleeping, never knowing if she was dreaming or if the medication was keeping her mind foggy.

She had pieced together that the older woman, her mother-in-law, was Eugenia Cahill and that Eugenia's husband wasn't around, maybe dead or incapacitated or just not interested; at least he'd never been to visit that she could remember . . . but her memory was the problem. A major problem.

Her mother-in-law seemed sincere, caring and had visited often . . . or at least Marla thought she had. Cissy hadn't been here before . . . or had she? Marla couldn't remember. Then there was her husband. Alex. A stranger and a man she should feel some tender emotion for, yet didn't. Her head began to pound again, setting off a pain so intense it felt as if skaters were turning triple axels on razor-sharp blades in her brain. The powerful medication that helped her drift in and out of consciousness but kept her groggy definitely had its pluses.

"What if she doesn't . . . you know . . . remember . . . or the scars don't go away or . . . she's not the same?" Cissy whispered, and inwardly Marla cringed.

"You're worrying again. From here on in she's going to get better and better."

"I hope so," the girl said fervently, though there was a hint of disbelief in her voice. "Will she need more plastic surgery? Dad said she already had a ton."

"Just enough to repair the damage. Now, really, we shouldn't talk about this any more."

"Why? Do you think she can hear us?"

"I . . . I don't know."

There was a pause, but Marla sensed someone edging closer to her bed, felt warm breath waft over her and realized she was being studied much like a single-cell organism under a high-powered microscope. Again Marla struggled to lift a finger. If only she could indicate that she was aware.

"She can't hear nothing—"

"Anything, 'she can't hear anything,' is the proper way to say it," Eugenia was quick to reprimand.

"Oh, is it?" the kid countered, and Marla figured the girl was jerking her grandmother's chain. "I'll try to remember, okay?"

"Just remember, your mother's lucky to be alive after that nasty accident," Eugenia intoned. "And of course she doesn't look the same, but you'll see, once she wakes up and they take the wires out of her jaw and the swelling subsides, she'll be good as new."

"Will she be able to walk?"

Marla's heart nearly stopped.

"Of course she will. Nothing's wrong with her legs, you know that. As I said, she'll be fine."

"Then why doesn't she wake up?"

"It's what the body does to heal. She needs this rest."

Cissy snorted softly, as if she didn't believe a word her grandmother was peddling. "She never liked me anyway."

What! No way! What a horrid idea and a wrong one. So very wrong. It was just a teenager's warped perception. Surely she would like, no, *love* her daughter.

"Of course she likes you." Eugenia laughed nervously. "Don't be ridiculous. She loves you."

Yes!

"Then why did she want a baby so bad? A boy? Why wasn't I good enough for the both of them . . . oh, just forget it," she grumbled, moving away from the bed.

"I will because it's nonsense," Eugenia said as if through pursed lips.

There was a loud, long-suffering sigh as if the girl thought all adults in general, and her grandmother in particular, were idiots. "I don't know why I'm even in this family. I just don't fit in."

You and me both, Marla thought, though her heart went out to the girl. Had she been so cruel and thoughtless to her own daughter?

"You try hard not to fit in, but you, you just have to apply yourself. Everyone before you was an honor student. Your father went to Stanford and then to graduate school at Harvard and your mother was at Berkeley. I went to Vassar and—"

"I know, Grandpa was at Yale. Big deal. I wasn't talking about being a brainiac anyway, and what about Uncle Nick? Didn't he drop out or something?"

There was a tense moment. Marla sensed Eugenia bristling. "Nick took his own path, but let's not talk about him now," the older woman suggested. "Come on, it's time to meet your father . . ." Eugenia must have shepherded the girl out of the room, for Marla was left alone. She relaxed, heard a nurse enter the room, then take her pulse. A few seconds later that warm, familiar haze of comfort seeped into her veins, chasing away the pain, the anxiety, the fear . . .

She dozed for a time . . . how long, she couldn't tell . . . but she heard the door creak open then shut with a quiet but firm click. She expected one of the nurses to walk to the bed and say something to her, to try to rouse her, or at least fiddle with the pillows, take her pulse or temperature or blood pressure again, but whoever entered was uncommonly silent, as if he or she was creeping toward the bed.

Or wasn't in the room at all.

Perhaps she'd been mistaken, or dreaming, only thinking she'd heard the door open. Maybe no one had come inside. Her mind was so fuzzy. She should drift off again, but couldn't and she thought she heard the scrape of a leather sole against the floor. But . . . no . . . maybe not . . . then she smelled it; the faint tinge of stale cigarette smoke and something else . . . the smell of a wet forest . . . earthy, dank . . . out of place and, she sensed, malevolent . . .

The hairs on the back of her neck rose. Fear shot through her. She tried to cry out but couldn't. Tried to pry her eyes

open, but they stayed steadfastly and firmly shut. Her heart
was drumming madly, and surely she was hooked up to some
monitor. Some member of the staff would come running into
the room. *Please! Help me!*

Nothing.

Not one sound.

Her throat was dry as sand.

Oh, God, what was he doing here?

Why didn't he say anything?

Who was he? What did he want?

On nearly silent footsteps he backed away. The door clicked
open again then whispered shut.

She was alone.

And scared out of her mind.

"I know this is crazy," Nick said to Tough Guy as he threw
a couple of sweaters into his duffel bag. He walked through
his bedroom to the bathroom where he searched under the sink,
found his shaving kit and stuffed in his electric razor and a
stick of deodorant. From the bathroom door he pitched the kit
into the open bag.

The mutt was lying on a braided rug at the foot of his bed,
head on his paws, sad eyes watching Nick's every move.

"I'll be back," Nick said, as if the dog could understand.
"Soon." He found two pairs of jeans that he added to the
bundle. "Ole's gonna take care of you and you'll like that,
believe me. He's got a lady Doberman who is one helluva
woman."

Tough Guy wasn't interested.

"You'll be fine," Nick told the dog. "Better'n me." He
zipped up the duffel and took a quick look around. This cabin,
all of four pine-paneled rooms, had been more than his home;
it had been his sanctuary, a place where he'd found peace after
the rat race. Somewhere between adolescence and now, he'd
managed to rid himself of the chip that had been so firmly

attached to his shoulder, the burden of being a Cahill and living up to family expectations.

"It was all bullshit," he explained to the dog as Tough Guy got to his three feet and hobbled after him to the living room where the cold ashes of last night's fire lay in the stone grate and the smell of burnt wood lingered in the air. Nick scowled as he thought that he'd never really measured up to Cahill standards; his father had expected Nick to break free of Alex's shadow, to best his older brother.

Samuel Cahill had wound up disappointed. It served the bastard right. The old man could rot in his grave for all Nick cared.

The phone jangled and Nick swore. He considered not bothering to answer. Instead, he dropped his duffel bag on the floor and in three swift steps picked up the receiver on the second ring, then growled, "Hello."

"Nick?" a woman with a slightly agitated and whispery voice asked. "Nicholas Cahill?"

"Who's this?"

"Cherise."

His cousin. His heart sank. No matter what she wanted, it was bound to be bad news.

"Boy, you're a difficult person to track down. I almost had to hire a private detective to find out where you were." She laughed nervously.

"But you didn't."

"No . . . Directory assistance."

Nick scowled, sat on the edge of his corduroy couch. He pictured Cherise as he'd last seen her, with blond hair, pale gold eyes, and not an ounce of body fat on her tiny body. She'd had a perpetual tan, overdone her makeup, and had puppy-dogged after him when they were kids. He'd liked her then, before both she and he had found their own separate brands of trouble and drifted apart. The good times were over; had been for twenty years. "So, Cherise, how're ya?"

"I'm fine," she said in a voice that didn't instill confidence. "Actually, I'm wonderful these days. I've found the Lord."

Great, he thought cynically. Just damned great. "Is that right?"

"My life . . . my life's been turned around."

"I guess that's good." Nick wasn't religious, and didn't really think much about it; but if Cherise wanted to be born again, that was all well and good. She'd always been one to follow the latest trend. The way he figured it, if Cherise were proclaiming her love for the Son of God, Christianity must be in vogue.

"Yes, it is. I thank Jesus every day."

"And the kids?" He glanced out the window to the gray day.

"Oh, they're . . . fine. Good. Teenagers." She sighed theatrically. "The Lord certainly has his work cut out for him with those three, I'm afraid."

Nick waited. Pleasantries were over. Surely there was a reason she'd hunted him down. He hadn't talked to her in over fifteen years. There was a few tense seconds of silence and then she drew in a breath.

"I, um, I'm calling about Marla."

His gut tightened but he wasn't surprised. "I heard about the accident," he admitted. "Alex came to see me."

"Oh."

That caught her off guard, cut her short for a second. But Cherise was a quick thinker; she always landed on her feet.

"Well, we can all thank Jesus that she's alive."

Amen.

"Her friend wasn't so lucky," she went on. "Did you know Pam? Ever meet her?"

"Nope."

"Oh, well." A sniff of disapproval caused Nick to wonder about the passenger in the car. But then, he wondered about a lot of things when it came to his sister-in-law. "Listen Nick, I'm calling you because you're family and I thought you might understand. You and Marla, you were close once, and you know she and I, we always got along. I love her like my sister, well, if I had one and I . . . well, not just me, but Montgomery, too,'' she added quickly, as if her brother was an afterthought. "I . . . we'd like to see her. The problem is Alex won't allow it. He keeps insisting that she shouldn't have any visitors aside from *immediate* family.''

So there it was. He glanced at the old Seth Thomas clock that hung near the kitchen alcove. "Isn't she still in a coma?''

"I know, but I'd love to sit with her, read some passages to her. The Bible has a way of healing, you know.''

"As I remember it, Marla wasn't too religious.''

"It doesn't matter,'' Cherise said quickly. "Jesus hears all our prayers, *all* of them.''

Nick didn't comment.

"Anyway,'' she went on rapidly, like a train gathering steam. "I've been praying for her, you know. And . . . and Pam. And that poor man who was in the truck, the one with all the burns who they think won't make it . . .'' She paused for a second. "I'd just like to see her, Nick, just hold her hand and tell her I love her and remind her that the Lord loves her, too.''

"Maybe when she's better.''

There was a painful, long-suffering sigh and he sensed the gears turning in Cherise's mind. She was like a dog with a bone, never giving up, always finding a way to get what she wanted. Three husbands, all once-upon-a-time confirmed bachelors, were proof enough of her skills of persuasion. "Look, Nick, I assume you'll be coming to visit, after all you've known Marla . . . well, a long time.''

The insinuation was there, left dangling.

Nick gripped the receiver a little tighter and didn't dare wade into the treacherous waters of that particular memory.

"I'd thought *you'd* want to visit her,'' Cherise suggested, and Nick felt the undercurrents, the silent accusations, running through the telephone wires.

"Maybe,'' he hedged, leaning back on the couch, eyeing the

yellowed planks that made up the walls of his home. Tough Guy bounded onto a beat-up chair, caught Nick's glare and immediately jumped down to crouch under the coffee table and observe him through the glass top where rings from the previous nights' drinks still remained.

"Well, if you talk to Alex, *please* tell him I want to see her. Try and get him to understand that we're family. Despite anything that happened between our fathers, we're still all blood. Kin."

"That we are," Nick said, standing.

"So you'll talk to Alex?"

"Yep."

"Good. Good. Thank you. The Lord works in mysterious ways, you know."

"So I've heard." A trace of irony tinged his words as Nick managed to disentangle himself from the conversation and hang up. He picked up the glass he'd left on the table and deposited it in the kitchen sink. Tough Guy hitched his way across the old linoleum.

"I'll be back," he said to the dog again as he shouldered his bag and walked onto the back porch. Pausing to check that the shepherd had food, water and a bed in the corner of the porch, he locked the door. Tough Guy raced to the truck, but Nick shook his head. "Not this time, fella." He scratched the dog behind his ears, one of which was a little chewed-up, as it had been when the dog had limped, bloodied and half-dead, to his porch not long after Nick had moved in.

"Must've tangled with a raccoon or other dog," the local vet had said. The result was that the shepherd had lost a leg, saved an ear, and found a new home with Nick. They'd gotten along just fine.

Now, Nick straightened. "You stay out of trouble," Nick ordered as he climbed into the cab and started the engine. The sky was a somber shade of gray that matched Nick's mood to a T.

He jammed the truck into first and thought about Cherise's

call and her proclaimed faith. He supposed a little dose of that wouldn't hurt him right now. A little divine help would be appreciated, but he wasn't holding his breath. He glanced in the side-view mirror, caught a glimpse of the black-and-white dog watching him from the back porch and felt like he was leaving the only real family he'd ever known.

"Great," Nick muttered under his breath. He reached the county road that would lead him, eventually, to the Interstate. From there it was due south to San Francisco.

And to Marla.

There were voices, several hushed voices that she thought she knew as she rose to the surface of consciousness. The urge to sleep was strong, her mind thick and dull, but she struggled to open lids that refused to budge and forced herself to stay awake, well, as awake as she could.

"Yeah, he said he'd show up, but I really had to twist his arm," Alex was saying.

Who? Who's going to show up?

Alex chuckled, but the sound seemed forced. "He looks like hell, too. Really bought into all that counterculture, north woods look. You know, faded jeans, old shirt, baggy parka, shaggy hair, the whole nine yards. He hadn't seen a razor for more than a week, unless I miss my guess. He'd been out fishing or crabbing or something in a boat that looked about as seaworthy as a sieve."

"But he *is* coming," Eugenia said, returning to the point.

So her mother-in-law was in the room, too.

"He said he was, but who knows? He's not exactly dependable."

"You were at his place?"

"I stopped by, but he wasn't at the cabin. I tracked him down at what I would loosely call a marina." Again the mirthless chuckle.

"Why do you want him here?" Cissy asked, and Marla

realized for the first time that her daughter was also in the room. "Y'know, if you hate him so much?"

"I don't hate him, honey. I just don't . . . approve."

"Jeez, Dad, why do you care what he does as long as he's not bothering you?"

Good question, Marla thought, and felt herself drifting away again, the deep, comforting sleep that was so seductive pulling her under again, but no one responded and she felt a tension in the silence.

"Why won't anyone talk about him?" Cissy finally demanded. "Y'know sometimes it's like his name is a four letter word or something."

"It is," Alex said.

"So is yours," the girl said just loud enough to be heard.

"There's no reason to argue about it." Eugenia sucked in a soft breath. "Brothers don't always get along."

"Like with Grandpa and his brother?"

"Fenton, yes," Eugenia said stiffly. "And his children. Cherise and Montgomery, oh, I think he goes by Monty or something like that these days."

"Why aren't they part of the family anymore?"

"They don't want to be."

There was a snort of disbelief and Cissy said, "Uncle Monty called the other day. For Dad."

"I talked to him," Alex said with a trace of irritation that Marla didn't understand. But then there was so much that was beyond her comprehension, beyond her memory . . . she tried to move, to let them know that she could hear, but felt herself drifting away again.

"Okay, so what about Nick?"

Nick was the one they were discussing . . . the brother who hadn't finished college or high school or something . . . there was something she should recall about him, but her head was so thick . . . oh Lord, what was it?

"Doesn't Uncle Nick want to be in the family?" Cissy

pressed, refusing to be put off, her voice beginning to sound far away.

Eugenia said, "Oh, honey, you wouldn't understand."

"Try me."

A pause. Marla imagined Eugenia and Alex trading looks, wondering how much of the family's sordid past they could spill. "All right, Cissy," the older woman said quietly, "since you asked. In times of family crises, like this one with your mother, it just seems right for everyone to stick together and kind of circle the wagons, show signs of family unity."

"Circle the wagons against who?"

"*Whom*," her grandmother corrected. "Don't they teach you basic English at that school?"

"Okay, *whom*," the girl repeated. "So who are they—the bad guys? This doesn't make any sense. I just want Mom to wake up and be the same, okay? And . . . and I want her to look the same." Her voice rose an octave. "Look at her, I mean, she doesn't even look like herself." Cissy sniffed loudly, then cleared her throat and Marla's heart skipped a beat. If only she could say something to comfort her daughter, but she was so tired . . . "Nana, it's like . . . it's like you and Dad, you're both afraid of something or someone. I just don't get it."

Alex stepped in. "We're just worried about Mom, honey. That's all. But she's going to be all right. I've talked to Dr. Robertson, we just have to be patient. And there aren't any bad guys," Alex added, his voice surprisingly soft. Always before Marla had sensed a hardness underlying his words, but not this time, not while dealing with his daughter. "Nana was just using an analogy. Now, come on, isn't there a soda machine down the hall? Here's some change, run down there and get yourself a Coke or something."

Marla felt a stab of tenderness for this man she couldn't remember, but Cissy was having none of his platitudes.

"I think you're keeping something from me. It's because that woman was killed, right? That Pam woman died in the crash and Mom . . . Mom might be charged with murder or something, right? That's . . . that's why all the police are hanging around.''

Murder? What were they talking about? In a spurt of adrenalin, her mind cleared.

"Manslaughter. Not murder.''

What?

"Detective Paterno is only trying to figure out what happened. It was an accident, honey. No one was murdered. Your mom's going to be fine. She'll get better and come home, the police will ask her to tell them what happened and, I suspect, that will be the end of it.''

"Then why did you go and get Uncle Nick if it's not a big deal?''

"It's time Nick returned, okay?'' he snapped, then caught himself. "Now, here . . .'' There was the sound of jangling metal, keys or coins chinking softly. "Why don't you run down to the machine in the cafeteria and bring Nana and me each a soda. Slice or Sprite, or whatever they've got. Get something for yourself, too.''

A clink of change.

Marla expected another argument, but there wasn't much of one.

Cissy, grumbling under her breath, made her way to the door, her footsteps disappearing as the pain in Marla's head began to return with a vengeance.

The temperature in the room had dropped twenty degrees. *What was this talk of murder and manslaughter? Who was Pam? Oh, God, did I kill her?* Marla's heart raced, she felt sweat break out on the back of her neck. If only she could remember. If only she could ask questions and get some answers. If only she knew something!

"I hate to admit it,'' Eugenia said, "after all he is my son, but I'm starting to doubt if it was a good idea to insist that Nick come home.''

"Wait a minute. This was your idea.''

"I know, I know," she said as if shaking her head at her own folly. "I was upset with the accident and everything else . . . but there was that business between him and Marla."

What? What business? Marla tried to open her mouth but couldn't and though she was fighting the pull of unconsciousness, she felt herself being dragged under the weight to slip into the soft void of unawareness so overpowering she had to strain to hear the conversation.

"That was fifteen years ago."

"He never got over it."

"Of course he did, there were lots of women since." Alex sounded impatient. Edgy. As if the subject cut too close to the bone.

"None of those others lasted more than a few months. He and Marla—"

"I remember." Alex's voice was ice and Marla knew she should be concerned, but was sinking too quickly. "However we don't have much choice, now, do we? I told him she spoke his name and he agreed to come."

Did I speak? How? She didn't remember being able to say anything and she ached to communicate in any way possible. Marla had thousands of questions to ask her family, questions about the baby, her daughter, her life. She tried to say something, to cough, to get their attention . . . Why couldn't she speak? Her fingers curled in frustration.

"Did you see that?" Alex said quickly.

"What?"

"She moved. Look at her hand."

Yes! Yes! I can hear you! Do you understand?

"Get the doctor," Alex ordered. "Finally. Maybe she's finally waking up!" There was an edge of excitement to his voice.

Her throat tightened with the thought that she was loved by this man to whom she was married, a man she couldn't visualize.

"You mean she's heard our conversation?" Eugenia asked, an icy fear in her voice.

"I . . . I suppose so."

Then there was a silence, as if they were looking at each other, maybe mouthing words of caution, or just exchanging knowing glances.

Marla slowly let her hand relax and heard soft footsteps sidle to the bed. "Marla?" Alex asked, gently. "Honey, can you hear me? Just move your hand, sweetheart. Let me know that you're okay. God, I've missed you."

He sounded so sincere. She wanted to believe him. Oh, God, she wanted to trust that he loved her. He picked up her hand and held it in his.

"Squeeze my finger if you can hear me, darling. Come on. Give it a try."

Marla willed her fingers to move, but her hands were stiff, her muscles unable to bend or shift.

"I think . . . I think I felt something," Alex said.

"Good. Oh, maybe she's finally waking up." Eugenia's voice was closer. "Marla? Can you hear us, dear? Just nod, or open your eyes." A pause. Marla couldn't move, felt herself losing the frail hold she had on consciousness. "Honey . . . ?"

With a sigh of disgust, he let her hand fall onto the bed. "It's no use."

"Of course it is," Eugenia said calmly. "We just have to be patient. She'll come around."

"And if she doesn't?" Alex said coldly.

"Then . . . we'll have to adjust. All of us. It'll put a crimp on things, but it won't be the end of the world. Don't borrow trouble. You saw her hand move, felt her try to squeeze your hand. This is progress."

"If you say so," he grumbled, obviously disbelieving.

Bayview Hospital was one of the city's finest, or so he'd been told, but as Nick walked down the carpeted hallways where recessed lighting played on copies of famous pieces of art, and nurses, doctors and aides hurried by at a clipped, professional pace, his skin crawled. He'd never liked the feel of a hospital. Any hospital. The odors of antiseptic, talc from the latex gloves, and disinfectant burned in his nostrils. Piped-in music, meant to be soothing, scraped against his nerves, and the smiles of patients, visitors and staff all seemed tarnished and false. In Nick's opinion, not much good ever happened at a hospital. This one wouldn't likely alter his position.

But he was here. Like it or not. And he was going to do his damned duty.

Gritting his teeth he made his way up in the elevator to room 505 and found the door slightly ajar. Soft music—an instrumental version of an old Beatles piece—played from hidden speakers in the corridor that was surprisingly empty of nurses, aides or visitors. But then maybe his brother had segregated this wing for his wife; after all he was some kind of muckety-muck on the board of this hospital. Samuel Cahill, then his son Alex after him, had donated enormous amounts of money to Bayview's building fund, all through the Cahill Foundation. So, Alex could probably call the shots here when it came to his wife's care. Just the way Alex liked it.

Nick pushed the door open to the darkened room where a patient, Marla, he presumed, was lying in a hospital bed. She was alone. Alex hadn't shown up yet, but then, Nick was a few minutes early.

The room was pretty much standard. Polished metal bed rails reflected the dimmed illumination from a single fluorescent fixture recessed in the ceiling. An IV, like a thin sentinel, stood guard at her bedside, dripping glucose water and God-knew-what-else into her veins. Bouquets of cut flowers, boxes of candy, and potted plants gave splashes of color to the otherwise drab surroundings. Cards from well-wishers overflowed from a white wicker basket with a bright orange bow. Half-drawn blinds were slanted enough to cast shadowy stripes over the bed.

Gritting his teeth, Nick strode to the bed and felt like a damned intruder. Marla was lying on her back, her face bruised and swollen beyond recognition, her jaw wired. "Jesus," he whispered.

This was Marla?

His gut clenched. He'd told himself he was long over her, that the anger and pain of her betrayal had been buried years before, but standing over her as he did now, he couldn't help but feel a sliver of empathy for the pathetic creature who was his sister-in-law. Damn, she looked bad. Barely alive. Her head had been shaved on one side and there were visible stitches in the dark stubble.

His fingers curled over the rail. As he stared down at her he remembered the woman she'd once been, all the beauty and pure feminine allure that had been Marla Amhurst in that carefree time before she'd become Mrs. Alexander Cahill, before she ceased to be his lover and became his brother's wife.

The memories he'd locked away were suddenly unleashed and recollections of a young, long-legged, flirty woman who oozed sex appeal and knew it, came to mind. God, she'd been intriguing, with mischievous green eyes, haughtily arched brows and cheekbones that wouldn't quit.

Now she was reduced to this, a battered hospital patient, lying half-dead in a cold bed, hooked up to monitors and an IV, unaware of the world around her; a far cry from the woman who had snuggled under the rumpled covers of an iron bed in a cozy cottage in Mendicino and teasingly kissed the tip of his nose before giving him a naughty wink and slowly working her way downward.

"What happened?" he said, gripping the rails of the bed. "Damn it, Marla, what the hell happened?" Shaking his head, he dismissed his nostalgic memories. They were all lies anyway. She'd used him. Pure and simple. And he'd let her.

The damned thing of it was, he would probably do it again. In a heartbeat.

No matter how wretched she looked right now, in a drab cotton gown that she would have disdained as a rag, Nick had to remember the woman within. "How the hell did you end up here?" he whispered.

Behind her lids, her eyes moved.

Wasn't she supposed to be in a coma? The hairs on the back of his neck rose. "Marla?" he whispered, his throat nearly closing on her name. "Marla?"

Slowly, as if with all the effort in the world, her eyes opened a crack and then wider. She stared straight at him, impaling him with huge black pupils ringed by a tiny slice of green.

His heart jolted.

She squinted, blinked, but continued to keep him in her line of vision.

"I thought you . . . I'd better call a nurse or a doctor." His knuckles turned white as he gripped the rail.

She lifted a hand to touch his and struggled to speak, but her lips moved over teeth that were laced together with wires and the words when they came were muffled. Nonetheless they rang distinctly through his brain and touched a nerve.

"Who are you?" she demanded, eyebrows drawing down over those harsh green eyes.

So she didn't remember. A thorn of disappointment cut through his soul but he ignored it. His gut clenched. "I'm Nick."

She dropped her hand and gave off what he supposed was a sigh. Still no hint of recognition lighted her gaze. "Nick?" she whispered with obvious difficulty. "The . . . brother?"

So she did know. "I think you refer to me as an outlaw."

She didn't respond.

"You know, as opposed to in-law," he explained, lifting a shoulder. "Your in-law." Nothing registered in that swollen black and blue face. "It was a joke."

"A bad one." Her eyes began to close again. "A really bad one," she mumbled around the wires, her voice fading.

"I'll come up with something better next time," he said and she didn't respond. "Marla?" Oh, hell, she couldn't drift off again! The last he'd heard she hadn't woken up at all; that's what Alex had said on the phone earlier when he'd suggested they meet here in the hospital room, which, as it turned out, hadn't been such a hot idea.

He shoved his hands deep into the pockets of his leather jacket and walked out of the room in search of a nurse. Being alone with a woman who seemed to drift in and out of consciousness wasn't his idea of a party. Especially when that woman was Marla Amhurst Cahill. He glanced over his shoulder to the open door and saw her lying, unmoving, on the bed. She looked real bad. But, now that she was rousing and healing, that would soon change.

No doubt she'd be beautiful again.

Not that he cared.

What was the old saying? Once burned, twice shy? Well, he'd already been burned big time. This time he'd be shy—shy as hell.

Chapter Three

"I'm telling you she woke up, stared me straight in the eye and asked me who I was," Nick said, still unnerved. Leaning against the window casement in the sitting room of the hundred-year-old mansion where he'd grown up, he yanked at the collar of his shirt and glanced at his mother. "I was explaining what had happened to a nurse just as Alex flew in. Once I filled him in, I left. I figured he and his wife might want to be alone. They have a lot to catch up on."

"Well, thank goodness she's had a breakthrough," Eugenia said from her favorite high-backed chair. "I've been so worried, you don't know. This has been a nightmare, Nick, an absolute nightmare."

"It's not over yet."

"Oh, I know." She shook her head and not one strand of apricot-colored hair moved.

The phone jangled in another part of the house, but Eugenia didn't budge, just glanced toward the archway leading to the foyer of the house. Located on Mount Sutro, with a commanding view of the city and Bay, the gated estate with its imposing house—Craftsman rather than Victorian, he'd been reminded more than a dozen times—had been a source of pride to every member of his family. Except for him. He hated it.

The phone jangled sharply again, then became silent. "Carmen must have gotten it," Eugenia said. "Probably reporters or the police. Ever since the accident, they haven't left us alone. Some even camped out near the front gate for a while, until another more interesting story came along." She rolled her eyes. "I never thought I'd see the day when I was glad there was some political scandal afoot at the governor's office."

"The price of fame," he said.

"Yes, well . . ." She cleared her throat and fiddled with the strand of pearls around her neck.

Quick footsteps hurried down the hallway and within seconds a slim woman with shining black hair and almond-shaped eyes rounded the corner. Dressed in a crisp white blouse with the sleeves rolled up and narrow black skirt, she offered Nick a confident smile as she carried a cordless phone to his mother.

"It's Mr. Cahill from the hospital."

"Good." Eugenia took the proffered phone and waved her fingers in Nick's direction. "Carmen, this is my other son. Nicholas." She looked over the top of her glasses. "Carmen just about runs this place. What with everything that's going on, I don't know what I'd do without her."

Carmen smiled. "It's just part of the job," she said, pumping his hand with a surprisingly firm handshake. "Glad to meet you."

"Same here."

Eugenia was already speaking into the phone, her eyes, behind wire-rimmed glasses, focused on Nick. "Yes, but . . . Nick said . . . yes, well . . ." She let out a long, defeated breath. "I suppose you're right." For as long as he could remember his mother had deferred to a man, first to his father and then to Alex. He guessed it was happening again.

"Fine. Yes . . . you want to talk to him? . . . No? . . ." She shook her head in Nick's direction to silently tell him he was off the hook. For the moment. "That'll be all right, then. Yes. We'll be here . . ." She clicked off the phone and set it on a beveled glass table. Her lips twitching downward, she glanced at her watch. "He's on his way home from the hospital. Unfortunately, Marla didn't waken again."

"What?" Nick scowled. "Why not?"

"I don't know. Alex said she was totally unresponsive. Not only to Alex, but to the nurses and Dr. Robertson as well." Eugenia's shoulders drooped a bit and she stared out the window. "I suppose this is to be expected."

"Like hell."

She lifted a plucked, gray eyebrow. "Swearing won't help."

"Sure it will," he grumbled as Carmen, who had obviously been lingering on the other side of the archway, came back into the room.

"I didn't want to disturb you earlier when you were resting," she said to Eugenia as she picked up the phone and stuffed it into her pocket. "I took messages and left them on Mr. Cahill's desk in the den."

"Do you remember who they were?"

"Mrs. Lindquist again and Mrs. Favier."

"Cherise," Eugenia said icily. "Of course. Anyone else?"

"Someone from a newspaper and an attorney, a woman, who said she represented Mrs. Delacroix's estate."

"Wonderful," his mother said, the little lines around her mouth more evident as she pursed her lips. "Just what we need. Well, Mr. Cahill will deal with them when he gets home." She folded her hands in her lap. "Carmen, would you mind getting me some tea . . . Nick, anything?"

"Maybe later."

"It'll just be few minutes." Carmen flashed a quick smile and hustled toward the kitchen.

"Efficient girl, but we're going to lose her," Eugenia observed. "She's going to night school, studying to be a bilingual teacher. It was my suggestion that she continue her education, after I met her at Cahill House . . . well, you know about that.''

Of course he did. Cahill House had been established nearly a hundred years ago for girls who found themselves ''in trouble.'' A board of directors ran the philanthropic establishment and a Cahill had always been chairman of the board. Some things just didn't change. And that, in Nick's opinion, was the problem. Samuel had served on the board and now so did Alex. A large donation was made every year in the Cahill name.

''I wish people would quit calling. Everyone knows Marla's still in the hospital . . . oh, well, Joanna Lindquist's a friend, but a horrid gossip and I suppose you can't stop attorneys and then there's Cherise . . .'' Eugenia's eyes met Nick's. ''I assume that Alex told you that Fenton's children are coming around again.'' She rested her chin on her hand and Nick noticed the age spots, evidence that his mother wasn't too stubborn to grow old.

''I heard. Cherise even tracked me down. Wants to see Marla.''

''I'll bet. If she does, there's a reason behind it, let me tell you. I've never really believed in the old 'bad blood' theory, but those two are enough to change my mind.'' She pushed herself out of her chair and walked stiffly to the window where Nick was sitting. ''Well, there's nothing I can do about it. Alex will have to deal with Monty and Cherise. If they want to sue us, so be it. They haven't a leg to stand on.'' Straightening the hem of her suit jacket, she added, ''They're like vultures around a dying lamb, you know.''

''Except no one's dying,'' he said, making sure he caught her drift.

''Not yet,'' she teased with a deep chuckle as she took her chair again and Carmen brought the tea service, poured Eugenia a cup and, after asking if she needed anything else, left.

''Tea?'' Eugenia asked, as there were extra cups on the tray.

''No thanks. I think I need something stronger.''

''Help yourself.'' She took up her cup.

"Later." Nick walked to the fireplace and from beneath Eugenia's chair came a low, nervous growl.

"I wondered when she'd come to life," his mother said, then leaned over the arm of her chair. "Coco, hush!"

A little scruff of a white-haired dog stuck its nose out of the shadows. Glittering black eyes regarded Nick with distrust. Again the tiny beast growled.

"Just ignore her," Eugenia advised. "Coco's all bark and no bite." She let one hand trail off the arm of her chair, her manicured nails tracking through the dog's fur, her gold bracelets clinking softly. "You're just a coward, deep inside, aren't you?" she asked in a higher pitched voice, then glanced at her son again.

"So, where are your bags?"

"On my way back from the hospital, I took a room at the Red Victorian."

"Oh, for the love of St. Mary, you checked into a hotel? When your family lives just up the hill?" Eugenia threw up a hand as if she couldn't understand what went on in her younger son's head. "You can stay here, in your old room."

When hell freezes over, Nick thought. This place held too many ghosts from his past, and soon Marla would be returning. He glanced around the sitting room. A few new chairs had been thrown in with the antiques and period pieces he remembered. This house had survived two major earthquakes as well as the rigors and tests of several generations of Cahills. The shake and brick walls, pitched roof and original windows exuded old money and San Francisco elegance at its finest. Or worst.

Nick wasn't certain which.

He felt no sense of homecoming in this behemoth with its chandeliers that dripped cut glass and glittered against hardwood floors that gleamed with the soft patina that only comes with age and the scuff of expensive shoes. Carved paneling, painstakingly tooled by a meticulous German immigrant over a hundred years earlier, had darkened with age.

Yep, it was quite a place. If you liked a house that seemed to have no soul.

The front door opened and Alex strode into the foyer. He dropped his briefcase on the lowest step of the staircase. Yanking off his gloves, he glared through the archway at his brother. "You said Marla was awake," he accused, his gray eyes harsh and disbelieving.

"I said she woke up and stared at me, said a few words and fell asleep or whatever you want to call it again." Nick wasn't about to be intimidated.

"Well, she never so much as moved while I was there and I stayed over an hour." Alex unbuttoned his coat. "Dr. Robertson told me waiting around was futile. They'll call if there's any change." Tossing his coat over the banister, he walked into the sitting room. "Helluva thing, isn't it?" He reached into his jacket pocket and pulled out a pack of Marlboros. "After over six weeks of nothing, not one solitary sign of life, Marla opens her eyes, speaks to *you*, then relapses into a coma. All in the five minutes you were there." Alex crammed a cigarette into his mouth and, with a click of his lighter, lit up.

"It's a start, Alex. Just be patient." Eugenia set her cup in its saucer, then stood as Alex planted an obligatory kiss against the smooth parchment of her skin. Even in four-inch heels, she was a head shorter than her sons. Her apricot-tinted hair was fixed in place, her suit—always some designer suit—impeccable, without so much as a wrinkle.

"Be patient? Hell, I have been!" Alex yanked on his tie and shot a stream of smoke from the corner of his mouth. Raking stiff fingers through his hair, he grumbled, "Christ, it's frustrating. Frustrating as hell." He leaned a shoulder against the mantel where gilt-framed pictures of the family cluttered the mantelpiece. Resting one arm on the smooth oak, he let his fingers dangle toward the grate. Smoke from his cigarette curled lazily towards the ceiling. "This is a disaster," he whispered in a voice that was barely audible. "A goddamned disaster."

Nick said, "I thought you said she woke up once before."

"No." Alex shook his head, drew hard on his cigarette and his lips twisted as if at a private irony. "She whispered your name, but she never regained consciousness that I know of. Her eyelids didn't so much as flutter. It . . . it was like some kind of weird dream she was having."

"Dream?"

"Or something. I don't know. I'm just sick of this." Alex massaged his forehead with his fingertips. "Hell, I want a drink. You?" He nodded toward his brother and crossed the room to a rosewood cabinet with beveled mirrors across the back. Inside were the finest blends of Scotch, bourbon and rye whiskey that money could buy. Alex dug a ring of keys from his pocket and unlocked the antique cabinet.

"Maybe we should wait at the hospital," Nick suggested.

"Nah. They said they would call." Alex threw a look over his shoulder, and the first hint of a smile tugged at the corners of his lips. "The nurse kinda threw me out again. I guess I was being . . . a little what did she call it . . . 'unfeeling and argumentative,' yeah, that was it. The upshot was that I pissed her off. So what do you want?" he asked Nick.

"Scotch. On the rocks."

"Mother?"

"Nothing for me," she said tartly, but then she'd always been a little bit of a teetotaler, never imbibing more than a glass of wine, which, Nick assumed, was a direct response to their father's deep-seated love affair with gin. She held up her cup. "This'll do."

"Did you talk to the doctor?" Nick asked.

"Yeah. I met with Phil Robertson in the hospital room—before I pissed off the nurse. He thinks that Marla's coming around. It might be hours or days, he couldn't say, but, and this is important," he extracted a couple of bottles, "when she does wake up and all her vital signs are normal, Robertson will release her." With a flick of his wrist, Alex twisted open the cap of a new bottle. "I've already got a live-in nurse and a relief nurse waiting."

"Good news all around," Nick said, trying to keep the sarcasm from his voice as he stared through the window at the lights of the city. Rain spattered the glass, drizzling in rivulets that inched down the panes and smeared the view.

"It's not good news, Nick. But it's the best I can do." Alex looked older than his forty-two years. Weary. Sick of the whole damned mess. He clinked a couple of ice cubes into the bottom of an old-fashioned glass engraved with the family crest, a ridiculous symbol of Cahill self-indulgence. A hefty splash of Scotch followed and within seconds the drink was deposited into Nick's hand.

"To better days." Alex took a long swallow from his glass and some of the strain around his eyes seemed to ease as the liquor hit his stomach.

"Amen," Eugenia agreed, her eyes shaded with disapproval as Alex finished his drink in one swallow.

"A helluva homecoming, isn't it?" Alex said. "Marla in the hospital, another woman dead, a trucker burned and hanging on by a thread, a new nephew you haven't met yet and the family business in trouble."

His mother offered him a smile that was somewhere between tenderness and crafty calculation. "Whatever the reason, it's good to have you back, Nicholas."

He took a sip of his drink. The smoky Scotch slid down his throat as easily as water, an acquired taste he'd been told, but one he seemed to have been born with.

"So tell me about Marla's accident," Nick suggested, as Alex turned his attention back to the bar and poured himself another stiff shot.

Nick was edgy. Marla had been awake; he'd seen it with his own eyes. It seemed as if they should be doing something, *any*thing rather than sitting around this stuffy room and sipping drinks. "What exactly happened that night?"

"We assume Marla and Pam Delacroix, a friend she'd met recently, were going to visit Pam's daughter down at UC Santa Cruz as they were headed that direction. It was just over six weeks ago, right after James was born. The day she was sup-posed to come home from the hospital. Why she decided to leave then, is beyond me.'' Alex frowned into his drink, study-ing the amber depths as if he were a fortune-teller reading tea leaves. ''Anyway, she just met Pam, got behind the wheel for God-only-knows-what reason, and took off. It was a nasty night. Fog and rain. And that stretch of Highway 17 is treacherous. It winds through the mountains. Lots of accidents all the time. Somehow Marla lost control of the car. No one knows why. Maybe because she wasn't familiar with Pam's Mercedes. Any-way the road was slick and wet and the car slid along the guardrail, finally broke through at a weak point and hurtled over the cliff. Pam was killed instantly. Wasn't wearing the seat belt. Marla barely survived. Crashed her head on the side window, fractured her jaw in three places, lacerated the hell out of her face, but the air bag inflated and she didn't end up with any other broken bones or internal injuries. She even lucked out with her teeth—none broken.''

''I doubt if she'd consider that lucking out,'' Nick argued.

Alex finished his cigarette and tossed the butt into the fire-place. ''The result was the broken jaw, a concussion, and a broken nose. Bad enough, when you get down to it, especially with the coma. The police identified her from the hospital bracelet that she was still wearing at the time of the accident—she must've forgotten to take it off.''

''That doesn't sound like Marla.'' The woman Nick remem-bered was always fastidious about her looks.

''Maybe she was upset. Who knows?'' Alex walked to the bar, poured himself another shot or two. ''The left side of her face is pretty mangled, but the surgeons are optimistic. They've already done a little reconstruction, to keep her face symmetri-cal, and she'll probably want more once the wires are off and she wakes up.'' He shook his head at the magnitude of it all.

Nick shifted from one foot to the other. Why the hell didn't the hospital call? This standing around and doing nothing was driving him nuts. Nick glanced at his mother calmly sipping tea, her eyes cast on the edge of the Oriental rug where Coco was lying, chin resting between her white paws, her wary black eyes fixed steadily on Nick. "I think I should shove off—"

Footsteps sounded on the stairs and Cissy, dressed all in black, burst into the room. "I thought we were going to see Mom," she said, stopping dead center when she spied Nick.

"Cissy, this is Nicholas. You remember him, don't you?" Eugenia asked.

All petulant lip and suspicious eyes, Cissy gave him a quick once-over. "Don't think so."

"It's been a long time," Nick said, giving the kid an out. "Maybe ten years."

She shrugged. Obviously didn't care. "Are we going or what?"

"As soon as we hear from the hospital. Nick, here, said she woke up and talked to him. But I stopped by to see her and she'd lapsed back into the coma."

"What? Can she do that?"

"She did it."

"No way." Cissy blinked hard. "I mean, once you wake up, you wake up, right?"

Alex downed his drink and touched her on the shoulder. "Dr. Robertson thinks it'll be soon now."

"He's been saying that ever since the accident." Cissy looked from one adult to the next, searching their faces, expecting to find lies. "This is nuts!" She dropped onto a camel-backed sofa of pale green velvet. "I just want her to wake up and everything be the way it was."

"That's not going to happen," Alex said with more tenderness than Nick would ever give him credit for.

"Why'd this have to happen?"

"Cissy, we've been over this. It just did." Alex's nerves were beginning to fray and Nick was surprised. His brother had always been a cold, level-headed bastard; someone who could handle any situation with surprising calm. An old girlfriend, the one before Marla, had once accused him of having ice water rather than blood running through his veins. Alex, at the time, had considered it a compliment.

But tonight he was shaken. Big time.

Maybe he really does care about Marla. Maybe he'd married her because he loved her, not because he was only interested in besting his brother.

"I could be at the ranch right now," Cissy complained.

Eugenia snorted contemptuously. "You have school tomorrow. And it's raining."

Cissy muttered "Big deal" under her breath and stared out the window. The girl reminded Nick of a house cat sitting on a windowsill, tail switching, eyes focused on the birds sitting on a branch just on the other side of the window pane.

The phone rang and Alex jumped, strode around the corner to the foyer and grabbed the receiver before the second ring. "Alex Cahill. Yes . . . good, good . . . wonderful. We'll be there directly." He slammed the phone down. "About time," he growled as he reentered the room.

"Mom?" Cissy asked, and some of her fake snotty teenage attitude melted into the woodwork. Without her sneer and the mistrust in her expression, she was pretty and probably would blossom into a beauty. Like her mother. "Is she okay?"

"Let's hope so," Alex said but managed a smile. "That was the hospital. It looks like she's finally rousing."

"Thank God," Eugenia said as she rose to her feet and Nick felt a mixture of relief and trepidation. "Fiona and Carmen are here to look after the baby, but I'd better let them know what's going on." She marched quickly to the back of the house.

"We'll take the Jag," Alex said, reaching into his pocket for his keys.

"I'll drive my own rig." Nick didn't wait for any further arguments. He needed his own set of wheels, his "out" if things got too intense in the hospital. There just wasn't any telling what would happen when Marla finally came around.

* * *

She opened one eye a crack but the shaft of piercing light forced her to shut it again. Her headache was a low throb, and the pain in her jaw more pronounced. She was vaguely aware of some music, a tune she should remember, floating in the air around her.

"Mrs. Cahill?" a soft female voice said.

That name again. Oh, God, why did it seem wrong? Her eyelids fluttered open and she winced against the blaze of light, then realized the lamps were turned down low, the blinds drawn, the room semidark.

"Do you know where you are?"

Marla nodded. Her mouth tasted terrible, her skin itched from lying in bed and her hair felt stringy, her scalp gritty. Good Lord, she must be a sight. Slowly, the blur that was the nurse's face came into focus.

"This is Bayview Hospital, and I'm Carol Maloy." The name tag on her pale blue jacket verified the information with an RN tacked on. Tall and blonde with crystal blue eyes, she offered a smile of straight white teeth. "Glad to have you with us."

Marla swallowed against a throat as dry as sand.

"So, how do you feel? Are you thirsty?"

With more effort than it should have taken, Marla managed to nod, but Nurse Maloy had already turned away and returned with a glass of water equipped with a straw. "I suspected you'd be waking up today, just had a feeling. We'll start with this, then move on to juice if you really want to go wild."

With the nurse's help, she managed to suck up some water. It tasted like heaven as it slid past lips that felt cracked and dry, through the wires binding her teeth and down her parched throat.

Her stomach clenched. Threatened to upheave.

As if anticipating the action, the nurse said, "Whoa. Slowly. Just sip, okay? You've been out for quite a while now. It's going to take your body a while to adjust to being among the living again.''

Marla took her advice, sipped slowly. Her head began to clear.

"See, you're getting the hang of this already!" She took Marla's temperature. "Nasty things, those wires," she prattled on, "but necessary, I'm afraid. The good news is you won't have to deal with them too much longer. Maybe a week or two." She took Marla's blood pressure and pulse with the quick efficiency of someone who could strap a cuff around someone's arm in her sleep. "I've already called Dr. Robertson and he'll be down to see you shortly." She hung the blood pressure cuff on the wall. "He's called your family."

Her family. The people without faces. Maybe now she would remember them.

"Would you like to sit up?"

"Yes," Marla said, glad for a change in position. Any change. The nurse showed her the bedside controls and the head of the bed elevated enough so that she could see the rest of the room. It was small, efficient and would have been sterile had it not been for the profusion of bright, fragrant flowers crammed onto every available surface while boxes of candy and unopened packages were stacked on a shelf near the closet. Cards overflowed from a basket on a bedside table. "Your mother-in-law wanted you to wake up to all this, just so you knew how much you were missed," Carol explained as she listened to Marla's heartbeat with her stethoscope. "Normal, I'm afraid. Temperature, blood pressure, pulse . . . all normal." She pocketed the stethoscope, then picked up a pair of wire cutters that were lying on the table with the water glass, pitcher and a box of tissues. "These probably seem out of place, but if you ever, ever, think you might vomit, page us immediately and start clipping the wires in your mouth as if your life depended on it." She was instantly sober. "Because it does. We don't want you to choke or suffocate."

Marla shuddered, horrified at the mental image that came to mind.

"Not a very pleasant thought, I know," the nurse said, as if she'd read Marla's mind. "And in all likelihood, nothing's going to happen, but I just thought I'd let you know."

"Better safe than sorry," Marla guessed.

"You got it." The nurse jotted some quick notes on her chart. "Okay, everything looks pretty good. I'll get the juice and have someone give you a bath in bed, okay? As soon as the doctor says it's okay, we'll get rid of some of the tubes running in and out of your body and let you clean up." She winked again, then swung through the door.

Marla couldn't wait to be free of this prison. She sipped the water and looked around the room. A window offered a view of a parking lot, and farther away stretched an expanse of green water, probably part of the Bay, considering the name of the hospital. She reached over and thumbed through the cards left at the bedside, reading them and wondering who the people were who had signed their names. Bill and Sheryl, Gloria and Bob, Joanna and Ted, Anna, Christian, Mario. Not one rang a bell, but then neither did her own. Marla Amhurst Cahill. Dear God, why did she wear the name like a pair of oversized shoes?

Her head was throbbing and as she set the water glass on the table and leaned back in the bed, she suddenly remembered a face, a man's face. Rugged and rough-hewn with tanned skin, chiseled features, and thick black eyebrows on a ledge over intense, laser blue eyes.

Her throat tightened at the memory.

There had been something about him that was unnerving and rough; an edge about him that she'd sensed. He'd joked, but hadn't smiled. He'd been in this room and he'd said he was Nick. The outlaw . . . That's what he'd called himself. And there was something about him that had been . . . distrustful or sinister; she'd sensed it even in their brief encounter.

Her pulse pounded. He hadn't been lying. He'd looked like

some sort of twenty-first century Jesse James with his leather jacket, tanned complexion and jeans.

But this was crazy. She was a married woman. She had only to look at her left hand to prove it. There, winking under the dimmed lights, wrapped around her third finger was a ring that glimmered with diamonds set deep into a wide gold band. Her wedding ring. Staring at the shiny piece she remembered nothing about the day it was placed on her finger or of the man who had presumably said "I do," and slipped it over her knuckles.

Think, Marla, think!

Nothing.

Not a clue.

She wanted to scream in frustration.

Looking at the band was not unlike staring into Nick Cahill's eyes. No quicksilver flashback of another time and place, not one glimmer of recollection, no reaction other than a keen sense of curiosity. About the man. About her marriage. About her children. About herself.

"So you did wake up." A tall man wearing wire-rimmed glasses and a white lab coat had pushed open the door and was walking inside. He wore a pencil-thin moustache that set off his thin face. Completely bald with too many teeth crammed into a small mouth, he said, "Do you remember me?" then must've read the dismay in her eyes. "Don't worry about it. Amnesia sometimes follows a coma . . . it should clear up." His smile was meant to instill confidence. "Just for the record, I'm Dr. Robertson." He leaned down and shone a penlight into her eyes. "How do you feel?"

"Awful," she admitted. No reason to sugarcoat it.

"I imagine. Any pain in your jaw?"

"Tons."

"Your head?" He was eyeing the top of her crown.

"It aches like crazy."

"We'll get you something for it. Now, tell me about your memory."

"What memory?" she asked, trying not to wince as he moved his light from her left eye to the right.

"That bad?"

She thought, and even the act of concentrating increased the pressure in her head. "Pretty bad. Saying I was foggy would be optimistic." She forced the words out through teeth that felt clamped into cement.

He leaned back, clicked off his light and folded his arms over his thin chest. "Tell me about yourself."

Wow. She thought. Dig deep. "It's . . . it's weird. I know some things, like, oh, I can read, understand, think I'm pretty good at math, but I don't remember taking it. I think I like horses and dogs and the beach and scary movies . . . but . . ." She swallowed the lump forming in her throat, and forced her lips to move around her immobile teeth. ". . . I don't remember my family, not my children, not my parents, not even my husband." Her voice was failing her and tears filled her eyes and she felt absolutely pathetic, a sorry, needy creature without a past. She tried to grit her teeth but they were already locked shut.

"Just remember, this isn't abnormal," he said with a comforting glance as he double-checked her vital signs, then tested her reflexes. "Here, now hold on to my fingers and squeeze as hard as you can," he said, holding up the index finger of each hand. She gripped for all she was worth. "Good, now release." He made another note on her chart. "As for your memory, it should return. Your brain took quite a shock with the concussion and you've been comatose for a while." He flashed her a grin. "But everything should come back to you."

"When?" she demanded, desperate to know that she would be all right.

"Unfortunately, I can't predict that." He frowned and shook his bald head.

Well, it had better be soon, she thought, *or I'll go out of my mind—or at least what's left of it.*

"I wish I could."

"You and me both."

"You'll have to be patient. Give yourself time to recover."

"Why do I think I'm going to get tired of hearing that?" she asked and he shrugged.

"Maybe you know yourself better than you think."

"That's the trouble, doctor," she said, looking him straight in the eye. "I don't know myself at all."

True to her word, the nurse had bustled into Marla's room, given her a quick sponge bath, and straightened the sheets. She'd just breezed out the door when Marla's family arrived en masse. Smiles, hugs, kisses that seemed strained were rained upon her by strangers. All strangers. Marla forced a grin she didn't feel and tried like crazy to remember these people, only to fail. Just as their voices had seemed foreign to her, their faces sparked no memory whatsoever.

"It's so good to see you awake and have you back with us," her mother-in-law said, dabbing at her eyes with the corner of a handkerchief. A petite woman with apricot-shaded hair and small even teeth, she wore high heels that matched her purse, a gray wool suit, pearl-colored silk blouse and a print scarf in tones of red and gold.

"Thanks."

Eugenia cleared her throat. "That big old house has been empty without you."

Marla's heart melted.

Cissy, her daughter, planted an obligatory kiss on her cheek and backed away. She was tall for her age, slender, and dressed from head to toe in black. Her skin was somewhat tanned, sprinkled with a few pimples that her makeup didn't quite hide and her eyes were rimmed in thick, black mascara. "Hi," she offered up tentatively.

"Hi backatcha." It was all Marla could do to wrap her lips around the words. *This girl* was her daughter? Why didn't she feel something, have any inkling of a memory of . . . anything? Where was the motherly tug on her heartstrings—the lightning quick flashes of images of giving birth, or of diapering Cissy as an infant, or recollections of skinned knees, the loss of a baby tooth, or the heartache of watching her daughter suffer from her first adolescent crush? Surely all those events had happened, but Marla had no memory of her life at all. It was almost as if she was dead inside. And it was scary. Scary as hell.

"I knew you'd wake up!" Alex's voice boomed across the room. She turned her head, bracing herself for another blank slate, but as she laid eyes upon her husband, she had a faint sense that she'd seen him before—an elusive image that nudged at her brain then scampered back to the dark netherworld that was her memory. "Oh, honey, it's so good to see you again." Dressed in a navy blue suit and an overcoat that was unbuttoned, the belt ends stuffed in his pockets, he was tall and strapping, with gray eyes and a smile as wide as his jaw. He reached over the bed rail and hugged her fiercely. "I . . . we've . . . we've missed you." His voice was deep and he smelled of smoke and some kind of musky aftershave. Holding her firmly he planted a soft, fervent kiss upon her cheek.

She felt absolutely nothing for him.

Nothing.

Oh, God, she couldn't be this hollow. This unfeeling. Tears burned in her eyes and blurred her vision. Reaching up, she held him close, wanting desperately to feel some twinge of tenderness, some sense of belonging, of loving him, but she could only hope that, soon, she would remember. *It takes time,* she told herself, but was frustrated at the thought. She wasn't given to patience, Marla realized, and along with a smidgen of gladness for divining something of her personality, decided that it might not be such a good trait.

The phone rang sharply and every one of Alex's muscles tightened. "I told the hospital that you weren't to get any calls," he said, extricating himself from her and reaching for the receiver. As Cissy sat braced against the air-conditioning unit under the window and Eugenia plucked some dead blossoms from a Christmas cactus, he picked up the receiver.

"Hello . . . Hello? Is anyone there . . . shit!" He slammed the receiver down.

"Was no one there?" Eugenia asked and Marla felt a shiver of dread.

"Wrong number," Cissy said with a bored expression.

"Not when the calls go through a switchboard." Alex rubbed his jaw and his eyes darkened thoughtfully as Eugenia stopped plucking the brittle pink blooms. "I'll check on that. Have there been any other calls?"

"No . . . well, not that I remember, but then I don't remember too much." She offered what she hoped would pass for a smile.

He sighed. "We heard. We talked to Phil . . . your doctor . . . Robertson before we came up to see you. He warned us that you might be amnesic for a while. The good news is that it should be temporary."

"Should be," she repeated on a note of sarcasm. "Let's hope."

"Don't worry about it." He leaned over and kissed her forehead. "You just concentrate on getting better. Phil thinks you'll be able to come home in a couple of days."

She thought she'd go out of her mind if she spent another day lying around doing nothing. "No. I want to go home now."

"Of course you do. But it's impossible."

"Why?"

"I think he wants to run a couple of routine tests. Your vital signs, that sort of thing. No big deal."

"A big enough deal to keep me in here," she snapped.

"You just woke up, honey," he reminded her.

"But I want to go home," she repeated. "Now."

No one said a word. Alex glanced at Eugenia, who had moved from the Christmas cactus to a vase of flowers and was removing the dead roses and dropping them into a small wastebasket near the closet. Cissy suddenly found the parking lot interesting and stared out the window, avoiding eye contact with both her parents.

"Listen, dear," Eugenia stepped closer to the bed. The woman who had been teary-eyed moments before was suddenly all steel and determination. "When you're better, you'll come home, of course you will, but right now you need to concentrate on getting well." She touched Marla's hand gently, but her eyes, behind her wire-rimmed glasses, silently commanded her not to say a word, as if there was some secret they all shared, a secret that didn't dare be voiced, here, in the hospital, and Marla felt a new sense of dread.

"Where . . . where's my baby?" Marla asked.

"At home. We couldn't bring him here. The pediatrician's orders," her mother-in-law said and her gaze softened a bit. "You'll see him as soon as you get home."

"And when will that be?"

"Soon, honey. When the doctor releases you. He's just as anxious for you to go home as you are to get there. We've known Phil and his wife for years." Alex's voice was meant to sound kind, but there was an undertone she thought she heard and she wondered if he was placating her; keeping the truth from her. There was something about him that just didn't ring quite true.

Or maybe you're just paranoid!

"We have? Then why did he introduce himself as Dr. Robertson?" she asked, trying not to feel paranoid, but beginning to sense that the entire world was against her. Dear God, maybe she was going crazy. Hadn't she thought she'd sensed someone at her bedside, an evil presence . . . for the love of God, was she losing her mind? Sweat dampened her palms and her nerves were jangled, yet she couldn't stop herself from asking, "Why didn't he call himself Phil? Say something?"

"Who knows? Probably out of a sense of professionalism. He has to keep up a certain sense of decorum. He probably just puts on his—" Alex held up his hands, signing air quotes with his first and second fingers—"'doctor face' when he's at the hospital."

"It's odd, if you ask me."

"Maybe so, but there it is."

This was getting her nowhere, and she was tired. Weary. Feeling as if she was running in circles on legs made of lead.

As if sensing her despair, Alex hugged her again. "I know this is confusing and exhausting and you still feel like hell," he said and again she felt the sting of tears. "But slow down, give yourself time. You're going to be fine," he whispered into her ear and she wanted to believe him, to trust that. Oh, God, if only he was looking into a crystal ball and foretelling her future rather than offering her platitudes to ease her mind. Swallowing her anxiety, she wrapped her arms around his neck and looked over his shoulder to the doorway. The man she'd seen earlier, the outlaw, stood apart from the rest of the family, his jaw dark with a day's growth of beard, one shoulder propped against the door frame.

Beneath black eyebrows that had slammed together, Nick stared at her.

He didn't so much as smile, didn't offer any words of encouragement. Instead, he folded his arms over his chest, his leather jacket creaking and stretching as he observed the tender scene between husband and wife through his narrowed, jaded eyes. What was it he witnessed? What caused his square jaw to clench so hard?

Suddenly she had to know what she looked like, how everyone else saw her. Was it what had happened between them, or her appearance now? She yanked her gaze from his and silently called herself a dozen kinds of fool. "Is there a mirror over there anywhere?" she asked.

For a second, no one said a word.

"Don't either of you two have one?" Marla's gaze moved from her mother-in-law to Cissy.

"A hand mirror?" Eugenia shook her head, apricot curls unmoving under the overhead light. "Well, only in my compact."

"Could I see it?"

"I don't know if that's such a good idea . . ." Eugenia was

nervous and Marla realized she must look worse than she imagined.

"Is it that bad?"

"No, dear, but—"

"Give her the mirror," Nick cut in.

She glanced his way again, saw an emotion akin to anger dart through his gray-blue eyes. "Yes, get it. Because if you don't, I swear I'll climb over the rail of this damned bed and crawl to the sink and its mirror if I have to." She flung a hand toward the cabinet mounted above the basin, then pushed the button that elevated the head of the bed even higher.

"But your IV and, well, you're still . . ." Alex gestured to the bed and she realized that he was probably indicating her catheter and urine bag hidden discreetly under the sheets.

Heat washed up her cheeks and she groaned inwardly, then squared her shoulders. "I don't care."

"Give it to her." Nick's lips were blade thin.

Eugenia swallowed hard. "Well, I suppose it's only a matter of time before you're able to get up anyway, but remember, you're still healing and soon you'll look much better and . . ." She started riffling through her little purse. "Oh . . . here we go." She withdrew a shiny gold compact and handed it to Marla.

Cissy winced.

Eugenia stiffened her shoulders.

Alex turned away.

Only Nick's posture didn't change. He continued to watch her as, with trembling fingers, Marla snapped the compact open and stared into the tiny mirror.

Oh, God, she thought, sucking in air through teeth wired shut. It was worse than she'd imagined. Not only was she bruised and swollen, discolored in shades of yellow-green and pale purple, but the face staring back at her was that of a stranger.

Chapter Four

Watching Marla, Nick gritted his teeth. With the hand not attached to an IV, she gently touched her face, her fingers tracing the bruises and scabs, even the stubble over the part of her head that had been shaved. To her credit, she put on a brave show, not giving in to tears that he suspected were just beneath the surface. She swallowed hard and tenderly fingered a row of stitches that showed through the fuzzy growth of new hair. "Oh, God," she whispered, blinking several times before finding some grit and visibly stiffening her spine. "I . . . I don't think I'd even pass as the Bride of Frankenstein . . . you know what they say, always a bridesmaid, never a . . ." Her words were mumbled, said with difficulty. She tried to smile, but failed and her chin trembled ever so slightly.

Nick could barely watch this woman he'd sworn to hate, the one who had used him, betrayed him, and ended up his brother's wife.

"It'll be all right," Alex said, taking the compact from her hand and snapping the gold case shut. "Just give yourself time."

"That's right. In a couple of months, you'll be yourself and you'll laugh . . . well, at least put this behind you," Eugenia forced a grin that showed a hint of gold fillings. "We all will."

"I will *never* laugh about this," Marla shot back.

"None of us will." Alex shot his mother a warning look.

Nick silently agreed. In his estimation, the truth was better than false hope and the facts spoke for themselves: Marla Amhurst Cahill had nearly died and right now she looked and probably felt like hell. The road to her recovery was bound to be long and bumpy.

"I . . . I don't know if I'll ever be myself." Marla, still stricken, glanced at Nick, her gaze skating across his for only an instant, as if he alone understood. "I just don't feel that I'm . . ." She let her voice trail off.

"You're what?" Alex said.

She looked from one person to the other. When she met Nick's gaze, a shadow of an emotion he couldn't read chased across her eyes, only to quickly disappear. "I don't know who I am."

"Oh, brother," Cissy intoned and was rewarded with a don't-even-say-it look from her father.

"You'll be fine," Alex predicted.

Nick didn't believe it. She'd never be fine. Never had been. Yet a needle of guilt pricked his conscience as he saw her bruised face. For years he'd shoved her out of his mind and when he had thought of her it had only been with jaded disregard. Now he witnessed her wan and battered and fighting for some grain of dignity.

Cissy pretended to be staring out the window as she ran her fingers absently over the vents of the air-conditioning unit, but Nick could almost see the gears grinding in the teenager's mind. From the corner of her eye she was watching her mother. Something was definitely going on there.

"Don't you worry, things are going to be just fine. Once you get back home, with the baby . . . and the rest of us. You'll see.'' Eugenia took the compact from her son and dropped it quickly into her purse.

Nick wanted to get the hell out. This was about as much family togetherness as he could take for one day.

''You were here before.'' Marla was looking at him again. He gave a cursory nod and held her gaze. ''A few hours ago.''

''I remember.'' She said it as if awed and then lines deepened on her forehead. ''The outlaw.''

''That's right.'' Was it his imagination or was there a flicker of more than idle curiosity in her gaze?

''There was someone else here, too,'' she said.

''With me?'' Nick shook his head.

''No . . . no . . . I mean before you came in. At least . . . I think . . .'' Her eyes clouded and she looked away, studied the folds of the blankets that were bunching at her waist. ''Yes, I'm sure of it. Someone who didn't say a word, he came in and . . . and stood right there by the bed . . . Oh, damn it, I know this sounds paranoid, but it . . . it seemed real.''

''Nonsense,'' Eugenia said with a high-pitched, isn't-that-a-silly-notion laugh. ''It was probably a nurse.''

''No.'' Marla was frustrated. Agitated. ''Maybe I was dreaming. But I do remember, or . . . I think I do . . . that I actually heard all of you here . . .'' Her eyebrows drew together over a face that had once been breathtakingly beautiful. ''You were here another time . . . or was it twice before? Oh, God, I can't remember.'' She lifted a hand to shove the hair from her face and then stopped suddenly when her fingers encountered the bald spot above her left eye and the stitches in her scalp.

''Many,'' Eugenia said kindly. ''We were here many times.''

''And you sent Cissy down for soda. Sprite?''

''That's right. We did once,'' Alex agreed, smiling, though from Nick's perspective, the grin seemed strained and out of place. ''We thought you were in a coma, that you couldn't hear us.''

Eugenia fiddled with the clasp of her purse, and before she

offered up a cheery grin, the corners of her mouth turned down for just a second, just the way they did when she was perturbed. "So, you could hear us. Why didn't you respond?"

"I tried. But it was impossible."

"Don't worry about it."

"But I can't remember anything else, not the accident, not . . . anything." Still holding Alex's hand, she turned to look at Cissy, who rolled her eyes theatrically. She sent her father a look that said more effectively than words, *Can we just go now?* Nick didn't blame the kid.

Alex didn't take the hint. He leaned closer to his wife and said, "Now, listen, honey, even if you can't remember much—"

"No, it's not that I can't remember much, Alex," Marla cut in, her tongue tripping over his name, "I don't remember *any*thing about *my* life, though other things—general things are fairly clear. But my parents, my birthday, if I have brothers and sisters, or—"

"You mean you don't remember us?" Cissy asked, suddenly getting it.

Marla didn't reply.

"This is temporary," Alex cut in.

"It had better be." Marla turned her eyes to her husband as if seeking answers, and Nick's gut clenched. "I'm sorry about all this . . . trouble and Pam . . . oh, God, I feel awful that she died."

"You remember her?"

"No," she whispered, struggling not to break down. "I . . . don't recall the accident . . ." Her voice strangled as she tried and failed to control herself.

"You'll be better soon," Eugenia said.

Marla turned to face her mother-in-law. "Promise?"

"No, but—"

"Then don't give me any platitudes, all right. I have to get out of here, to do something. I need to talk to Pamela's family. I want to remember all of you."

Cissy blinked hard and sniffed, then turned away as if embarrassed.

Nick wanted to think that for some unnamed reason Marla was playing a game with them all, but she seemed incredibly sincere. He wouldn't have believed it of her, of being capable of caring for anyone but herself, but then maybe she'd changed. Maybe when she'd lost her memory, she'd lost her manipulative edge.

Or else she was faking them out.

Alex grabbed his wife's hand. "Why don't you try to get some rest?"

"I will, but I have so many questions. What about *my* family? Where are they?" she asked. "My parents? My siblings? I must have someone? Do they live nearby or far away?"

"Oh, honey," Alex said, sidestepping the questions. "There's so much to tell you, but now isn't the time."

"Why?" she asked, her voice low. She seemed to steel herself. "Are they all dead?"

"No, no . . . just your mother, but your father isn't well."

"Oh." Confusion crossed her features. Sorrow. Grief.

"We'll discuss it all, go through pictures, visit your dad, anything you want. But not until you're home and well, okay?"

She didn't answer but seemed to shrink a little in the bed, become smaller. Insanely, Nick wanted to comfort her and tell her everything would be all right; but he reminded himself of his place. And this was Marla they were dealing with, she could handle herself. If not, she had a husband to do the honors.

It was time to end this agony. "Look, I'll be shovin' off," he said to Alex and hazarded one last glance at the woman in the bed before striding out of the room. Away from his family. And Marla. God, he needed to get away from her.

He couldn't help but feel a twinge of pity for her. Once upon a time she'd been young, vibrant and sexy as any woman on earth. Now, she was just another patient, lucky to be alive, and destined never to be the same.

Shit.

He jabbed the button for the elevator and the doors whispered open. He nearly bumped into a tall, broad-shouldered man with a trimmed beard, dark glasses and thin lips compressed into a hard expression. Wearing a parka, jeans and hiking boots, he brushed past Nick, walking with a slight limp past the open door to Marla's room. Then he quickened his pace down the corridor.

For a reason he couldn't name, Nick hesitated. Had the guy swept a quick look inside room 505, seen the family and decided to keep going? Or was he visiting someone else in the wing? He seemed familiar, but Nick couldn't name why.

Not that it mattered. Probably his imagination working overtime.

On the first floor, Nick found his way through the general reception area and was out the doors to an evening where the first wisps of fog were gathering and the mist dampened his cheeks and forehead. He hazarded a glance up to the fifth floor and found Marla's room. Cissy was still in the window, staring out to the parking lot, probably wishing that she, too, could escape. Well, he couldn't blame her. He climbed into his pickup and glanced at his watch. He had a few hours to kill.

So maybe he should go take a look at the accident site, then check out the crashed Mercedes. He twisted the ignition and the old engine sparked.

As he looked over his shoulder to back out of his parking space, he caught a glimpse of a man running with an uneven gait through the fog, the same vaguely familiar guy he'd nearly bumped into outside the elevator just a few minutes before.

Nick followed the guy with his eyes, saw him climb into a dark Jeep and wondered why he'd gone up to the fifth floor only to come down again so fast.

"You're borrowing trouble," he told himself. "And you've got enough as it is."

* * *

Two days later, she was getting ready to be released. Dr. Robertson had given her every test imaginable, seemed satisfied with the results and now she was just waiting for the paperwork and a ride when the door to her hospital room creaked open. "Mrs. Cahill?" a man said, poking his head inside. "I'm Detective Paterno. San Francisco Police Department."

Her heart plummeted as he, dressed in dark slacks and jacket tossed over a casual shirt, eased into the room. He would be full of questions. Questions for which she had no answers. Her head was clearer, but the glimpses she had into her past were like the flame of a lighter running out of fuel; images would spark and sputter, flicker and die, leaving her with nothing. He flashed his badge and Marla's heart sank.

"Sorry to bother you here at the hospital," Paterno apologized. With a hound-dog face, deep brown eyes and a solemn, concerned expression, he seemed like a nice enough guy, yet Marla was wary. She couldn't help remembering her daughter's concerns that she might be charged with murder or negligent homicide or God-only-knew-what. And the police were masters at getting a person to say something they shouldn't . . . Dear God, where did *that* attitude spring from? He was studying her with dark suspicious eyes that were at odds with his rumpled, I'm-just-one-of-the-guys attitude. "I'm helping with the investigation of the accident. A favor to the California Highway Patrol. I'd like to hear what you remember about what happened."

"It won't take long," she muttered.

Ignoring her sarcasm, he placed a pocket recorder on the rolling table that held her water glass, a box of tissues, and the wire cutters, then flipped open a small notebook. "Tell me anything you recall." He smelled of the rain that darkened the shoulders of his jacket and there was a faint odor of Juicy Fruit gum that he chewed slowly. His hair was curly and black with a few gray hairs visible. Short and thick, he had the start of a belly hanging over his belt.

"That's easy," she said. "Nothing."

"Nothing?"

"Haven't you already talked with my doctor?"

"Yeah, he mentioned you had amnesia." Was there just a trace of disbelief in his voice? Another cynical cop.

"It's true, Detective, and a real pain in the neck." Shoving the sleeves of her robe over her forearms, she added. "Believe me, I'd love to help you, but I just don't know much." With a sigh, she glanced at her wrist where her plastic ID bracelet hung.

"You don't even remember what ran out in front of you to make you swerve, if anything?" he asked.

"Nothing." Marla tried to concentrate and was rewarded with a blinding headache.

"You were driving south on Highway 17 through the Santa Cruz Mountains. It seems from the skid marks, you saw something and hit the brakes. Maybe it was the truck, or a deer, or . . ." He let the sentence trail off, inviting her to finish.

"You don't understand, Detective," Marla said, trying to put a rein on her temper. "I don't even recall my own name, or either of my children or my husband . . . nothing. Just . . . just every once in a while a little flicker of something, an advertisement, a jingle, a . . . scene from an old movie, but nothing . . . nothing real."

The look in his eyes said, *how convenient,* but he didn't remark, just moved his wad of gum from one side of his mouth to the other.

"Well, since I'm here, just humor me, all right?" He lifted a bushy eyebrow and she nodded. "You were with Pam Delacroix."

"So I was told."

"And you knew her from . . . ?"

"I, uh, my husband said she was a friend of mine. But . . ."

"You don't remember."

"That's right." She frowned, angry with herself. "I think I'm going to sound like a broken record."

"Yes."

She reached for her juice and sipped as the detective went through a series of questions for which she had no answers. Outside the room, medication carts rattled, people talked, the bell for the elevator doors chimed. Inside 505, the feeling was tense and Marla didn't like the detective's attitude—as if she'd caused the accident and nearly killed herself intentionally. "You know, this feels a little like an inquisition," she finally said. She fiddled with her straw, then set her glass aside.

"Just tryin' to sort out everything."

"I really can't help you." Her back was beginning to go up, she was tired and her head was pounding like crazy.

"You were driving Pam Delacroix's car, right?"

"I . . . I guess so. That's what everyone says, so I assume it's true," she said hotly. "Now, listen, don't you have to let me talk to an attorney, Mirandaize me or whatever it's called?"

"*That* you remember?"

"I told you . . . little strange things. Maybe I saw it on an episode of . . . of . . ."

"*NYPD Blue? Law and Order?*"

"I . . . I don't know . . ."

He studied her through quick, intelligent eyes. "You really want to call a lawyer? I'm not here to arrest you, you understand."

"I don't have anything to hide." *At least nothing I can recall,* she thought, but bit back the words. She just wanted this interview to be over, to close her eyes, to hope that her medication would kick in and fight the pain throbbing in her jaw and hammering at her skull. And she wanted to shake this feeling that her life was spinning out of control, that there were unspoken questions hanging in the air, questions that were somehow too evil, too incriminating to utter aloud.

"Okay." Paterno chewed his gum furiously between his back teeth. "How about the semi careening toward you? It jackknifed, went off the far side of the road and the driver—

Charles Biggs—is barely holding on in a burn ward at a hospital across town. We're hoping he wakes up and can remember something.''

Marla went cold inside at the thought of the trucker. "The poor man," she whispered, glancing out the window to the gray afternoon. Her fate suddenly didn't seem so bad. She silently prayed that she hadn't been the cause of the accident, that her negligence hadn't killed her friend, a woman she couldn't remember, as well as maimed a stranger she'd never met. A cloud of depression threatened to settle on her shoulders. How would she ever live with herself if it turned out the accident was her fault? *Oh, God, please . . . no. I won't be able to survive the guilt . . .* Swallowing a thick lump in her throat, she gave herself a quick mental kick for this case of the "poor me" blues. "Why don't *you* tell me what happened that night," she suggested, deciding it was best to face the ugly truth rather than hearing what could very well be her family's sugar-coated version. She impaled Paterno with her gaze. "I want to hear the facts.''

"Just the facts, all the facts and nothing but the facts?''

What was that, some kind of dumb joke? She lifted a shoulder. "I . . . I suppose.''

"It's part of an old TV cop routine," he said, and she realized he'd tried to gain a reaction from her. He was testing her to see how much she really did remember. As if what—he didn't believe her? Why would she fake amnesia? Was there something she didn't know about herself, something that would make him distrust her?

Paterno lowered himself into the single plastic chair stuffed into one corner of the room. "From what we can tell from the skid marks, you were driving Pamela Delacroix's Mercedes south, presumably going to Santa Cruz where Pamela's daughter, Julie, attended college. You rounded a corner going uphill and swerved. The truck, coming from the opposite direction, braked hard to avoid you or whatever it was you were trying to miss. It jackknifed and went through the guardrail on one side of the road, your car broke through on the other. Pamela wasn't wearing a seat belt and was thrown out of the car. Her neck was broken and she died instantly.'' Marla's stomach tightened. Bile rose in her throat at the sheer horror and the guilt of it all. ''The semi rolled down the hill through the woods before hitting a tree and exploding. Someone saw the fireball and called 911 just before the first witnesses, an older couple heading north, arrived.''

Marla closed her eyes, shaken, the images he sketched painted in vivid colors in her mind. Tears burned her eyelids and she felt suddenly ill, as if she might throw up. ''I'm sorry,'' she whispered clumsily.

''Me, too.'' The detective didn't sound as if he meant it, and when she met his eyes again she saw a hardness within their dark depths, disbelief and accusation shimmering just below the surface of his gaze. Another cop who'd seen too much.

Getting to his feet, he fished in his pocket and placed a card on the table. He snapped off the recorder and jammed it into his pocket. ''That's it for today, but if you remember anything, contact me.''

''I will,'' she promised, then noticed movement in the partially open doorway. She'd been concentrating so hard on Paterno and the accident she hadn't seen Nick arrive. She wondered how long he'd been there, how much he'd heard.

''Isn't she supposed to have a lawyer present when she talks to the police?'' he asked stepping into the room. His black hair glistened as if he'd been in the rain, his eyes touched hers for a heart-stopping second, then his gaze skated away to focus on the detective. Paterno flipped his notebook closed and dropped it into a pocket.

''Mrs. Cahill and I have already been through this. She hasn't been charged with anything.''

''Alex said something about possible manslaughter.''

Her blood ran cold. Her head thundered. Was that possible? Prison?

"We haven't ruled anything out," the detective said, rubbing his jaw. "You're not the husband?"

"No." Nick's voice was firm and he glanced at Marla for a second, sending her a silent unreadable message that even in that short instant made her realize that he was making a point. "I'm her brother-in-law. *'The husband's'* brother. Nick Cahill." He offered the detective his hand.

Paterno's fingers surrounded Nick's larger hand. He gave it a quick, sharp pump.

"You're from Oregon, right?"

"Devil's Cove." Nick didn't bother to smile. "Don't ask. I think it was named by a drunken lumberjack or sailor."

"You come down just to see the family?"

"I was asked to. Business."

"Not because of the accident?"

"That had something to do with it." Nick's face was a mask without emotion, his features set, his jaw beginning to darken with five o'clock shadow.

Paterno chewed his gum in earnest as he digested the answer. With a square finger, he tapped on the card he'd left on the table and glanced back at Marla. "Remember—if you recall anything, get in touch with me."

"I will," she said and meant it. As painful as it might be, she wanted to know the truth, to rid herself of the torment.

Once Paterno was out of sight, Nick closed the door completely, and the sounds of the nurses' station and elevator suddenly disappeared.

"What're you doing?" she asked.

"Insuring that we have privacy." His eyes were dark, the skin stretched over his cheekbones tight.

Her pulse jumped and she caught the intensity of his gaze. "You act like I'm some kind of criminal." She shoved a strand of hair from her eyes, her fingers grazing the spot where her hair was shorn close. "Or that you are."

He sliced her a look, and the sterile box of a room seemed suddenly far too intimate—too close.

"I just want you to be careful."

"Look, Nick, I appreciate your concern. But you can forget all these theatrics. I don't have anything to hide."

How do you know? He didn't say it, but she read it in his gaze.

Tired, cranky, her head throbbing, she was sick of the questions, the hospital, the not knowing, the pain and the damned wires holding her mouth shut. More than that, she was really, really irritated that everyone she talked to was a stranger.

"That's what I thought." Folding his arms over his chest, he leaned against the closet and stared at her with eyes that held secrets. "So, have you got everything you need to blow this joint? Alex said the doctor was releasing you today."

She shook her head. "What I need now is an aspirin. One about the size of Montana will do."

"I'll see what I can rustle up," he said, starting for the door.

"Wait," she said, not wanting him to leave . . . not when there was so much she didn't understand.

He paused, hand on the doorknob.

"Why is it that I feel . . . I don't know . . . that you don't trust me or that you know something about me that I don't . . ." She paused. "I mean everyone seems to know more about me than I do, but with you it's different."

He lifted a dark brow and turned from the door. His expression had all the warmth of an arctic blast. "What do you mean?"

"You tell me," she suggested. "Because you know and I don't."

He rubbed the day's growth of beard with the thumb of one hand and sized her up, as if . . . as if he didn't *believe* her. Slowly he said, "I just came here to check on you because Alex asked me to. I don't think we should get into anything heavy."

"Why not?"

"Because it serves no purpose."

"Maybe I should be the judge of that."

His jaw tightened and he studied her, as if weighing her reaction. "Okay, Marla, since you asked, I'll give it to you straight." His lips flattened over his teeth. "You and I, we were lovers."

"What?" she gasped. No, no, no . . . this wasn't right. It couldn't be. She'd had an affair with her husband's brother? And yet, deep inside she realized that a part of her found him attractive . . . even sexy.

"Don't worry about it. It's ancient history," Nick added. "You threw me over for Alex."

She felt the blood drain from her face and heard her heart thudding. She wanted to argue but the look in his eyes, the dare she saw in their smoky depths, convinced her that he was telling the truth. She sank back on the pillows and felt sick inside. "How long ago?"

"Fifteen years."

"And in the interim?" she asked, bracing herself.

"Nothing."

She let out a slow breath.

"You asked," he reminded her.

"Yes, I . . . I know." She was sick inside. What kind of a person was she?

For the first time since she'd woken from the coma, she wasn't sure she wanted to know.

"You said a hundred grand." He was irritated and jittery as he spoke into the pay phone. The streets were wet, shimmering under the streetlights near the waterfront. The smell of salt water mingled with the fresh scent of rain. "Twenty-five doesn't cut it."

"She didn't die," was the cold response. "The deal was an accident that killed her."

"The deal was that there wasn't supposed to be another

person in the car," he reminded the man on the other end of the connection. "I want the rest." Traffic shot past, tires humming along the waterfront. Someone flicked a cigarette butt out of a window of an old Nova. Heavy metal music screamed through the wet night, the thump of bass cranked to the max.

"You'll get your money. But she has to die. And it has to be an accident."

"I could go to the police."

"Try it."

"I will."

"Not with your record."

Shit. There wasn't even the tiniest bit of concern in the bastard's voice. A police cruiser rounded the corner, splashing through the puddles, easing along the curb. He turned away instinctively, hid his face as the dampness of the city invaded his bones.

"You'll get your money, once the job's done and done right. No fuck-ups. Got it?"

"Yeah, yeah." For the time being he had to go along. He was in too deep not to go through with the hit. And he had his own, personal axe to grind in this one. The woman goddamned deserved to die. "I need a number where I can reach you." His nose was beginning to run. He swiped at it with his sleeve and sniffed.

"No. I'll contact you."

"But—"

Click.

The connection was severed.

"You son of a bitch. You goddamned rich son of a bitch." Jaw clenched, he slammed the receiver down. He checked the coin return slot out of habit, then shoved his hands into his pockets and ducked against the rain as he jaywalked to his Jeep. His ankle, the one he'd ripped up still ached, but he felt a moment's satisfaction that the cocksucker would get his and get it soon.

A neon Budweiser sign glowed in the windows of a seedy tavern one block up and he hesitated, then decided he deserved a drink. And a woman—any whore would do.

Dealing with rich bastards usually made him thirsty.

Besting them always gave him a hard-on.

Chapter Five

"I remember this place," Marla whispered as the Bentley sped up a narrow, winding street to the summit of Mount Sutro. Her heart leaped as she caught her first glimpse of the house mounted at the most prestigious point on the ridge. Yes, yes, yes! She'd been here before; she was sure of it.

She'd been in a bad mood since leaving the hospital, but some of that was disappearing as bits of memories—tickles of her past flashed behind her eyes. There was a ring . . . she looked at her hand and frowned because it wasn't the diamonds on her left hand, but a simpler ring that she recalled, and walking along a beach and riding horses . . . yes, yes, yes. Bits and pieces, but still her life.

Less than half an hour ago when she'd been pushed out of the hospital in a wheelchair, she'd had a sense of trepidation even as Alex had helped her into the buttery leather interior of the Bentley. The chauffeur, a behemoth of a blond man with a fragmented smile and cold blue eyes, had held the door for her. Lars Anderson. Nordic. Silent. Harsh looking, like some evil presence in a James Bond film, Lars had been with the family "for years" according to Alex. With only a tip of his hat and that eerie smile, he'd driven unerringly from the hospital, past the lush greenery of Golden Gate Park and the gingerbread Victorians of Haight-Ashbury to this gated fortress.

Home.

Electronic gates opened and the huge mansion, dozens of windows cut into the shake, brick-and-mortar exterior, glowed in the twilight. Ancient rhododendron and azaleas guarded the brick paths and stone steps to a front door that was familiar.

Relief brought tears to her eyes. "I remember this," she whispered, feeling like a maudlin fool.

"Do you?" Alex's smile was wide, but there wasn't much warmth in his eyes, as if he didn't quite trust her.

"Did you think I would fake it?"

"No, of course not." Seated in the plush rear seat, he took her hand and linked his fingers through hers. But the short feeling of elation that her memory might be returning slipped away as Lars nosed the car into a basement garage and the glimmer of recognition faded. A silver Jaguar was parked in one spot and there was still room for another vehicle—undoubtedly her car.

"Where's—"

"Your Porsche is in the shop, waiting for a part."

"I drive a Porsche?"

"You did," he said. "You will again. As soon as you're well and we get the car back. But you might want to wait a while . . . because of the accident."

She swallowed hard. Shivered. If only she could live that one night over again. "And if wishes were horses, beggars would ride . . ."

"Pardon me?" Alex asked.

"Oh, it's nothing, just something my mother used to say . . ." *Yes!* Her mother, she had a vague image of a woman, but it wasn't clear.

"You remember her?"

"Yes . . . no, not quite, but I will."

Alex reached into his pocket for a cigarette.

"You said she was dead."

"That's right . . . Years ago."

Too bad, she thought. Right now she could use a mother. *And so could your children. You'd better go inside and take care of them.* Her heart beat a little faster when she thought of the baby. She ached to hold him, and yet she couldn't even recall his little face. *A fine mother you are.*

The thought was discouraging, but she pushed it aside as Lars cut the engine, then hurried around the Bentley and opened the door for her. He offered her a hand as she climbed out of the car and into a garage that smelled faintly of diesel, oil and dust. She felt foolish and awkward, as if she'd never accepted his help before.

But then why would she have? She'd probably always driven herself.

"Thank you," she muttered automatically and saw a flicker of surprise in his wide-set eyes.

"Over here—the elevator," Alex reminded her as she glanced around the concrete walls of this basement garage. She studied the hubcaps and tools mounted over a workbench in an adjacent room, and experienced the gnawing feeling that she'd never set foot in here before.

But you remember the house! You did! Don't worry about it. "Do you want to go straight to the bedroom so you can lie down?" he asked, and she shook her head.

"What I'd like to do is see my baby." Marla followed him and a stream of smoke to the elevator.

"He's probably sleeping."

"But I want to see him. Now." She turned to stare her husband straight in his eyes. "You *do* understand that, don't you?"

"Of course. But I thought you might want to acclimate yourself with the house, reacquaint yourself with where things are before you see James and . . . ." The elevator door opened and he jabbed his cigarette out in a canister in the garage. They stepped inside and he pushed the button for the third floor.

"And what?"

"Nothing." His lips compressed as if he were irritated.

"No. You were going to say something," Marla insisted, her jaw aching.

"It might be hard for you if you don't recognize him," he said slowly, as if she were a child, "or conversely, if he doesn't immediately bond with you . . . I was only thinking of your well-being."

"My well-being is just fine," she snapped, tired of everyone treating her as if she were some fragile hothouse flower even though she was leaning against the interior of the elevator car as she was tiring already. Damn it all. She didn't know a lot about herself, but she was certain she'd never been a wimp. "Let's go see our son."

"Are you sure you're strong enough—?"

"Just show me the way, Alex," she insisted.

Her husband didn't say another word as the old elevator ground slowly upward and Marla was sorry she'd snapped. After all, he was only looking out for her; it wasn't his fault her memory was shot to shreds.

On the third floor she stepped into a carpeted hallway that circled a center staircase. Alex led her to double doors. "Our suite," he announced as they entered a sitting area complete with a corner fireplace, small couch, and reading table between two chairs. "My bedroom is that way," he said, indicating a doorway to the right, "and this is yours." He opened narrow French doors and allowed her to walk into a bright room decorated in navy, peach and beige. A rosewood bed, canopied in lace dominated the room and matched several other pieces. Leather-bound volumes filled a bookcase, two vases of fresh cut flowers were arranged on tables, pictures in gilt frames were hung on a wide expanse of wall and the room had the feel of a showplace, as if it should be roped off for the guided tour later in the afternoon.

"You and I, we don't sleep together?"

"Not often, anymore." Alex yanked on the knot of his tie and undid the top button of his shirt. "We do sometimes, of course, but no, not in general."

"And you don't think that's odd?" A headache was starting to form at the base of her skull.

He shook his head. "Not really. We've been married a long time. The situation's just kind of evolved over the years." He shrugged. "It's not such a bad thing. We have separate lives."

"But we managed to conceive a baby." This seemed wrong to her.

"Yes." He smiled and Marla thought she saw a flicker of boyish charm beneath his veneer of wealthy sophistication. "That we did manage. Come on. You're right, it's time you met the little devil." At the far end of the room, he led her through a glass-paned door to the nursery, a tiny room painted a soft baby blue and trimmed with a wallpaper border of pastel animals and Noah's Ark.

This room felt lived-in and warm. Just right for an infant. Pillows and stuffed animals were clustered in the corners, a bookcase was filled with toys and a night light glowed from a lamp shaped like the Ark.

From the crib the sound of a baby's soft snoring could be heard. Marla beelined to the crib, and swallowed a thick lump in her throat. In the crib an infant lay sleeping on his back, his little legs curled, his tiny hands clenched into fists. Downy soft reddish hair barely covered his scalp and his lips moved as if he wanted to suckle.

Her heart squeezed, not from motherly love, but in despair. How could this little cherub not have engraved his way into her heart, into her memory? Why could she not recall anything about him? She blinked against tears. Carefully she reached into the crib and gently lifted him and the blanket surrounding him into her arms.

This is your son, Marla. Yours! The thought was as heart-warming as it was frightening. What did she know about babies?

Obviously she'd raised one child to adolescence but right now her own sense of innate motherhood escaped her.

James let out a soft little cry as she put him to her shoulder. It felt so right to hold him, to place him close over her heart, and yet there was something . . . on the very edges of her memory . . . teasing her.

Rousing, the baby opened his eyes and stiffened. He stared straight at her for a split second, eyes round.

"Hi there," Marla whispered, her heart swelling in pride. The baby was just so . . . precious.

He blinked, then as if he found her scarred face frightening, he opened his mouth and wailed for all he was worth. His face turned red with the effort of screaming at the top of his small lungs.

"Shh, little one," she whispered, cradling his tiny head with her hand. "You're fine."

James was having none of it. His back went ramrod stiff and he only stopped screaming long enough to catch his breath.

"I was afraid of this," Alex said, for once looking as if he had no idea what to do. "I'll call the nanny."

"No." Marla tried not to panic. This was her baby. *Hers.* She had the right to hold him, to wake him from his sleep, to try to bond with her son.

"Quiet, sweetheart. Shh. Mommy's here and everything will be all right," Marla said, lying through teeth that couldn't move.

Somewhere far off in another part of the house, a dog started barking like crazy.

"Great," Alex muttered, raking stiff fingers through his hair. "I knew we should have let him sleep."

Ignoring her husband, Marla slowly rocked side to side. "Just take it easy, James," she said, though she felt like a complete klutz with her own child. Maybe he was hungry, or needed to be changed, or maybe he was just cranky and ticked off that she'd woken him. Her headache was hammering through her brain, but she wasn't about to give in to the pain right now. "I'll take care of you," she promised the baby as she moved to a changing table and let his blanket drop to the floor. Placing his little body onto a tiny mattress, she fumbled with the snaps of his pajamas. All the while he screamed loud enough to wake the dead.

"I'm comin', I'm comin', just hold yer horses, Jimmy boy," an unfamiliar voice called from the hallway.

"Thank God," Alex muttered under his breath.

The door to the hallway burst open and a slight woman with wild red hair and granny glasses bustled into the room. She cast a disparaging glance at Marla and without so much as a hello, took charge, almost bodily pushing her to the side. "I'll take care of him," she said with the authority of one who knows her position.

"And you're?"

"Fiona. The nanny, Mrs. Cahill. Don't you recognize me?"

Of course she didn't and felt embarrassed as the woman tended to her son. Along with her curly flaming hair, Fiona sported large teeth that overlapped a bit in front, and white skin dusted with freckles.

"I'm sorry," Marla apologized, the pain in her head beginning to pound. "I don't remember much."

"So I've heard. Everyone here's been worried sick over ya," she said with a trace of an English accent. "But don't worry about it, yer memory, it'll come back. My uncle's did. He was in a skiing accident, nearly killed him it did, and when he finally came 'round, he was his old self again . . . well except that he never did quite get rid of that limp of his." With incredibly deft and efficient fingers, she stripped the baby of his diaper, flung it into a diaper pail, whipped out another disposable from a drawer and amid a cloud of baby powder, had him changed, dressed again and was cuddling him on her shoulder within seconds. Worse yet, he actually stopped crying. "He's a fussy one, he is," she said, rocking side to side and holding the quiet infant as if he belonged to her. "Ain't you supposed to be restin' or somethin'?"

"Marla!" Eugenia said as she entered the room, a scowl of disapproval drawing her features together. "What're you doing up?" She turned on Alex. "She just got out of the hospital, for goodness' sakes. Fiona's right. She should be resting."

"Marla wanted to see James."

"Well, of course, of course, but all in due time." Eugenia turned concerned eyes in Marla's direction. "The baby will still be here, you know. They don't disappear, not for a good twenty years or so," she chided, but there was a hint of steel in her soft words. "Now, Fiona, you're to always use correct English around the children, you know that." She glanced at her grandson and a prideful, beatific smile eased the little lines around her lips. "He *is* adorable, isn't he?"

"He wasn't too adorable a few minutes ago," Alex countered, then grinned. "Just kidding, Mother. Look, I've got to run back to the office, but I'll be back in a couple of hours. Look after my wife for me, will you?" he said to Eugenia before planting a swift kiss on Marla's cheek and winking at his mother. Then he was out the door.

"Alexander doesn't slow down for a minute, and this one," Eugenia indicated the baby, "he's going to be just like his father, aren't you, little man?"

Fiona, satisfied her duty had been fulfilled, placed the baby back into his crib as Marla reached down and picked up the blanket from the floor. Carefully she tucked it around him as he searched for and found his thumb.

Eugenia was still beaming. "He's special, that boy is. We waited so long and finally, finally, we have a Cahill to carry on the name."

"You mean a grand*son*."

"Yes."

No wonder Cissy was so upset. "You've been waiting for one?"

"Let's just say I consider James a blessing of the highest order." She leaned over the crib and ran an age-spotted finger along his chin. "The highest order."

"And Cissy?"

"She's a blessing, too. Of course. All children are gifts from God."

"But some are Rolexes and some are Timexes, is that what you're saying?" Marla demanded, irritated beyond belief at the antiquated notion that females were less valuable than males. What archaic, deluded waters did that spring from?

"Of course not. Everyone has a purpose. Cissy's is different from James, but no less important," Eugenia said quickly, correcting herself as two points of color tinged her pale cheeks.

Marla didn't believe her mother-in-law for an instant. No matter how she tried to rationalize it, Eugenia's mentality was straight out of the Dark Ages.

The older woman cleared her throat. "Now, dear, you really should take a little nap, if you can. Or read. There's an intercom on the bed stand and just ring when you want something. I already asked Carmen to bring you tea, a pitcher of water and your medication, already mixed in with a little orange juice."

For the first time since leaving the hospital, Marla accepted the fact that she was tiring; that she hadn't yet regained all her strength. Her head was thundering and she needed some time alone, to lie in her own bed, fight the pain and try like crazy to make some sense of this life that seemed so foreign, to force herself to recall any jagged little piece of memory. "Maybe I will lie down," she said after taking one more look at her baby. Suddenly bone-weary, Marla walked to her room and kicked off her shoes.

Eugenia closed the shades. "Rest now," she suggested.

"Thanks," Marla said as she eyed the elevated bed with its lace canopy.

You don't live here; you've never lived here. This isn't your house; this isn't your bed. No way. The thought seared through her brain, but Marla ignored it; she was just too damned tired. She would remember. Soon.

"If you need anything else, anything at all, just use the intercom here, it's one of those plug-in types, but it works well." Eugenia motioned to a bedside table and pushed on a black button. "Carmen?" She lifted her finger.

"Yes, Mrs. Cahill," came the reply.

Eugenia pushed the button again. "We're fine. Don't need anything . . ." she said, lifting an eyebrow at Marla who caught the signal that if she wanted anything now was the time to ask. She shook her head and her mother-in-law spoke toward the box again. "I was just showing Marla how to reach you. Thank you." Eugenia lifted her finger.

This is a test, only a test. The words flew through Marla's mind, but she couldn't remember where she'd heard them before. And right now, tired and aching, she didn't give a damn.

"I'm staying in tonight," Eugenia said. "Is there anything else you'd like? I see the juice is already here. No doubt it's got your dose of medication in it." She motioned to the night table where a tall glass of orange juice was sweating on a lace cloth.

"Nothing."

"Well, just let Carmen know. Now, lie down and don't worry about a thing."

Fat chance. It seemed as if all she did was worry about who she was, the accident, her family, her damned memory. Her head was thundering again. "Where's Cissy?"

Eugenia fumbled with the pearls at her neck. "Well, I let her go over to a friend's. She waited around for a while, but you were late . . ."

"Red tape at the hospital. Some foul-up with the release forms," Marla said, remembering her own impatience at being detained even a second longer than she needed to have been.

"Anyway, I shouldn't have let her go over to the Thomases, but you have seen her the last couple of days and frankly, I was tired of her grumbling about being bored and all . . . I didn't let her go riding, and Lord did I hear about that." She clucked her tongue, as if the thirteen-year-old was already too much to handle.

"It's all right."

"I'll make sure she's home when you wake up."

"Thanks."

"Glad you're back, Marla." Eugenia smiled as she shut the door and Marla let out her breath. She drank from the glass of juice and winced at the bitter taste. The pain medication. Good. In a few minutes her head would stop aching. Maybe her mother-in-law was right. Maybe things would be better after a good night's sleep in her own bed.

Stripping down to panties and bra, she tumbled into the bed and felt the cool sheets caress her skin. The bed was comfortable, the soft down quilt heavenly and her eyelids felt as if they each weighed a ton.

Exhaustion overtook her. She was grateful to forget about the questions that had been plaguing her ever since she'd woken up from her coma. Everyone was right; she was just confused. That was it. Because of the accident. That had to be what it was.

Otherwise everyone was lying to her.

The lab coat was a couple of sizes too big, but it didn't matter. It was all the camouflage he needed. One of the burn ward nurses hadn't shown up for duty tonight as her car had been disabled, her cell phone stolen and the other two were run ragged as the hospital was searching for staff to fill the void.

By the time they managed that, he'd be finished.

The lights were too bright for his liking, but there wasn't much he could do about that, and he shoved a pair of tortoise-rimmed glasses onto his nose. Slipping into his role of intern easily, he walked with confidence. The name tag on his lapel and picture were of Carlos Santiago. He figured no one would notice that the image on the card didn't match his face as he strode with the authority of someone who knew what he was doing. That he belonged.

What a joke.

He'd never belonged anywhere. Had always been on the outside looking in. Well now he wasn't only looking, he was fucking pounding on the window.

Near the burn ward, he lingered in an alcove, then waited until the overworked nurse on duty was called into a room. As she disappeared through the door he crept on silent footsteps to Charles Biggs's room.

Lying in the bed, the man looked like a monster. Any skin that was visible was red and oozing. Bandages swathed part of his body. He was unmoving, tubes going in and out of his body, an IV dripping pain medication and God-only-knew-what else into his bloodstream.

Too late.

Biggs wasn't going to make it.

He eased to the bedside of the unlucky bastard. *That's what you get when you happen to be in the wrong place at the wrong time. Too bad, Biggs.*

Biggs drew a rattling breath into his scorched lungs.

You cost me, you son of a bitch, he thought, then took a small, rubber sheet from his pocket and placed his gloved hands over Biggs's mouth and nose. The man stiffened, tried to gasp in another breath, struggled in his unconscious state.

His muscles strained with the effort of holding the big man down, but it was over before it really started. Charles Biggs had been loitering on this side of death's door for much too long. He just helped the bastard over the threshold.

As he moved silently away from the bed and the damned monitors started beeping wildly, he smiled and walked on silent footsteps to a back stairwell. He opened the door and disappeared down the concrete steps.

The way he looked at it, he'd done the sorry son of a bitch a favor. A big one.

He stepped out of the stairwell on the first floor and ran into a nurse running full tilt in the opposite direction.

"Excuse me," she said, her gaze flying to his name tag,

then up to his face. A quizzical expression crossed her features. "Carlos?" she said. "Hey!"

He turned quickly. Dashed through the glass double doors and prayed the woman didn't get too close a look at his face, as he nearly tripped over an elderly woman being pushed in a wheelchair.

"Son of a bitch," he growled, stripping off the lab coat and cutting across traffic. He glanced back, saw the nurse at the door. She was talking animatedly to another woman. Her fingers were jabbing in the direction of the street. Still running, he rounded a corner, ignored the pain in his ankle, crossed another couple of streets and found his Jeep just where he'd left it.

Adrenalin surged through his blood as he climbed in, flicked on the ignition and, sweating despite the cool temperature, nosed the Jeep into traffic. He lit a cigarette and left the hospital behind. His heartbeat slowed as he put some distance between himself and the hospital.

He'd nearly gotten caught.

But hadn't.

Grinning to himself, he glanced down at the white lab coat with its ID tag and the picture of Carlos Santiago staring up at him. He jabbed his cigarette onto the tag and the smell of charred plastic filled the Jeep.

"Muchas gracias, amigo."

"Had Marla been drinking on the night that she lost control of the car?" Nick asked. He and Alex sat in an Irish pub a few blocks from his hotel. Alex was on his second scotch and water. Nick was nursing a beer.

"Nope. She'd just gotten out of the hospital."

"What about Pam?" Nick asked, wondering about the woman who no one seemed to know. Marla's friend.

"No one knows what she'd been doing but there was a little alcohol in her bloodstream. Not much." From the booth where they sat, Alex's gaze followed a couple of guys who were throwing darts near the back of the bar.

"Marla and she were close?"

"As close as Marla gets I suppose," Alex swirled his drink. Ice cubes danced in the weak light. "She didn't have a lot of friends."

That surprised Nick. "She sure as hell got a lot of cards and flowers."

"It's expected. We're pretty high-profile around here." Alex yanked at the knot of his tie and Nick wondered if his brother ever wound down. Competitive to a fault, Alex had always been a classic type-A personality, following in the old man's footsteps as if they'd been made by God Himself. Never questioning, always proving to the bastard that he was indeed more than qualified to be Samuel J. Cahill's heir. A football scholarship to Stanford, undergraduate degree there and then law school at Harvard. Alex knew how to play the game.

"High profile but not well liked?" Nick asked as glasses clinked and conversation buzzed around them.

"It's hard to say. People tend to kiss ass when you have money." Alex pinched his lower lip thoughtfully, then motioned to the waitress for another round.

"So you really don't know who your true friends are?"

"Something like that." Alex tossed back the rest of his drink and set his glass on the glossy table. He rubbed his face and looked a decade older than his forty-two years.

"Cherise called me before I left home," Nick finally admitted.

Alex's expression changed from congenial to guarded. "Don't tell me. She whined about me not letting her see Marla."

"That was the gist of it, yeah."

"Shit." Alex snorted, wiped his nose with the back of his hand. "She and Monty. They won't give up. Like hyenas at a lion's kill." He frowned at the analogy. "Or better yet, wasps that won't go away. They bug the hell out of you, make a lot of noise, and threaten to sting.'' He tossed his brother a dark look. ''I'll deal with Cherise. And Montgomery.''

The subject seemed closed and Nick had done his duty, so he slid lower on his spine and observed his brother. ''I drove out to the scene of the accident,'' Nick admitted.

Alex didn't show much reaction. ''And what did you find out?''

''Not much. But I can't figure out why both vehicles broke through guardrails in opposing directions. The truck, well, that's nearly understandable, just from the sheer weight and speed of the rig. It was, after all, going downhill, but the Mercedes . . . how did it manage to tear through that kind of steel?''

''Good question.''

''I saw the car,'' Nick admitted. ''Found a policeman who was more than happy to let me take a look in the yard where it's being held.'' His lips rolled in on themselves as he remembered the crushed metal, blood-stained seats and shattered glass. ''It's a wonder anyone survived.''

''Marla's always been tough. You know that.''

The muscles in the back of Nick's neck tensed. ''Tough is one thing.'' He stared straight at his brother. ''Seeing the car made me almost believe that she had a guardian angel watching over her.''

''Almost?''

''I have a problem with organized religion.''

''I remember.''

''But no one should have survived that wreck.''

One side of Alex's mouth lifted. ''Well, Marla's always been lucky, hasn't she?''

Nick didn't answer, didn't want to go there. ''Why do you think Marla panicked and lost control of the car?''

''Hell if I know. She was always a decent driver. Never even a traffic ticket. I guess only she can answer that one . . . if she gets her memory back.''

''You mean when,'' Nick corrected.

"Do I?" Alex smiled to a pretty waitress with a knockout figure and big brown eyes.

She hardly looked old enough to be serving drinks. Dressed in a short skirt, white blouse and red bow tie, she picked up his empty glass, deposited another full one and left Nick a beer that he wasn't quite ready for. But he didn't complain. Figured he'd find a way to down it.

"I'm not sure if she'll ever remember anything," Alex said. He met the questions in Nick's eyes and sighed. "Sure, I play the game and tell her she will. Of course I do and Phil Robertson, her doc, he seems convinced that her memory will return, but right now, it doesn't seem like it." He took a long sip from his new drink and settled back against the tufted seat. "It's just hard to predict."

Grudgingly, Nick had to agree.

"And maybe I'm just sick of all this shit."

"Maybe." Nick sipped from the long-necked bottle and wondered about the accident. Pam Delacroix had died instantly, Biggs had never regained consciousness. Marla remembered nothing, surviving in her own personal netherworld. "You never met Pam?"

"Nope." Alex reached into his jacket pocket, withdrew a pack of cigarettes and said, "I need a smoke. Wanna join me outside?"

"Sure." They finished their drinks, and Alex insisted on paying by offering the waitress his credit card. After signing the receipt, and shrugging into his overcoat, he and Nick walked outside to an alley where several men were gathered, smoking, laughing, laying down odds on the 49ers' chances for a play-off berth, barely glancing in Alex and Nick's direction. Alex lit up and blew smoke from the corner of his mouth and Nick zipped his jacket against the chill that was San Francisco in mid-November. "All I know about Pam is what Marla told me, that she and Marla met at the club a few years back, though I never heard about it at the time." He shrugged. "But that could be expected." He looked up to the sky. "There have been times in our marriage that we didn't talk a lot. We've separated a couple of times . . . oh, nothing official, but the marriage, well, it's had a few bumps in the road.'' He turned thoughtful, inhaled deeply on his smoke and Nick didn't comment, didn't want to tackle the dangerous subject of his brother's marriage. ''As for Pam, I'm not really sure. I assume that they played tennis together, and maybe bridge . . . but, come to think of it, I never heard her say she was going out to meet her. Other names I heard—Joanna and Nancy, I think. But not Pam.''

''But you must've heard something since.''

''From the insurance company and a lawyer for Pam's estate. I sent flowers to the funeral, of course, donated to some charity in Pam's name, but haven't had much contact. She was divorced, and had gotten her real estate license I think, but she just dabbled at that. I think she lived off her ex. He's some hotshot computer engineer who made it big in Silicon Valley. They had one kid, a daughter, and she was down at UC Santa Cruz.'' He drew hard on his cigarette as the men clustered near the doorway laughed nearly in unison, as if someone had cracked a particularly hilarious joke. Traffic whizzed by. High in the heavens the moon was partially hidden by wispy, slow-moving clouds.

''So what was Marla doing that night?''

''That's the sixty-four thousand dollar question. Shit, I wish I had an answer to it. But the truth is I have no idea why Marla and Pam took a notion to go down there. For Christ's sake, James was only a few days old and Marla just gets a wild hare and takes off down Highway 17 in the middle of the night? It was nuts.''

''Maybe she'll tell us when she gets her memory back.''

''Maybe.'' Flicking ashes onto the pock-marked street, Alex gazed up the hill, past the Victorian buildings of Haight Street toward the Cahill house, the place they had once, as children, thought of as home. As far as Nick was concerned, Alex could have the mansion and all the problems that came with it.

Alex tossed his cigarette into the gutter, where it died quickly. A bicyclist darted in and out of the traffic and cars rushed through the narrow streets. "I wish I had met Pam," Alex said. "Then maybe I could have made some sense of this. It looks like her family is suing us—their lawyer's already called— but I contend that everything should be handled through the insurance company. Christ, what a mess." He stuffed his hands into his pockets and nodded toward the street where he'd parked his car. "Just one of many, I'm afraid." He flashed a mirthless smile at his brother. "And speaking of which, I have a few files in my briefcase—kind of an overview of the company," he said, obviously anxious to change the subject. "I thought you might like to review them before you came down to the office."

"Probably a good idea," Nick allowed as Alex used his keyless lock that opened the driver's door of the Jag. He snapped open his briefcase and withdrew a small, slim case which he handed to Nick.

"If you have any questions you can call me at the office, but I'd rather we didn't discuss details in front of Mother or Marla or anyone at the house." In the lamplight, Alex looked older than he had, his features more drawn. "I won't kid you, Nick. The company's got problems. Big ones. Mother knows there are some difficulties of course, but it would be best if we left it at that."

"What about Marla?"

"Let's keep her out of it. She's got enough to deal with."

No shit, he thought, but said nothing and gave a curt nod of agreement.

"Good. I appreciate it." Alex's face was grim. For the first time Nick realized that Cahill International might be in serious trouble, that Alex, as CEO was taking the heat. There was even a chance that he'd somehow screwed up, that the company was struggling because of his decisions. Alex clapped him on the back, his hand smacking against the damp leather of Nick's jacket. ''Thanks,'' he said, and for the first time in his life, he sounded as if he meant it.

Nick felt the Cahill noose tighten another notch. As he watched his brother slide into the Jaguar, punch it and roar up the hill, he only hoped that he hadn't just agreed to become the fall guy.

Chapter Six

"Charles Biggs died."

The announcement heralded Janet Quinn's arrival at Paterno's office. She flopped into a chair wedged between a file cabinet and the window.

"Shit."

"My sentiments exactly." She slapped a file down on the edge of Paterno's already jammed desk. A detective with the department for years, Janet was a tall, no-nonsense woman who endured a constant ribbing for her mannish looks—short cropped brown hair now shot with gray, square jaw, thick eyebrows and pensive blue eyes that she didn't adorn with anything but a functional pair of glasses. She didn't gussy herself up and she didn't give a shit. No doubt she'd heard herself referred to as a bull dyke or the sneered suggestions that she took steroids by those who were jealous. And there were quite a few. She'd climbed the ranks swiftly because she was a helluva detective and she didn't give up.

"When?"

"Late last night—or early this morning. His heart monitor

went off at three forty-seven. Couldn't be revived. Considering his condition, maybe it's a blessing.''

"Considering our case, maybe it's not.''

She lifted a shoulder and leaned against the file cabinet. She wore Dockers, a shirt and Rockport shoes.

"Don't suppose he said anything before he died.''

"Nope.''

"Death certificate?''

"Not yet.'' She shook her head and Paterno tented his hands, looking over the tips of his fingers, thinking. The accident bothered him; it bothered him a lot. Now two people were dead and, he supposed, he could chalk the whole thing up to bad timing, but he didn't like the feel of it. It didn't fit.

He saw a gleam in Janet's eye.

"Something else?''

"Yep. There was a disturbance right after Biggs' heart monitors went off. Some guy in a stolen lab coat plowed into a nurse on the first floor and took off. She saw his name tag and realized he wasn't Carlos Santiago, an intern who'd been working swing shift. On the way out, the guy nearly knocked over a woman in a wheelchair being pushed by an aide.''

"Jesus.''

"I already spoke with Santiago,'' Janet said. "Sure enough his ID tag is missing.''

"You think he had something to do with Biggs' death?''

"Could be. I've already asked the nurse, Betty Zimmerman, to come in and talk to the composite artist. The aide couldn't remember much. He was too concerned about his patient and didn't get a look at the guy. But we'll see what happens after the nurse talks to the artist. We could have something by the end of the day.''

"Was the guy in Santiago's coat seen in the burn ward?'' Paterno leaned back in his chair, glanced out the window to the morning fog still rolling in off the Bay.

"No. But they were short staffed. One nurse's car wouldn't start, another was sick. The rest of the crew was run ragged.''

"What about Santiago?"

"He looks clean. Really pissed that he got dragged into this. I talked to him and I think he's legit, but he's testy, and let me know that he wouldn't let his civil rights be violated, that just because he's Hispanic, well, you know the drill."

"But he did cooperate?"

"Yep." She nodded, her face screwing up.

"Do you think this is all coincidence?" he asked.

She snorted, then sent him a twisted, mirthless smile as she settled back in the plastic chair. "I thought you didn't believe in coincidence."

"I don't." His mind was turning fast. The feeling that the accident on Highway 17 with Marla Cahill at the wheel was starting to look more and more like a setup. But what? Why? Who? And what would Biggs know about it? The way Paterno figured it, Biggs was just an unlucky player in this game—a guy driving a semi in the wrong place at a very wrong time. He found a pack of Juicy Fruit, offered Janet a stick and when she shook her head, unwrapped a piece and folded it into his mouth. "Got anything else?"

"Yeah, something strange," she admitted, deep lines etching across her forehead, the way they always did when she was trying to piece together a puzzle that didn't quite fit. "The lab says that they found three kinds of broken glass at the scene. Windows from the truck and the Mercedes." She held up two fingers. "And a third." She wagged her index finger. "Near as they can tell it's shards from some kind of mirror and not a rearview mirror or a side-view mirror. We checked."

"They're different?" Grabbing the paper cup on his desk, he took a sip of now-tepid coffee.

"Yep, it's the backing . . . this glass was hand-painted with some kind of reflective material." Leaning forward, she thumped three fingers on the manila folder she'd dumped on his desk. "It's all inside. In the report."

He thumbed through. Sure enough. Bits of glass that didn't

fit either make or model of the vehicles in the wreck. "So what's it mean?"

"I don't know. It could've been on the road before, but it's a coincidence."

"Another one," Paterno said, frowning. "Way too many for my liking."

"Same here."

"Any word on why the guardrails gave way?"

"Not yet. The semi just blew through one. Big rig, heavy load, but on the other side, that's still debatable. There were welding marks, fairly recent, I think, as if the rail was weak and had been repaired, but the highway department can't locate any work order for the past five years for that stretch of road."

"So it just gave way." He bit on the end of his thumb and scowled. The whole damned thing didn't make any sense. And it just didn't feel right. Two people were dead and the driver who started the whole mess had conveniently lost her memory. Now there was evidence of another player, someone who could have killed Biggs. Could it be that Charles Biggs was the target, if there was one? Had Paterno been reading this wrong from the onset?

"Do a thorough check on Biggs."

"Already done. He's clean as a proverbial whistle. No arrests, one outstanding parking ticket, married for forty years to the same woman, put both his kids through college and aside from owning the independent trucking company that consists of the one truck he drove, he owns a small Christmas tree farm in Oregon and doesn't even cheat on his taxes. He and the missus have socked away nearly two hundred grand for his retirement and he spent his free time fly-fishing on the Metolius River near Bend and teaching his grandkids how to hunt and fish. No history of drugs or domestic violence or anything. The guy was a real Boy Scout."

"So we're back to Marla Cahill and Pam Delacroix." He finished his coffee, wadded the cup and tossed it into an overflowing basket.

Christ, what a mess.

"Too bad Biggs didn't wake up," he grumbled, chewing hard on his wad of gum and feeling his heartburn kick in. "Let me know when the autopsy report comes in. It's just a damned shame he didn't tell us what he saw."

"I guess we'll have to count on Marla Cahill for that," Janet said with a cold smile and no trace of humor. "When she gets her memory back."

"Which might be about a second before hell freezes over."

Where am I? Marla dragged her eyes open to a strange room and she was disoriented for a second before she remembered that she was home. This was her room. Her bed. Her . . . everything.

How long had she slept? Gray daylight showed through the shades, but Marla had the impression from the fullness of her bladder and her groggy mind, that she'd slept around the clock. Her mouth tasted bad and her hair, what there was left of it, felt lank and dirty. She hadn't heard Alex come into the suite, hadn't heard her baby cry, had slept as if she were dead.

In bra and panties, she staggered into the bathroom, used the toilet, splashed water over her face and avoided looking at her pathetic reflection. There were fresh towels on the bar. She stripped, then stepped into a glass shower large enough for two and turned on the spray. Hot water needled into her skin, soaking her muscles. Gingerly, avoiding touching her stitches, she washed, shampooed and found a safety razor to tackle the hair on her legs and under her arms. Then, still feeling as if her mind was shrouded by cobwebs, she braced herself and cranked the spray to the right. Icy water shot out of the showerhead and she sucked in her breath, leaning against the slick tiles.

Slowly she began to feel human again, stronger than she had since she'd woken from the damned coma. Twisting off the spray, she reached for a towel and in that moment she had a flash of memory, of another time and place.

She'd been at the beach . . . and there had been friends with her . . . or her husband . . . or . . . Cissy? Her daughter . . . no, that wasn't right . . . but the sun had been shining and she'd come running out of the ocean, her feet nearly burning on the hot sand as she took a towel from . . . from . . . whom? Her head hurt from the effort of concentration. It had been a man . . . Yes, a man. He must've been Alex . . . or . . . Nick? Her throat tightened at that particular implication and she rubbed the thick terry cloth over her arms and legs. Maybe it had been someone else. *Or maybe it hadn't happened at all.* Propping herself against the tiles with one arm, she shook her head and tried to focus, to call back that fleeting, tantalizing memory, but it had faded as quickly as it had appeared.

Determined to discover more about herself, she stepped out of the shower and faced her reflection. Jesus, she was a mess. The bruises were disappearing, the swelling nearly gone but she didn't recognize herself. And her hair! What a catastrophe! The blunt cut at her chin on one side of her face would have to be cut short, maybe even spiky, to try to blend with the new fuzz that was just covering her scalp. If nothing else, she and her newborn son would be sporting similar hairdos.

Wasn't there some famous singer who had shaved her head . . . part of some kind of religious protest or something . . . or was she wrong about that, too? Damn the amnesia! "This is a start," Marla reminded herself as she squeezed some toothpaste on her finger and ran it over her interlaced teeth. These little bits of memory certainly were precursors to her recovery. "Rome or even San Francisco wasn't built in a day." But she couldn't wait to piece together her history and as she rinsed her mouth, she grew impatient.

On impulse, she searched the medicine cabinet and drawers. She came across two prescription bottles, one for tetracycline with two pills still in the tiny plastic jar, the second empty of premarin. On the second shelf she found a pair of scissors and started snipping her locks. Shorter and shorter, one tuft after another, bits of mahogany-colored hair fell into the sink. When she was finished she didn't look any worse than when she'd started, so she opened a can of mousse, worked some around her stitches and fluffed up what she could. Salon perfect it wasn't, but it would grow and fill in, covering the scars. Her hair was the least of her problems. She didn't bother with any of the makeup she found carefully arranged in the top drawer of the vanity. What was the use? Instead she headed for the closet.

It was immense, a row of perfectly coordinated suits, slacks and jackets. A rainbow of shoes, each pair placed neatly in an individual cubbyhole, filled one wall, another was reserved for evening gowns that sparkled within zippered plastic bags. Tennis outfits and warm-ups owned one corner, while purses lined two shelves. A full-length mirror was fitted next to the door and inside a tall, slender cupboard was an ironing board.

"Wonderful." So where were the jeans? The old sweats? Her purse? Yes . . . where was her purse with her wallet and checkbook and maybe even an address book, all the things important in her life?

She went through each and every handbag, clutch, tennis bag and suitcase on the two shelves. All empty. Clean. As if they'd been vacuumed, for crying out loud. "Damn." She threw them back onto the shelves in disgust, then riffled through the drawers of an armoire and found a stiff pair of jeans that were a size too big and a pink sweater that was soft enough to make her believe it had been her favorite.

Or had it?

"Don't even go there," she warned herself, slipping on a pair of battered tennis shoes she found in one of the cubbies. She thought of her daughter, her son, her husband and Nick, the man who had been her lover. Her lips folded in on themselves as the questions about her life started coming fast and furiously again, bringing with them the inevitable headache.

Outside the closet in this bedroom that felt so odd, she paused at the bureau and swept her gaze over the pictures arranged in front of a bevel-edged mirror. One snapshot framed in gold caught her eye. There she was, long before the accident. Mahogany hair shining in the sun, a little girl of about three balanced on her hip. The ocean spread out behind her like a shimmering sequined blanket. Marla stood barefoot on a boulder, her head thrown back, her eyes squinting. A rose-colored sundress was caught in that split second of time and billowed up past her knees, showing a length of tanned thigh, while Cissy's chubby little arms encircled her neck.

Marla picked up the picture, her fingers holding the frame so hard her knuckles showed white. *Think, come on,* remember! *This is you and Cissy and . . . and the person taking the picture, the one whose shadow is partially visible at your feet, must be Alex!*

But try as she would, she couldn't recall the day at the beach. Or any specific day for that matter.

"Give yourself time," Marla said again, replacing the photo and nearly dropping it as her fingers didn't move with the dexterity they should. She still felt clumsy and awkward, out of sync. Edgy, she made her way to the nursery. James wasn't in his crib, but she didn't panic. The nanny probably had him downstairs, or Eugenia, "Nana," as she called herself, could be *doting* on him for she certainly acted as if the boy's birth was nearly as important as the Second Coming. Or maybe even the First.

Outside the nursery, she heard voices floating up from downstairs, but decided, while she was alone, to do a little exploring—get the feel of the place. Whether it was paranoia or just a need for self-preservation, she wanted to learn as much about herself and her family as possible, and not always by asking questions and getting answers she felt had been premeditated and carefully constructed so as not to upset her. She'd have to straighten that out, and fast. She was home now. Ready to get on with her life, eager to put the past behind.

But you can't. Not yet. You still have so much to remember and the police to deal with . . . Marla's thoughts turned dark with regret, but she pushed them from her mind. She would have to call Pam's daughter and her ex-husband, try to express her grief and regret and she'd have to do it soon. Regardless of the police. Or the attorneys. Or the damned insurance companies that she'd heard Alex whispering about.

She walked through the suite, a sitting area with its own fireplace and verandah, then tried the door to Alex's room and found it unlocked.

Without thinking twice she stepped inside. The room was as neat as if he expected a military inspection. A king-sized bed, dresser, small couch and armoire hiding a television and stereo system were placed around the room. A bay window offered a view of the grounds, and farther off, the lights of the city. Through a walk-in closet filled with suits and sports clothes hung with precision was an exercise room and the equipment that kept him in shape. Marla ran her fingers over the handle bars of the exercise bike and eyed the treadmill, weight bench and NordicTrack, wondering if she'd ever used any of this stuff. She was in reasonably good shape, but she couldn't imagine spending hours in this room working up a sweat. No, something told her she'd rather be outside . . . walking, running, playing tennis, riding . . . maybe even rowing.

Through another door she stepped into a private office, paneled in dark wood, accented with brass fixtures. Forest green leather furniture, potted plants, and beveled glass windows mounted high, near the ceiling, offering light but no view.

This, she supposed, was her husband's sanctuary. It smelled faintly of smoke and his aftershave. Oils of racehorses graced the walls. Horses . . . In her mind's eye, Marla caught a glimpse of herself riding, through open fields, her hair streaming behind her. Her lungs had been near bursting, the wind rushing at her face in a torrent, and beneath her, there had been the feel of powerful muscles stretching under her legs . . . bareback? She rode *bareback?* Like a wild tomboy or American Indian in old movies . . . ? *Yes!* As if she'd done it a thousand times, she suddenly remembered the chafe of horsehide against her legs. Stunned, she swallowed hard. Her palms were instantly sweaty, her heart racing. She shook her head. How did that imagery fit in with everything else around here? With the pictures of sleek racehorses, thoroughbreds held on reins by liveried handlers or ridden by jockeys in racing silks and jodhpurs along manicured tracks? Nothing wild . . . or reckless or . . . free. All contained. Constrained. By convention and society.

Her knees threatened her and she dropped into Alex's desk chair to get a grip. "This is good," she said, but she wasn't certain she could believe it. The leather chair squeaked and she cringed. It wasn't that she was trying to do anything behind her husband's back, she told herself, but she just plain needed answers and she needed them ASAP. Yet she felt a niggling tickle of guilt as she flipped through the open desk calendar, as if she were invading someone else's private space. "Stupid woman, he's your husband, for crying out loud. There are no secrets between you."

But she knew the statement was false. She'd felt the secrets, saw them in his eyes though he tried to hide them. There were lies and deceit and . . . "Stop it!" She was making herself nuts. Certifiably nuts! Stiffening her spine, she riffled through the pages of the calendar, studying the dates, places and names, hoping something, any little haphazard doodle or notation, would jog her memory.

Her accident had occurred nearly eight weeks earlier, so she turned back to the date when her entire life had nearly ended.

That square was blank.

"Damn it," she muttered, feeling as if yet another obstacle had been thrust onto the road to her recovery. Most of the calendar squares were covered with pen and pencil marks, notations in two different hands—dinner party at the Robertsons, the Friday before, Cissy's riding lesson on the day after the accident were written in a soft, easy-flowing script. Alex's business meetings or squash and golf games were slashed in a bolder scrawl.

She picked up a pen. Wrote her name on a note pad. Compared the handwriting. It was different, a stronger, harsher script

than Marla's . . . or was she going crazy? She wrote her name
again. Alex's name. Then Nick's.

Maybe it was the accident that had caused the difference.
But an eerie sensation crept under her skin and she dropped
the pen.

She fought the feeling that something was wrong.

She was jumping at shadows, for no good reason.

So what about the trip to Santa Cruz? Why wasn't it on this
marked-up calendar?

*Maybe you were leaving Alex. But the baby? And Cissy . . .
perhaps it was a last-minute, spur-of-the-moment trip?* No. She
wouldn't have just left the kids. It didn't fit. Anxious, she turned
to the Rolodex. What were the names she knew? Robertson?
Phil and his wife, Linda, were listed. Lindquist . . . Joanna Lindquist, yes, she was in the cards as well. Joanna and Ted. Mill-
er . . . Randy and Sonja were listed but Sonja had been crossed
out as if she'd died or left. . . . With fingers that were still a bit
sluggish, she flipped to the Ds and searched for Pam Delacroix,
but there wasn't a listing for anyone with that last name.

"How odd," she thought aloud, tapping an old card at the
back and then, starting again. Slowly, card by card, she flipped
through, thinking that Pam's name and number might have
been misfiled. Some of the people who had sent her cards and
flowers were listed: Bill and Sheryl Bancroft, Mario Dimetrius,
Joanna and Ted Lindquist and . . . Kylie Paris . . . Her heart
stopped. That name was familiar . . . very familiar . . . as
if . . . as if she were a close relative . . . someone near and dear.
But the address and phone number meant nothing to her. *Think,
Marla, think. Why does this woman's name ring a bell and
none of the others do?*

But nothing came. Not one lousy recollection. "Damn it
all," she muttered and turned her attention back to Pam Delacroix. Why wouldn't she have listed Pam's name in this master
file of friends and business acquaintances?

Because she never existed. She's a lie.

The thought struck her hard. Like a hammer blow to her chest.

Of course she did exist, the rational side of her mind argued. *But she's dead.* You *killed her.* In her *car! The police are investigating her death. So, be rational. Use your head. Figure this out, damn it.* Pam had existed, was her friend, so there should be something in this house that would serve as a reminder.

A computer, monitor glowing, hummed softly on one corner of the desk and she wondered if she had the time to check the computer files. *Later,* she told herself, *when you know you won't be caught.*

"Don't get paranoid," she told herself. "Or you'll end up in the loony bin."

Marla touched the keyboard. The screen saver of tropical fish shifted and icons blinked up at her. With surprising ease she found the word processing program, nearly jumping out of her skin when she saw *Marla's files.* So she had used this machine! Good. That thought should have been reassuring and she tried to open the file only to discover she needed a password. Her heart sank. She glanced around the drawers, searching for a hint of the password and found none. She tried to retrieve her e-mail. Same problem. Attempting every combination she could think of—her name, her children's names, anything, she finally gave up. Her fingers beat a sharp tattoo on the arm of the chair and she heard footsteps on the stairs.

She jumped, for no reason she understood, knocking over a mug holding pens and pencils. It rolled onto the floor, spilling its contents. "Great." As quickly as possible, she scooped up the pens and pencils and crammed them back into the mug with its Harvard logo.

She heard the door to the suite open, the footsteps fading away. "Mrs. Cahill?" a woman's voice—one she didn't recognize—called, muffled.

"In here," she replied, determined to stay put. "In the office." She reached up from the desk, opened the door to the hallway and spied the open door to Cissy's room on the other side of the staircase. Her heart was drumming, her hands clammy, but she forced herself to stay calm. This was her house, damn it, her husband's room. She had every right to be here. So why did she feel as if she were trespassing?

A few seconds later a slim woman with flashing brown eyes and dark skin stuck her head through the doorway. "Hi."

"You . . . you must be Carmen."

"Yes."

Marla felt the urge to apologize. "I'm sorry I—"

"I know. Amnesia. Don't worry." Carmen stepped into the office and if Marla's change in appearance affected her, she managed to hide it. Dressed in a slim navy skirt and white blouse with the sleeves rolled up, Carmen said, "Mrs. Eugenia sent me to check on you and ask you about dinner. When I didn't find you in your room, I was worried."

"I'm fine . . . well, considering. Right now it's all relative, I suppose." Marla glanced at the computer screen again. "I don't suppose you know my password for this?"

"Sorry." Carmen shook her head. "I don't remember that you used it that much."

"How about where my purse might be—the one that was with me the night of the accident?"

Deep lines grooved the woman's high forehead and she pursed her lips thoughtfully. "I haven't seen it . . . or anything else from that night for that matter."

Marla's heart sank. She pushed the chair back. "How about my personal things, pictures of me as a little girl, or when Cissy was a baby?"

"Sure." Carmen brightened. "That I can do."

Marla's head snapped up. "Really?" This was something. Not much, but something tangible to link her to her past.

"Sure. All the photo albums are in the library."

"Maybe I should look through them and I know this sounds a little weird, but would you mind showing me around?"

"No problem at all. Now, about dinner?"

"Is it dinner time already?" She glanced at the skylight high over the staircase and noted that the sky was darkening.

"No, not until eight. But Mrs. Eugenia likes things organized."

"That, I believe," Marla said imagining her unbending, socially conscious mother-in-law. She doubted if Eugenia ever bent a rule, much less broke one, and she couldn't imagine the little woman ever adjusting a schedule.

As they walked across the hall, Marla said, "I checked. James isn't in the nursery."

"He's downstairs. With Fiona and Mrs. Eugenia."

Good. One less concern for the moment.

As deftly as a museum director, Carmen showed her the rooms on the third floor—Cissy's bedroom, painted in yellow and, it seemed, forever a mess with books, computer discs, CDs and magazines strewn all over the floor. Her vanity was covered with jars and tubes of makeup, her walls plastered with posters of teen idols . . . some of the faces looked familiar, but none of the names came to mind.

Another room on the floor was the guest room and Marla looked for any trace of Nick. There was none, of course. The room was as precisely decorated as her own. Too perfect with its matching oil paintings, color-coordinated drapes and carpet and casual, understated elegance. Fake. Phony. Why she felt this way, Marla didn't understand but she felt that her life and this house were a sham.

"What about Fiona—where does she sleep?" she asked as they walked along a corridor banked by soft lights.

"The live-ins are upstairs on the top floor," Carmen explained. "The cook, maid and probably the nurse when he arrives."

"Nurse?" she repeated.

"Mr. Cahill hired a round-the-clock nurse."

"For me?"

Carmen winced and rolled her dark, expressive eyes. "Maybe I wasn't supposed to say anything."

"No, it's fine. I would have found out sooner or later." They walked to the elevator. "You said 'he.' ' "

Carmen held up a hand and stepped inside the elevator. "I thought Mr. Cahill said the nurse was a man. Tom something or other, I think, but don't quote me."

"I won't," Marla promised, and as the car ground down to the second floor, she felt, for the first time, that she'd actually bonded with someone in this towering, beautiful, cold house that was her home.

They walked along a wide corridor that Marla assumed was the heart of the house. It was dark except for a few lamps that burned on tables. Soft music flowed from hidden speakers, and paintings that she suspected were originals decorated the walls. Floral print runners covered the hardwood floor and branched into several rooms.

She followed Carmen into what appeared to be the living room with intimate clusters of chairs and couches, potted philodendron and ferns nestled between small tables and a massive stone and brick fireplace that rose to a tooled copper ceiling that reflected the lamplight with a warm, mellow glow.

Through sliding doors, Carmen showed her a music room. Antique instruments adorned the walls and a concert grand piano gleamed in a corner surrounded by windows overlooking the city.

Another door led to the library, complete with glass-enclosed shelves that climbed to the ceiling. A wooden ladder attached to the bookcase rolled on casters from one end of the collection to the other. A globe was nestled in a corner near the fronds of a potted fern, and an aquarium, complete with neon-colored tropical fish, gurgled near the bay window. Marla doubted she'd ever withdrawn one of the leather-bound volumes, never stood at these windows, never curled up on one of the soft-looking pillows on the love seats . . . but then how would she know?

"Here are the photo albums," Carmen said, pointing to a shelf in a corner. Marla picked up the first volume, opened it and stared at her wedding day fifteen years ago. She and Alex, younger looking, he in a black tuxedo, she dressed in a white lace dress with a train that went on for miles. Other pictures of the church, the wedding party, the cake and reception.

An entire family assembled, with the exception of Nick. He wasn't in a single shot. But then he'd claimed to be the "outlaw" and she suspected that translated into black sheep as well. Rogue. Outcast. A man who kept his own set of rules which, she imagined, were often at odds with those of his brother and mother. No wonder she found him fascinating at a very basic and dangerous level.

Cloistering those particular thoughts, she studied one of the family assembled at the wedding reception. Eugenia, dressed in indigo, her chin thrust forward in pride, stood near a tall, gray-haired, distinguished-looking man who seemed bored by the festivities. Samuel Cahill, Marla knew instinctively. Along with Alex and Marla, there was another older couple as well. No doubt her parents. Marla's throat closed as she stared at the couple. The woman was reed-slender, with a pointed chin and haughty expression. Short dark hair, piercing eyes and a beaded dress of pale pink showed off her slim figure. The man at her side was tall and rangy, a John Wayne type who looked out of place in his expensive suit. His smile, if you could call it that, was forced, as if he were always impatient.

Hardly the warm family she was looking for, Marla thought with more than a shred of disappointment. Worse yet, she didn't recognize her own parents. The woman especially. There was nothing about her that touched her memory, and the man . . . no . . . she felt a flicker of something stir deep inside her, but she wasn't certain and she didn't like the feeling. It wasn't warm or familiar, no . . . it was more like hatred . . . a deep-seated loathing.

"No," she whispered, feeling sick inside.

"Mrs. Cahill?" Carmen's voice jarred her out of her reverie. "Is something wrong?" she asked, and Marla, embarrassed, snapped herself back to the present. The look on her face must have mirrored her thoughts because Carmen's smile fell away.

"I . . . I'm sorry. This is probably too much for you. I shouldn't have—"

"No, no, I'm fine . . . just a little disoriented and please, enough with the Mrs. Cahill, call me Marla."

"If you say so," Carmen said as Marla snapped the wedding album shut and replaced it.

"I say so, and just remember, I *need* to know. Everything."

"Of course."

At the far end of the library there was a sizable nook surrounding a wet bar and the scents of brandy and cigar smoke lingered in the air. They crossed the hall to another door. It had been left ajar and with one glance inside, Marla guessed the room belonged to Eugenia. Her mother-in-law's perfume lingered in the air. A carved wood bed dominated one wall near a private bath. French doors with sheer curtains opened to a private balcony. In the far corner an antique secretary and love seat crowded around a small fireplace decorated with hand-painted tiles.

"They're waiting for you in here," Carmen explained, touching Marla on an elbow and shepherding her into a long room with a television, two couches and a recliner. The baby was propped on Eugenia's lap, his wide eyes focused on everything and nothing. Marla smiled at the sight of his fuzzy head.

"Good Lord, what did you do to your hair?" Eugenia asked, eyes wide and mouth open like a dying, gasping fish.

"Gave it a trim."

"I'll say . . . well . . . don't worry about it."

"I'm not."

"I'll call my hairdresser. I'm sure she wouldn't mind stopping by and''—she fluttered her fingers anxiously in the air near her own head—"well, evening it up a bit." Then, recovering slightly, she leaned down and stage-whispered to James. "Look who finally woke up."

"What time is it?" Marla crossed the room, took a seat next to her mother-in-law and reached for the baby.

"After four, dear. You practically slept around the clock. How're you feeling?"

"Groggy," she admitted as she chucked her son under his little chin and wrinkled her nose at him. The scents of baby powder and oil tingled in her nose. "How's Mama's big boy, hmm?" she asked, her voice automatically rising an octave as she spoke to the little cherub.

"Cranky, is what he's been," Fiona supplied, as she walked into the room. "And he needs feedin' and changin'."

"I'll do it."

"But—" Fiona began to protest.

"Trust me, I need the practice."

"He *wasn't* cranky or irritable. His tummy was upset," Eugenia corrected.

Carmen, still hovering near the door, said, "Mrs. Cahill says she'll take dinner with the family."

"Really?" One gray eyebrow shot up over the rim of Eugenia's glasses. "Are you certain you're up to it? Dr. Robertson wanted you to get as much rest as possible."

"I'll be fine . . . as long as whatever's served is blended."

"Steak Diane, I believe, is on the menu, but we'll make an exception for you." She chuckled to herself.

Marla's stomach growled at the thought of real food, and she wondered as she changed the baby on a nearby table, then wrested James's bottle from a reluctant Fiona. She had the nagging feeling that something was wrong in the family.

Eugenia, seated on the couch, her high heels propped nearby, a tapestried bag of knitting needles and yarn at her feet, looked every bit the doting grandmother. Baby toys were scattered over a blanket spread upon the floor and Fiona, though seemingly not the sweetest person in the world, seemed completely relaxed and competent. Everyone had treated her well, yet she harbored some suspicions about them all.

She felt that everyone was hiding something from her; something vital.

She forced that ugly thought aside while feeding the baby,

her heart opening to the little imp who seemed to be accepting her . . . if just a little. Coco, the scruff of a dog, lying on a pillow near Eugenia's knitting bag, was another matter and regarded Marla as if she were Mata Hari. Dark eyes followed her every move and despite repeated warnings from Eugenia, the dog growled deep in its throat.

"Where's Cissy?" Marla asked, ignoring the animal.

"She went shopping with friends after school, and, of course"—she glanced at the slim gold watch strapped on her wrist—"Alexander isn't home from the office yet."

What about Nick? Marla wondered, but didn't ask, and winced as she rubbed her jaw.

"You're getting those wires out in a couple of days," Eugenia said, her eyes fastened on her knitting.

"It can't be soon enough."

"I imagine. You have an appointment to see the doctor who did the surgery and the plastic surgeon later in the week. If he takes them off, you can have your teeth checked, but it looks as if there isn't work to be done."

"Thank God for small favors."

"You'll be just like new," Eugenia predicted.

Marla hardly felt new. More like rebuilt, similar to a wrecked car that had nearly been totaled, but somehow salvaged. She held her tongue and tried to shake off any lingering feelings that she was being manipulated. By whom? And why? She had no answers and to take her mind off the wearing questions, she played with her son.

The baby started to cry and Fiona was up like a shot, removed him from Marla's arms, and announced she'd put him down for a nap. She was out of the room before Marla could protest.

The phone jangled and within seconds Carmen, carrying a portable receiver, bustled into the room. "It's for you," she said to Marla. "Mrs. Lindquist."

"You don't have to take the call—" Eugenia said, but Marla snatched the receiver from Carmen's outstretched hand.

"Hello?" she said around the stupid wires holding her teeth together.

"Marla! You *are* home!" an enthusiastic female voice nearly yelled over the background noise of voices. "You must've been going out of your mind in the hospital. How *are* you?"

"Still kicking."

"What?"

"I said, I'm all right," she qualified.

"Sorry, I'm at the club and it's kind of noisy here and your voice sounds funny. The wires, right? Anyway, I just thought I'd take a chance at catching you at home. When can I come see you?"

"Anytime," Marla said and saw the corners of Eugenia's mouth turn down in disapproval as she reached for her knitting needles and a skein of coral yarn.

"You can have visitors?"

"Of course." Why wouldn't she be able to see her friends? Her mother-in-law's lips moved as she counted stitches, then the needles started softly clicking.

"Well, I thought so, but Alex was very firm that no one was to visit the hospital. I tried, but ran into a security guard of a nurse who looked like she should have been a contestant in the World Wrestling Association or whatever it's called now. Anyway, she wouldn't let me pass."

"Is that so?" Marla slid her glance to the side where Eugenia was knitting as if for her very life. "Probably because of the coma."

"I imagine."

"But I'd love to see you now," Marla said, though she couldn't remember Joanna's face for the life of her. From the corner of her eye Marla noticed Eugenia's jaw clench. The older woman slowly shook her head in objection. Marla ignored her mother-in-law. "How about this evening? Drinks?"

Eugenia's head snapped up, lines of worry stretching around her eyes.

"Sure. Yeah. I won't be able to stay long, but I could drop

by when I'm finished with my next set. Say in about . . . An hour and a half?''

"Perfect. See you then." She said good-bye and hung up before her mother-in-law could voice the objections that were so evident in her eyes. Eugenia muttered something under her breath, then began ripping out her last row of her knitting, as if Marla's wayward conversation had caused her to miss a stitch.

"This isn't a good idea," Eugenia finally said, taking up her needles again.

"Why not?"

"You're in no condition to entertain. And you can't drink anything with the medication you're on . . ." Eugenia was knitting furiously, metal needles clicking to beat the band.

"Not even one glass of wine?"

"Absolutely not."

"I need to see my friends . . . and by the way, do you have any idea where my purse is? The one that I had when I was in the accident?"

Eugenia sighed. "I wondered when you'd ask about that. There wasn't one, at least none that the police could find. No overnight bag. Nothing."

"But surely . . . now wait a minute."

"I know, I know, it sounds odd, but that's all I know about it."

Reluctantly, her mother-in-law set aside her knitting. "Nothing's settled. You know, because of the accident . . . Maybe the police really do have it and are lying."

"No way . . . I mean that's too bizarre."

"Is it?"

"Yes! Why would they do that? Because they suspect me of something?" Marla asked as the phone jangled in her hands. She answered before thinking. "Hello?"

"Marla. You're awake. Good." Alex's voice had a sharp edge to it. "I just talked to Detective Paterno. Charles Biggs died this morning."

"Oh, God, no." She felt as if her bones were crumbling, as if she couldn't possibly support herself any longer. Now not one, but two people dead.

"Marla? Are you okay? I just wanted to let you and Mother know what was going on. The police will probably be calling again. There're some questions about how he died, maybe it wasn't just from his wounds." He paused for a second. "They think it might have been murder, that someone helped him along."

"I don't understand," she said, but suddenly felt as cold as death.

"Neither do I, but I wanted to warn you." Alex was irritated and worried; she could hear the tension in his voice, imagined the strain on his face. "Paterno won't give up until he's dug up something. I've dealt with him before."

"You have?"

"You remember . . . oh, no . . . he was looking into some trouble we had down at Cahill House . . . the situation resolved itself, but he kept sniffing around . . . anyway, you'd better brace yourself. No doubt he'll be calling you. With more questions. A lot more."

"But I can't tell him anything—"

"I know, I know, just be careful."

"But he's with the police."

"The San Francisco Police. Your accident occurred in the mountains, far away from the city and yet he somehow lands in charge of the investigation. Look, I don't trust him, okay? Just keep your cool."

"I don't have anything to hide," she said and sensed Alex hesitating.

Her heart galumphed.

"Do I?" she demanded.

"Of course not, darling. I didn't mean to rattle you. Just be careful."

Shaking inside, fearing something she didn't understand, Marla nodded, as if Alex could see through the telephone wires.

"What is it?" Eugenia asked, her lips drawn into a knot. Marla passed her the phone, tried to quiet the dull roar in her head. What was happening to her? Her stomach turned over at the thought of the poor man who'd been burned so horribly, then died.

Because of her.

Things couldn't get worse, she told herself, but she had the nagging suspicion that she was wrong. Dead wrong.

Chapter Seven

"Nice do," Joanna quipped as she stood on the front porch. She motioned to Marla's hair with sleek fingers decorated with rings.

"Thanks, I did it myself."

"That I believe."

Still reeling from the news that Charles Biggs had died, Marla ushered her friend into the sitting room off the foyer. Joanna breezed in as if she'd been inside dozens of times. A petite woman with short, streaked blond hair, dark eyes and thin lips, she was dressed in a white warm-up suit trimmed in gold, and white tennis shoes. Several gold chains circled her tanned throat and a tennis bracelet studded with hefty diamonds surrounded one slim wrist. Marla stared at the sculpted lines of Joanna's face looking for some clue, hoping she could remember something, but it was as if she'd never seen this woman before in her life. Disappointment assailed her yet again.

Joanna plopped onto an overstuffed sofa and dropped her hands between her knees. "So, how're you feeling?"

"Better, off and on. I still get headaches and these"—Marla

drew back her lips to expose the wires—"are the pits." She settled into a side chair.

"But necessary." They paused in the conversation while Carmen brought in a bottle of wine, two stemmed glasses and a small tray of fruit, cheese and crackers.

"Anything else?" Carmen asked, setting the tray on the coffee table.

"This should do it. Thanks." As Carmen eased out of the room, Marla poured them each a glass and handed one to Joanna.

"So you've got amnesia?"

"Big time."

"You don't remember me?" Arched brows lifted and as if to lighten the mood she turned her face side to side, showing off her profile. "What about now?"

"Nope, but then it's not an exclusive club. I don't remember anyone."

"Gee, just when I was beginning to feel special."

Marla couldn't draw up a smile. "Well, don't. I can't even . . . even remember my own kids. Isn't that sick?"

"Well, yes . . . that's the whole point."

"I know and . . ." Marla swallowed a lump in her throat and shook her head. "I keep reminding myself it's getting better. I have flashes of things that have happened to me, some a long time ago, others more recently. But, no, I'm sorry, I wish I could say, 'Oh, *yeah,* I remember you,' but I don't. Damn. It's so weird. I don't remember playing tennis at all."

"Good. Then I can pretend that I always cleaned your clock on the court."

"That's a lie?"

"A major lie. You've got a serve that scared the devil out of me." Sipping her chardonnay, she stared at Marla over the rim. Her dark eyes twinkled. "You should get it back."

"Along with my face?"

"Well, at least along with your hair."

Marla laughed a little.

"As for your face . . ." She lifted a hand, spread her thumb away from her fingers as if she were an artist measuring for symmetry. "Hmm. That'll take a little time, I suppose," she teased. "But my husband's a plastic surgeon, remember. Ted specializes in faces, primarily cosmetic, but he's done some reconstruction. Let me see—remember, I used to work for him." She paused for a second, little lines forming between her eyebrows as she thought. "Oh, that's right, you wouldn't remember. Well, good. It wasn't a great time." At Marla's perplexed expression, Joanna let out a sigh. "Ted was married to his first wife then. I was the evil other woman who stole him away." Joanna lifted her eyebrows and smiled as if a little proud of herself for sneaking a prize from a competitor.

"Oh."

"That was twelve years ago. Water under the bridge."

She placed her finger under Marla's chin and cocked her own head to one side. "You look so different, and my guess— now that's an educated guess, mind you—says that you're going to look great once the swelling and bruises disappear, but you're going to look different."

"Maybe better?"

"Maybe, but I don't know why you'd want to be. You had more male attention than you could handle as it was."

"What?" This was news. And yet she had a vague sense that it was true.

"Oh, yeah, you were always . . . well, you know, men noticed you." Joanna said it with a touch of acrimony, a hint of jealousy, and Marla wondered what kind of friends she and Joanna had been.

Or what kind of woman you were. Joanna isn't saying it, but she's hinting that you basked in the male attention lavished your way, even maybe went out seeking it. That particular thought made her stomach turn sour.

"I'm really sorry about Pam," Joanna said, plucking a strawberry from the tray. "I know she was your friend."

"Yours, too, right?"

"Never met her."

"But she was a member of the club."

"Was she?" A pause as Joanna ate the strawberry and her mouth moved to one side of her face, as if she was really concentrating. "I . . . I don't think so. I mean, I never saw her there."

"I didn't play tennis with her?"

"No . . . well, not that *I* knew of, but it's been a while, you know. You were gone for a while . . . on a trip to Mexico, I think, and then you got pregnant, so . . . well, *I* never played tennis with her and you were in our league . . . To tell you the truth, I don't remember you ever mentioning her. I just heard that you were her friend after the accident . . ." She turned a palm toward the ceiling. "Well, it's a big club. Lots of members. I don't know everybody, but no one in our group had ever met her."

Marla felt a trickle of dread. She was certain Alex or the police officer or someone said she'd played tennis with Pam Delacroix . . . or had she just thought so? Maybe her mind was playing tricks on her. It was all so damned frustrating and fuzzy. But there was one way to find out. "I don't suppose you happen to have an address book for the club?"

"Mmm. I do." Joanna licked her fingers and nodded frantically, as if eager to be of help. "In here." She set her glass on the table and dug through an oversized purse that was large enough to double as an athletic bag. "Now, if I can just find it." After searching through several compartments, she opened a zippered pocket and withdrew the address book. "Voilà!" she said, slapping the book onto the table between them. "Sometimes it's a miracle that I find anything in this mess."

Marla, feeling a sense of uneasiness, flipped through the pages, found the Ds and ran her finger down the names. Not one was familiar. None rang any distant bells. Delacroix wasn't listed. No name. No phone number. *As if she never existed.* "Damn." Somehow Marla had expected this—sensed it. She read through the roster again, and again, each time more slowly. It didn't help.

"Nothing, right?" Joanna lifted her shoulders as she cut off a piece of cheese and placed it on a water biscuit. "I'm telling you, I didn't think I'd ever heard her name before. We talked about it, Robin, Nancy and I—but none of us had ever heard you mention Pam." She popped the piece of Brie and cracker into her mouth. "You know, we used to play doubles together a couple of times a week. You'd have thought one of us would have remembered you talking about her."

"But she was with me that night and now ... now she's dead. Along with the trucker."

"He died?" Joanna asked, cringing a little, her petite nose wrinkling in distaste. "Probably a blessing, considering."

Tell that to his family, Marla thought, sick at the thought. "It's just so ... hard."

"I know."

Do you? How can you possibly? Two people are dead, dead, *because of me and I don't remember a damned thing about it!* Marla gripped her glass so hard she was afraid she might snap the stem, but managed to hold her tongue. After all, Joanna was her friend, here to offer support, a link to the outside world.

Joanna's neatly plucked eyebrows drew together as she bit into the cracker again. "So, really, how do you feel?"

"Pretty damned bad." Marla, despite everyone's warnings, took a drink of cool wine. So it didn't mix with the medication—so what? Was it going to fry her brain or something? So she couldn't remember? So what if she was a little fuzzier? Big deal? Hoping some of the names in the club's roster would mean something to her, she slowly turned the pages again, her eyes sliding down the names, addresses and phone numbers, but though some of the names seemed familiar, she conjured no faces with Smith, Johnson and Walters ... all common names. No faces. "But, as I said, it's supposed to get better."

"Let's hope." Joanna lifted her glass in a mock toast and she used her index finger to point to Marla's hand.

"What happened to your ring?"

"I'm wearing it."

"No, not your wedding ring, the other one, the ruby ring. You got it from your father, I think, and you never took it off, called it your 'lucky' ring."

"I don't know . . ." She rubbed her finger, looked for an indentation in her skin to see if there was an impression where a ring she'd worn for years had been . . . there was none.

"They didn't steal it, did they? At the hospital? It happens sometimes."

"I don't know . . . I was wearing this one." She was perplexed.

"Well, you check into it; that ring's an antique. Worth a fortune and with your dad being so sick and all . . . well, I know you'll want it as a memento." She touched Marla on the arm. "How's he doing?"

"I haven't seen him," she admitted, feeling a little guilty.

"I know you've been worried about him," Joanna said. "We talked on the phone and you said you were afraid he might not last to see James's birth."

"He's . . . he's that ill?" Marla asked, surprised Alex hadn't said as much.

"You told me he was only given a few weeks . . . and that was over a month ago."

Marla felt ice form in her soul. "He's dying?"

Little worry lines formed between Joanna's eyebrows. "Yes, Marla. I guess you've forgotten that, too."

"I guess."

Joanna finished her wine in one gulp and checked her watch. "Look, this has been way too short, but I've got to run. Kids to pick up from tae kwon do, you know."

"Thanks for stopping by."

"No problem. Thanks for the wine, but why don't you, as soon as those wires come off, have lunch with us? Nancy and Robin would love to get together. We could hit some balls, or if you're not up to that, we could play bridge or just sit and yak. Whatever you want.''

"I'd love to," Marla said. "This elegant dental work is supposed to come off this week." She thought about how horrid she still looked, but decided she'd brave going out in public. These were her friends, for crying out loud, and right now she needed all the friends she could get to help her through this.

"Good, I'll set it up."

"Thanks."

"And Marla?" Joanna placed a hand on Marla's arm. "I'm really sorry for all this . . . trouble. When it rains it pours, I guess. First all those problems down at Cahill House and now this . . . you've certainly had more than your fair share."

"What problems?" Marla asked.

Joanna blushed to the roots of her hair, as if she was suddenly horribly embarrassed. "Well . . . It was probably nothing more than bad press . . . I'll see you later. Now, don't forget to check on that ring!"

With a wave, she was off, leaving Marla with an unsettled feeling in her stomach and a need to know more. So much more. Standing at the window, Marla watched through the rain-spattered glass as Joanna climbed into a flashy red BMW. Within seconds the sports car roared through the gates and down the hill.

"That woman's a viper," Eugenia said from behind her.

Marla jumped. She hadn't heard her mother-in-law enter.

"A viper?" Marla repeated, turning her head to see Eugenia glaring through the window. "How so?"

"A snoop, a gossip, ready to bite you when you least expect it. Poor white trash who had big ambitions. Set her sights on Ted Lindquist and broke up a twenty-five-year marriage without so much as a thought of Frances or the kids." Sighing loudly, Eugenia stepped away from the window, removed her glasses and polished the lenses with an embroidered handkerchief she pulled from her jacket pocket. "Well, I shouldn't gossip, I know, but Frances was a friend of mine."

"Joanna said something about trouble at Cahill House."

"Yes, I heard," Eugenia said in a sigh and Marla wondered how much of the conversation her mother-in-law had been privy to. Had she eavesdropped intentionally? "Well, I suppose you may as well know the truth."

"That would be nice," Marla agreed, her words sounding brittle.

Eugenia dropped into her favorite chair and behind her glasses, she looked old and weary. "It's nasty business. There were some charges leveled last year at the director of the house, a preacher who was charged with . . . being involved with one of the girls. Nothing came of it. All the charges were dropped, and the girl, who was under age at the time, remained anonymous. But you know how these things go. The press blew it all out of proportion. Alex handled everything, of course, but there were rumors that persisted, lingered like a bad smell, tainted Cahill House's reputation." She wiped the corner of her eye, though she didn't seem to be crying. "Anyway, it happened over a year ago—maybe eighteen months." Eugenia stuffed her hankie in her pocket and set her glasses onto her nose again. "People like Joanna feed on that kind of gossip, never let it die." She lifted her gaze to Marla's. "I believe it's because they have guilty consciences of their own and they always feel relieved when someone else is taking the heat. But, let's not dwell on it now," Eugenia said, as if to close the subject. "Now, don't you think you should rest for a while before dinner?" She checked the clock in the foyer. "And it's about time for your medication, isn't it? I think Carmen took it upstairs and left it in your room."

Marla wanted to argue, but she couldn't muster the energy. She was tired, her head beginning to pain her again.

"Carmen can help you upstairs."

"I think I can make it on my own."

"You shouldn't overdo," Eugenia advised, glancing at Marla's empty wine glass. The older woman's lips puckered in disapproval, but she didn't admonish Marla any further. "Alex has hired a nurse, you know. He starts tonight."

"I don't need a nurse."

Eugenia's smile was patient as she straightened from her throne. "We'll see," she said, and clipped out of the room. Marla, though her head was beginning to throb, made her way up to the library on the second floor, picked up several photo albums and hauled them another flight to her room.

Dutifully she drank the juice sitting by her bed, hoping that the headache would lessen. She kicked off her shoes, then slid between the sheets and began paging through the leaves of the photograph albums. She'd seen the wedding and moved on to snapshots taken in the first years of her marriage with Alex. Pictures of her in a convertible with Alex by her side, holding a drink aloft while sunbathing at some tropical beach, hamming it up with her tennis racquet and then with Cissy . . . and the man she now recognized as her father. The baby on his lap, he staring into the lens without a smile. She didn't like him. She knew that now. She'd never liked him. He was cold and distant and the woman who was her mother, she felt nothing for the wasp-waisted woman with the perpetual frown.

Think, Marla, think. There were pictures of the man standing on an expansive lawn and backdropped by a palatial brick house, Georgian style, complete with white columns, broad front porch, three square stories in the center, flanked by shorter wings of two stories. This was the home where she'd grown up?

Barely able to keep her eyes open, Marla flipped through other pages and each time she saw her father, something inside her recoiled, as if she were afraid of him, as if . . . as if whatever she'd done in her life, it wasn't good enough for him.

"This is crazy," she mumbled, blinking hard, but so damned tired she couldn't stay awake a second longer. She shoved the albums aside and sank into the pillows. She'd just doze for a little while, and then when she was clearheaded again, she'd tackle the problems, but when she slipped into sleep she dreamed, and none of the people in the dream had any faces, they walked around her, spoke out of mouths connected to no eyes or noses, laughed and joked, never including her.

She was an outsider. Alone. Isolated. She heard voices, but couldn't speak. It was as if she were invisible . . . somewhere far off a baby cried . . . and a voice, one she should recognize, saying, "I know, I know, but from now on, just jot down who called and I'll give her the message. Don't bring her the phone. It's too soon and too embarrassing for her. She looks dreadful. The poor thing can barely speak with her mouth wired as it is. Really, it's in her best interest."

Marla wanted to protest . . . the woman was talking about her. The baby stopped crying and Marla, nestling into the bed, rolled onto her stomach. She was so tired, so blasted tired. When she woke up, then she'd fix things, the people would have faces again . . . when she woke up . . .

"So Tough Guy's all right?" Nick asked, sitting on the edge of his hotel room bed and nudging off one shoe with the toe of the other. Cradling the phone between his ear and shoulder, he leaned back on the pillows and stared up at the tie-dyed canopy of his four-poster.

"Ye-up, as well as can be 'spected," Ole said. "I've got him with me and he's purty good, jes' keeps lookin' down the lane fer ya."

"I thought I'd be back sooner," Nick said. "Bit it might take longer."

"It figures."

Nick frowned as he thought how deeply he was getting ensnared in this Marla mess. But then, he supposed, his entanglement had been inevitable. As it always had been when it came to that woman. It was odd, though, seeing her in the hospital all battered and bruised, his bitterness at war with the pity he felt for her. *Poor little rich girl.* Or, more likely, *Poor, wretched, rich bitch.*

"Don't ya worry about Tough Guy none," Ole was saying. "I'm watchin' him and the *Notorious* as if they was my own."

"Thanks." Stretching the phone cord, Nick walked in his stocking feet to the window overlooking Haight Street. "I'll let you know when I'll be back."

" 'Preciate it." Ole hung up and Nick rubbed the crick from his neck. He'd been tense from the moment he'd seen Alex in the parking lot at the marina in Devil's Cove. It had only increased with each passing day. He looked up the hill. Somewhere up there Marla was recuperating, hopefully starting to remember. His conscience twinged a bit for there were certain parts of his life that would best be forgotten. But they lingered, just under the surface where memories of dark corners, hot skin and the musky smell of sex was ever-present. Marla had been the most provocative woman he'd ever known.

The only one who had really gotten to him.

No matter what the circumstance, whenever they'd been together, passion had sizzled around the edges of their conversation, in the sultry glances she'd cast in his direction, in the butterfly soft touch of her fingers against his neck or chest. Never had any woman affected him so. Not before. Not after.

He'd been foolish enough to think that it wasn't her, but them. The two of them with some kind of cosmic, unique chemistry. Of course, he'd been wrong. And he'd been old enough that he should have known better. Twenty-four wasn't exactly a kid, but he'd lost all sense of sanity when he'd been around her.

"Shit," he muttered under his breath as he returned the receiver to its cradle. He was supposed to go up to the house for dinner. Eugenia had issued one of her commands masked as an invitation. He plowed stiff fingers through his hair.

Knuckles rapped softly against his door.

Scowling, he crossed the room and yanked hard on the knob. On the other side of the threshold, a tiny fist raised to beat on the door again, stood Cherise. "Oh, good, I was afraid you

might not be in,'' she said, and without an invitation, breezed
in on a cloud of some kind of perfume he'd smelled before—
a long time before. She was nervous, though she tried to play
it cool in her black leather jacket, jeans and matching sweater.
Her blond hair was swept up and pinned on the back of her
head with glittery clips and she wore more makeup than she
needed. Gold eyes, rimmed in thick black eyelashes, stared at
him. ''I came here because I have something I want to talk to
you about.''

''Wait a minute, how did you know where I was staying?''
Nick asked, and she lifted a shoulder as she set a damp umbrella
under the table.

''Monty found out somehow.''

''How would he know?''

''Beats me, but . . . he has connections.''

Whatever that meant. But then Montgomery Cahill had
always been on the sneaky side. Uncle Fenton had been known
to say that his son had a little snake oil in his blood. Nick
believed it. He also thought everyone named Cahill had been
blessed with that same genetic flaw. Nick let the comment slide
as Cherise dropped into a chair near the window and glanced
through the half-drawn curtains.

''You want a drink?''

''No . . . I . . . well, I gave that up when I accepted Jesus.''
She shook her head vehemently and the little clips in her hair
twinkled in the lamplight.

Fine. ''But you won't mind if I have one?''

''Suit yourself. I try not to judge.''

''Good idea,'' he said, remembering her as a teenager and
her affinity for marijuana, speed and LSD. Eventually she'd
become a cocaine addict and between husbands two and three
had gone through treatment. Now, it seemed, she'd found the
Lord, through her latest husband. Nick opened the minibar and
grabbed a can of beer. ''You said you came here for a reason.''
He popped open the tab and sat at the foot of the bed.

"It's about Marla." Cherise perched on the edge of the chair as if she expected to bolt at any second.

"What about her?"

"I was hoping you had talked to Alex about me visiting her."

"I brought it up. He thinks she shouldn't have visitors."

"But we're family," Cherise complained. "You know she and I were always close."

This was news. *Or a lie.* He took a long pull on the can. "I hadn't heard."

"Come on, Nick. You remember. We always hung out together when you . . . well, when you and she were together."

"I really don't recall."

"Well, it's true. I counted her as one of my best friends." She fiddled with the clasp on her tiny purse as she talked, fidgety little fingers with purplish polish working the gold button. Click, click, click. "And now Alex refuses to let me see her. I don't know if it's just me or all her friends, but I don't think it's right."

"I said he's not big on the visitor thing. I doubt if I can change his mind."

"Then go around him, for goodness sake. Tell Marla I want to see her."

"This . . . affection or friendship you have with Marla, it has nothing to do with the fact that you and Monty are making noises that you were cut out of the inheritance?"

Was it his imagination or did her eyes narrow just a fraction? "I suppose that's what Alex is peddling."

"Among other things." He drank half the can, watched her squirm a bit.

Her little face screwed up in vexation. "Wouldn't you know?" Disgust contorting her pretty features, Cherise tossed one hand in the air. "That's another issue," she said in a long-suffering sigh. "I know Alex is your brother, but if I were you, I wouldn't trust him as far as I could throw him."

I don't. "Why?"

"Because, because . . . he's running the company into the ground and he's a liar. Always has been and he won't change now. He's guarded. Secretive. And some of the secrets you wouldn't believe."

"But *you* know them?"

"Some of them," Cherise admitted, her eyes darkening with challenge. "But not all. No one knows all of Alexander Cahill's secrets. Not even his wife."

"I suppose you think he could use a good dose of Christianity."

"Everyone could." Her smile was as phony as her eyelashes. She batted them coyly. "Even you, Nick."

"I'll remember that."

"Jesus forgives us all of our sins. Me. Alex. You."

Nick's jaw slid to one side as he eyed his cousin. "I don't know, Cherise, my list is pretty long. It could take him a while." To prove his point he opened his throat and chugged the Coors.

"Trust me. He's a very patient man."

Nick laughed and wiped his mouth with the back of his hand. There was something about Cherise he'd always liked; then again she was a real pain in the butt. Chameleonlike, Cherise seemed to blend into her surroundings, whether it had been the Junior League, drug scene, or now, her latest venture, into the world of evangelism.

"I'd just like to see Marla," she said, reaching for her umbrella as she stood. "I thought maybe you could arrange it."

"I'll talk to her."

"How is she?" Cherise asked as if she really cared, but Nick noticed it had taken her nearly fifteen minutes to ask.

"Comin' along."

"Good. Give me a call. I'm staying at the house right now. The number's the same as it always was." Balancing her umbrella with one hand, she dug in the small purse with the other, then withdrew a business card. "Here ya go." She handed it to him, and Nick noted the praying hands embossed in one corner while her name, address and phone number, linked with the Reverend Donald, her husband's, along with their church affiliation, adorned another. "And," she said, placing a soft, smooth hand upon his, "know that I'm praying for Marla. For Alex. For you. Donald is praying as well."

"Isn't that heartwarming?" he mocked.

"It is, if you think of it."

"Hell, Cherise, I think you're wasting your breath." He dropped the card onto the nightstand near the phone. "I'm a sinner from way back. Remember?"

"A lost lamb . . ."

"Or a damned wolf in sheep's clothing."

"You can't convince me not to pray for you, Nicholas."

"Wouldn't dream of it."

"You're impossible."

"I try."

"I know." She started for the door and Nick followed her in his stocking feet. "So . . ." she said, holding her umbrella in a death grip. "Next time I'll try harder to convince Montgomery to come with me."

"Do that. I haven't seen him since I was a kid."

"He's still the same," she said, her eyes darkening a bit. "Still playing the part of the bad boy. Still fighting his demons."

"I guess he hasn't found the Lord yet," Nick said, remembering Monty's fondness for fast women, fast cars and a variety of pharmaceuticals.

"I'm working on him. Donald is, too."

Bully for Donald, Nick thought.

Cherise changed the subject. "It'll be good to see Marla again. It's been too long. She and Alex were having some rough times, you know. They'd split up a couple of times."

"Is that so?" This was news to Nick.

"I think so. Once or twice maybe . . . but I shouldn't gossip. It's their business, but I do pray for them."

"I'll bet."

"I'd just like to reconnect with Marla. She must feel awful. I heard on the radio that the truck driver died, too."

Nick nodded. Alex had called him with the news. "I didn't know that Alex and Donald were close," he said.

She didn't meet his eyes. Swallowed hard. "They're not. But . . . well, Donald did some work at Cahill House, was even on the board of directors for a while. And he was the pastor at Bayside at one time. He's wonderful, Nick, a true Christian. Always volunteering where there's a need, you know," she said quickly, then, as if she was suddenly anxious to leave, reached for the knob of the door. "Just see if I can visit her, okay?" She hesitated, then added, "It's been good to see you, Nick. Really." Biting her lip as if she was afraid she'd blurt out something she shouldn't, Cherise touched a hand to his cheek. "Take care." And then she was gone, out the door and down the hall, the scent of her perfume lingering in the air.

Nick finished his beer in one final gulp, then tossed the can into the wastebasket wondering what the hell Cherise really wanted. He just couldn't buy into the sitting at Marla's bedside and reading the Bible bit. No way.

He slid his wallet from his pocket and found a beat-up business card from his days of playing God with corporations. Turning it over he read several numbers scrawled on the back and, hoping that Walt hadn't moved, Nick reached for the phone and punched the old number.

A gravelly voice picked up on the third ring. "Haaga here."

"Walt, it's Nick. Nick Cahill."

"Well, I'll be buggered, what the hell are you doin' callin' me after all these years?" Walt asked from his apartment in Seattle.

"I need some help. Want you to do some digging for me." Nick heard the click of a lighter on the other end of the phone, testament to Walt's three-pack-a-day habit.

"I thought you gave up the business," Walt said.

"I have for the most part." He gave Walt a quick rundown on just how he'd happened to land in San Francisco.

Walt barked out a laugh that ended in a coughing fit. "So it's true. Blood *is* thicker than water."

"Thicker than a lot of things in my case. Look, what I want is as much information as you can get on the accident, on Pamela Delacroix and I don't know anything about her except that she's got a daughter down at UC Santa Cruz. The kid could even have a different last name for all I know."

"Y'know a social security number, or driver's license or husband's name. Even a friggin' address would help."

"That's why I pay you."

Walt sniggered.

"Okay, so get as much info as you can and fax it to me or send it through e-mail. I'll link up my laptop here. Scan me photos if you can find them."

"Is that all?" Walt asked, not bothering to mask his sarcasm.

"Not quite." Nick was on a roll now, and he felt the same surge of adrenalin in his bloodstream as he had years ago when he'd made a healthy living as a consultant to companies in trouble. "I'll fax you a list of the employees of the company tomorrow along with some family friends that I want checked out." Nick stretched the cord of the phone to the window and peered through the curtains. He saw Cherise on the corner, glancing at her watch and holding her umbrella against the rain . . . or was it Cherise? She'd left his room over ten minutes earlier and the black jeans, boots and leather jacket were common garb here in the city. On top of that, it was dark—city dark, the lamplight weak and ethereal. She glanced back at the hotel just as an SUV pulled up to the curb and she shook out the umbrella. Her blond hair with those glittery clips caught in the illumination from the streetlights as she disappeared into the rig. She was still closing the door when the impatient driver gunned the engine, running an amber light, water spraying from his wide tires. "Check on all the members of my family," Nick instructed Walt. "Alex and Marla, and my cousins, Cherise and Montgomery—he goes by Monty sometimes."

"All have the last name of Cahill?"

"No, wait." He walked to the night table and picked up the card his cousin had left. "Cherise's last name is Favier." He spelled it and added the home phone number. "Her husband is Donald; he's with the Holy Trinity of God church in Sausalito." Frowning, Nick rattled off the number of the church.

Walt grunted, indicating that he'd gotten the information. "What about your mother?" he asked. "Eugenia? What should I do about her?"

Nick didn't miss a beat. "Check her out, too."

Chapter Eight

Tony Paterno stared at the computer screen where images of Pam Delacroix looked back at him, photos taken for her driver's license, passport, and a couple of more glamorous head shots she'd used for her business cards when she'd worked at a real estate company in Sausalito. Pam wasn't a dead ringer for Marla Cahill, but they certainly resembled each other. He'd seen the photos before, of course, but the longer this case dragged on, the more the two women seemed to resemble each other.

So what did that mean? That they were related? That the woman behind the wheel wasn't Marla and the real Mrs. Cahill had already been cremated? But why? And if so, there had to have been a real fuck-up at the scene. It was impossible. And yet . . . Drumming his fingers on the arm of his chair, he glanced at the other images of Pam Delacroix, not nearly so flattering, pictures taken at the scene of the accident. Lying face up on an embankment, her body was little more than a bloody heap, her neck broken, her face nearly scraped free of skin, her broken arms flung wide on the forest floor. Other pictures showed the wreckage of the Mercedes, windows shattered, metal twisted, leather upholstery ripped and covered in blood. Impact had blown the tires, shattered the glass, twisted the shell of the car and sprung the spare clean out of the trunk. It was a sheer stroke of luck that Marla Cahill had survived.

If she really was Marla.

Was the resemblance a fluke? Another coincidence? Could she be faking her amnesia? He snapped his gum and scratched at his jaw, his fingers scraping over a day's worth of stubble. Charles Biggs was dead—pushed into the grave by someone who'd slipped into the hospital, disguised himself and suffocated the poor bastard. Pam Delacroix or some other woman who looked a helluva lot like Marla Cahill had also been sent to her maker. The "accident" was looking more like a setup. But how? Why? Who was behind it? Who was the intended victim?

He thought hard. Motive. That's what he needed. Who wanted one or more of the three people involved in the wreckage dead?

"Son of a bitch." He pushed a button on the keyboard and leaned back in his chair as the printer whirred to life. There was something about the accident involving Marla Cahill that had never felt right, but he hadn't been able to put his finger on it. He'd inherited the case. As both victims who had survived the crash had been life-flighted back to the city, SFPD was handling the investigation on this end, helping out the California Highway Patrol who were first to arrive on the scene and in whose jurisdiction the accident had occurred.

No crime had been proven. No drugs, no alcohol in her system. There was no reason to believe that she'd been driving in a negligent manner as there were no witnesses.

But one woman had been killed outright and Charles Biggs, the only witness, had been murdered.

He twisted in his chair and picked up reports on all the people related to Marla Amhurst Cahill. What a bunch of bluebloods. Marla came from a wealthy family in Marin County. Her father, Conrad James Amhurst, was living in an expensive care center with a view of the marina at Tiburon. If Paterno's information was correct, the old man had one foot in the grave already. Pancreatic cancer. Conrad Anhurst would be lucky if he lived another three months.

From all reports the old man had been a womanizing bastard in his youth, his wife, Victoria, Marla's mother, a cold fish. She'd died a few years back, complications after cosmetic surgery—a liposuction that had gone bad. Paterno snorted but kept scanning the files. Their only son, Rory, had been injured as a toddler and had ended up in an institution. That left Marla as the wealthy old man's only heir. And she couldn't remember anything. Or so she claimed. Paterno's fingers tapped out a nervous tattoo on the arm of his chair. Maybe she was lying. But what the hell for?

He pulverized his gum as his eyes narrowed on page after page of reports.

The Cahills didn't exactly epitomize the *Ozzie and Harriet* image of the American family. Nope, they seemed a little more like something straight out of *Dynasty*. Eugenia was the matriarch—prim, proper with all the warmth of a smiling snake. As phony as the proverbial three-dollar bill.

Alexander, the eldest son and Marla's husband, was, from the outside, every woman's dream husband. Handsome and fit, educated at Stanford and Harvard, he'd practiced law some years before stepping into his ailing father's shoes and assuming command of Cahill Limited, an international corporation. When the old man had kicked off, Alex had inherited everything.

But Paterno didn't trust him. Rich, arrogant and sarcastic, Alex Cahill seemed to think he was above the law. Paterno had dealt with him before; didn't like the supercilious son of a bitch.

Alexander's brother, Nicholas, seemed to be the black sheep. While Alex had excelled in school and garnered athletic and scholastic awards, Nick had gotten himself into trouble with the law, deep enough that the old man had to bail him out more than once. None of the charges, everything from stealing cars to possession of alcohol to vandalism—had ever stuck. The charges had always been dropped. Probably because Daddy had paid off everyone involved, not that it said as much in the report.

Nick had finished high school and left home at eighteen, worked as a trucker, on an oil rig, even tried his hand at ranching in Montana where he'd later been a fishing guide. He'd owned his own fishing boat, ran a company that made truck parts, built up a small fortune and began buying and selling small businesses in the Seattle area. Somehow, he'd become a corporate troubleshooter, then quit abruptly about five years ago and settled down, presumably with enough cash, in some rinky-dink town in Oregon. Devil's Cove, for crying out loud. Somehow it fit.

Now he was back.

Because of the accident? Or, as he'd said, to help his brother with the company? What, Paterno wondered, could possibly be wrong within the lavish and hallowed halls of Cahill Limited?

Paterno leaned forward and spat his gum into a wastebasket. He tossed the report on Nick aside.

Then there were a couple of disgruntled cousins who felt that they'd been cut out of the family wealth. Montgomery Cahill and his sister, Cherise Cahill Martin Bell Favier, had been fairly vocal about being mistreated at the hands of their father and uncle. "Monty" had landed in juvenile hall a couple of times as a kid. Apparently his father, Fenton, hadn't had quite the same amount of influence with judges and cops that Uncle Samuel had. Or maybe he wanted to let the kid take the fall for his own crimes.

There was also the chance that Fenton just hadn't given a shit. That wasn't uncommon. Paterno had only to think of his own father to know how it felt to be overlooked or ignored. He reached for his coffee cup, took a swig and felt the burn of acid crawl up his throat.

What was the deal with Marla Cahill and Pam Delacroix?

Pam's ex-husband was screaming for justice, but Paterno suspected the guy smelled money.

And why had Marla Cahill, rich to the bone, been friends with a woman who didn't seem to fit into her social circle. He scoured the information on Pam again. She was supposed to have belonged to the same tennis club as the Cahills, but Paterno found no proof of it. But she was unpredictable. Had a law degree that she didn't use, though at one time she'd been a family practice attorney. When the marriage had fallen apart, she hadn't gone back to practicing law and instead started selling real estate in Sausalito.

Why?

Plucking the pages from his color printer he stared at the images of Pam Delacroix . . . or was she Marla Cahill? Had there been a misidentification? Could the police at the scene have screwed up so badly? The woman's ID had been on her, her body identified by her ex-husband.

And then there was the matter of Marla Cahill, who'd been wearing a hospital ID bracelet at the time of the accident. Now, even if she was amnesic, wouldn't her husband or mother-in-law know she wasn't who she said she was? She couldn't be bluffing the whole damned world, could she? There were physical traits and mannerisms, voice patterns . . . unless everyone was in on it.

A conspiracy.

Jesus, he was starting to think like Oliver Stone.

Paterno snorted at the turn of his thoughts. No reason to speculate. It was time to reevaluate the facts. He'd start with blood types.

Little James let out a cry and Marla, having overslept again, sprang from the bed. She was in the nursery in seconds, picking him up and holding him close. "It's all right," she said automatically as she cuddled him for a few seconds before changing him. She drank in the sweet baby smell of him as she snapped up his pajamas and watched his little legs kick. He fastened blue eyes on her and her heart soared. "You're cute as a devil and you know it, don't you?"

His little fists moved jerkily and he cooed.

"Oh, yeah, James, you're gonna be a heartbreaker." She finished changing him just as Fiona appeared with a bottle. "I'll do it," Marla insisted and as the nanny straightened the room, Marla sat in the rocker and, humming softly, fed the baby. He drank greedily, pausing only to stare up at her once in a while. "I know, I know, you're looking at me and hoping you're adopted, aren't you?" She winked at him and when he'd finally had his fill, she set the nearly-empty bottle down, hoisted his body to her shoulder to burp him.

"He's a good baby, he is," Fiona said as she folded a blanket over the end of his crib. "I've been with others who ain't as sweet as yer little James." She hesitated. "Now, Cissy, I imagine she was a fussy baby."

I wish I could remember.

"A headstrong girl she is," Fiona added, "going to get herself into trouble." She picked up the bottle and frowned slightly, as if she realized she'd stepped over a line. "Not that it's any of my business. Now, I'll take this little guy down to his playpen," she said and Marla didn't protest.

She felt better than she had in days, her head clearer, her body stronger. She knew instinctively that she would bond with the baby, but she had some major damage to repair with her daughter, who still stared at her as if Marla had stepped right off a space ship from Mars.

She took the time to shower and change, then decided to check the computer again, to read each name on the Rolodex. But she couldn't.

Alex's room was locked. Just as it had been the last time she'd tried to open the door. Was he trying to keep intruders out? Or did he have secrets he couldn't afford to let anyone, most of all his wife, see?

The sense of well-being she'd felt while holding her newborn disappeared.

She opened the door to Cissy's room. It was empty, the lights turned out, tidier than she'd ever seen it. No doubt while her daughter was at school, the maid had picked up after her. Marla felt a prick of guilt. As a mother, she should have been up earlier, greeted Cissy, checked her homework, asked if she needed clean clothes for physical education, found out what her after-school schedule was then seen her off to school, just as she should have fed and changed her baby before his morning nap.

Except you have servants for all those tasks.

Still, she was bothered. Joanna's visit replayed in her mind . . . *You had more male attention than you could handle as it was . . . none of us had ever heard you ever mention Pam . . . What happened to your ring?*

Marla paused at the landing and looked over the railing to the foyer two flights below. Faintly she heard the sound of conversation and rattling pans from the kitchen and the ticking of the clock downstairs. Other than that the house was still, no click of Eugenia's heels on the hardwood, no barks from that suspicious little dog, no strains of classical music wafting from hidden speakers.

Aside from the servants and baby she was alone. She walked the short distance down the hall to the office and tried to open the door. It was locked tight. Without a key no one could gain access to Alex's bedroom, exercise room or the office. He'd locked everyone out.

But why? What was he afraid of? That someone on the staff would riffle through his things? Or was he hiding something? But how could the maid clean up after him if he kept his room off-limits? Was he hiding something from the staff? Or from his mother? Or from her?

Marla rested her hand on the doorknob, tried to turn it again and failed. She even pressed her shoulder into the old panels, grasping at straws that the old lock might give way, but the door didn't budge.

The door is locked because of you, Marla, and you know it. He didn't like you snooping in his desk. He doesn't trust you. You've sensed it. She headed back to her room and eyed her bed, the one she slept in apart from Alex. *Somehow this is all because of Nick and what you feel about him.* Her throat tightened and though she wanted to deny what she felt, she caught a tiny glimpse of the woman she'd once been.

What had Joanna said? *You were always . . . well, you know, men noticed you.*

Joanna had said a lot of disturbing things. Where was the damned ring Joanna had mentioned? The gift from her father. At the thought of Conrad Amhurst she felt a dark weight in her heart, a pain she didn't understand. She couldn't remember the man and yet she was certain their relationship was far from loving, maybe even estranged.

So why wear the ring?

More important, where was it? In her room? In Pam's wrecked Mercedes? Locked in some safe? There was only one way to find out: find the damned thing. She started with her bathroom and the jewelry box on the counter. No ring. She checked the nightstands, then searched through every drawer in her bureau. Nothing. "Think, Marla, think," she muttered under her breath and walked into the closet, hoping to spy another cache for her favorite pieces of jewelry, but found nothing.

Maybe Alex had it removed when she'd gone to the hospital.

But he didn't ask that your wedding ring be taken off, now, did he?

She swept her gaze over the contents of the closet once more and stopped short when she spied the case for her tennis racquet. Maybe inside. She unzipped the leather case, looked through the one flat pocket and found no ring, nothing but a credit card receipt from a store downtown.

She stuffed the receipt in her pocket, then pulled out the

racquet and held it in her hand, hefted its weight, lifted it up and down, testing its feel.

You've got a serve that scared the devil out of me.

"Okay, ace, let's see it," she said to herself.

Pretending to toss a ball in the air with her left hand, she drew back her right. In a split second she swung the racquet up high over her shoulder, then slammed it down. Hard. The racquet whooshed and felt awkward as hell. The grip was too large, the weight uncomfortable. Had she really won tournaments? She tried to concentrate, but failed miserably. Again.

"Big surprise," she mocked. The closet was suddenly too tight, filled with clothes and memories that didn't seem to belong to her. She had to escape, to get out of this unfamiliar house with all its dark secrets and locked doors. She needed to breathe again. To find herself. Snagging a peacoat from a hanger, she hurried down the back stairs and through a mud room to a covered porch. Another few steps and she followed a garden path that wound through the grounds. A thin mist shrouded ancient rhododendrons, ferns and azaleas while tall fir trees rose ever upward to disappear into the fog and this patch of land, on the top of a city hill, seemed oddly isolated.

Burying her fists in the deep pockets, Marla walked along a brick path slick with rain and littered with fir needles. Her breath fogged and she shivered as she passed a series of tiered ponds. Beneath half a dozen lily pads, spotted koi swam lazily.

She was nearly certain she'd never gazed at the pools before. Nearly.

Frustrated, she glanced upward to the highest peaks of the house where the lights glowed in the windows. Moisture gathered on her cheeks and she caught a glimpse of movement, a dark shadow in an upstairs window. Was that her room? But she'd just come down from there . . . she recognized the print of the drapes . . . but who would be in her bedroom? No one was at home except the servants.

That was it. Whoever was in her room was probably just cleaning up, the maid going about her daily rounds and besides, who cared? It wasn't as if she was hiding anything. And yet . . . Marla glanced up at the window again and the figure was gone.

Angry with her overactive imagination she yanked her hood over her head and she edged around a garden spot where roses had been pruned, all hint of blossoms long disappeared, only short thorny stalks remaining.

The hairs on the back of her neck rose. She felt as if she was being watched. Turning, she looked up at the house again. There he was. The dark figure. He was lurking in another room . . . on the other side of the suite . . . Alex's? But Alex's room had been locked. She'd tested the door herself. Her heartbeat kicked up a notch. Surely it was only a servant, one with a master key, and yet she had the uneasy feeling that she was being silently observed . . . guarded. A raindrop fell from the edge of her hood and she blinked. In that second the image was gone—no sinister figure lurking in the darkened room. No eerie threat.

You're jumping at shadows, she told herself, but felt her skin crawl with goose bumps as she walked through an arbor and spied a swing set that was beginning to rust. Had she ever pushed Cissy on one of the swings? Ever caught her daughter as Cissy had laughed and slid to the bottom of the short slide?

Think, damn it, Marla. Concentrate. Remember!

She sat in one of the swings and pushed herself with her toe. There were grooves in the gravel beneath the swing, deep impressions made by tiny feet where puddles had begun to collect. She closed her eyes and heard the sounds of the city, the hum of traffic, clatter of a cable car, a dog barking his head off not too far away. Beyond the brick wall there were neighbors. Down the hill was the city, but here, in this fenced estate, she felt cut off from the world.

But San Francisco was just outside the electronic gates.

All she had to do was walk through.

And go where?

"Anywhere," she murmured, her hands chilling against the

cold links of the chain supporting the swing. *Nick's hotel is only a few blocks down the street.* No way would she go there, she told herself, but maybe, once outside this elegant fortress, she would find some peace, force her damned memory to return. She had to uncover what she could about Pam Delacroix— who the woman was, how Marla knew her and why they were driving to visit Pam's daughter.

Her head pounded with a zillion questions, and guilt, ever lingering just beneath the surface of her consciousness, was with her when she thought of the two people who had died in the crash. Two people. With families. She felt that she should pray, but knew instinctively that prayer wasn't something she did very often. Today, however, she figured she might make an exception. A little spirituality couldn't hurt. But she couldn't call up a single word as she balanced on the child's swing and the rainwater that had collected on the seat seeped through her jeans.

She heard the crunch of shoes on gravel and stiffened. Her fingers tightened on the wet chains supporting the swing.

"Marla?"

Her heartbeat accelerated at the sound of Nick's voice.

He poked his head through the arbor and did a quick scan of the play area. "I wondered where you were." Wearing a battered leather jacket and a pair of disreputable jeans, he appeared to stand beneath the canopy of a twisted leafless clematis. "What're you doing out here?"

"Thinking. Or trying to."

"Figure anything out?"

"I wish," she admitted with half a smile. "What about you? What're you doing here?"

"Looking for you." His face was all angles and planes with a hard jaw, blade-thin lips and a nose that wasn't quite straight. Standing dead center in the arbor, feet planted as wide as his shoulders, as if he didn't dare step any closer, he said, "I wanted to catch you alone."

The muscles in the back of her neck tightened. She met the

intensity of his gaze through the morning mist. Forbidden images of kissing him crept stealthily through her mind. For a second she wondered what it would be like to make love to him, to touch his skin, feel his muscles beneath the surface, run her fingers along that square, beard-darkened jaw. Her stomach did a slow roll of anticipation and she mentally berated herself for the lust that raced through her blood. He was her brother-in-law. She was a married woman. *Married.* She couldn't have these taboo fantasies. Wouldn't.

"I knew no one was supposed to be home this morning. Cissy's at school, Mother is with the board of Cahill House, Alex has a meeting downtown, so I figured that I'd pretty much find you by yourself."

She cleared her throat and imagined she recognized dangerously erotic thoughts running through his eyes. The same illicit visions that she was battling. "Why?" she asked over the steady drip of the rain and her voice sounded strangled. She told herself it was just because her teeth were wired together, but knew differently. "Why were you looking for me?"

"I had a visitor the other night," he said. "Cherise. She wants to see you."

"Why doesn't she just drop by?" Marla asked, and tried to ignore the fact that his jeans hung low on his hips, and that his shoulders stretched the width of his jacket, or that he was incredibly sexy—treacherously so.

"Alex nixed it."

"He doesn't much like her or her brother," Marla observed, dragging her eyes away from him as she recalled conversations between Alex and his mother about the cousins—bloodsuckers, money-hungry leeches, isn't that what he'd called them?

"Because they have a bone to pick with him. A sizable bone. Anyway, she asked me to pass the request along." Nick folded his arms over his chest and his leather jacket creaked as it stretched over his shoulders. Raindrops slid down his bare head and along his throat to disappear beneath his collar. Her eyes followed the motion.

Marla's mouth was suddenly as dry as the Sahara.

"I figured you had the right to know," he added.

"I—did. Do." She took control of her tongue. "Of course she can visit. Any time."

"She wants to read you Bible passages."

"Oh. Well." She cleared her throat then cast him a wry grin. "Maybe God's trying to tell me something. You know, that I should get some religion or something."

He snorted. "Cherise and her husband would be only too glad to accommodate you."

"I'll keep that in mind."

He dug into his jacket pocket, withdrew a card and walked forward, his boots crunching in the gravel. Handing her the card, he added, "You can call Cherise yourself. No need for me to be a go-between." Again his eyes touched hers and she knew that if the moment was right, if things were different, she would have reached out, touched him, silently invited him to kiss her.

A few seconds stretched out and she heard the hum of traffic, the steady drip of moisture from the tree branches and the erratic beating of her heart.

"Thanks." He turned, but she couldn't let him go. Not yet. Climbing out of the swing she stepped around the puddles that had collected near the play set and hurried to catch up with him. "Nick, wait. There's something I've been wanting to ask you."

She saw the cords stand out in the back of his neck before he turned to face her again.

"Yeah?"

"You remember how it was before . . . how I was."

"Before what?"

"Before I was married," she said and the skin over his face muscles stretched taut.

"I try not to."

"But . . . did I play tennis?" Her hood slipped off her head.

"You tore up the court."

"Ride horses?"

"I don't think so." He shifted and she stepped closer, tilting her head up to look deep into his eyes.

Every muscle in her body tensed, but she forced herself to ask the question that had been plaguing her since her conversation with Joanna. "What kind of woman was I?"

"That's a loaded question."

"Tell me."

His lips folded in on themselves. "You were a spoiled brat," he said. "Your parents gave you anything you wanted."

"And what was that?" she asked and thought she heard the scrape of a shoe on the brick path, but ignored it.

Nick's eyes darkened seductively. "Everything."

"Everything?"

"You had it all, Marla. Money, brains, beauty and it wasn't enough. You wanted it all . . . the whole damned world." One side of his mouth lifted in self-mockery. "And you damned near got it."

"Did I . . ." She began, stumbled, then pushed on. "Did I want you?"

He snorted. "No." His eyes narrowed and raw emotion played upon his strong features. His hands shot forward suddenly. He grabbed her by the shoulders, his fingers like steel through the jacket. He drew her so close that she could feel his heat, smell the hint of aftershave upon his skin, saw the slight, disgusted flare of his nostrils. "But I wanted you," he said through lips that barely moved. Contempt edged his words. "More than a man with any brains should want a woman, more than I'd wanted anything in my whole damned life. Is that what you wanted to hear? Are you satisfied?"

"N—no," she admitted, more confused than ever.

"Then things are just as they should be, because, Marla, you never were."

Footsteps crunched on the other side of the arbor. Nick dropped her arms as if she was suddenly too hot to handle.

Lars rounded the corner. Dressed in old jeans and a sweatshirt, he carried a shovel in one hand and a rake in the other. His face was hard, his eyes darting from Nick to Marla and she wondered how much he'd heard of the conversation, how long he'd been in the garden. Had he been watching them through the rising mist, hiding behind the walls of rhododendron and fir?

"They're looking for you inside," he said, motioning toward Marla with the handle of the rake.

"Who is?" she asked.

"Mr. Cahill," Lars said as he approached. His expression was hard. Condemning. "Your husband."

She couldn't stop the flush that crawled up her neck.

"He brought the nurse he hired with him." Lars's voice was flat but there was disdain in the curve of his lip, silent accusations in his steely eyes. He nodded to them both, then walked past the swing set to a gardening shed.

"I guess I'd better meet my new keeper."

"Is that what you think he is?"

"Don't you?" She didn't bother to hide her agitation. "Come on, Nick, does it look like I need a nurse?" She walked through the arbor and tossed her head. "You may as well come inside and watch the fireworks."

"You think someone's going to explode."

"You bet I do and it might be me," she said, hiking up the steps to the back door. "If Alex thinks I'm going to let him tell me what to do, he'd better think again." She wiped her feet on a mat and walked inside. "I'm not letting anyone put a leash on me. Especially not my husband," she said hotly, working herself up to an argument.

Together they hurried up the stairs to the sitting room where Alex and a tall, thin man with a short clipped beard were talking.

"There you are!" Alex said as he sat on the edge of a wingback chair, his hands clasped between his knees, his attention on the other guy. "Christ, Marla, where were you? I checked your room and called for you and I was just about to have the place searched."

"I was in the backyard."

"In this weather?"

She didn't answer. The wet shoulders of her jacket and raindrops on her face and the flush from the cold air should have been testament enough to her whereabouts.

"I thought you were in a meeting," Nick said to Alex as he positioned himself near the fireplace. Flames crackled in the grate and the smell of burning wood wafted through the room.

"It was canceled so I thought I'd show Tom around. Marla, Nick, this is Tom Zayer. He's Marla's nurse."

"Do I know you?" Nick asked, his eyes trained on the nurse. "Have we met?"

"Could be," Tom said. "I see a lot of people. I worked Emergency at Bayside and I had a job with Cahill House."

Nick's eyebrows became one. "You look familiar."

Tom snorted and lifted a shoulder. "It's a small world."

"It was at the hospital. I'm sure I saw you there."

"Could have been."

Marla managed a smile she didn't feel. Though her fists strained to clench she stretched her fingers and tried to keep a tight rein on her temper. "It's good to meet you," she said to the nurse. She offered her hand and shook his. "Unfortunately my husband's made a big mistake. Despite my appearance, I really don't need someone to look after me. I'm sure that Alex will be more than glad to pay you for your trouble, but I really won't be needing your services."

"Of course you will," Alex cut in, and Tom, dropping Marla's hand, stepped back, held up his hands as if surrendering, and looked from Marla to Alex.

"Hey, I'm not stepping into this."

"It's not a problem." Alex shot Marla a look that was meant to drop the argument in its tracks. It didn't.

"I'm fine. I *don't* need a nurse. It would be a waste of Tom's time, my patience and your money."

"This was Phil's idea," Alex said, his jaw clenched, a vein beginning to throb over his eye. Marla guessed it wasn't often anyone stood up to him . . . especially not his wife. "*He's* the doctor."

"Then I'll talk to Phil," she said, the reins of her temper slipping through her fingers.

"Hey, if this is a problem," Tom interjected, "maybe you two should work it out."

Alex pointed a finger at Tom. "It's not a problem. I obviously just should have discussed it with my wife in more detail."

"A lot more detail," Marla said, just as Eugenia's footsteps and Coco's nails could be heard in the hall. *Great, just what she needed.*

The older woman was stripping off her gloves as she rounded the corner and Coco shot into the room, barking like mad, making a pest of herself. "Hush!" Eugenia snapped as the dog yapped at Tom. "Now! Or you'll go to your kennel. Sit!" For once the animal obeyed. "Alex, Nick . . . Marla," she greeted. "I see you've met Tom."

"You know him?" Marla asked.

"Oh, yes, at Cahill House when he volunteered for us. How are you?" she asked the nurse.

"Fine, fine," he said nervously as Coco started barking again. "Maybe I should just go."

"Marla doesn't want a nurse," Alex explained.

"But why not?" Eugenia was crestfallen. "You do want to get better, don't you, dear? As fast as you can."

"Of course."

"Then it's decided."

"No way," Marla shot back.

"Hey, I don't need this." Tom was reaching for his briefcase. "You folks should sort this out."

Alex stood his ground. "There's nothing to sort out. You're hired and that's that. We'll take your things up to the servants' quarters and if you give me a minute, my wife and I will discuss it."

"Sure. Whatever."

Eugenia picked up the bad vibes. "Why don't you come

with me and I'll give you a tour of the house," she offered.
"Nick . . . would you like to come along?"

"I've seen it," he said stiffly, but caught the hint and walked
out of the room as Eugenia ushered Tom upstairs.

Coco barked wildly.

"Shut up!" Marla growled at the dog and stamped her foot
hard enough to jar her bones. "No more! Do you hear me?"

Dark eyes sparked. The little pedigreed thing seemed about to
yap again, but with a disgruntled woof turned and, tail tucked
between her short white legs, scuttled after Eugenia and the nurse.

"Miserable beast," Marla muttered as she turned her attention to Alex. "I don't need a nurse or a babysitter or whatever
it is you think you hired," she whispered, once she thought
she was alone with her husband. "And don't give me that
garbage about me not knowing what's best for me or that the
doctor insists, okay, because I'm not buying it. Not one word."

"Maybe this isn't just about you," Alex said, a vein becoming pronounced over his left eye. "Maybe it's about Mother
and Cissy and my peace of mind. How do you think I feel
leaving you here with just my elderly mother or teenage daughter to look after you?"

"I don't need looking after."

"Of course you do," he snapped, anger flaring in his eyes.

"I'm a grown woman and this house is crawling with servants. There's Carmen and Fiona and Lars and God-knows-
who-else!"

"None of whom have any medical training to speak of!"
His expression was beyond exasperation and he, like Nick only
moments before, clapped his hands on her shoulders. His eyes
snapped fire. Marla had the feeling he wanted to shake some
sense into her. "For God's sake, Marla, for once in your life,
think of others, will you?" he demanded. "This is a rough
time for all of us. And things aren't getting any better. I've
still got the demands of the business, you know."

"You don't have to worry about me," she said, but some
of her anger was dissipating, her self-righteous martyrdom

flagging at the desperation etched across his features. Was it for her? Or himself? A thousand emotions tore through her, and in an instant she remembered another time, on this very floor, the feel of his hands over her upper arms. She flashed to the rage in his flushed face, the vein, the very same vein throbbing in his forehead. *Bitch,* he'd snarled, or had it been someone else? The fingers digging into her forearms had been there before, hard, steely, causing a white-hot pain. How many times had they replayed this same ugly scene?

She must've paled, her horror shining in her eyes because it was as if he suddenly realized what he was doing and dropped his hands to his sides.

"Hell, Marla, would you just, for once, not fight it?" he asked and ran shaky fingers through his hair. The fire crackled and hissed in the grate and some classical strains of music wafted on the air, at odds with the tension in the room and the rain spitting against the windowpanes. Alex reached into his pocket for a pack of Marlboros and shook one out. "Let me take care of you."

Sagging into a chair, Marla dropped her head to her hands. "I . . . I remember . . . that we fought," she said as she heard the click of his lighter. She looked up to find him inhaling hard on the cigarette, then walking to the mantel. "And now . . . now you lock your doors." She glanced up at him, her head beginning to throb. "I wanted to get into the office, to use the computer, but I couldn't."

"Sometimes I have sensitive files in my office. Files from the office or the hospital or Cahill House. I don't want the staff to find them."

She flashed on the file cabinets she'd seen in his office. Couldn't they be locked? He didn't have to shut off the entire suite of his rooms, did he?

"I would like to think the staff is honest," she said.

"They are. I'm just cautious. Because of my position."

Or because you have something to hide—something else?

"It makes me feel more like an outsider."

"It shouldn't." With the hand holding his cigarette he rubbed his temple, as if fighting a nagging headache.

The clock downstairs ticked off the seconds and Marla felt miserable, wondered how far from her husband she'd drifted, how much further she would continue to drift.

"Look, honey, you're right. We did fight," he admitted. "More often than I like to remember. But I don't lock my doors or my files because of it." He shook his head. "No way, and . . . and I . . . was hoping . . . oh, Christ, Marla, you could have died in that accident, left me and the kids all alone and I was hoping, shit, I even prayed that you and I, we could find our way past all this." He spewed out a long stream of smoke. "We have two children. They didn't ask for any of this mess we created."

"No, no, they didn't." She felt miserable about the kids and yet she wouldn't let this man or any man for that matter tramp all over. "You can't expect me to just . . . sit here in this house, to not try to find out who I am, to not try and remember." Hot tears burned her eyes and she looked down, her fingers laced as her hands hung between her knees. What was wrong with her? Why did she feel the need to fight with him, to assert her independence? She remembered her response to Nick in the garden and closed her eyes for a second. What kind of woman was she, lusting after her brother-in-law, while she felt nothing for this man she'd vowed to love, honor and obey. Well, she was having one helluva time with the obeying part. It just wasn't her nature. She knew in her gut that it never had been. "I'm sorry for starting the argument," she said, lifting her eyes and fighting the tears that were determined to slide down her cheeks. "But I . . ." She lifted a hand. "I'm frustrated."

"I know, I know." He flicked ashes into the fire. "This is going to take some getting used to. For all of us. And it's going to get worse before it gets better. The police seem to think that Charles Biggs was murdered. They're certain of it. Someone posed as an intern and suffocated him and walked out of the hospital. Got away clean."

Marla felt cold inside. "Why?"

"Who knows? Probably some nutcase." Alex was tense. Worried. "It probably has nothing to do with you, or the accident, but I think we should err on the side of caution. I want to beef up security around the house."

"You think someone's going to try and do us harm?" she asked, rubbing her arms as if suddenly cold as she thought of Charles Biggs, a man she'd never met, a man she'd unwittingly helped to his grave.

"Frankly, I don't know what to think," Alex admitted and she thought of the figure she'd thought she'd seen lurking in the window.

"I thought I saw someone in the house today."

Alex's head snapped up. "Who?"

"I don't know. I convinced myself it was my imagination or one of the servants. I was in the garden and felt someone watching me, when I looked up, there was someone in the window, but I couldn't recognize him . . . or her."

"Jesus, Marla," he whispered. "Why didn't you say something?"

"Because I wasn't sure. It could have been one of the staff."

"But it freaked you out."

"A little," she admitted. "I blinked and he was gone."

"That does it. I'd rather err on the side of safety, okay? I'll tighten security and we'll try it with the nurse, okay? In a few days, or weeks, when you're stronger, when things calm down, I'll give him a paying job at Cahill House or pull some strings at the hospital to get him a job."

"You can do that?"

"Oh, yeah." He drew hard on his Marlboro, then jettisoned the butt into the fire. "One thing Dad taught me was that money can buy just about anything. Take Nick for example. If our old man hadn't bailed him out way back when he'd probably still be behind bars."

"He was in jail?" This surprised her.

"For eight hours. Assault charges. Someone got fresh when he was dating you. Nick didn't take kindly to it."

She sat still, stunned.

"He had a temper back then," Alex added. "And he's damned lucky he didn't end up pulling five to fifteen." Alex lifted a shoulder. "Water under the bridge now. He's cleaned up his act." He walked to her, placed his hands on her shoulders once again and this time the pressure was urgent but not painful as he drew her to her feet. His breath was smoky, his expression unbending. "Now . . . come on . . . Tom stays. For a while. Just for a while. Until you're better. Okay?"

Wondering if she was making a mistake of epic proportions, she nodded slowly, allowing him to draw her to her feet and pull her into his embrace. Her cheek rubbed against the fine wool of his jacket and her eyes closed for a second. "All right. For a while," she agreed, trying to dig deep and find some feelings of love for this man, her husband, the father of her children. All she needed was a little spark of passion, a kind memory, *any* damned sensation that there was something special between them. She fought tears and a tightness in her chest that told her this was all so very wrong.

She placed a chaste kiss upon his smooth cheek, hoped that she could somehow reconnect the frayed strands of their relationship. Alex's arms surrounded her, held her tight against him and again she felt nothing. Not one damned thing. Her fists clenched in futility and slowly she opened her eyes.

Looking over Alex's shoulder, she spied Nick standing in the archway, one leather encased shoulder propped against the wall, arms folded over his chest, his hair still wet and gleaming beneath the chandelier. Blue eyes regarded her with cold accusation and she remembered their meeting in the garden, the passion that had lurked just beneath the surface of his gaze. Now, his mouth twisted into a wry, self-deprecating line, as if he'd walked in on a scene he'd been expecting for quite a while.

"Marla," he drawled with more than a touch of sarcasm, "welcome home.

Chapter Nine

If he had any brains at all, he'd leave now, get out of Dodge and reclaim his life, Nick thought as he grabbed a beer from the minibar, snapped on his laptop and checked his e-mail. There it was. Walt Haaga's report, ready to be downloaded. Fine. Much as Nick hated the electronic age, how he'd sworn to never again be a part of the Internet community, he was, while here in San Francisco, a slave to it.

As he waited for the transfer of information to his disk, he popped open the cap of his beer and glowered through the window. What had he been thinking today when he'd found Marla in the garden seated in that child's swing, swaying gently as the mist had seeped through the vegetation. He should never have let himself be alone with her, never have touched her, never have considered kissing her.

But he had. And while he'd fought the urge he'd remembered in vivid Technicolor the way her burnished hair had fallen over her naked shoulders, the soft rise of her breasts with their dark nipples, the way her long legs had come together beneath a perfect thatch of springy curls.

"Idiot," he ground out and tossed back another long swallow. What was it about that woman that got to him? She'd changed over the years, matured, and her face was different, still scarred from the accident. The hot, sexy intensity in her gaze had been replaced by a different kind of passion. Deeper. Emotionally dangerous. But just as captivating.

"Shit." He finished his beer as the file was complete, then he called up the images, scanning Haaga's report page by page until he ended up staring at a picture of Pam Jaffe Delacroix.

"Son of a bitch," he muttered as he studied a woman who resembled Marla. She could have been Marla's sister . . . not her twin, but certainly a close relative. The same mahogany-colored hair framed a beautiful face, but her forehead was wider than Marla's, her eyes a bit rounder, her chin more pointed. There were other differences as well, of course. Was it just coincidence?

Or had Marla changed? Not just emotionally, but physically as well. Alex had mentioned that she'd had reconstructive surgery after the accident that had altered her looks so she was bound to look different from the woman he remembered. Were they the same person? Had they switched places? Identities? *What?*

He stared at the images. Pictures of Pam taken over the years—with her husband before the divorce, with a small child on a sailboat and then, later at the girl's graduation from high school.

His blood turned to ice water. What the hell was going on here?

"Think, Cahill," he told himself while dozens of questions assailed him. What had happened on Highway 17 that night? Who was this woman whom no one had met and yet was alone with Marla on the night she was killed? Why were the police still investigating if it was a simple accident?

He didn't like where his thoughts were leading him. He touched the computer screen where Pam's face stared back at him. She wasn't nearly as beautiful as Marla, but she could hold her own.

"Damn," he growled and snapped the disc from the computer. It was late, after midnight, but he'd seen an all-night copy center a few blocks away and wanted the reports and the images transferred to paper. He threw on his jacket, took the stairs and, with the disc tucked into a pocket, turned his collar against the wind blowing off the Bay. Traffic was slow and a fine mist caused the city lights to shimmer and blur. Stuffing his hands deep into the pockets of his jacket, he thought about Marla; how she'd nearly died on that winding mountain road.

And Pam Delacroix had lost her life.

He skirted a puddle, then jaywalked across the street to CopyWrite and a pimply faced kid of about eighteen who was far more efficient than he looked.

It didn't take long. Within the hour he had pictures, typed reports, financial statements, resumes, a list of traffic violations and enough information on Pam Delacroix and the members of his own family to keep him up all night.

At the hotel he spread the information on the bed, separating the piles and including the files he'd gotten from Alex about the business and Cahill House. Then he settled in.

Somewhere in this mess there might be a clue to what exactly he was being sucked into. He just had to look hard enough to find it.

Tony Paterno had hoped for a miracle.

He hadn't gotten shit.

He eased his '69 Cadillac, a wide-bodied convertible he'd inherited from his father, into heavy traffic and headed north toward the Golden Gate. Paterno usually played by the rules. Unless they got in his way. Then he'd been known to bend a few. Just as he planned to now. Even if it included breaking and entering.

Pamela Delacroix's blood type was O positive, the same as

listed on her death certificate. Marla Cahill's was O negative, which agreed with Bayview Hospital's charts. He'd talked to the officer in charge of the accident scene again and was satisfied that there hadn't been a major fuck-up. Pam Delacroix was dead.

So much for his switcheroo theory.

He flipped on his blinker and changed lanes just before the approach to the bridge and wondered why nothing was breaking in this damned case.

The composite sketch of the man wearing Carlos Santiago's ID tag on the night Charles Biggs had died could have been any white, six-foot male of about a hundred-seventy-five pounds who'd been in the San Francisco area that night. There had been nothing to distinguish the man from hundreds of thousands of others. The guy had brown hair, not long, not short, a moustache and glasses.

The suspect could have dyed his hair, shaved his moustache, found himself a pair of contacts and put thousands of miles between himself and the hospital by now.

So Paterno was back to square one.

Chewing on a wad of stale gum, Paterno watched the bumper of the Honda in front of him as the Caddy's wipers slapped raindrops from the windshield. On the radio a phone-in psychologist was telling some poor woman whose husband was cheating on her to "wake up and smell the espresso." Frowning, lost in his own thoughts, he saw the rust-colored cables flash by in his peripheral vision, and was only vaguely aware of crossing the neck of greenish water linking the Pacific Ocean with San Francisco Bay or of the fact that his old ragtop was leaking again.

He nosed his Cadillac toward Sausalito, and tried to ignore his sixth sense that swore to him that Marla Cahill wasn't who everyone claimed she was. But if so, then surely Marla's husband would see a difference in her.

Amnesia couldn't cover up old physical scars, couldn't change appearances, couldn't alter a voice . . .

"Hell." He nearly missed the turnoff on the north end of the bridge and had to gun the old car's engine to cut in front of a U-Haul truck and make the exit. Pam Delacroix had lived alone in a floating home on Richardson's Bay in an old artists and writers community in Sausalito. Her daughter was off on her own and her ex, Crane Delacroix, was an engineer of some kind who had worked for a software company that, when it had gone public, made everyone rich. Including Crane. From all accounts his ex-wife lived on her divorce settlement, never bothered practicing law again and dabbled at everything from glazing pottery to writing. She sold real estate part time, but hadn't had a sale in over six months and worked mainly from her home, not even paying for desk space at the company she was associated with.

A lot of people knew of her, he'd decided, but not many people really knew her.

He parked the Caddy in a guest area, then found Pam's floating home docked between a sailboat converted into a permanent abode and another platform home. It was quiet on the marina, the gray skies and soft rain offering some cover, which was just as well for what he had in mind. Paterno rapped hard on the door. Waited. No one answered, so he tried the door. Locked tight. But there wasn't a deadbolt. Glancing over his shoulder to make sure he wasn't being observed, he let himself inside with his credit card. Next time he'd get the damned search warrant; right now he couldn't be bothered.

Pam Delacroix's death was still considered nothing more than an accident, but Paterno was working from a different angle. Too many things didn't add up in his mind and two people were dead. Charles Biggs and Pam Delacroix would never be able to tell their sides of what happened that night and Marla Cahill was claiming amnesia. Someone hadn't been patient enough to let nature take its course with Biggs. Why?

There *had* to be a connection, a thread he could start pulling so that the entire tapestry of lies surrounding Pam's death could be unraveled.

Careful to disturb nothing, he walked through the lower level, two bedrooms, a bath, and a family room turned into a den. Complete with a freestanding fireplace and surrounded by bookcases filled to overflowing with Pam Delacroix's personal law library, the room was walled in dark paneling. A sliding door opened to a deck, beyond which was the bay.

Her computer sat on a corner desk and images of her daughter marched across the monitor.

Paterno didn't hesitate and snapped on a pair of latex gloves, then, careful so as not to disturb anything, looked through Pamela Delacroix's personal files. Neither Marla Cahill's phone number nor address was listed. There were no notes about her. On the date of the accident, nothing was scribbled on the calendar.

"Great."

There were books spread on the desk, legal references and manuals on police procedure and adoption, case histories of parental rights and, in the word processing programs, several chapters of a book that Pam had been working on. It looked like another legal thriller. So Pam Delacroix was hoping to cash in on the trend as so many other ex-lawyers before her.

The answering machine was blinking, so he hit the switch. Whoever had called had hung up without leaving a message.

Paterno made a mental note to check Pam's phone records.

He left the den and climbed a spiral staircase to the second floor living area. Kitchen, living room and master bedroom and bath were as neat as her office was messy. Not a floral pillow out of place, not a crumb on the counter.

He glanced at the pictures in the bedroom, scattered along the bureau top. Sure enough there was the kid, Julie, in her graduation cap and gown, holding a white cat with black and orange patches.

Nothing else seemed out of the ordinary. The closets were so neat as to have outfits arranged by color, the kitchen cupboards and drawers looking as if Pam had been expecting a photographer from *House Beautiful* or her mother-in-law to make a surprise appearance.

But not so the den.

Returning to the work space, he did a little more digging, checked into the files that were listed as having been last used on the computer's menu, but found only the roughed-in chapters of her book. Then he printed out the computer's address book and calendar.

Pocketing the papers, he let himself out and locked the door behind him. The next time he showed up he would play by the rules.

He walked up the ramp to his Cadillac and glanced across the Bay to the Tiburon Peninsula, a posh, scenic jetty of land. Marla Cahill's father, Conrad Amhurst, lived over there in a rest home. Paterno's eyes narrowed and he slid into the Caddy, throwing it into gear and driving out of the parking lot. His kids called the car a boat and wanted him to trade it in on a newer model, but he loved the red leather interior and the spot on the dash where his father's little statue of the Virgin had stood for nearly thirty years.

He didn't think he'd sell the car. Not for a while.

"*Mon dieu!*" Helene, Eugenia's personal hairdresser, took one look at Marla and nearly fainted right through the floor of the foyer. "But what happened?"

"I told you about the accident," the older woman said.

"No. I mean . . . her hair."

"Did it myself," Marla said, somewhat amused at the tiny woman's expression of sheer horror.

"Well, well, we will see . . . Oh, I will need to think on this." Then, as if she realized how her words might affect her new client, she smiled. "It will be no trouble, though. I can do wonders. You have a beautiful face, one you should not hide, let me see . . . You are satisfied with the color?"

"I just need a trim," Marla said, "something to even it up."

Helene sent her a sly, if-you-only-knew look as they took the elevator to the suite and the hairdresser set about working her magic. She insisted upon shampooing, conditioning and cutting what was left of Marla's hair. Her expression grim, as if her job was tantamount to sculpting a fifth face at Mount Rushmore, she worked, muttering under her breath, shaking her head and finally drying what, in Marla's estimation, was a masterpiece. Soft wisps of mahogany locks nearly covered her scar then tapered in layers to her nape.

"You are lucky," Helene said, tilting her head to admire her work. "Natural beauty."

Marla cast her a wry look in the mirror where her face was still swollen and slightly bruised.

"Oh, yes," Helene insisted. "This discoloration will soon disappear and with your cheekbones and eyes—you will be gorgeous. This I know." She threw up one hand and rolled her expressive eyes. "You should see what I have to work with at times."

"Thank you," Marla said, and felt herself blush, warming under the compliment. Tonight, damn it, she'd actually take dinner with the family. So she had to have soup. So she still had the wires. It was her family and she needed to feel part of it, to connect with her daughter and her husband.

And she did look better, she thought, catching her image in a hall mirror as she walked Helene to the front door.

The telephone rang and she didn't think twice about answering.

"Hello?"

"Marla is that you?" a woman asked.

"Hello?" another voice cut in. Carmen had answered before the second ring.

"I've got it," Marla said quickly. There was a click as Carmen hung up the extension. "Yes, this is Marla," she said and from the corner of her eye, saw Eugenia, still standing at the doorway saying her goodbyes to Helene, snap around.

"Thank Jesus I finally got through to you," the caller

breathed on a heartfelt sigh. "It's me. Cherise. I've been trying to reach you ever since the accident."

The front door clicked shut and Eugenia turned, her eyes narrowing on Marla as if she were a stern teacher and Marla was a naughty fifth-grader caught passing notes in class.

"Every time I've called I've been put off, but Nick said to keep trying and . . . well, the Lord must've intervened. How do you feel?" Cherise asked, her voice filled with concern.

"Better." Marla caught her mother-in-law's disapproving expression and ignored it. Upstairs the baby began to cry.

"I know this has been hard," Cherise was saying. "The injuries and the loss of your friend. It's a terrible, terrible time. The Lord's challenges are sometimes difficult to understand."

No kidding.

"The Reverend and I would love to visit you."

"The Reverend, meaning your husband?" Marla asked.

"Yes. Oh, that's right . . . I forgot about your amnesia." There was a smile in Cherise's voice. "He goes by The Reverend Donald."

An image of Donald Duck—one complete with halo and angel wings, one she was certain she'd seen sometime long ago—flashed through her mind. The Reverend Donald probably wouldn't like the comparison. "Come on over." The baby cried again and Marla cast a glance up the stairs. Where was Fiona?

"How about tomorrow? In the afternoon?" Cherise suggested.

"As it happens, I'm free," Marla joked, refusing to give in to a sense that she should have checked with someone before inviting guests. This was her house, damn it, and right now, judging from the wails rippling down the stairs, she needed to get off the phone and check on her baby. "I get the wires off my jaw in the morning, so I'll actually be able to speak clearly again."

"Perfect. Then I'll check with The Reverend and we'll be

there between three and four. Maybe I can even talk Monty into tagging along.''

"The more the merrier,'' Marla said before hanging up and facing Eugenia's scowl.

"You invited someone over tomorrow?''

"Just family,'' Marla said, rankled at her mother-in-law's superior, disapproving tone as she headed up the stairs. "Cherise and her husband. The Reverend Donald.''

"Dear Lord.''

"Her words precisely,'' she called looking down from the second floor landing. "Her brother might be coming along.''

The baby stopped crying.

"Montgomery. Wonderful,'' the older woman intoned through lips that barely moved. "This should be interesting.''

Amen, Marla thought caustically as she started up the stairs to get James. *A-friggin'-men!*

"Marla's different.'' Nick was slouched in the passenger seat of his brother's Jaguar as Alex navigated the car down Market Street toward the Bay. The sky was a light gray, the pavement wet from an earlier drizzle.

"Of course she's different. You haven't seen her in years.''

"That's not what I meant,'' Nick said, surveying the financial district of San Francisco with more than a slightly jaundiced eye. High-rises of concrete and steel towered to the heavens, traffic clogged the streets and pedestrians hauling bags, briefcases, backpacks and umbrellas hurried anxiously along the sidewalks. Traffic signals blinked as engines rumbled and people shouted. Pigeons and seagulls flapped on the busy sidewalks.

Nick hated it. All of it.

"Well, okay, so Marla is different,'' Alex admitted, pushing in his lighter as they stopped for a red light and a stream of people bustled both ways as they crossed the street. "She's just survived the birth of her second child and a traumatic accident that killed her friend and a complete stranger. Now she's got no memory, had plastic surgery and her mouth wired shut for nearly two months. You haven't seen her for years. Yeah, I imagine she seems lots different.'' Fingers searching, he reached into his jacket pocket, pulled out a pack of cigarettes and shook out a Marlboro just as the lighter clicked. He lit up. ''I hope she recovers . . . I mean not just physically, but mentally, that she shakes this amnesia.'' He braked for a stop light and traffic swarmed around the Jag. ''I doubt if she'll ever look the same.''

''She can have more surgery.''

''Yeah, why not?'' He stepped on the gas. The Jag shot forward. ''You've probably figured out that our marriage had more than its share of problems.''

Nick's jaw tightened. ''Cherise mentioned you split a couple of times. What went wrong?''

Alex cut him a hard glance. ''Marla's not the easiest person to live with.''

''But you are.''

''Yeah, right.'' Alex snorted. ''I guess it doesn't matter any more. Things are fine now. I only mentioned it because it was bound to come up and I wanted you to hear it from me.''

Nick didn't comment. He'd seen Alex and Marla embracing in the sitting room just yesterday.

And in the garden you'd damn near kissed her.

Alex guided his car into a parking garage under a gigantic building located just off the Embarcadero. All steel, concrete and glass, the building abutted the financial district and had housed the offices of Cahill Limited for the past seven years when Alex had decided that the small brick building the company had owned for nearly a century wasn't prestigious enough.

Nick figured the move was one of the major mistakes that had slowed the flow of black ink and turned it into red. The move alone had cost nearly a million dollars, and that was just the start. The lease was astronomical, an amount even an upscale address couldn't justify. Not in Nick's mind.

Alex parked in a narrow, reserved space in the basement

garage, then Alex led him to an elevator and they were whisked to the third floor and double glass doors etched with the company logo.

Alex paused long enough to introduce Nick to his secretary and collect his messages, then showed Nick to an expansive corner suite that held a large desk, grouping of couch, table and two chairs, full bar and credenza that angled around a corner. Alex Cahill's private domain, Nick thought. Behind the desk, a bank of windows made the most of a view of the city. Rooftops in varying elevations allowed glimpses of the Bay through the drizzling fog.

"There are worse places to work," Alex observed, ridding himself of his coat and scarf.

"Much."

"I know what you're thinking. That this is all eyewash, costs too much, and that the offices should move to a low rent district somewhere around the Bay, or maybe at the old place." He hung his things in a closet that was larger than Nick's at his house. "Believe me, I've considered it, but the convenience of being here, in the heart of the city, the contacts I've made in this building alone, the prestige of being a part of the financial district all have their rewards. And I'm close to the house, can be involved with the kids more than I could have before. Now, with Marla recuperating, that's a real plus." He shut the closet door and slid behind the desk, automatically flipping on his computer as he motioned Nick into one of the leather chairs.

As Alex glanced at the stock quotes on the computer screen, Nick noticed an array of pictures displayed on the credenza. Pictures of Alex shaking hands with the governor, standing in front of a Lear jet, in golf attire with a group of men, and then there was the family portrait. Marla, Cissy and Alex, taken over ten years ago, against a pure white backdrop. Cissy wasn't quite a toddler and rested, in full, frilly, pink regalia, on Marla's lap. Round-eyed and innocent, with apple cheeks and raised eyebrows, the baby had curiosity abounding in her expression. In direct opposition to her father. With one hand on Marla's shoulder, Alex, dressed in a black suit, stood behind her, his pose proprietary, his spine stiff, pride oozing from his smug, well-practiced smile. But Nick's gaze was drawn to the woman in the center of the photo. Not a lock of rich, mahogany hair was out of place. Her arms surrounded her daughter and her eyes, vibrant green, twinkled. Her smile offered just a hint of white teeth as she posed, the perfect corporate wife in a sedate black dress, creating an illusion that Nick knew hid the real woman deep inside.

"That was taken on Cissy's first birthday," Alex observed. "Twelve years ago."

"The happy family."

"Most of the time."

"You'll have to have another one taken."

Alex's eyebrows drew together for a second as if he didn't quite catch on. "Oh, because of the baby. Right. I suppose so." Tenting his hands under his chin and leaning back in his desk chair, he scowled. "Guess with all my other problems, I wasn't really thinking about a photo shoot. Now, I've told the staff that you're to have full access to anything you need and you can either work in the boardroom, or I can find a spare office."

"The boardroom'll do as long as I can take files out of the office."

Alex scratched his chin. "On the condition that you move into your old room in the house. I'd rather not have company records at the hotel, lying around for anyone to see, or move, or maybe even steal. It's not that I don't trust you, you know, but it's a matter of security."

"You already gave me some of the files," Nick said, not buying the excuse for a second.

"I know. I've had second thoughts."

"Bullshit." Nick's jaw slid to one side and was reminded that his brother, before joining the family business, had been a successful corporate lawyer. "Why are you and Mother so hell-bent that I move into the house?"

Alex hesitated.

"It's a control issue, isn't it? Not over the files, but over me."

With a snort, Alex said, "You've always been a suspicious bastard."

"That's why I'm on the payroll. So that you can put my suspicious brain to work. Or is it?" Nick demanded. "What is it you really want from me, Alex? You could have hired any one of a dozen reputable troubleshooters in this city. It doesn't take a rocket scientist to figure out that the way to save money is to cut overhead and raise prices, create a higher profit margin or sell more product at the same one. And as far as your family situation is concerned, you could have hired governesses, nurses, companions for Marla and Mother and the baby to free your time. You really didn't need me down here." He eyed his brother in his crisp tailor-made suit and two-hundred dollar tie. "So why the hell did you think it was necessary to drive all the way to Oregon to plead your case?"

Alex's lips rolled in on themselves and he paused either for theatrical effect or because he was hesitant to speak the truth. He glanced at the pictures on the credenza. "Because of Marla."

There she was again. Caught between the two of them. As always. Unspoken insinuations seemed to creep across the thick carpet and slide against the walnut and brass fixtures.

Alex leaned forward and his chair squeaked. "I knew there was a good chance she would lose her memory. Dr. Robertson had warned me about that. I also knew that seeing you might jog it. With everything going on, I wanted you here."

"You've never wanted me here."

"Maybe I've changed."

"Not until hell freezes over." This was all wrong. Alex was the last person on earth to pull a one-eighty.

"Marla might not snap out of this . . . malaise. It started before the accident, a couple of weeks before James was born, and it has something to do with you, Nick, whether you like it or not."

"I don't see how."

"There was something between the two of you and we both know it. Marla's always had a 'thing' for you and even though she married me, it was never quite over." He sighed and tugged at the knot of his tie. "It was your name she said before she woke up. Not mine." He frowned thoughtfully, then shrugged. "I thought you might help her heal."

"I'm not buying this. None of it. If she needs to get well, you can hire doctors or shrinks or whatever it takes, but dredging up something that happened fifteen years ago isn't going to help. No," Nick said, feeling guilt wrapping around his lungs, making it hard for him to breathe. True, he and Marla had been lovers but that was before Alex and she had married. Slowly he pushed himself to his feet, but his gaze never left Alex's eyes. "There's something more goin' on here. More than you're saying. I can feel it."

"And what would that be?"

"I don't know," Nick admitted, "But I sure as hell intend to find out."

Marla realized a little too late that she should never have come down to dinner. The entire family had collected around an expensive linen-covered table replete with china, crystal and silver. Candles had been lit, soft music played and a centerpiece of freshly cut roses, irises and daisies had been placed beneath a chandelier that had been turned down low. Alex was at the head of the table, she at the opposite end. On one side Cissy sat next to her grandmother, on the other Nick had taken a chair, sent her a cold glance, then appeared to merely tolerate the conversation around the clink of silver and soft music. Prime rib, potatoes with parsley, thin spears of asparagus garnished each plate, the aromas blending deliciously.

Marla felt completely out of place with her bowl of specially concocted bisque. This was the first formal meal she'd taken with the family and it felt wrong. Maybe it was the amnesia, or the prescription she was taking, she thought, grasping at anything that would explain her feeling of separation, from this, her family. Maybe it was paranoia returning. Or maybe it was because she remembered meeting Nick in the garden and wanting him to kiss her.

Awkwardly using a spoon she took a sip of her shrimp bisque and her stomach, tight with nerves as it was, felt worse.

The conversation had been stilted, stiff as a corpse. Alex had brought up the stock market and the business while Eugenia had mentioned Cahill House and the problems they were having trying to find a supervisor. Cissy, mostly quiet, had endured it all with long-suffering sighs and a bored expression. Marla hadn't blamed her. Nick had kept his comments to one-word responses and sliced into his slab of prime rib.

You were involved with him. He'd said as much. They'd been lovers. She felt her cheeks burn because she could well imagine it. Though she had no memory of making love to him, not one glimmer of his naked body in her mind's eye, she believed it. There was something about him she found irresistible. Unconventionally handsome, weather-beaten, with a cutting sense of humor that was downright irreverent, she found him sexy as hell and hated herself for it. Surely it was the drugs, her own state of confusion, this damned amnesia that screwed up her thinking, and yet, as she noticed the stony set of his features, his tanned skin stretched taut over high cheekbones, a broad forehead and square jaw, she felt that same pull she'd felt in the garden and in the hospital room.

She took another sip of soup, tried to concentrate on the conversation and didn't hazard another glance his way. Her stomach rumbled at the sight of real food and she couldn't wait to get the damned wires off. *Just one more day.*

"Mother says you invited Cherise and her husband to the house," Alex finally said on the other side of the flickering tapers.

"That's right. She called. They're coming over tomorrow."

"Do you think that's a wise idea?" Alex was cutting the

fatty edge off his prime rib. He sliced off a morsel then dipped it into a mound of horseradish.

"You know how I feel about guests," Marla said.

"But . . . well, Cherise and Montgomery, they aren't really friends."

"They're family."

Eugenia set down her fork. "There's some bad blood, you see."

"Oh, brother." Cissy took a long gulp of water from a crystal goblet where ice cubes and a slice of lemon danced.

"We'll talk about this later," Alex said as he glanced at his daughter.

"Yes, yes, of course." Eugenia flushed. "No reason to bring it up at the dinner table."

"Why not?" Nick asked.

"Cissy doesn't want to hear it." Eugenia forced a smile and reached for her glass of wine.

"That's right, I don't."

"I think it's a good thing they're coming by," Nick said, leaning back in his chair, his eyes a darker blue in the dimmed light. "Maybe it'll clear the air."

Alex scowled and shook his head. "It'll just be trouble. It always is. Even after I tried to help Cherise's husband out and gave him the job down at Cahill House—"

"Well, that's water under the bridge," Eugenia said frostily, and Alex scowled.

"Right."

Nick shoved his plate aside; looked as if he wanted to bolt from the room as the tense seconds ticked by. Marla set down her spoon and decided this was as good a time as any to make her request. "As soon as the wires are off, I'd like to visit my dad," she announced.

Eugenia was pronging some potato with her fork. She didn't flinch, but Alex's head snapped up. His gaze narrowed on her. "Conrad? Why?"

"He's my father for one thing. And it might help. For me to remember. I—I understand he's very ill."

"That's true and I'd love to take the family over to Tiburon to see him. Especially the baby. But I have to think of the poor guy." Alex shoved his plate aside, leaned his elbows on the table and rested his chin upon his knuckles. "What would it do to him, to see you this way?"

She caught a glimpse of her image in the cut glass over the sideboard, but she didn't cringe. She was healing. The bruises were fading, the swelling diminishing, her hair neat in the candlelight. "I think . . . I think he would be relieved to see that I was all right."

Eugenia washed down a small piece of prime rib with a swallow of wine. "I guess I could run over to Tiburon. Not this week, I'm afraid. I've got errands and meetings but maybe next . . ."

"I could probably go on my own," Marla said, sick of being treated like an invalid. She was beginning to think of this house as some kind of glamorous prison, which, of course, was ridiculous. But she wanted to see her father alone, without the trappings of the family.

"You can't drive," Alex reminded her.

"Why not?"

"The Porsche's in the shop for one thing and you've been in a coma—"

"And I'm not anymore. There's no reason to bother your mother with my errands. Or for you to make a special trip with me. He is, after all, *my* father." It was all Marla could do to hang on to her patience. Beneath the veneer of civility, the soft music, flickering candles and polished silver in this huge looming house, there was a thick, inescapable tension, secrets hidden in the dark corners. "And if driving is the issue, then Lars could take me." That thought wasn't particularly pleasant but she didn't care. And she felt the need to see her father and she needed to see him alone.

"It's no bother," her mother-in-law assured her with the patient smile that was beginning to grate on Marla's nerves.

Since subtlety wasn't working, she decided to be more direct. "Look, I need answers. I want to be well so that I can remember . . . all of you . . . everything and it's time I became independent. I'd like to see my friends, go to the club, and as soon as the wires are off, out to lunch." She watched for a reaction and Eugenia, cutting her prime rib, only elevated her eyebrows a fraction over her glasses. Alex tossed his napkin onto the table.

"Of course you do. As soon as Phil gives his okay, then you can do whatever you want. Besides, didn't Joanna come by and visit the other day?"

"Yes, but I didn't remember her." Marla looked from one face to another as Cissy reached for her water glass again and Nick didn't say a word. "Now, wait a minute. Am I under some doctor's orders to remain housebound?"

Eugenia sighed and adjusted her fork and knife on the edge of her plate. "Dr. Robertson just wants to make sure that you're up to any activities. And then there's your memory loss to consider—"

"I've considered it and I'm sick to death of it," she said, surprised at her own vehemence. "I think seeing other people, getting out of the house, reacquainting myself with some of my usual haunts, finding some stimulation might just trigger something, and I might remember." More than anything, she wanted to know more about herself. Her life. Her family. Why did she feel like such an outsider?

"I'll talk to Phil tomorrow," Alex promised as if that were the end of it.

She nearly shot to her feet. Instead she grabbed the edge of the table and forced her voice to remain calm. "No, I'll talk to him. I think it's time I did some things for myself."

There was a moment of tense silence, then Alex laughed. "Bravo!" he mocked with sarcastic enthusiasm. He clapped his hands as if he were at a tennis match. "That's the spirit! Now that's the Marla I remember!"

Eugenia frowned. Nick leaned back in his chair. Cissy rolled her eyes expressively.

"Why don't you call him in the morning?" Alex suggested.

"I will," she said, wondering why she'd thought even for a second that her husband was trying to somehow hide her from the world. No, not hide her, but coddle her, treat her like some kind of porcelain doll that he thought might break. Or crack. As if she were fragile.

"Do we really have to talk about all this stuff?" Cissy demanded, and Marla cringed inwardly. "I mean, all this memory stuff, it's all so weird."

Eugenia tossed Marla an I-tried-to-warn-you look.

"Cissy's right, this isn't the place," Alex said, a note of warning evident in his voice.

"Then after dinner," Marla insisted.

Carmen appeared as if on cue.

"But, really, there's no reason," Eugenia said, shaking her head and scooting her chair back. "I think I'll have my coffee in the sitting room," she said to Carmen who quickly disappeared again.

Nick leaned forward. "If Marla wants to discuss this, she should," he said. "It's *her* memory."

"Oh, God," Cissy mumbled.

Marla plowed on, grateful for some support, even if it came from Nick. "And I want to go to the ranch and see you ride," she said to her daughter.

Cissy rolled her eyes. "Oh, pulleeez, when have you ever cared about riding?"

"I told you before," Marla insisted and all eyes turned her direction. "I remember riding. It's just a hazy little image, but I know I used to ride horseback. I thought maybe you and I . . . at the ranch . . ." her voice nearly failed her at the censure in Cissy's gaze. "Maybe we used to ride together."

"Are you kidding?" Cissy shook her head and she almost

laughed. "Now you're really jumping off the deep end! Mom, you're afraid of horses. Something about being thrown off as a kid. Right?" Cissy implored her father with a searching look.

"That's right honey," he agreed, and her heart sank. "A nasty spill. No broken bones, but you've been deathly afraid of horses ever since."

Could she have been so wrong about herself? Were those flashes of memory nothing but ... what? Dreams? False images? No! She was certain. "I can't explain it, but I feel like ..." Her voice fell away as everyone had stopped eating and was staring at her, as if expecting her to say something. "I think ... I think I liked to ride." She looked at her daughter. "With you."

"Give me a break. Don't you even remember your phobias? God, Mom, this is really pathetic and weird and—"

"Cissy, that's enough!" Alex interjected angrily, his voice commanding and harsh over the quiet strains of classical music.

"No, she's right." Marla met her daughter's worried gaze. "It is weird and pathetic and scary and I wish it would just go away. But it's going to take some time, so please, just be patient with me, okay?"

"May I be excused?" Cissy asked, tears forming in her eyes, then without waiting for an answer shoved her chair back so hard the legs scraped against the floor. She was up in an instant, her napkin falling as she dashed from the room.

"You've upset her," Alex charged, staring at his wife.

"And you've upset me," Marla flung back, her fingers curling in frustration. "I can't stand this anymore. This not knowing. I'm not going to hide up in my room until I look presentable enough to go out and I'm damned well not going to shun my friends who want to see me, nor am I going to ignore my father and brother or Cherise and her preacher of a husband or anyone else. I'm going to get well, come hell or high water."

"You'll have to be patient," Eugenia said.

"I'm sick of being patient, okay? Now, I think I will start

remembering if I get out of this house and start doing some of the things I did before the accident."

"I think she's right," Nick agreed.

"Won't you be embarrassed?" Eugenia asked. "I mean your friends are . . . well, socially prominent women and—"

"And they must be snobs or idiots or a bunch of phonies if they can't accept me for what I am. Joanna Lindquist didn't run away and cower at the sight of me, did she?"

"This is ridiculous," Eugenia muttered, standing, yet lingering at the table.

Alex was staring at Marla. "I'm sorry," he said. "You're right. Maybe you should get out. I . . . I've just been worried about you." He leaned back in his chair and sighed. "You know we always host a party the week after Thanksgiving at Cahill House. This year I figured you'd want to pass, but maybe that's not such a good idea. We still have what two, nearly three weeks? Maybe you and Mother can see to it."

Some of Marla's bravado slipped. Her stomach soured at the thought of dozens of guests, all expecting her to be hostess. And yet, she had a staff to help her, surely she could do something. "I'm not sure that I'm up for a huge party."

"Of course you aren't," Eugenia said, glaring at her firstborn. "That's way too much for you. You can skip it this year. Everyone will understand."

"Wait a minute. I didn't say no, I said I wasn't sure." But the idea was beginning to grow on her and she wasn't about to play the poor little invalid and know that because of her condition, family traditions and social gatherings were being sacrificed. Already her daughter thought she was nuts. Besides, she needed to meet the people who were her friends. "Okay," she finally said, nodding to herself. "I'll do it."

Eugenia opened her mouth as if to protest, then sat down in her chair again.

Was there a bit of trepidation in Alex's smile? Or was it just her imagination working overtime? "Wonderful," he said with a trace of sarcasm.

Marla second-guessed herself. Maybe she was being rash. Suddenly she felt ill.

"Now," Alex said, "if you'll excuse me, I've got a meeting downtown. Drinks at the Marriott. Japanese businessmen interested in investing. This could be the shot in the arm we need." He walked around the table and planted a kiss on his wife's cheek. "You'll stick around a while, won't you, Nick? Entertain the women?"

Nick seemed uncomfortable but lifted a shoulder in half-hearted agreement. "For a while."

"Thanks." Obviously relieved, Alex checked his watch and strode out of the room.

"I don't need entertaining," Marla clarified as she pushed her chair out and stood.

"Well, I do." Eugenia arched a commanding eyebrow.

"If you don't mind, I think I'd better go up to see if Cissy's all right."

"She's just being a teenager," Eugenia said.

"I think she needs to talk to me." Not only did she want to straighten things out with her daughter, but she needed to get away from her mother-in-law *and* Nick—the outlaw, the man who made her question her marriage, her emotions, her convictions. She should avoid him like the plague, for she sensed, deep in the darkest parts of her soul, that he was a temptation she couldn't resist. She didn't need the undercurrents of emotion she caught in his glance, didn't want to speculate what it felt like to kiss him or make love to him or . . . She cleared her throat. "And then I think I'll rest."

"Are you certain you don't want a little tea or coffee?"

"I'm sure," she said firmly.

"Then Nick will be glad to help you upstairs, won't you dear?" Eugenia asked, and Marla had to press her lips together not to argue.

Nick sent his mother a guarded look. "Why not?"

"Afterwards come down and have coffee with me," Eugenia

invited. "I'm sure the cook can rustle up some cobbler or cheesecake or something."

"Coffee'll do," he said, but walked with Marla to the elevator. Her head began to ache again, her stomach was uneasy and it was all she could do not to sag against the elevator car's rail.

As the door closed, Nick pushed the button for the third floor then leaned against the side of the car. Again they were alone. In a cramped, far too intimate space. She tried not to notice his rugged good looks and irreverent damnably sexy attitude. He was tougher than Alex, perhaps more sinister. He wore his I-don't-give-a-damn attitude as if it were a badge. And, damn it, it intrigued her. While her husband was polished and Ivy-league educated, a successful businessman who entertained clients from all over the world, she guessed Nick was a loner, a man who could do just as well in a crowd or by himself. "Why're you here?" she asked as they reached the third floor. "I mean . . . not here in the house, but here in San Francisco."

"I thought you knew. Alex thinks the corporation needs some help." His jaw slid to one side. "At least that's what he says."

"But you don't believe him?" she asked as she walked into the hall surrounding the staircase. Music blared from behind the closed door to Cissy's room, and when she tapped and stuck her head inside, the girl, a telephone receiver to one ear, scowled.

"What do you want?" Cissy demanded.

"To talk."

The girl bit her lip. Looked as if she wanted to scurry into a corner and hide. Flipping her hair over her shoulder, she managed a bored expression. "Can it be later? I've got home-work."

Marla glanced at the phone and stereo. There wasn't a book in sight. But this wasn't the time to start nagging. Not when there were more important issues between them. She met the challenge in her daughter's rebellious gaze. "Okay. When?"

"I don't know." Cissy lifted a shoulder.

"But you'll let me know."

"Yeah," she said shortly, adjusting the phone to her ear. "Mom, *puh*leez . . ."

"Okay, okay. Tomorrow," Marla said, then closed the door and sighed. Nick was standing near enough to touch her. "I guess I'm going to have to sharpen my parenting skills."

"Is that possible?" Nick asked.

"I don't know," she admitted, wishing she felt any sense of kinship with her daughter. She checked on the baby, found him sleeping, then returned to the hall. Nick was waiting for her.

Rain bounced off the skylight far overhead and gurgled in the gutters. "I asked you if you believe Alex."

"Don't you?"

"Of course," she said quickly, unable to face the mind-numbing truth that she didn't trust her own husband.

Nick rubbed the back of his neck. His gaze was dark. Stormy. "I'm not sure what to believe."

"You don't trust him," she said as they reached the double doors to the suite. "Why?"

"That's between him and me."

"Yes, but I have this feeling that it has a lot to do with me," she guessed, and saw a flicker of emotion in his gaze.

His gaze dropped to her lips for just a second, then returned to her eyes. "You always were an egomaniac, Marla."

"Was I?" She managed a nervous laugh that seemed to ring hollowly. "Funny, I don't remember that." As she reached for the knob of the door, she shook her head. Exhaustion was taking its toll. She wanted to lie down, go to sleep, and when she woke up, hope this nightmare had vanished.

"What exactly do you remember?" he asked.

"Not enough, but . . . I get glimpses of the past, just tiny flashes, nothing concrete, nothing I can hold on to. Kind of like the spark in a lighter that's running out of fuel. Just a quick glimmer and then it's gone even though I try like hell to call it back.'' Her gaze swept around the hall with its thick carpet, the dark rail of the stairs, brass light fixtures and porcelain pots of philodendron and ferns. "But I have a feeling that my memory's coming back," she said, and tried not to notice the scent of his aftershave, or the dark promise she imagined she saw in his eyes.

"That's good news."

"The best."

His look was intense. Heart-stopping. "I'm pulling for you."

"Are you?"

He reached forward as if he intended to touch the curve of her face, then let his hand fall to his side. "You bet."

She felt a sudden rush of unwanted tears but fought them back. What was it about him that when he offered a tiny hint of kindness, she wanted to fall apart like some foolish woman, the kind she disdained? Forcing a smile she didn't feel, she tried to lighten the mood. "That might not be such a good idea, because when I remember everything," she added, opening the door and stepping through the crack, "everybody, including you, better watch out."

"What's gonna happen?"

A wry smile twisted her lips. "In your case, maybe I'll finally recall what it is that makes you so defensive around me."

He lifted a dark uncompromising eyebrow. "You know, Marla, some things are best left forgotten."

"I don't believe it and neither would you if you were me," she argued. "Not knowing is pure hell. Pure hell."

"I suppose." Again he focused on her lips.

Her pulse jumped stupidly. "Anyway, who knows what I'll remember? But it could be interesting, don't you think?"

"That's one word."

"And another?"

"Damning." His eyes searched hers. So blue. So intense. So knowing. Her breath caught in the back of her throat. What was it that bonded them so tightly, yet forced them apart?

Staring at the slant of his cheekbones and the set of his jaw, she swallowed hard, felt her mouth turn dry as dust and hazarded a quick glance to eyes as seductive as they were condemning. Oh, God, this was so wrong. And yet . . . There was something, a secret, a deep, erotic secret that she sensed existed between them. Wayward, taboo thoughts of lovemaking crept unbidden through her brain and yet they were fantasies, not memories.

"Good night, Nick," she said firmly, shutting the door quickly before she said or did anything rash, anything she might regret. This was crazy. *Nuts!* Nick was her brother-in-law and she was imagining what it would be like to touch him, to kiss him. She'd even gone so far as to tease him, *flirt* with him for crying out loud. As if it was second nature. What was it about him?

She sagged against the door of the suite. She was a married woman. *Married—as in* until death do us part. "Stop it," she chided, kicking off her shoes, then padded to the bathroom where she stripped and splashed cold water over her face. Maybe her fascination with him was the reason there had been problems in her marriage. Maybe she'd had an affair with him *after* she'd married Alex. Maybe he'd lied and the time-line was vastly different. Maybe . . . oh, God, no . . . maybe her baby was *his* child, the result of an illicit affair and . . . and . . . And she'd pawned James off as Alex's.

"Stop it!" she ordered, staring in horror at her reflection in the mirror over the sink. Her fingers grabbed hold of the marble edge of the counter in a death grip. Drops of water ran down her face and her skin was pale, but healing. And the woman in the mirror wasn't unattractive. No . . . If anything, she sensed that she would be beautiful. Just as Helene had predicted. She might not look *exactly* like the photographs that were strewn around this house, but she'd be pretty in her own way. *A Jezebel.* Good Lord, was it possible? Her hands shook as she snapped a towel out of its ring and dabbed at her skin. She couldn't . . . *wouldn't* let her mind run wild with fantasies about Nick or anyone else for that matter. No, she just had had to get a grip, let her memory take its course.

And then what?

"Deal with it. No matter what it is."

She found a pair of pajamas—white satin, of all things—and slipped them on, then ignoring the rumbling in her stomach, and the questions pummeling her brain, she climbed into bed, sipped the glass of juice dutifully waiting for her and didn't even bother turning on the television or leafing through the photo albums she'd stacked by the side of the bed. She knew she'd fall asleep instantly and she wasn't disappointed. The minute her head hit the pillow, she drifted off so deep that she didn't hear the footsteps enter her room less than an hour later, didn't know that she was being watched . . .

Chapter Ten

"Die, bitch!" The voice was low, gravelly. Filled with hate.

Marla froze in the bed. Her eyes flew open. The room was dark. So dark. Her heart jumped to her throat. Panic surged through her blood.

Oh, God, was someone there?

Squinting hard against the shadows, she scanned her room, her eyes adjusting to the slits of light sliding under the door to the suite. But no one was looming over her bed and yet . . . yet . . .

A cold clammy sweat enveloped her. Marla swallowed her fear and turned on the bedside lamp. The room was suddenly awash with soft golden light. Everything was just as it had been, right down to the matching pillows on the bed. She'd been dreaming; that was it. Probably because she didn't feel well. The soup she'd had at dinner, mixed with the tense conversation, had given her a bad case of nerves and a jittery stomach.

There was no one in the room.

She let out her breath and heard something—a muffled footstep? *What?* Heart thundering in her ears, she threw back the covers and shot out of bed. *Calm down,* she told herself, but couldn't stop the sweat that beaded on her skin as she slowly scanned the room—bathroom, closet, curtains, searching for any hint that a sinister presence had threatened her. She found nothing.

Rain lashed against the windowpanes and wind rattled the glass, but she was alone. "Get a grip," she told herself, but inside she was shaking. Her stomach clenched nervously, its contents roiling.

Had she heard someone or had the snarling voice been part of a fast retreating nightmare? She shoved a hand through her hair and, mentally scolding herself, walked through the suite where the lights were turned down low. Feeling a fool, she rapped lightly on her husband's door. "Alex?" she called through the panels. No answer. She tried the knob. The door didn't budge. "Alex?"

Locked out again.

Calm down, no one is here. It was a dream. Nothing but a damned dream! Alex hasn't gotten home yet. That's it. Relax.

But she couldn't. It was all too real. She checked the clock. Not quite eleven. She hadn't even been asleep all that long. *You were just imagining things, that's all. Your nerves are shot, Marla. You're jumping at shadows. No one was in your room. It was the tail end of a nightmare, one you don't remember. Take a deep breath and get hold of yourself, for God's sake.*

Edgy, she walked into the darkened hallway, then snapped on a light and stared at the empty, carpeted corridor. At the railing, she strained to listen. Above the soft strains of classical music, there was a quiet whisper of conversation, Eugenia's prim diction and Nick's lower voice. Marla's knees nearly buckled in relief. Nothing was out of the ordinary. She heard no scurrying footsteps. No heavy breathing. No sounds of Coco barking loudly at an intruder. *You're not going to hear the report of a gunshot, or the splinter of glass.*

Face it, Marla, you're just a basket case. No dark, ominous figure is lurking about. No sinister presence is scuttling away.

And Nick's downstairs. Somehow that thought was reassuring though Marla hated to admit it, even to herself. She wasn't one of those insipid, frail women who needed a man to feel safe. She was as certain of that small fact as she was of anything, which didn't say a lot these days, she thought.

But she couldn't depend on Nick. Or Alex. No. She had to rely on herself. Her stomach still ached and beads of sweat were chilling on her skin. This wasn't the first time she'd thought someone was at her bedside. She'd felt the same eerie, malicious presence in the hospital.

"Stop it," she ordered, her fingers curling over the railing. "There was nothing there. You're dealing with bad bisque mixed with an overactive imagination." Nonetheless, she had to check on the kids. What if there had been a stranger in the room? What if he was hiding in Cissy's room or James' nursery? What if cornered he would then grab one of the children? Hold either of them hostage? The family was wealthy and could easily be a target. Propelled by the turn of her thoughts, she shot across the hallway and threw open Cissy's door.

"What the—?" Cissy jumped up from her vanity stool, knocking over a bottle of fingernail polish. She dropped the brush. Purple polish splashed onto the vanity. "Shit!" she yelled loudly as she was wearing earphones. "Are you nuts?" She ripped off the headset and motioned angrily at the spilled polish.

Marla swept the room with her gaze. It was a mess as usual, books, sweaters, CDs and stuffed animals scattered all over the carpet, but there was nothing sinister about it. "I had a bad dream. Wanted to check on you."

"By scaring me to death?"

"I'm sorry, I should have knocked."

"No, duh! You're losing it, Mom."

"I hope not."

Cissy rolled her eyes, but her anger was replaced by teenaged concern. "Are you okay?"

"Fine," Marla lied. "Just . . . nervous."

"Maybe you should take some Valium or tranquilizers or whatever. That's what Brittany's mother does. All those kids drive her nuts."

"I'll think about it," Marla said, feeling like an utter fool. "Good night, honey. I'll see you in the morning."

"Yeah." Cissy nodded, but her eyebrows were still pulled together in one concerned, disbelieving line. She dabbed at the spilled polish with a Kleenex as Marla closed the door behind her and hurried across the hall to the nursery.

The night light set on dim allowed her to see into the room. James was sleeping soundly on gingham sheets and gratefully oblivious to any evil in the world. "Oh, sweetheart." Tears of relief filled Marla's eyes. Everything was all right. Her children were safe. No one had attacked her. Nothing was wrong in this guarded fortress of a mansion.

And Cissy's right. You're losing it. Big time. Get a grip, Marla. Now! She sniffed, swiped at her nose and fought tears. No one was in the house who shouldn't be. Life here was normal . . . well, as normal as it could be considering. Her stomach gurgled and ached, but other than a trace of nausea, she was fine. *If you don't stop this ridiculous paranoia you could wind up locked away in a mental hospital.*

"No," she whispered quietly, stiffening her spine. She couldn't bear the thought. This house was enough of a prison, but an institution . . . no way. Not ever. She wrapped her arms around herself and told herself that her nerves were just strung tight tonight, tighter than usual.

She glanced down at the baby again and a flash of memory sizzled through her brain. In an instant she remembered the hospital and the delivery room with its bright lights, the intense pressure and pain of the birth, a masked doctor delivering the boy and . . . and . . . the baby . . . her precious son . . . coming into the world. The labor had been long. Tedious. Worse than she'd expected. But in the end she'd delivered her son. *Yes! Yes! Yes! James was her child. Hers!* She remembered his crown of red hair, wet and plastered to his head beneath a coating of white and his face all screwed up and angry in the seconds before he was placed onto her belly and she held him to her breast.

I will love you forever, she'd thought at the time, *and no one's going to take you away from me. I swear it. No matter what.*

Vivid images were burned in her brain and along with the elation of birth there was something darker involved, something intense . . . fear . . . A deep-seated and mind-numbing fear that someone would take the child from her, wrest this precious baby from her arms . . . but that was insane . . . wasn't it?

She picked up the tiny bundle and held him to her shoulder as if she expected someone to rip him from her at any moment. Tears streamed down her face and her stomach spasmed. "Oh, sweetheart," she whispered, kissing his thatch of hair and drinking in the sweet baby scent of him. He cooed, nuzzled and sighed in a soft breath against the crook of her neck, evoking more tears in her eyes. God, she loved this tiny child. "It's gonna be all right," she said, rocking from side to side. "Everything's gonna be all right. Mama's here. I . . . I won't let anything happen to you. Not ever." *And how are you going to stop it?*

"However I can. Whatever it takes." She sniffed back her tears, and refused to be intimidated. No one was going to help her; she wasn't certain who she could trust. She'd have to combat her fears by herself. As she stood in the semidark for a few minutes, needing to hold the baby far more than he needed to be cuddled, Marla pressed her lips to James's downy crown. Outside a branch scraped against the roof and the wind rushed through the trees, but inside it was safe. James made tiny smacking noises with his lips and Marla smiled, reluctantly placing him in his crib.

She left the connecting door to the nursery slightly ajar as she made her way back to bed. Holding her son had chased her fears away, but she was still a little queasy. Her emotions were ragged, her mind jangled and frayed, her stomach in knots. She considered going downstairs, searching out the damned nurse, but felt like a wimp. Besides, it was only a case of nerves; nothing more. She couldn't imagine telling Eugenia or Nick that her tummy was upset and that she'd thought a stranger had stood over her bed and threatened to kill her, here, in her own home.

"Toughen up," she scolded herself, then downed the rest of the water in her bedside glass. She slid between the covers and told herself that tomorrow she wasn't going to sit around this house. No way. No how. Not one more minute. As soon as the damned wires were off, Marla would visit her father, her brother and the tennis club. She'd meet with Cherise, see if she remembered her. Her mind spun with plans of reaching someone in Pam Delacroix's family, finding out more about the woman she couldn't remember and the hastily arranged trip that no one understood. Maybe she could explain how horrid she felt about friend's death. Then there was Charles Biggs's family. She'd have to talk to the bereaved.

There were no two ways about it. Starting tomorrow, she'd take the bull by the horns and gain control of her life again—find out exactly what made Marla Cahill tick.

And what about Nick? Are you going to explore your relationship with him, too? "You bet I am," she said as she plumped her pillow. She couldn't get well until she knew the truth.

Reaching over for the lamp, Marla glanced around the room one last time. Elegant as it was, it still felt strange to her, awkward, as if it didn't fit, just the way she'd felt as a teenager, slipping into a beautiful, expensive dress, two sizes too big and belonging to someone else . . . the memory tore through her mind. Sizzling. Bright. Harsh. It wasn't just an analogy. She *had* tried on a fancy dress, one that hadn't belonged to her. She remembered it clearly. And yet . . . how? According to everyone she'd grown up pampered, the only daughter of an extremely wealthy man, treated as if she were a princess . . . surely she'd never have worn hand-me-downs . . . no way, and yet the dress, a soft blue beaded confection, was imprinted upon her mind. She remembered running her fingers along the skirt, feeling the smooth lining against her skin, knowing the expensive dress had belonged to another girl . . . one she didn't like . . .

When? How?

Her stomach clenched.

Was this a real memory, or all part of the dreams she was having? *Call for Nick*, Marla's mind screamed silently. *Alex isn't here and you need someone to confide in.*

But not Nick, oh, God, no . . . she couldn't . . .

Closing her eyes, she tried to concentrate. She'd been about fourteen at the time, not much older than Cissy. "Won't she mind?" she'd asked her mother. "Won't she care that I'm in her dress?"

There had been a sharp bark of laughter from the other room . . . the kitchen with its smells of grease and stale cigarette smoke. "She's got so many, she won't miss one."

"Mother," Marla whispered now, cold sweat breaking on her skin. She'd been talking to her mother. A fan swirled lazily overhead and flies buzzed at the half-open window. But why would Victoria Amhurst be in a shabby bedroom with yellowed curtains, a rag rug and dusty blinds?

Where had they been? Why had she felt like it was home?

Marla held her breath, thought hard, her fists clenching in the smooth sheets of her bed—this elegant canopied, rosewood monstrosity—and tried to call up her mother's face. She'd seen the pictures in the photograph albums, but she couldn't remember her mother at all. Why in the world had she given Marla a hand-me-down dress fit for a debutante? A *used* gown?

Unless she wasn't Marla Cahill. Wasn't Alexander's wife. Wasn't Victoria Amhurst's daughter.

Was it possible? She touched her face, traced the scars that were receding. Why would everyone insist she was a woman she wasn't? What about the wreck and the amnesia? Coincidence? Or were there darker forces at play—sinister plans embodied in the man who had threatened her? The voices in her mind kept reminding her that this wasn't her room, that there was just no way she would have draperies and pillows that matched, a bed big enough for two but only occupied by one, a sitting area and bookcase filled with leather-bound volumes that, she guessed, hadn't been opened in years. Where were the magazines? The crossword puzzle books? The hand-stitched throws? The *mess* that she instinctively felt was a part of her life?

But the baby. He's your own flesh and blood. You remember him. In time you'll remember this room, too.

You have to.

Her stomach rumbled again and cramped. She took in a deep breath. The pain would pass. She was still just upset; that was it. She passed a trembling hand over her lips. This was all too much. But tomorrow . . . tomorrow she'd start sorting everything out and she wouldn't take any more well-intentioned advice. She was going to do things her way.

Turning off the light, she closed her eyes, told herself that she'd imagined the horrid voice condemning her to death and that her memories of that blue gown were all part of her confusion. She needed to sleep. To rest. To start all over in the morning. That was it. Sleep.

Her stomach quivered.

Calm down, for God's sake.

She wanted to spit.

Don't let this upset you. You'll be fine.

Nausea threatened.

Just breathe deeply, think quiet thoughts, relax . . . oh, no!

Bile climbed up her throat.

She was going to throw up!

Panicked, she slapped at the lamp. Hit the switch but knocked the base with her arm. Illumination flashed. The lamp fell onto the pitcher. Water splashed. The bulb splintered into a million shards. The room sizzled into blackness.

No!

Her stomach churned. Scrabbling for the wire cutters with one hand, she pushed the button on the intercom with the other.

"Nick! Carmen!" she yelled, knowing she was about to vomit. "Help!"

Oh, God, she couldn't stop it. Nausea overtook her.

"Can you hear me? Help!" *Please, Nick, please!*

She dropped the pliers, picked them up and then doubled over with the cramps. Bile spewed up her throat and into her nose. Burning. Choking. Hunched over, she stumbled through the suite and onto the landing. Her fingers clamped around the wire cutters and she ripped at the bindings on her teeth.

Footsteps thundered two floors down.

Too far away. They couldn't make it.

The door to Cissy's room burst open. She took one look at her mother and screamed. "Mom! Oh, God, Mom! Help!"

Marla was on the floor, writhing and gasping, choking, working the cutters. Her nose burned, her lungs were on fire, water streamed from her eyes. The hall began to spin and darken. Footsteps. She heard thundering footsteps.

Suddenly Nick loomed above her, his face a mask of concern. "Jesus Christ!" Straddling her, he yanked the cutters from her hand and yelled to Cissy, "Call 911. Now!"

The teenager didn't move.

"What the hell happened?" he demanded, forcing her mouth open, snipping wildly at the wires as Marla retched and struggled for air. She choked, convulsing, her eyes feeling as if they were bulging from their sockets.

"Hold on Marla, for God's sake, hold on," Nick ordered, as her jaw began to loosen. "Shit!"

Marla convulsed, certain she was dying, her lungs bursting. The world turned dark.

Wires snapped. Pain shot through her mouth. "For Christ's

sake call the paramedics!'' Nick bellowed. ''Where's the damned nurse?''

She couldn't breathe . . . it was so dark . . .

Snip! Snip! Snip!

''Hang in there, Marla, just hang the hell in there,'' he said and she was vaguely aware of his face, all tense angles, sweat running down his jaw as her body wracked and the blackness of unconsciousness swept over her. ''For the love of God, Marla, hang in there!''

With his hands, Nick pried the broken wires open and forced her jaws apart. He turned her on her stomach where she retched, choked, coughed and lost the contents of her stomach all over the carpet.

''Oh, my land!'' Eugenia's voice came over the frantic clip of her footsteps. ''What happened oh, my—''

Boots rang down the back stairs, echoing from the servant's quarters. Marla gasped, coughed, thought she'd be sick all over again. From the corner of her eye, through the dimness of her vision and the horror that she was lying in her own vomit, Marla saw Tom, Fiona and Carmen rushing to her. Her jaw ached, her stomach still twitched and for the first time since she'd gained consciousness she wanted to give herself into the comfort of a dark, black void.

Nick shook her. ''Stay with me,'' he ordered. ''Marla, stay the hell with me.''

''Get out of the way. I'll see to her,'' Tom commanded and his boots came into view. ''Mrs. Cahill?'' He was leaning over her, his hand on her shoulders. ''Let me help you . . .''

No! She wanted Nick. She didn't want this man, this stranger touching her.

''Call 911,'' Nick screamed at Eugenia. Then to Marla. ''You'll be all right.'' His gaze held hers as if he were willing her to stay conscious. ''You'll be okay.''

''I said I'd take over,'' the nurse insisted.

Nick didn't budge. ''I've got her.''

Blackness oozed in from the corners of her vision.

"Breathe, damn it. Open your mouth!" Nick's strong hands wedged her jaw open again and she coughed and heaved again, curling into a ball and retching until there was nothing left but pain.

"I'll call the paramedics." Carmen's voice was clear over the sounds of Cissy sobbing and Marla's own rasping breath. She opened her eyes, the hallway swam, then came into sharp focus. Nick was still straddling her, though his weight wasn't pinning her down as he balanced on his knees. His face grim, his intense blue eyes searching hers. "Marla?" Carmen had disappeared, but Eugenia, Tom and Cissy were standing around, needing to fuss.

"Oh . . ." She could barely speak, her mouth bruised and aching. "I . . . I'll be all right," she lied, the words hard to form.

"The ambulance is on its way." Carmen appeared from the suite.

Marla shuddered and wrapped her arms around herself.

"The paramedics will take her to Bayside," Carmen added.

"We'll have Phil Robertson meet her there."

"No." Marla struggled with the word. At the thought of being hospitalized for even a few hours, Marla panicked. She couldn't, wouldn't go back to the hospital again, not to that place where she had no control of her life, no answers to the questions plaguing her. "No . . . I'll be . . . I'm all right." Still coughing, she dragged herself to her knees. Her stomach was quiet, she'd quit heaving, but the pain in her mouth was excruciating, the clipped wires cutting her lips, her jaw not working right as atrophied muscles refused to come alive.

"You're not all right. You just got out of the hospital a few days ago," Nick insisted, getting to his feet and regarding her through dark, worried eyes.

"And I'm not going back." She knew the sane thing to do would be to be examined at the hospital, and yet she felt that it would be a vast mistake.

"Marla, don't even argue." Nick's voice was firm, his jaw tight. "Look at you."

She couldn't see the mess she was; didn't want to. Leaning against the rail, she tilted her head to stare up at him. She knew she was a horrid sight with splotchy skin and vomit staining her pajamas, but she didn't care. Didn't care that the servants and her mother-in-law saw her in such a state. She took in another long breath and coughed for a second. Her mouth tasted horrid, her nose was filled with the acrid scent.

"Here." He sat her on a chair in the hall. "Let me see if I can help." Again he worked on her mouth, removing the remaining pieces of jagged wire, extracting any tiny piece of metal, so that there was nothing left but the pain of atrophied muscles and cut flesh. "Now when the ambulance gets here—"

"Just take me to a doctor and have him look me over," she insisted.

He hesitated. "I think—"

"Please, Nick, can you do this for me?" she asked and saw raw emotion darken his eyes. A muscle worked in the corner of his jaw. Blade-thin lips flattened as he studied her.

"You're sure?"

"Yes." She was in no mood for arguments. She could barely speak her mouth hurt so badly. "If . . . if I thought there was any danger, believe me, I'd have you take me back to Bayside."

"You nearly died," he insisted.

A chill swept through her. "I know," she whispered. "Now please . . ."

"For the record, I think this is a big mistake."

"She should be hospitalized," Tom interrupted and there was an edge to his words as he leaned down to look at her mouth. Marla didn't trust him. Not for a minute. And yet she could use the fact that Tom was on the payroll.

"If anything happens again, you'll be here, won't you?" she asked. "That's why my husband hired you, isn't it?"

"Yes," he admitted, his eyes narrowing a fraction, "but I'd like you checked over by a doctor."

"I'll go see Dr. Robertson. At his house or the clinic." God, it hurt to talk.

"The ambulance is already on its way," Nick said.

"Then cancel it." Marla insisted just as she heard the first scream of a siren, far down the hill. Her eyes beseeched Nick's and she tentatively touched the back of his hand. "Please."

"For goodness sake, I'll do it," Eugenia said. "And then I'll call Alex and have him meet you down at the clinic. I'm sure Phil won't mind." She glanced at the stains on the carpet. "I'll have this mess cleaned up while you're gone."

Marla hadn't expected an ally from her mother-in-law, but was grateful for the older woman's support. For any support.

Eugenia fluttered commanding fingers at her son. "Nick, you can drive her to the clinic and I'll have Alex meet you there."

"For Christ's sake—"

"Just do it, Nick. For once, don't argue."

"That okay with you?" Nick asked, swinging his head back to Marla.

"Yes." Anything but the hospital.

"Good. Then we're in agreement." Eugenia sent Tom a glance daring him to argue, then marched down the hallway to Alex's office, withdrew a set of keys from the pocket of her jacket and unlocked the door. In a few seconds her voice could be heard through the door she'd left slightly open.

"I guess we're gonna do it your way," Nick said as he straightened.

Was it her imagination or had she seen a glimmer of tenderness in his gaze, a shadow of compassion? "Just give me a second and I'll try to look decent." As if that was possible. Damn, but she felt awful.

On wobbly legs, Marla made her way to her room, turned on the overhead light and saw the mess near the bed. Skirting the shards of glass and stain of water, she made her way to her bathroom. Grimacing, she splashed cold water over her face, rinsed her mouth gently, blew her nose, then stripped and gave herself a hasty hit-and-miss sponge bath.

She heard the ambulance's wail scream ever louder, then fade in the distance. By the time she'd thrown on a jogging suit, the sirens had stopped. Her stomach was still queasy, her mouth on fire, but she knew she wouldn't throw up again and she cringed at her hair and face in the mirror. Not that it mattered. She just wanted this ordeal over with. Nick was waiting for her in the hallway, but the servants had dispersed.

"The ambulance?" she asked, forcing her jaw to work.

"I sent it on its way. The paramedics weren't happy."

"Neither am I," she threw back.

"Let's roll."

"Just a minute," Marla said and made her way to Cissy's room where her daughter was lying in her bed, her arms holding a stuffed lion cub missing a set of whiskers as if her life depended upon it, her upper teeth worrying her lip. "Are you okay?" Marla asked though the inside of her mouth felt as if it was hamburger.

Cissy rolled her eyes. "Sure. Just great." She blinked and struggled against tears.

"I mean it."

"Then, no. I'm not. Okay? This is all so weird, Mom," she said, her chin wobbling and Marla glanced at the vanity where smears of purple nail polish still lingered. "Why can't you just be the way you were before . . . before you got pregnant?" she demanded. "That's when it all started, all this strange stuff. Before that . . ." her voice drifted off and she clamped her jaw shut, as if she'd said too much. "I . . . I just want you to be normal again."

Marla's heart cracked. Tears sprang to her eyes, but she fought the urge to break down. "Believe me, Cissy, I'm trying."

"Yeah, right."

"I mean it."

"Sure." Cissy squeezed her eyes shut, hugged the lion fiercely, and sniffed as tears drizzled down her cheeks.

Marla started for the bed, but, as if she sensed the movement, Cissy opened her eyes and whispered angrily, "Just leave me alone, okay?"

"Honey, please—"

"Don't, Mom. Just . . ." She dashed away her tears with the back of her hand, leaving dark smears of mascara on her cheek. "Just . . . go."

Marla didn't. She couldn't. Not yet. When the rift between them was growing wider by the minute. She sat on the edge of her daughter's bed and smoothed Cissy's bangs from her eyes. The girl stared out the window at the black night, turning her head and lifting a shoulder, silently ostracizing her. Marla plunged on, vaguely aware of Nick waiting on the other side of the threshold. "I know this is hard. For you. For me. For Dad . . . but I'm trying, honey, I'm trying really hard, and soon things will be better. I've been remembering things. Just today I remembered James's birth."

Cissy stiffened. "Did you?" she sneered, still clutching the stuffed animal and staring out the window.

"Yes."

"What about mine? Did you remember that, too? I was your first." Gold eyes dared her to deny the truth.

Marla felt a jab of guilt and wanted to lie, but didn't. Cissy would see right through any fabrication and it would only make things worse. "Not yet."

Cissy sent out a short disgusted breath. Her lips twisted as if at some private, painful irony. "You probably won't. Not ever," she said.

"Of course I will. Just give me time." Marla touched Cissy's cheek again but the girl winced as if she'd been burned.

"You know you came running in here a little while ago. You . . . You were like some kind of maniac, acted like you'd seen a ghost or something and scared the crap out of me."

"Oh, honey—"

"And then," Cissy cut in, her voice rising an octave, "and

then . . . and then . . . I found you in the hall puking and crying and . . . Mom . . .'' her voice suddenly cracked.

Marla's heart bled. She wanted to gather her daughter in her arms and hold her fiercely and promise never to let go, but as she reached for Cissy's arm, the teenager scooted to the far corner of the bed and Marla, sighing, rolled to her feet. She was getting nowhere with her daughter, was only making a horrible situation worse.

Nick was waiting for her, one shoulder propped in the doorway to Cissy's room. He fell into step with Marla in the hall.

"She hates me," Marla whispered as he walked her to the elevator.

Nick held the door open and Marla stepped inside to sag against the back wall of the small car. "She's a teenager. You're her mother. All teenagers act like they hate their mothers." He pressed the button for the first floor.

"No, it's more than that."

"Don't worry about it tonight." He touched the bottom of her jaw with one finger and lifted her chin, forcing her eyes to his.

"You think I have more important things to do?"

"Concentrate on getting your memory back."

"Believe me, there's nothing I want more."

He glanced down at her lips and for a second she thought he might kiss her bruised mouth. The air in the little car was suddenly thick, hard to breathe. The elevator stopped. Nick dropped his hand.

The door opened and Eugenia stood waiting in the foyer. Bony fingers fiddled with the strand of pearls at her neck. She glanced from her son to Marla and censure tightened the corners of her mouth. "I've called Lars. He'll drive you."

"I'll handle it," Nick insisted, helping Marla with a raincoat from the front closet.

"But he's already got the car warmed up and—"

"I said I'm taking care of it," Nick stated more forcefully, then threw on a battered leather jacket, helped Marla into a long coat, then, with a strong hand on her elbow guided her out the door and along the brick walk to the circular drive where his beat-up truck, an old Dodge that probably leaked oil and God-knew-what-else, was parked.

"What is it with you?" Marla asked. "Why are you such an outsider?"

One side of his mouth twisted up. "That's the way I want it." He helped her into the cab, then climbed behind the wheel. With a flick of his wrist and a double pump on the gas pedal, the old engine sparked to life.

"You like being the outlaw."

"Love it."

"Why?"

He eased to a post supporting a keypad, pressed a series of numbers and the electronic gates hummed as they opened. "I never was one to follow the beaten path."

"The black sheep. Rogue. Maverick."

He shrugged. "Whatever. Never thought about it much. Just did my own thing." He sliced her a look. "It seems to piss people off."

"I imagine." The truck's cab seemed suddenly too close. Intimate. The glass fogging to block out the rest of the night, the rest of the world.

"How're you feeling?"

"Like hell and don't tell me I look worse. I know." Aching all over, Marla cast a glance over her shoulder and through the back window to the house. A golden patch of light streamed from the sitting room windows and Eugenia's dark silhouette was visible. Two floors above, in Cissy's room, another light burned but the window remained empty. Marla's daughter didn't bother to watch them leave and Marla wasn't surprised. Their relationship was tenuous at best. What kind of mother was she? Why couldn't she remember a child who had been a part of her life for nearly fourteen years?

God help me.

Resting her head against the passenger-side window, Marla

sighed. Her jaw ached, her head pounded and she was alone with Nick. Again. He shifted the gears, his thigh, so close to hers, flexing as he pushed in the clutch, the fingers of his right hand gripping the gearshift and nearly brushing her leg.

He was near enough to touch. But she didn't. Would never. Or so she told herself as Nick maneuvered the truck, changing lanes on the shimmering wet streets. Raindrops splashed the windshield, the wipers slapped them away, and some kind of country music wafted through the speakers.

"So what was it that made you get sick?" Nick asked as he shifted down and braked on the steep grade that cut between skyscrapers and smaller buildings, the lights of the city blazing bright. Pedestrians hurried in the rain, traffic rushed through puddles and a deep mist seemed to creep through the alleys.

"I don't know. Bad soup? Nerves?" She lifted a shoulder.

"You didn't feel it coming on?"

"A little. I thought it would go away."

He sent her a look that called her a dozen kinds of fool. "So you just woke up and—"

"No." She stared at the taillights of a minivan as it rounded a sharp corner. She decided to tell him the truth. "I didn't wake up because I felt ill. There was more to it." She slid a glance in his direction, saw his fingers tighten on the steering wheel. "I woke up because I thought I heard something."

"What?"

In for a penny, in for a pound, she thought fatalistically. "I know this sounds completely wacko—paranoid—but I woke up because I felt, I mean, I thought someone was in the room with me. A man. He was hovering over the bed and he said something like '*Die, bitch!*'"

"*What?* Jesus Christ, Marla, are you serious?" His head jerked and he stared at her hard. He took a corner too fast. The back tires slid before catching. "There was someone in your room?"

"It's crazy, I know, I know," she said quickly. "Of course no one was there when I turned on the light and I walked, well, ran around upstairs, checked on the kids—that's what Cissy was talking about. But I didn't see anyone, so I told myself it was all part of a bad dream and went back to bed.'' Goose bumps rose on her skin as she remembered the terror she'd felt, the conviction that someone had actually gained access to her bedroom. She cleared her throat and stared through the windshield. "I told you it sounds paranoid.''

"You should have called down to me.'' The lines around his mouth and eyes grooved deep.

"I said I thought I was dreaming. Anyway, when I was in the nursery, I had a breakthrough. I *remembered* having the baby.''

"You did? Anything else?''

"No . . . not yet, but I felt like it was going to happen, that I was going to regain my memory, so I held the baby for a while, then went back to bed, still feeling pretty awful. The next thing I knew I was throwing up.''

"Jesus,'' Nick whispered.

"I think everything will come back. Soon. That's one reason I didn't want to go back to the hospital. I didn't want to backslide. I don't want any drugs that might slow this down.'' She reached for his arm then. "I have to remember and soon. Or I will lose it.''

"Can't say as I blame you.''

She dropped her hand, leaned back in the seat.

"We're almost there.'' He cranked on the wheel, turning down a side street. A car rounded the corner from the opposite direction. Headlights blazed bright. Harsh. Blinding.

Just like before! On that mountain road!

Marla's heart stopped. The air was suddenly trapped in her lungs.

A jagged piece of memory sliced through the lining of her mind. In a flash she remembered other twin beams, right ahead of her, blinding her. In her mind's eye she relived the horrifying moment. Witnessed the impact. The windshield shattering into a million blazing shards, a woman screaming as if she was being tortured, the sound of screeching, wrenching metal.

"The accident..." she whispered, shaking. Horror tore through her. She relived that terror-riddled moment and tried to step on brakes that didn't exist. Vividly she replayed the scene, saw the semi careening down the hill—faster and faster, roaring down Highway 17 and out of control. She screamed. The eighteen-wheeler swerved wildly, catching a man in its headlights. *NO! OH, GOD, NO!* The man would be crushed.

Marla's eyes slammed shut and she was breathing, panting, crying... Again she saw metal wrenching upon metal, sparks flying... No! No! No! The guardrail gave way and the tires blew. The car hurtled down the embankment and... and then hit. Then there was blackness... nothing...

"Marla!" Nick's voice was strangled with fear. A hand was on her shoulder, shaking her. "Marla!"

Her eyes flew open. She was in the pickup in San Francisco. With Nick. Trembling and sobbing. "I...I..." Tears rained from her eyes as she turned to Nick. "I remember the accident," she said. "It was horrible... there was something..." She squeezed her eyes shut, remembered Pam. "Oh... oh... No, don't die, don't die!"

Nick stood on the brakes. He cranked on the wheel and nosed his truck into a loading zone on a side street. Marla was barely aware of him cutting the engine, but she felt his arms wrap around her and didn't resist when he dragged her close to him. "Shh. It'll be all right," he said, though she knew he was lying.

He kissed her crown of short hair, folding his arms tighter around her.

"I killed her, Nick," she said, her soul scraped raw as she remembered the horror of Pam's body flying into the windshield. The blood. The screams. The darkness. She clutched Nick's jacket in one fist and cried brokenly, gasping and sniffing, trying to find some bit of composure as she remembered being blinded by headlights... but there had been no car driving in her lane . . . or were the headlights from the truck that had suddenly rounded the corner? Was she confused? Her memory contorted? Her head throbbed, her jaw ached.

But the image painted in her mind was vivid. There had been a man in the road. A dark figure in the glare of her lights, and then suddenly, as if he'd pulled a switch, he was ablaze in light, harsh, blinding, painful light . . . shining so bright that she couldn't see . . . And she'd swerved, just as the truck had rounded the corner and caught the man in its bright headlights.

Now, in the safety of Nick's arms, she drew in deep ragged breaths. She realized how desperate she'd become, how she was clinging to Nick's jacket, and slowly she uncurled her fingers and tried to push her body from his. Strong arms held her fast. "It's all right," he said again. "Now, what is it? Tell me what's going on."

"Please . . . let me go."

"Is that what you want?" he asked, his voice low and she looked into eyes as dark as midnight. Somewhere deep inside she felt a stirring, a want, a need to connect, but she swallowed hard and nodded.

"Yes."

His grip loosened and she extricated herself. Leaning back against the seat, she ignored the feel of him still lingering on her skin, the musky scent of him, the need she felt for his strength. Her blood was racing, her heart pounding, her nerves tingling with a million conflicting emotions.

"What I want," she said slowly, "is to get my life back. Whatever that is." She looked out the side window, watched raindrops fork down the glass. "Just now I finally remembered the accident, how I was driving, talking, laughing, I think, and then I rounded a corner and there was the truck coming down the hill in the opposite direction, but that wasn't it, there was something more. A man, I think. In the road. And he . . . and he was suddenly as bright as day." She rubbed her arms, chilled to her bones. "And then the truck swerved and I hit the guardrail and then . . . and then . . ." She squeezed her eyes shut again, the memory horrifying.

"Jesus, Marla, you don't have to be so damned strong. It's all right to fall apart." He held her tight again and breathed into her hair.

"No, I can't."

"Let it go."

Her throat closed and she stopped struggling, just sagged against him.

"Now. Tell me."

"I lost control. Pam died." Marla swallowed hard, knew she'd forever hear those horrid, tortured cries of agony as Pam gave up her life. "I . . . I shouldn't be doing this," she said, but didn't try to pull away.

"Just relax."

She laughed without any mirth. "Is that possible?"

"Probably not. But try."

He guided her forehead to the crook of his neck and his skin was warm against hers. For once she gave up the fight. Closing her eyes, she heard the strong, steady beat of his heart and she melted against him. His thumbs rubbed her arms and she thought of kissing his lips, of touching him where she was forbidden, of lying naked with him . . . oh, God, she couldn't think such wanton, dark thoughts as the minutes clicked by. A car drove past slowly and disappeared at the far end of the narrow street. From out of the shadows a cat pounced on the hood of the truck, then disappeared into the night.

"Now," he said, his breath ruffling her hair. "Just calm down. Take it slow. Think." Then as if realizing what he was doing, he slowly released her. "Try to remember, but don't push too hard."

She nodded, feeling suddenly alone as she leaned back in the seat and willed her skyrocketing pulse to slow. "It's coming back. Oh, God, Nick, it's all coming back."

"You remember Pam?"

"Yes." She nodded. "But not as a close friend, no . . . she

was more of an acquaintance and we were driving south
to . . . to . . .''

"See her daughter?" Nick prompted, "at the university?"

"Maybe, I don't know." She thought hard. "There was a
reason but . . ." She felt a chill as cold as death run through
her blood. ". . . I think it had to do with the baby."

"James."

"Yes."

"But he wasn't with you."

"No . . . maybe we were just discussing him, but . . ." Deep
in her heart, she sensed there was more to it, but couldn't quite
put the pieces together. "I don't know," she admitted.

"It'll come." He looked at his watch. "We'd better get
going." He glanced in her direction as he reversed from the
curb, then jammed the truck into first. "Are you gonna be all
right?"

"I don't know," Marla admitted and laughed without mirth.
"I don't even know what 'all right' is."

"Maybe none of us do." He melded his truck into the stream
of traffic moving toward the waterfront.

"Maybe not." Squaring her shoulders, Marla hazarded one
last glance at his strong profile. His gaze was fastened on the
street, his hands on the wheel and she felt ashamed because
she sensed that she was closer to him at this very moment than
she'd ever been with her husband. She ran a hand over her
forehead in frustration. "I don't think I've said 'thanks' yet."
He slid one eye in her direction. "You saved my life, you
know. Back at the house. I could have died."

"I did what I had to do."

"Well, I owe you one. Probably more than one."

"I don't keep score."

"Maybe you should."

"It wouldn't do a helluva lot of good," he said and turned
into a parking structure attached to Bayside Hospital and the
surrounding clinics by means of a sky bridge. Alex's Jaguar
was idling next to a Cadillac on the first floor of the lot.

Spying the pickup, Alex shot out of the Jag and was at the truck's passenger door in three swift strides.

"Are you all right?" he asked Marla, his face contorted in concern as she stepped out of the cab. He looked through the open door to Nick, still seated at the wheel. "What the hell happened?"

"Marla can fill you in."

"You're leaving?" Alex asked, draping an arm familiarly over his wife's shoulders and giving her a little squeeze.

Nick's lips compressed. "Yep. I figure you can handle it from here." His gaze found Marla's again and her pulse jumped as she remembered how close she'd come to kissing him.

"I'll catch you later, then," Nick said and Marla looked after him, feeling that she was being abandoned. But that was silly. Stupid. Irrational. Alex was her husband. Just because Nick saved her life didn't mean anything special. He would have done it for anyone. And the scene in the truck, that was all because of the rush and jumble of the trauma of the evening. Nothing more. Right?

Nick's gaze centered on Marla. Midnight blue eyes held hers for a heartbeat, then he turned toward his brother. "I figure you're right, Alex. Since I'm down here anyway, I may as well move back to the house."

"What changed your mind?" Alex asked as Marla thought about living under the same roof as her renegade brother-in-law.

Nick flashed his thousand-watt grin and lied through his damnably straight teeth. "I just figure it's time."

Chapter Eleven

"Here, this will help with the pain," Dr. Robertson said as he gave Marla an injection, then disposed of the needle. He was in a sport coat and slacks, his eyes serious behind his glasses as he examined her mouth and jaw. The clinic was quiet at this time of night, the staff having left hours before. Overhead fluorescent fixtures glowed and hummed, reflecting harshly on the chrome fixtures of the sink and the instruments gleaming on a spotless Formica counter. "Now, why don't you tell me what happened."

Marla was seated on a tissue-covered bed, her heartbeat finally slowing, the taste in her mouth and nose still foul, the pain screaming through her face beginning slowly to lessen.

Alex stood at the door of the examination room, his arms folded tightly over his chest as the doctor finished the job that Nick had started. The clinic was empty, the outer hallways dark.

"I . . . I got sick. Probably nerves or bad soup or both, I don't know," she said with difficulty. The muscles in her jaw had atrophied and she could barely open her mouth. Ignoring the pain, she forced her lips to move. "I've been pretty tense lately. Anyway, I felt a little queasy after dinner, went upstairs to lie down and . . ." She hesitated and decided not to confide in the doctor about the malevolent presence she'd felt in her room. Not right now. Not until she was clearheaded, certain the man hadn't been just part of a nightmare, and she had determined whom she could trust. "I . . . I woke up . . . probably because of a bad dream, then I had to throw up. There was nothing I could do . . ." She shook her head. "It . . . it was awful."

"Then, considering, I guess you're lucky," he muttered under his breath as he stepped away from the examination table and stripped off his latex gloves. "You could have choked to death or suffocated."

"Funny, I don't feel so lucky." In fact she felt like hell on a bad day. No doubt she looked worse.

"I suppose not." He cut a glance at Alex, then handed Marla a hand mirror so she could view the damage. Yep, the phrase "death warmed over" fit her description to a T. Tentatively she stretched her jaw. Excruciating pain tore through her face and she sucked in her breath. Dr. Robertson said, "You're going to feel your mouth for a few days—probably even weeks, but I'll prescribe something for the pain. Now, the good news is that your jaw's healed nicely."

"I'll take any good news I can get," she grumbled.

He chuckled and winked at her. "But take it easy, okay? Rest. Recover. And if I were you I wouldn't play hockey without a mask for a while."

"I'll take that under consideration," she said.

One side of the doctor's mouth elevated slightly. "Good. Now, keep your appointment with Dr. Henderson, though, as he did the initial surgery. He might want X rays to make sure the bones have knit, but it looks good to me."

"Thanks," she said, grateful the ordeal was over.

"So how's the stomach?" Robertson tossed his used gloves into a small chrome trash can.

"Better. A lot better."

"You should have told someone you were nauseous." Alex's eyes were dark with silent reproach, his brow furrowed, his lips pursed.

"Maybe you should have been home," she said irritably.

His eyes narrowed just a fraction. "I was working."

"It was after eleven."

The corners of Alex's mouth tightened and the look he sent her could have cut through granite. "I guess you don't remember. I work late a lot. That's why I hired Tom. If you weren't so bullheaded . . ." His words faded and the tension that had drawn his face into a tight mask diminished. "Look, I'm just concerned, all right?" He unfolded his arms and rubbed the back of his neck. "You scared the shit out of me."

"Me, too," she agreed, but decided not to push the argument. "I'm just sick of all this."

"We all are," Alex said.

Robertson washed his hands at a sink mounted in the wall. "Is there any improvement in your memory?" His gaze met Marla's in the reflection of the mirror as he dried his hands.

"It's still not great, but I am making some breakthroughs. Just tonight I remembered giving birth to James."

From the corner of her eye she saw Alex's spine stiffen slightly and a glimpse of surprise, no . . . was it worry . . . shadowed his eyes. "Did you?" he asked. "That's great. Fabulous." His smile seemed sincere. Almost.

"And I remember the accident," she asserted. "On the way over here, in Nick's truck, someone rounded the corner and his headlights were on high and all of a sudden the accident flashed before my eyes."

Alex paled a bit beneath his tan.

"There was a man in the road," she went on. "I was driving and I had to swerve to avoid him. That's when I hit the guardrail."

She shuddered and Alex nodded, encouraging her to continue though she sensed trepidation in his eyes. "Go on."

"It was horrible. A nightmare." Marla forced the words through her teeth as the memories of that night, the screaming tires, wrenching metal, slick road, the shattering glass streaked through her brain. Phil Robertson winced as she explained what happened. ". . . and yes, I finally remember Pam, not much about her but I know she and I . . . we were planning something . . . I just can't remember what."

"You're tired," Alex said. "Give it a rest."

"I will, but I need to talk to Detective Paterno."

"In the morning."

"Yes," she said, suddenly weary, exhaustion seeming to seep into her bones. The pain in her jaw was now a dull ache, but she was drained. "I'll call in the morning."

"Does Nick know about this?" Alex asked and Marla tensed, felt a twinge of guilt, as if she'd betrayed her husband.

"Yes."

"It figures."

"There's no reason to hide it."

"No, no, of course not," he said, but his smile was strained and he fiddled with the keys in his pocket. Her mind was starting to get fuzzy again, probably from the pain medication and she was tired . . . so damned tired. "Can we go home now?"

"Just let me give you a prescription," Dr. Robertson said as he pulled out a small note pad and started writing on it. He tore the top sheet off and handed the slip to Alex. "This'll help with the pain, but it might make you a little tired." He scribbled a note to himself and stuck it in a thick manila file.

Her medical file. All the information on her she'd ever want to know. A big part of the puzzle of who she was. "Can I see that?" she asked.

"What?" Robertson asked.

"The file."

"Nothing in it but medical information." The doctor's expression was kind enough, but there was something else behind the smooth exterior . . . it was almost as if he was patronizing her. Oh, God, she needed to sleep.

"About me," she said, reaching forward. "It's mine, right?"

"Don't you think you've been through enough tonight?" Alex cut in and waved the doctor to put the records away.

"But I want to know—"

"Marla, another time, okay?" Alex's voice had a tone that immediately put her back up. "It's late. You need to go home and rest. You said so yourself."

"I know what I need," she said, pushing herself off the examination table, "and that's to learn more about myself. About you. About our family. It's starting to happen, Alex. I'm really starting to remember and I'll do anything, *anything* to help my memory along."

"I understand—"

"Do you?" she tossed back, then glared at the doctor. *"Do you?"*

"Hell, Marla, stop it. Phil came down here in the middle of the night as a favor to you because you wouldn't go to the hospital. Now, he has a family to go home to and so do we."

Robertson clicked his pen and stuffed it into his pocket. "It's all right," he said, but didn't hand over the file. "So tell me what you do remember," he suggested, folding his arms over his chest, as well as Marla's medical records. There was no way she'd get to see her damned files tonight.

"Other than the accident and James's birth I only remember little things. Riding a horse, wearing a party dress, talking with Alex in the foyer of the house, nothing really very solid . . . just glimpses. I think seeing my records could jog other memories."

"You're probably right," he said with a change of attitude. "Why don't you come back to the clinic in a few days and if you want, I'll show you every scrap of information we've got on you?"

By that time it will be tampered with. Sanitized. Changed.

"I will," she promised and told herself that she wasn't involved in some great conspiracy. All the records would be intact. She'd just seen too many movies, that was all. She walked to the sink, found a paper cup and rinsed her mouth again.

"Good. By the time you call, who knows? Maybe your memory will have returned." He was so calm—nearly dead, it seemed. Because it wasn't his life, his memory he was discussing. Robertson could afford to be patient while Marla felt her life slipping by, like grains of sand sifting through her open fingers, and she couldn't clench her fist to stop it. She took a final swallow of water and worked at stretching the muscles of her face. Her tongue felt odd and oversized, her teeth still acting as if they were laced together, and after speaking with only her lips for over two weeks, she had to force her tongue, teeth and jaw to work together.

Alex helped her into her coat and Phil snapped off the lights to the clinic. Together, with Alex's arm around her shoulders, they walked across the sky bridge to the parking lot where Alex ushered Marla to the Jaguar. "We'll have you over for drinks," he promised Phil as he held the door open for her. "When Marla's more herself."

She couldn't help bristling at the insinuation, but bit back a hot comment that rose quickly to her lips as Alex settled behind the wheel. There was something about him that brought out a bitchy side of her and she was spoiling for a fight. With him. Though she didn't really understand why.

"Okay, so how're you feeling now?" he asked, giving her a quick glance as he fired the engine and wheeled out of the lot.

"Like someone took a jackhammer to my jaw."

"That good, huh?" He pressed on the lighter, then eased a pack of cigarettes from the inside pocket of his jacket.

"Yep, that good." She couldn't rouse a smile. His attitude rankled and the fact that she suspected he and Robertson were keeping something from her grated on her nerves. Worse yet, his attitude of stewardship—spousal concern when he was always away—bugged the hell out of her. Something wasn't right and it wasn't her imagination, but she was too tired to figure it out tonight.

The lighter clicked and he lit up, sending a cloud of smoke into the car's interior. With a push of a finger, the driver's window slid down and a gush of rain-washed air slipped inside. Smooth jazz played from the speakers as he eased the car into the late night traffic and the Jaguar sped up a steep hill.

The lights of the city burned in the surrounding skyscrapers. In the distance she recognized the historic district of Jackson Square and the Transamerica pyramid. As she'd seen it a hundred times before. And there was more . . . a flash . . .

In her mind's eye she saw herself at a desk, in a huge steel and glass office building. A computer monitor hummed, a telephone jangled and in the cubicles surrounding hers, other workers were on phones, at keyboards, staring into monitors. A bank of windows on one wall opened up to a view of the San Francisco skyline and a cerulean sky that stretched over the Bay.

But that was crazy. She wasn't an office worker. Never had been. Huddled in the far corner of the Jag she looked at her husband, his face grim and set in the glare of oncoming headlights.

"Was there ever a time when I worked?" she asked, knowing the answer before he even said a word.

Alex gave off a deprecatory snort. "You? Come on."

"I mean it."

"Of course not. Why would you work?"

"I don't know, I just had a vision of myself at a desk . . . in a loud, open room separated by half walls and filled with other workers, men and women bustling by, all wearing suits. . . ." Her voice faded and she rubbed her temple as she tried to remember.

"Marla, you've never worked a day in your life," he said and chuckled as if the thought were incredibly amusing. "You've been in dozens of office buildings, of course, but never as an employee."

"You're certain?" she asked. Why would she dream this?

"Positive." Some of the lines in his face softened in the dark interior. "You're imagining things."

Or paranoid. Not much difference.

"Why didn't you tell Tom or Mother or someone that you weren't feeling well?" he asked, touching her lightly on the knee. "That's why I hired the nurse in the first place, you know." Alex braked at a red light and sent her a look that silently accused her of being a fool.

"I didn't think it was anything."

"But you were sick when you went to bed?"

"It wasn't that bad and then . . ." She hesitated. Could she trust him?

"Then what?"

Go on. He's your husband. "This sounds so nuts," she said, but decided if she couldn't trust the man she was married to, she couldn't trust anyone. "I think someone was in my room tonight."

"Who? One of the servants?"

"No, Alex, there was a man leaning over the bed and he said, '*Die, bitch!*'"

"What?" His head whipped in her direction and the car eased over the center line. A sharp honk blasted from the next lane. Alex got control of the car again. "Christ, Marla, what do you mean there was an intruder in the house?"

"Just that." She told him the entire story and he gripped the wheel as if he wanted to tear it from the dash. ". . . I was so damned scared that I checked every unlocked room. I think I really freaked Cissy out, but once I was sure that everything was all right, that the kids were safe, I calmed down a little. I drank some water and went back to bed. The next thing I knew I was vomiting my guts out." She slid down in her seat, pressing her back against the passenger window and felt a chill as cold as death.

"Jesus, Marla, who did you think was in the room with

you?'' Alex sucked hard on his cigarette, the tip glowed bright in the darkness.

"I don't know . . . I'm not sure anyone was there . . . but it seemed real at the time.''

The light turned green. Someone honked behind them.

"Shit.'' Alex stamped on the accelerator and the Jaguar shot forward.

"It was scary as hell.''

"I bet.'' He gunned the engine. "Damn.'' His face had turned chalk white, his lips flattened over his teeth. "I'll have Lars check the house top to bottom.''

"No!'' she said sharply and shook her head. "I mean . . . it seems ridiculous now and even if there was someone there, he'd be long gone.''

"We have a security system and a gate. How'd the intruder get in?''

"Good question,'' Marla said and would have yawned but her muscles wouldn't stretch. She was so tired and it was difficult to talk. "Maybe he wasn't even there. Maybe I dreamed him up.''

"Did you call the police?'' Alex's voice was grim, his knuckles showing white.

"No.'' She shook her head. "It could have been a dream. You know, like the one at the hospital . . .''

"If you're frightened, we could have the police come out and investigate,'' he said. "You wanted to talk to Paterno anyway . . . but . . . shit, I don't know. Maybe we're all just tired and we can sort it out in the morning.'' He cranked on the steering wheel. "I could hire a security guard.''

"I don't think that's necessary.''

"Well, there is another option.'' His voice had softened.

"What?''

"You could sleep with me.''

No! She looked at him sharply, but he kept his eyes trained straight ahead. Her heart pounded and adrenalin surged through her blood at the thought of sharing a bed with him. She couldn't imagine kissing him, or even just lying close to him, spooned on his king-size bed, his arm around her. Her stomach clenched and she glanced through the window to the fog that was rolling in, seeping around the lampposts and buildings. Though the thought of being in his bed with him was repellent, she couldn't help but ask. "Why don't we sleep together?"

He snorted and stabbed out his cigarette in the ashtray. "That was your choice. A couple of years back." He glanced at her as if deciding whether to confide in her, then after waging a mental battle, lifted one shoulder. "The truth of the matter is that you . . . well you've been interested in other men."

"Men," she repeated aghast. Nick's rugged image and the memory of wanting to kiss him sizzled through her mind. It was true she was far from immune to Nick's innate sexuality or his damned irreverent charm. She even fantasized about feeling his work-roughened hands on all parts of her body, but she never for a minute considered the fact that she'd been involved with someone other than her husband, other than in a fantasy. Oh, God, what kind of woman was she? Clearing her throat, she picked at a button on her coat, then inched up her chin and pinned her husband with her gaze. "Men? Plural?"

"Yes."

"You're trying to tell me that I've taken lovers," she whispered, disbelieving. No way. But then her feelings toward Nick were impossible to deny and she knew somewhere in that most innately feminine part of her that she was a sensual creature. A passionate woman. Yet someone who slept alone. Or so it appeared.

"Okay, I won't tell you anything of the kind."

"But . . ." she prodded.

"You asked, Marla," he said angrily.

She felt a flush flame up her neck. "Who?"

"It doesn't matter." He took a corner a little too sharply. The tires chirped.

"Like hell it doesn't," she said angrily, her frayed nerves finally giving way.

"Let's not go into it now. It was quite a while ago." Alex fiddled with the radio, found a soft-rock station.

Marla snapped the damned thing off. "Then what about . . . what about James?" she asked, needing to know the truth. "Is he . . . is he . . ."

"Mine. James is mine." He slid her a glance and offered a tight smile. She felt more confused than ever.

"But, how—?"

"See what happens when you have too many gin and tonics?" His smile crept slowly from one side of his jaw to the other as if he somehow felt victorious. His laugh was just as vile, and she told herself she was imagining things. Overwrought. Drained.

A gnawing ache settled deep in the pit of her stomach. Could she sleep with this man? Her husband? Kiss him? Make love to him? Something inside her recoiled, but she ignored the feeling. They were married, had children . . . "Maybe, when I get my memory back, if we both think it would be a good idea, we could . . . try . . ."

"What? Sleeping together?" he asked, his lips twisting sardonically, the angles and planes of his face hard-looking in the coming headlights. "I don't think so, Marla. I'm really not into mercy-fucking."

She froze. Her stomach curdled like sour milk. "Is that what you'd call it?"

"Don't try to pretend that you're in love with me. I see it in your eyes. You don't even remember me. And when you do, well, then you'll know. So . . ." He braked for a corner and cranked hard on the wheel. "So let's just not push it. Not yet." He patted her knee again. "Unless you really want to bang my brains out."

She drew away.

"Didn't think so."

Good. She couldn't imagine tumbling into bed with him and kissing him, or . . . she couldn't think about it. "Neither one of us is ready to move into the same bedroom again." His fingers were tight over the steering wheel. "We'll take that one step at a time. Who knows? Stranger things have happened."

She didn't argue. Couldn't. She felt no spark of desire for this man who was her husband. Why, she didn't understand. Handsome and fit, at forty-two, Alexander Cahill was a successful lawyer-turned-businessman and yet there was something about him that didn't ring true, a coldness she felt beneath his charming exterior—a crudeness that wasn't covered by his spit-and-polish, Ivy-league, white-collar shine.

Or maybe it's all in your head. One way or another, Marla, you've got to find out. And Alex isn't going to help you. No one is.

Street signs flashed by as Alex drove up the hill. Stanyan, Parnassus, Willard . . . names that seemed familiar yet weren't. Streets she'd have to know. Even though Lars was always at her disposal, she wasn't about to use him for what she was planning. She needed independence. Freedom. Self-assurance.

Her breath fogged against the window as she turned to look at the shops lining the streets. Coffeehouses, small grocery stores, flower vendors, apartment buildings, climbing ever upward on the hill to the top. To the house.

With a press of a button on a remote control, the gates to the estate opened and Alex drove through. Marla stared up at the house rising high on the hill, steep gables pitched over dormers, paned windows glowing from the interior lights, chimney stacks rising proudly above it all. *Home,* she thought but really didn't buy it.

It still didn't feel right.

Nick drummed his fingers on the steering wheel of his pickup as he mentally kicked himself from one side of San Francisco Bay to the other. He stared out the windshield at the gloomy night and couldn't shake the feeling that he was being manipulated. But by whom?

Marla? His back teeth ground together as he thought of seeing her retching on the floor, nearly suffocating. She'd seemed so small and vulnerable and not for the first time he wondered why she'd gotten sick. A virus? Bad food? Or had someone poisoned her—slipped her a drug that caused her to heave?

Impossible.

But she'd thought she'd sensed an intruder.

Why would anyone want her dead?

And how had they gotten in?

Or out? The house was a damned fortress.

Maybe they hadn't left.

"Son of a bitch," he growled pocketing his keys and climbing out of his truck. He'd parked a few streets from the hotel and hoped a walk through the icy mist and rain would help clear his head.

For the first time in years he'd wanted to protect Marla, to wrap his arms around her and fend off any attack.

Like some goddamned medieval knight in . . . well, slightly tarnished armor. Shoving his hands deep into the pockets of his jacket, he crossed the street and ducked into the hotel. He was on the second floor in minutes and as he opened the door, his phone began to ring.

He snatched the receiver before the door shut behind him. "Nick Cahill."

"Glad I caught ya. I was afraid I'd have to leave another message." Walt Haaga's voice was rough and gravelly as ever.

"What's up?" Nick flopped onto the bed and kicked off his shoes.

"What isn't?" Walt said, coughing. "I've got more info. Let's start with Pam Delacroix."

"Start anywhere you please."

"Pamela, now she's an interesting lady. Lived off her ex, but dabbled at real estate, writing and the law. Seems that her primary interest was child custody cases. She was writing a book about it—parental rights, surrogate mothers, adoption issues. And that kid of hers—Julie—she dropped out of school a few weeks after starting. Just up and quit and moved in with a boyfriend in Santa Rosa. Has a job at a coffee shop serving up espressos. So her mother wasn't going down to see her.''

"Then why Santa Cruz?"

"Maybe everyone just assumed Santa Cruz because of the kid. For all anyone knows Ms. Delacroix and your sister-in-law could have been pulling a Thelma and Louise and just taking off down the coast. They could've been planning to go to L.A. or Mexico.''

"Another dead end," Nick grumbled.

"Or one less to consider."

"Why were they together?"

"Good question," Walt said. "But it probably wasn't to play tennis. As far as I can tell Pam Delacroix never belonged to Marla's club. I doubt if she owned a racquet much less a membership in an athletic club. She was more of a bookworm than an athlete.''

"Is that so?"

"I talked with her ex and a few friends. The only connection she seems to have with your family is that she attended the Holy Trinity of God church in Sausalito.''

"Where Cherise's husband is the minister," Nick said, his eyes narrowing.

"Yep."

Nick filed the information away, but it didn't quite fit. "I don't think Marla's a big churchgoer.''

"Nah, she's not a member. But my guess is that she met Pam through Cherise's husband. He was on the staff at Cahill House for a while. Counseled girls in trouble and got himself in a pot of hot water.''

"Did he?" Nick asked, a bad feeling beginning to gnaw at his gut.

"Seems he couldn't keep his hands off one of the unwed mothers.''

"Shit."

"Your brother fired him. About a year ago. There was a big scandal—lots of flak for a while. I've got copies of the newspaper articles and I'll fax 'em to you—but no charges were ever filed and the preacher went back to his congregation over in Sausalito.''

"And that was the end of it?" Nick was incredulous.

"Seems as if his flock and the girl he was supposed to have been involved with found a way to forgive him." Walt paused long enough to light up. Nick heard the distinctive click of a lighter.

"And that's just the tip of the iceberg. Man, are you related to a bunch of wackos."

"Tell me something I don't know," Nick said as he pulled the second pillow from the side of the bed and used it to prop himself. He grabbed a pen and notepad from the bedside table.

"Okay, how about this? Marla's old man, Conrad Amhurst, he's about to kick off.''

"That I heard.''

"I imagine," Walt said with more than an edge of contempt. "The rest of the family is practically drooling, waiting for him to buy the farm 'cuz he's worth millions and the kicker is that most of the estate is earmarked for that new baby.''

"What?"

"You heard me. Seems the old man has a thing against women, some archaic bent and even though Marla's son isn't able to carry on the Amhurst name, the guy is giving most of his wealth, estimated to be over a hundred million, to the kid. In trust, of course.''

"Of course." Nick leaned back on the bed, scratched at the stubble on his chin. "What about Marla, or her brother or her daughter Cissy?''

"Oh, they each get some of the pie, but a pittance. Rory, he'll be taken care of for life, Cissy gets her share when she's twenty-five *if* she finishes college and Marla will get something, but seventy-five percent of the estate goes to that newborn. How about that, just a few weeks old and a multimillionaire?''

"How do you know this?" Nick asked.

"I know it, okay?" Walt said with a laugh. "You pay me

to. You know, Marla's old man has always been an ornery bastard. Never played by the rules. Hard drinker. Big womanizer. It's a wonder Marla's mother stayed with him, but probably did for the money.''

"Who else knows the terms of Conrad's will?"

"Probably everyone. When there's that much money involved, heirs go to great lengths to make sure they're not getting the shaft and being cut out.'' He laughed long enough to cough. "It's just human nature.''

"If you say so.''

Walt snorted. "Look, you may have turned your back on a fortune a few years back, but most people don't. In fact they'll do anything for the kind of money we're talking about. Lie, cheat, steal. Even kill.''

Nick considered the list of dead and dying: Pam Delacroix, Charles Biggs, and tonight Marla could have lost her life. Just as she could have in the accident.

"I haven't figured out what's going on down there,'' Walt continued, his voice muffled as he drew on his smoke. "But I expect whatever it is, it might just get worse. Watch your ass.''

"Always do.''

"Good.''

He didn't like the turn of his thoughts. Marla was in danger. He could feel it. "Look, Walt, I know this is a helluva imposition, but I wonder if you could come down here for a few days, do some of the legwork. I've got a room at the hotel, you could take it over. I'm gonna move up to the house.''

"I'd have to tie up a few things here, but I could be down within the week.''

"Thanks. I'll keep the room until you show up, so you can leave messages here for the time being. Like I said, I'll be moving up to the house, so if you want to send me any more information, why don't you leave me a message on my cell phone or here. If you want to fax, you can do it to a little copy center—CopyWrite—I found not far from this hotel. Put it to my attention.''

"Why not the hotel?"

"Just a precaution. Everyone in my family knows I've been staying here."

"Don't trust them much, do you?"

Nick stared past the curtains that fluttered at the windows to the city lights beyond. "Nope," he admitted, thinking it a sad comment on his life. "Not at all." He hung up and started throwing his few belongings into his duffel bag. For over fifteen years he'd avoided the house on the hill like the plague, now he was eager to return.

Because of Marla.

That much was the truth. He wanted to see her again. Wanted to kiss her. Wanted his damned brother's wife. But more than that, he wanted to make certain she was safe. In the past few weeks she'd had two brushes with death. Accidents? Or was someone trying to kill her?

Chapter Twelve

The room had changed. Nick eyed the matching drapes, bedspread and throw rugs and decided it didn't matter a helluva lot. The memories he had here weren't all that great to begin with. It hadn't felt like home then, and it sure as hell didn't now. He dropped his duffel onto the brass bed. His stay here was temporary. Just until he figured out what was going on. He could live with the fluff and ruffles, but he didn't know if he could stand the thought of Marla only two doors down. Christ, that woman had a way of getting under his skin. Like no other. Even now, after all these years, while she was still recovering, she got to him.

"Hell." He felt claustrophobic and tossed his jacket over a bedpost. When that didn't help he walked to the window and opened it, letting in the cold November wind and staring over the lights of the city to the black sky where not a star was visible. How would he stand it, being this close to her?

When could he leave?

What the hell was going on?

He'd spent hours reviewing the company's books. Alex was

right, Cahill Limited was sinking deeper by the day into an ocean of red ink. Bad investments, expenses outrunning income, an employee who had been caught embezzling, an incredible amount of money spent on philanthropic causes such as Cahill House and Bayside Hospital's new pediatric wing, an excellent employee benefit package and an extravagant lifestyle of the CEO, all contributed to the problem. But these were simple, extremely basic facts that any snot-nosed kid with a two-year accounting degree could have figured out. Yet Alex had been insistent to draw Nick back into the fold. Was it to appease his aging mother who had, for years, pleaded with Nick to return? Was it because of Marla and her accident? Or was there another reason, something that escaped him, something, he sensed, was far deeper and darker.

For some reason Alex wanted Nick around Marla. And yet they had been rivals for her affection before.

He plowed stiff, impatient fingers through his hair.

Whatever Alex's motivation, Nick was trapped. Not because of the diminishing bottom line of Cahill Limited, nor because of his mother's needs to have both her children near her. No, he was bound here in this huge, soulless house, in a city he despised, because of Marla. Because he was scared shitless for her life and because, damn it, he'd never been able to use his head whenever he was around that woman.

He walked into the deserted hallway where the reflection of dimmed lights gleamed on the railing, and oil paintings of long-dead relatives peered from gilt frames, and where moments before his mother had told him how happy she'd been that he'd finally "come to his senses" and moved home. She'd even gone so far as to touch him on the sleeve, a major show of emotion for Eugenia.

"It's good to have you back, Nicholas," she'd whispered. "I know we've always been at loggerheads with each other, and, perhaps while raising you I made some mistakes, expected you to be more like Alex, but . . . in my own way . . . I've always loved you and missed you.'' Her lower lip had wobbled a bit and she'd quickly tightened her jaw.

Nick had been stunned, looking down at her. Without a trace of makeup, a red-and-black Japanese robe tied at her waist, the lines of her face so much more visible than ever before, she'd seemed, for the first time in his thirty-nine years, vulnerable. Real. That she cared.

He'd found it hard to believe. ''I won't be staying long.''

''I know. You never do.'' She'd sighed. ''I suppose I failed you. If I had it to do over, if I had the wisdom then that I do now . . . oh, bother.'' She managed a frail, pale-lipped smile meant to disguise the pang of despair that shadowed her eyes.

He'd felt like a heel.

''Well, we'll just make the best of things, won't we? But . . .'' she'd hesitated and fiddled with the tie of her robe. ''I just feel that there are things going on here that . . . well, I don't understand. Alexander, he's been so withdrawn and Marla . . . oh, the problems with that girl . . .'' Eugenia had worried her lip with her teeth as she'd thought. ''I suppose all marriages have trouble, their ups and downs. I certainly know that from my own experience. Your father, he . . . oh, well, I loved him. Far more than I should have, I suppose.'' For a second she was lost in her memories, then her eyes focused on Nick again. ''You're a lot like him in many ways, Nicholas. Self-righteous. Smart. And yet you're very different in other ways.'' She'd squared her shoulders. ''I just wanted to say thanks for coming.''

''I'll be staying until my job's done. Then I'm out of here,'' he'd reminded her.

She'd smiled as if she knew her second-born far better than he knew himself.

''We'll see,'' she'd said, starting for the elevator.

''I have a life in Oregon.''

''Do you?'' she'd asked, lifting a disbelieving eyebrow and leaving the question hovering in the air before disappearing into the elevator and returning to her room.

"Yes," he said to himself as he considered Alex's stash of liquor two floors below.

Nick figured he owed himself a drink. He took the time to place a call to Ole to find out that Tough Guy was doing all right, then with thoughts of the simple life at Devil's Cove at odds with the complicated mess here in San Francisco, he headed downstairs.

Fortunately Alex had left the key in the liquor cabinet. Nick found a bottle of Scotch and searched for a glass. Outside the wind rushed, while inside the only sounds were the tick of the grandfather's clock in the foyer, the soft drone of the ancient furnace and the creak of hundred-year-old timbers. A far cry from his cottage at the Oregon coast, he thought as he poured himself a stiff shot. Tiny, compact, with a roof he'd shingled himself, furniture that was old or purchased secondhand through the classified ads, and a three-legged dog who was a security system and best friend all rolled into one. Nick had enough money stashed in the bank and stock market set aside and enough income from his investments in apartments and office buildings he'd bought when he'd lived in Seattle to keep him happy. He could afford a more lavish life style. He didn't want one. It was just too much trouble.

Alex's life was testament enough to that sorry fact.

Yeah, Nick had a life, a life he wanted, a life that was his, a life of freedom.

So what the hell are you doing here?

He added a couple of ice cubes to his glass, then walked to the fireplace, where embers of a recent fire glowed in the ashes. Yet the room seemed cold. Sterile. Not the least bit warm or inviting. Like the rest of this damned house. Like his family. Like his life before he'd moved away after his affair with Marla. In his mind's eye he remembered how she'd kissed, as if she'd never stop, soft little moans escaping her throat. When he'd touched her, his fingers running up her bare arms, she'd lowered her eyes to half-mast, so that her seductive green irises were hidden beneath a fringe of dark lashes. She had trembled in

his arms, whispered that only he could make her feel so wanton,
touched her tongue to his ear and in a throaty voice had whispered, "Please, Nick, give me more ... I want so much
more ..."

Now, he slammed his eyes shut and took a long gulp of his
drink. He'd come full circle, leaving San Francisco because of
Marla and returning for the same damned woman. And though
she'd changed, he still felt that incredible pull to be near her
and he was even considering crossing the line, stepping over
the edge of decency and morality to the dark, inviting seduction
of the woman. She was different, yes. So very different. She
was kinder, gentler, her sense of humor more complete and
though he sensed a toughness deep within her, she was vulnerable as well, a woman he couldn't resist. It was so odd, as if
he was falling in love again, more deeply this time, and with
a different, deeper woman. Children had made her less self-
involved, more playful, more caring about those around her.
The things that had bothered him about Marla all those years
ago had faded with the years and yet, beneath her beautiful
skin, and deep into her psyche and libido, lay the same female
animal who had made him lose his mind, his common sense,
all reason, for a few stolen moments of sheer, sensual pleasure.

Their trysts, always alone and secretive, had been romantic
and wildly erotic. There hadn't been anything she hadn't done,
nothing she wouldn't experience, no boundaries. Her arms had
been open wide, her mind leaping ahead to the next sensual
pleasure, her skin so hot his sanity had melted whenever he
was around her, and her shimmering mischievous eyes, oh,
such sweet, dangerous invitation. The feel of her wet mouth
on his skin as her tongue explored all the indentations of his
muscles left him weak and wanting. No woman since had come
close to Marla.

He would have walked through hell for five minutes of
lovemaking with her. And one day, she'd met him, kissed him
chastely upon his cheek, tossed him a bright, I-know-you'll-

forgive-me smile, and told him it was over, that she'd met someone. The someone just happened to be his brother.

"Son of a bitch," he growled and tossed back his drink in one gulp. What the hell was he doing here, falling for her all over again. He should have his head examined—better yet he should be shot. He walked to the liquor cabinet and poured himself another over the ice cubes that hadn't yet melted. As he took a sip, he heard the gates hum open and walked to the window. Headlights flashed. Alex's Jag shot through. Nick's stomach tightened. He drained half his drink. Within minutes, the elevator rumbled and he started up the stairs. Glass in hand, he met his brother and wife at the landing of the bedroom floor. Marla looked like hell. Pale, her jaw swollen, her eyes sunk deep into their sockets, she tried to call up a smile for Nick, but failed. His heart wrenched, but he clamped his jaw tight.

"So you really moved in," Alex said as he held the door open to their suite for his wife. "I thought you might have changed your mind."

"I considered it, but didn't want to disappoint," Nick drawled. Marla sent him a quick look, then made her excuses.

"Forgive me, but I've really got to lie down," she said and there was a pained, haunted quality to her gaze that got to him. Frail and uncertain, so unlike that bold sexual creature who had wrapped her fingers around his soul.

Despite all else, Marla Cahill had been through hell tonight.

"Are you okay?" he asked.

A tiny spark of humor flickered in her eyes. "That depends on what you consider okay. Compared to being run over by a steamroller, I'm in pretty good shape, but otherwise . . ." she waggled her hand to indicate indecision ". . . I've had better days." She leaned against the door and chuckled without any humor. "I just can't remember many of them."

"You will."

"Let's hope." She glanced at the railing and the spot in the carpet where she'd thrown up. Aside from a dark water stain, all traces of her ordeal had been cleaned away. She visibly shuddered. "I owe you a big thanks, Nick. If you hadn't been here . . ."

"Someone else would have stepped in."

"No, no, Marla is right," Alex said stiffly. "Thank God you were here."

"It worked out." Nick shrugged.

There was an awkward silence, then Marla said, "I should check on the kids."

Alex was already crossing the hall to Cissy's room. "I'll handle it."

"Will you? Thanks," she said, then with a final look over her shoulder, she met Nick's gaze again. "Good night, Nick." God, she looked vulnerable. Unsteady. So unlike the Marla he knew, the woman he tried to avoid.

He lifted his near-empty glass in a mock salute. "Night."

Marla's heart twisted as she slipped through the door and on the other side, in the suite, she tried to force his image from her mind.

Don't do this to yourself, her tired brain nagged as she made her way to her room. *Yes, he saved your life, but you owe him nothing. Nothing. These conflicted feelings you have for him have got to end. You're married to Alex.*

At that thought her stomach curdled. There was nothing between them, no spark, no love. If she'd ever been in love with her husband it had been years ago, or lost in the fog that was her memory. *Give it time. Soon you'll remember, soon you'll know why you fell in love with Alex and this sexual attraction to Nick will seem silly.*

But she was lying to herself. The feelings Nick aroused in her, the basic female response was something that she knew was unique. "Don't even think of it," she told herself. The blue seduction of his eyes was unthinkable. She was married. She had children. She . . . she . . . oh, God, she was falling in love with him. "You don't really know him," she said aloud, seeing her reflection in the mirror and inwardly cringing, for though her face was still unfamiliar to her, she recognized restless desire in her own gaze. "Oh, you're an idiot." Her fingers drummed on the dresser and she stared at the jewelry box. The one without her ring. There were just so many things about her life that didn't seem right.

Frustrated, she unbuttoned her coat and flung it on the bed. She'd just unzipped the top of her jogging suit when there was a light rap on the door and Alex poked his head inside her room.

"I just wanted to report on the kids," he said and she resisted the urge to pull the zipper tab to her neck. Her bra was showing, the tops of her breasts and abdomen bare and she felt as naked as if she was wearing nothing. His eyes flicked down her torso, but he didn't comment. "They're both sleeping."

"Good." Hot embarrassment washed up the back of her neck.

"Is there anything else you need?"

"Not that I can think of." She just wanted him to leave. Now.

"I'll tell Tom about the medication. He'll see that you get it on time."

She shook her head. "Don't bother him, I think I can handle it myself. Just leave the pills and believe me, when the pain hits I'll take them."

Alex's calm disappeared. Irritation tugged at the corners of his mouth. "Let's not argue any more tonight, okay? Especially about Tom. He's a professional. He'll take care of this." Alex's voice was firm. Authoritative. Commanding.

Marla nearly snapped back a hot retort, but managed to hold her tongue. She was too tired to argue. For the moment. Tomorrow, she'd set things straight. "Fine."

"Now," Alex said, his tone softer and more conciliatory when he realized she wasn't going to fight. "I'll see you in the morning—"

"Wait," she said, a sudden thought striking her. He turned and she held up her right hand and wiggled her ring finger. "I don't suppose you've seen my ring?"

"You remember it?" He was incredulous.

"I wish. I only know about it because Joanna brought it up. I thought you might know where it is—where I might put it when I take it off."

"Probably in here somewhere, I'd guess." He motioned with a sweeping hand to her bedroom.

"It's not. I looked. Top to bottom. Isn't that strange? Joanna thinks that I always wore it and that someone at the hospital might have stolen it."

"I doubt it. Maybe you should look again." Alex shifted from one foot to the other, then checked his watch. "You've had a lot to take in the past few days, Marla. The ring is the least of your worries."

"Joanna said it was a gift from my father."

"Conrad gave you lots of gifts."

"Did he?" That surprised her. She'd seen enough photographs of her stern-faced father and when she'd looked at them, trying to conjure up some memory of the man, she'd intuitively felt that they'd never shared so much as a joke together, that he didn't really like her. She'd sensed that Conrad Amhurst was a self-driven man who had little time for his children and she had no sensation that he'd ever been close to her, that in fact, just the opposite was true. Though she couldn't recall him, she felt in her gut that he hadn't liked her, that she'd somehow been a disappointment.

Perhaps it was because she was his daughter; not a first-born son. That archaic way of thinking should have gone out with the Dark Ages, but she had the sense it still very much existed; her son James was a prime example of being the exalted prince while his older sister held a grudge, with a very large chip on her shoulder, for being ignored.

"Your father showered you with things," Alex said. He thrust his hands into the pockets of his coat, then leaned against the doorjamb.

"Like what?"

"Oh, God, Marla, cars, stocks, bonds, a building. You name it, he gave it to you."

"That's the problem, Alex, I can't name anything. Except the ring." She rubbed her neck and rotated her head. God, she was tired. "As I said before, I want to see my father," she said.

"I know, I know," he snapped. "You don't have to nag me. I'll arrange for you to meet the old man in a couple of days, okay, but let's not make any plans tonight. Tomorrow, we'll sort things out."

"I'll hold you to it."

"I imagine you will," he said without a trace of humor, then went into his room. Marla was too exhausted to come up with a response. She waited until she heard his door close, then tore off the rest of her clothes, leaving them in a pile on the floor. Despite the horror of the night, despite her conflicted feelings about Nick, despite the feeling that there was something very, very wrong here, she was asleep the second her head hit the pillow.

Nick finished his drink, stripped to his boxers and flopped onto the bed. Closing his eyes, he willed himself to sleep, but images of Marla, some of the younger woman he'd known so intimately, others of this new woman, older, but warmer, a woman without a memory, without a past, a woman who still responded to him, haunted him.

Had someone tried to kill her? But who? Why? And why did Alex want him living here in the house so badly? This all felt wrong, as if he were stepping into a carefully laid trap.

Why did Marla look so much like Pam Delacroix—the mystery woman. Friend? Acquaintance? Who the hell was she?

He heard the door to the suite shutting and then footsteps retreat down the hallway. Probably nothing more than Alex needing a drink just as he had. But he sat up in bed, instantly wary. Hadn't Marla claimed she'd felt someone near her bed? Hovering over her? Someone threatening to kill her?

Quietly Nick rolled to his feet, crossed the room and opened the door to the hall just as the elevator door closed. Heart pounding, he walked into the unlocked suite and to Marla's room where she, exhausted, lay sleeping as if dead to the world. Clenching his jaw so tightly it ached, he resisted the urge to touch her cheek. Gritting his teeth, he checked on the baby and even cracked the door to Cissy's room when he heard the soft purr of an engine and the clunk of the garage door opener being activated.

Someone was leaving? At this hour of the night?

Nick walked to the window of Cissy's room and saw the taillights of Alex's Jaguar flash brilliantly as he paused until the electronic gates opened. The Jag shot through and disappeared down the hill. Nick checked his watch. It was after one-thirty in the morning.

Where the hell was his brother off to?

To meet someone.

But who? And why?

It has something to do with Marla.

The next few days passed in a fog of pills and pain as Marla's atrophied muscles began to work. Tom, as Alex had told her, was quick with the medication, or a tray of pulverized food that she could barely swallow and every time her mind began to clear, she would become drowsy again. The shades were drawn, one dim lamp set on low, the room, she thought dazedly, seeming more like a death chamber than a bedroom.

She didn't know night from day, had no strength, could barely move.

But she sensed this wasn't right. Every time she began to think clearly, to gain some strength, the mental fog rolled in again and she was lost. Asea. Rolling in and out of consciousness and feeling a bleak, heavy despair.

"No more pills," she'd insisted groggily on the second, or was it the third day? "I'm . . . I'm too out of it."

"But you're healing." Tom was helping her eat some kind of pea soup.

"No . . . there's something wrong . . ." But he insisted and when she complained to Alex, he'd stroked her head and told her she was getting so much better. Nonetheless she was dazed, drugged, and aside from getting up to use the toilet, she'd been nearly confined to her bed.

"I'm worried about her," Eugenia had said when she'd come in to visit with the baby. Marla's arms ached to hold little James, but she couldn't move, couldn't so much as sit up. "Shouldn't we call Dr. Robertson?"

"I've already talked to Phil," Alex said. "This is normal."

"I don't think so." Eugenia shook her coiffed head and Marla tried to say something only to nearly fall asleep again.

"Marla's exhausted, needs rest, so Phil prescribed pain pills and a mild sedative, just to make sure that she's strong again."

"But—"

"Shh. Let her sleep." Alex had shepherded his mother out of the room, but Marla heard him say, "I've talked to Phil. Her reaction is fairly normal, but he's changing Marla's pain medication to something that won't make her quite as groggy."

That thought was heartening, but she really didn't care. Not even when she opened an eyelid and saw Cissy standing over her bed, her face a mask of worry, her teeth sinking into her lower lip. "Jeez, Mom, are you gonna be okay?"

"Yeah," she managed, her tongue thick. "I'll be . . . fine . . ." She said and fell asleep again, feeling herself begin to drool on the bed. She slept for hours . . . or was it only minutes . . . or even a day . . . when she heard the next voice. Nick's voice.

"This isn't right."

Marla cracked open an eye to see his concerned face. She caught the image of his bladed features and lips pulled into a thin line of vexation. "I'm taking her to see the doctor."

There was someone else in the room. The damned nurse stepped out of the shadows and into her line of vision. "Mr. Cahill left precise instructions that she wasn't to be disturbed," Tom countered and Nick threw him a defiant glare, daring Tom to challenge him again.

"Tough." Nick stuffed Marla's slippers into his jacket pocket.

"Mrs. Cahill is my responsibility."

"I'll remember that." Gently Nick reached down, gathered Marla into his arms and over her weak protests carried her to the elevator.

"You can't do this!" Tom yelled after them.

"Watch me." The elevator door opened and they stepped inside. Marla caught a glimpse of the nurse, his face mottling with rage, his lips thin and white. The door shut.

"You don't have to carry me," she protested.

"Like hell."

On the main floor he strode out the front door. The air outside was brisk. Cold. The chill of winter present in the morning air. Nick started down the front steps. Lars, gardening rake in hand, stepped from between two ancient rhododendrons, and blocked Nick's path.

"What are you doing?" Lars demanded.

"Taking Mrs. Cahill to see a doctor." Nick shouldered past him and Marla, feeling a fool or a wimp, tried to slide from his arms. He held her fast.

"Does Mr. Cahill know about this?" Lars asked suspiciously.

"I hope so." Nick's face was drawn, his features harsh, his stare uncompromising as he strode to his truck. "I hope someone had the presence of mind to tell the bastard that I'm taking his wife to the hospital."

"This . . . this is ridiculous. I can walk," she insisted though she wasn't sure that her legs would hold her or that her blurry mind could function.

"I doubt it."

"Really." But her head lolled back and she felt like a moron, letting some man determine her fate. "I'm . . . I'm not going back to the hospital."

"I think it's time we found you another doctor."

Her head was beginning to clear as he opened the door of his Dodge. He removed her slippers from his pocket and dropped them onto the floor, then took off his jacket and threw it over her shoulders. "Don't argue with me," he said as he slammed the door.

"I think I should make my own decisions," she said, cranking open the window a crack just as the roar of an engine caught her attention and she spied Alex's Jaguar through the foggy windshield. "Great," she muttered as she saw her husband, his face contorted in rage, climb out of his car, flick a cigarette butt into the shrubbery and stride up to Nick.

"What the hell's going on here?" Alex demanded.

Nick stood, feet planted shoulder-width apart, arms folded over his chest, in front of the truck. Didn't answer.

"What the hell do you think you're doing?" Alex demanded.

"Taking your wife to see a doctor."

"That's not necessary. Phil's on his way."

"He's coming here?" Nick asked disbelieving. "A house call?"

"Yes, here . . . now, what's wrong with Marla?" Alex started to walk to the passenger side of the truck, but Nick grabbed his arm and planted himself firmly between the passenger door and his brother.

"Nothing that a decent physician and a lot less pills won't fix."

Alex's nostrils flared. He jerked back his arm. "This has nothing to do with Phil."

"Like hell. He's the one who's overmedicating her. It's his fault."

"No, it's mine," Alex admitted with an edge of defiance. "I wanted Marla to take it slow and rest. To recover. Phil was only doing what I asked."

"Shouldn't that have been Marla's decision?"

"Probably but she was so freaked out and paranoid, I took charge. Remember she was seeing things—people in her room, for Christ's sake," Alex said. "I just thought she needed some time to pull herself together."

"You arrogant bastard," Nick growled.

"But it doesn't matter now, I've called Phil, he's changing the course of her medication and by morning she should be clearheaded again."

"You'd better hope."

"Or what? Don't threaten me, Nick. I made a mistake. It's over." He stepped around his brother and approached the truck. "Marla? Look, I'm sorry. I suppose you heard what was just said. I made a mistake."

"A big one," she said, fury streaming through her blood. She looked him square in the eye through the half-opened window.

"I said, 'I'm sorry,' okay? Phil will be here in a few minutes. He wants to see how you're doing and take you off some of the medications. Just trust me."

Never, she thought, *I'll never trust you for as long as I live,* but at the moment a Cadillac purred through the open gates with Phil Robertson at the wheel.

Nick's gaze turned murderous as Robertson slid out of his car. "You let my brother tell you what to prescribe for his wife?"

"What?"

"Some kind of sleeping pills? You let him decide?" Nick accused.

Alex grabbed hold of his brother's sleeve. "Now wait a minute, Nick, don't go jumping down Phil's throat."

Marla forced her feet into her slippers, opened the door of the truck and slid to the ground. Her legs were unsteady, but propped by the door, she managed to stand. "I want to know why I feel so . . . groggy, so dull . . . why I can't seem to wake up.''

Phil Robertson's lips tightened. ''Someone should have called me before today.''

''How long has it been . . . since I saw you in the clinic?'' Marla asked.

''Five days.'' The doctor turned up his collar.

''Five,'' she whispered, unbelieving.

''Let's go into the house, I'll take a look at you and I can give you something for your pain that won't make you so disoriented and sleepy.''

''I don't want anything,'' she said firmly. No matter what, she needed her wits about her. She couldn't rely on Nick to bail her out time and time again. ''I'll be fine.''

''I think you should listen to Phil. He's the one with MD after his name.'' Alex placed an arm over her shoulders.

She shrugged it off. ''No, I don't think so. Now, listen,'' she said her jaw beginning to ache as the medication wore off, ''I'm a grown woman. I'll make all the decisions about what's happening to me, to my body.''

''I was just thinking about your best interests,'' Alex explained, but there wasn't any warmth in his eyes and one of his hands curled into a fist before he jammed it into the pocket of his coat.

''Were you? I don't think so. Now stop treating me like some frail hothouse flower.'' She was still wearing Nick's coat, her pajamas and her slippers. Despite the chill, she flung Nick's jacket at him and he caught it on the fly, then she turned back to the house, her legs seeming to gain strength with each stride.

Men, she thought unkindly. Who needed them?

She climbed the steps and though still slightly woozy, yanked hard on the front door. One last glance at the threesome told her all she needed to know. Alex was reaching for his cigarettes, rage simmering in his expression, Phil Robertson looked worried, his brow knit, his lips in a tight little knot, and Nick just stared after her, his blue eyes bright with that same sexy, irreverent challenge that she'd found fascinating from the moment she'd woken from the damned coma.

He alone was the man she could trust.

Never in his life had Nick been involved with a married woman, hadn't ever considered it. He lay on the bed, stared up at the ceiling and tried to force Marla out of his mind. Impossible. She was wedged in tight, a seductive image that brought a sheen of sweat to his brow and caused his damned cock to ache. The house was quiet, everyone presumably asleep. Nick rolled over, tried to conjure up any other vision but Marla's seductive eyes, and couldn't.

And she's just down the hall.

But she's Alex's wife.

Their marriage is already in trouble. You can see it. He never pays her any attention. She doesn't remember him and she wants you as much as you want her. Go on, get out of bed. Just go check on her.

His gut clenched and he threw off the covers. This was nuts. He yanked on a pair of jeans, didn't bother with a shirt or shoes, opened the door and walked into the hallway where security lamps gave off a dim, barely existent glow that pooled on the carpet. He walked directly to the door of the suite, placed his hand on the knob and stopped. What would he say to her? What would he do? Nothing. He couldn't do a damned thing.

Gritting his teeth he went downstairs and poured himself a drink. What would be the price of his lust? A family broken? Two kids who would become the product of divorce? Marla would never want to move to Oregon and he wasn't sure that was what he wanted anyway. He just wanted to kiss her and touch her again, to feel that sizzling connection they'd experienced fifteen years before.

And you'd love to best Alex, get a little back, admit it. You don't like the way he treats her and you've never really gotten over the fact that she threw you over for your brother.

"Son of a bitch." He tossed back his drink, wiped a hand over his mouth and hiked back up the stairs. God, he was a fool. He'd reached the bedroom landing and had started toward his room when the door to the suite cracked open and Marla stepped into the hallway.

"Oh!" Her hand flew to her chest and her eyes opened wide. "Nick," she whispered. "You scared me half to death!"

"Sorry. I couldn't sleep."

"Me, neither. I thought I heard Cissy get up."

"It was me."

"Oh."

"Sorry to disappoint."

"You didn't." She seemed flustered and looked back through the door. God, she was beautiful in some kind of satin pajamas that were a size too large from the looks of them, her hair rumpled, sleep still heavy in her eyes.

"I—I'd like to talk to you," she said and he had trouble keeping this eyes off the V of her neckline where her pajama top buttoned. The hollow of her throat was visible, that feminine circle of bones he found so fascinating, as enticing as he remembered.

"I'll buy you a drink. Full bar downstairs."

"Just what I need with all the drugs in my body," she teased then flashed him a dazzling grin. "Give me a minute to get my robe." She was through the door in an instant and in the thirty seconds it took her to retrieve the matching wrap, he kicked himself a dozen times. This was stupid. Treacherous.

But he couldn't stop himself and as she slipped through the door, he caught a waft of her perfume and his gut tightened. She closed the door with a soft click, then cinched the belt of her robe as they walked down a flight to the darkened living room. Rain drizzled down the ancient glass of the windows. Nick struck a match to the logs stacked in the grate, then poured himself a drink. Marla, looking nervous, her fingers playing with the ties of her robe, stood by the crackling flames.

The room, illuminated only by the shifting firelight, seemed to shrink.

"Sure I can't get you anything?" he asked, dropping ice cubes into his short glass.

She hedged, didn't meet his eyes. "Maybe a brandy. A small one."

He grinned, found a snifter and poured a thin stream of amber liquor into a squatty crystal glass. "That's my girl," he said before he saw her reaction, the way she bit her lip anxiously. He handed her the drink and touched the rim of his glass to hers. "To better days."

"And nights," she said, then took a sip, her eyes regarding him over the rim of the snifter. Wide and green, they stared at him. Her face had healed, the scar in her hairline was barely visible and her hair surrounded her face in short mahogany waves.

"So, what's up, Marla?"

"I . . . I want to know what happened. I was out of my head for five days and all I remember are images, people coming in and out . . . nothing clear. I thought maybe you could catch me up. Has anyone contacted Pam's family?"

"Not that I know of. But then I've spent a lot of time up to my eyeballs in accounting records for the company."

"And what have you found?"

"Unless Alex does something drastic, Cahill Limited will go bust."

"But it's a huge corporation," she protested, and he watched as her lips parted and she took another sip.

"Privately held corporation and not really all that large, not in today's world."

"Can it be saved?"

"I think so. With the right number of cuts. If Alex is willing."

"He seems to work all the time," she said, walking to the window and staring out at the lights winking down the hillside.

"He's always gone to one meeting or the other. Either at the office or on the board at the hospital or Cahill House."

"Do you miss him?" Nick asked. She hesitated, then shook her head.

"Sadly, no. I don't feel any real connection with him." He watched the back of her neck turn rosy at the admission. "I can't explain it."

"Alex isn't an easy man."

"Nor are you," she observed, sending him a glance over her shoulder. It wasn't meant to be provocative but it was. Her robe slid to one side and his eyes were drawn to the column of her neck and the smooth skin at the curve where her neck met her shoulder. What he would do to kiss her there.

"How would you know? You don't remember."

"Woman's intuition," she said. "There's something about you that a woman can sense. A restlessness. You're not satisfied with much in life, I'd guess. And you don't settle. If you want something, you go for it."

"Not always."

"Oh, yes, you do."

"I want you."

Beneath the layers of satin her backbone hardened and she glanced at the floor, her neck bowing. "But you still don't trust me."

"Why would I?" he asked and took a step closer, condemning himself as he did. He'd sworn to be immune to her charms, that he'd never allow her close to him again, but as each day had passed he'd felt more drawn to her, more intrigued. He'd warned himself time and time again and yet when he got down to the bones of the truth, he'd like nothing more than to touch her, kiss her, caress her and thrust into the deepest, most feminine part of her.

"Did I hurt you so badly all those years ago?" she asked, studying the drizzle of raindrops on the windowpane.

"It was my fault." Another step closer.

"But you're punishing me."

"How?"

"By . . . by trying to keep your distance." She was still turned away from him, her drink now on the windowsill, her hands on the ledge as she stared through the ancient, watery glass.

"Self-preservation, Marla. It's just a basic animal instinct." *Like the other ones you arouse in me.* He was so close now he could smell the scent of her skin, see the tiny hairs on her nape, wonder about the secrets that lay beneath the folds of satin that encased her.

"You saved my life," she said and her voice was breathless as if she, too, could feel how near he was, the barest of inches separated his toes from her heels. Her perfume wafted to his nostrils, smelled faintly of lavender and reminded him how long it had been since he'd been with a woman.

"Saved your life? Maybe, maybe not. I did what I had to do. Don't make it more than it was, okay? Don't try to cast me as some kind of hero. Believe me, I'm not."

"You spend a lot of time trying to convince everyone that you aren't."

"It's not hard," he said, and knowing he was making a deadly mistake he reached forward and curled his fingers over her shoulders, grabbing smooth satin and supple flesh. Beneath his hands he felt her tremble, watched as she took in a swift breath but made no move to pull away.

Firelight played in her hair and gilded her skin, the innocent pink of her robe turned to a soft, warm peach color as his hands opened and closed over her upper arms. With a low moan, she leaned against him and he lowered his head, his lips pressing against the back of her neck. Desire ran hot through him, centered between his legs, caused him to think of nothing but the pure sensual pleasure of this woman. So hot. So wet. So wickedly wanton. So forbidden.

"Nick," she whispered so softly he wasn't certain she'd said it.

Knowing he was going too far, he let his senses take over,

nuzzling her neck, tasting her hot skin, pushing the silky fabric away from her body. He ran his tongue along her shoulder and she quivered. He reached around her waist, found the knot holding her robe together and loosened it.

Marla felt his heat. She arched against him, one hand reaching over her head to run her fingers in his hair. He kissed the length of that arm, sending tingles along her nerves, making her forget that she'd promised herself to never fall victim to his raw sexuality, that loving him would only cause her heartache, that making love to him would ruin her life.

The knot gave way.

Satin parted to reveal another layer.

Nick groaned in frustration, then unbuttoned her pajama top. His fingers delved inside and Marla gasped at the warmth of his touch, the sear of his hands on the underside of her breasts. Her skin tingled and she let her head loll to the side offering more of her neck to his greedy lips.

Deep inside she felt an ache, a yearning. The pajama top parted, fell off her shoulders along with her robe, bunched at the small of her back. Nick licked the shell of her ear, coarse hairs on his chest brushed the back of her shoulders as he pulled her hard against him. She pressed her buttocks even closer, felt his erection hard against the cleft between her cheeks.

"Ooh," she moaned, rubbing against him as his hands kneaded her breasts, his thumbs scraping her nipples, his breathing rapid and hot. Sweat sheened her skin. Her blood pulsed faster, ran hot as tallow.

"Marla, oh, God, Marla . . . I don't . . . want to . . ." He was moving against her, the fly of his jeans hard as it slid along the satin of her pajama bottoms. She couldn't help responding, pushing closer to him as he ground against her. Part of her knew she was making the biggest mistake of her life, the other part didn't care.

You're married, for God's sake!

But the marriage was a sham.

You're a mother!

But I want this man, I feel a connection to him, a need that only he can satisfy.

Don't confuse lust with love, Marla. Think!

One of his hands lowered, slid over the smooth satin, brushed past her belly button slowly until his strong hand cupped her mound, and his fingers curled between her legs, holding her firmly against him, making her feel his need, his heat, causing her to quiver with want. Through the fabric he touched, rubbed, probed, stoking a fire that was already white hot. Her skin was on fire, the ache inside her pounding.

Her knees weakened as his lips caressed the curve of her jaw. She closed her eyes, threw her head back, let him kiss her shoulders and throat as he kept up his rhythm. Her heart beat was an unsteady tattoo, her breath was short, desperate gasps. She wanted him, wanted to turn in his arms, feel his hard flat nipples, touch the muscles straining across his chest. Desperately she needed to experience the bittersweet union of his body joining with hers.

Images of him, naked, sweating, straining above her filled her head. Hard sinewy legs pushed, his muscular back flexed, her fingers dug into his buttocks, he thrust hard . . . long . . . over and over again . . . oh, God . . . she was spinning . . .

"Marla," he whispered, his voice hoarse with desire. "This is so wrong . . . I . . . we . . . I . . . should . . ."

She couldn't think . . . couldn't breathe. She was hot, beads of sweat dotting her brow, running down her spine, moistening her skin. His lips, oh, God, if she could just turn around and kiss him, lower his fly and . . .

Somewhere on the floor above a door creaked open, then clicked shut.

Nick froze.

Marla's head cleared instantly.

What in the name of God was she doing?

Nick released her as if she were molten. Her robe and pajama top slid to the floor and she snatched them up. "Damn," he whispered as on silent footsteps he crossed the room putting much needed space between his body and hers. The elevator motor whirred.

Marla slid her arms through pajama top and robe, fumbled with the buttons, then in frustration, yanked the belt tight around her waist. How could she explain herself, her mussed hair, red face, rumpled clothes and the desire she was certain was evident in her eyes? What had she been thinking? Why would she give into such, treacherous, forbidden temptation?

Nick stepped forward grabbed her arm and pulled her into an alcove near the bay window. His eyes, still glassy, found hers and he held a finger to his lips.

Her heart was hammering, her mind whirling. They would be caught and then . . . oh, how could she account for how she felt about Nick to her daughter, to her mother-in-law or . . . or . . . to . . . her husband?

Harlot. Jezebel. Whore. All the archaic condemning terms burned through her brain.

The elevator finally ground to a stop, at the basement garage below. Over the wild beating of her heart, she heard the electronic garage door clunk and open, then the firing of a smooth engine.

"Alex," Nick whispered against her ear and pulled her to one side of the window where they watched the brake lights of her husband's car flash bright and reflect in the raindrops. The gate opened and the Jaguar drove through.

"Where is he going?" she asked.

"To meet someone, I'd guess."

"Who?"

"I don't know, but it's not on the up and up. Nothing good happens after midnight."

"I think we just proved that," she said, furious with herself. How had she been so stupid, such a foolish woman to give into her basest of needs? "I've got to go to bed." She hesitated, then added, "Alone." She started toward the door, but he caught her wrist in his fingers.

"I'm not going to apologize, Marla," he said, his blue eyes dark with challenge.

She angled up her chin. "Good. Neither am I." Then, before she said anything she'd regret, she turned and took the stairs two at a time to the sanctuary of her perfectly decorated and oh, so cold, bedroom.

Slut! She was nothing more than a damned, dirty slut.

He stared up at the house, raindrops peppering his bare head, fogging his glasses as he watched the window where he'd seen the lovers. The man had been behind, caressing her, kissing her, his face hidden in the shadowy room. Through the drizzled glass he'd observed from a distance, his binoculars not allowing him to get the view he wanted, but he recognized Marla letting the man strip her and touch her and though it had been too dark to see just how far they'd gone, he'd gotten hard, had to touch himself, couldn't wait until he was the one fondling and touching her, he was the one rubbing his rough hands over those luscious breasts.

"Just you wait, baby," he whispered, then seeing the garage door open, he ducked quickly down the street, feeling the cold rain run down his neck and knowing that it was just a matter of time before it was his turn.

He licked his lips.

He couldn't wait.

Chapter Thirteen

You nearly made love to Nick.

"Damn it." Lying in bed, Marla smashed her fist into the mattress. "What's wrong with you?" She thought of his hot breath against her nape and the back of her throat went dry. "Fool, fool, fool!" she chastised, throwing herself out from under the covers and padding to the bathroom.

She stripped off her clothes, determined to force the erotic images from her mind, but under the shower's pulsing spray with the glass steaming, she thought of him and the way his hands felt on her breasts, how he'd rubbed the silken fabric of her pajamas against her fevered skin.

"Stop it!" she shouted, shampooing quickly and turning the water cold enough to chase all her wanton thoughts from her mind. Dear Lord, she was going to make herself crazier than she already was. "If that's possible," she muttered, turning off the faucet, grabbing a towel and drying as she stepped into the bathroom. She was determined not to think of Nick this morning, but images of his naked torso, tight abdomen and the way his jeans had been slung low over his hips, his crotch bulging, continued to chase after her as she threw on a pair of jeans and a sweater, slapped lipstick over her mouth, brushed mascara over her lashes and dabbed mousse in her short curls. A volatile mixture of emotions—shame, disbelief, as well as a tiny bit of satisfaction and a grain of hope—roiled within her. She knew a relationship with her brother-in-law was doomed.

Yet, she couldn't forget the feel of his lips, the heat of his touch and how violently and passionately she had responded to him.

Oh, God, what had she been thinking? She scowled into the mirror in her bathroom as she ruffled her wet hair with her fingers.

"You weren't," she told her reflection firmly and hated the gleam of mischief she saw in her eyes. "You've got tons of things to do today. Tons! You don't have time for any romantic nonsense." Yet she couldn't help but wonder as she slid into tennis shoes and hurried downstairs, if she was just naturally lusty and passionate, or was it only with Nick?

The truth of the matter is that you . . . well, you've been interested in other men. Alex's condemnation echoed through her mind.

"Don't think about it," she warned herself. She didn't have time for recriminations. "Just go forward from here."

For the first time since waking from her coma Marla felt alive. Energized. Ready to take on the world and figure out who the hell she was, what had happened on the night of the accident, and why she felt like a prisoner and stranger in her own home. Last night she'd suffered through Phil Robertson's apologies and her husband's angry silence before she'd encountered Nick coming up the stairs, but she couldn't forgive Alex for taking away five days of her life.

Fine. He messed up. But that's no reason to go sneaking behind his back with Nick.

What she felt about Nick had nothing to do with Alex. She tried to tamp down the rage that tore through her. She'd lost five days of her life. Nearly a week! Because her husband thought it best.

Bullshit. That's all it was.

The pain in her jaw reminded her that she wasn't completely healed, so she tossed back a couple of aspirin with a swig of water and wasn't going to let a dull ache stop her. She managed to reach the kitchen and coffeepot in time to say good-bye to Cissy as the girl, backpack in tow, breezed out the door.

Alex, she was told by Carmen, had already left for the office and she wondered if he'd even bothered to come home last night. Where had he gone? Who had he met? Why the hell was he sneaking around in the middle of night?

She'd find out. She just had to decide whether to confront him or do a little research first. She had a gut feeling that she was good at this sort of thing, though she couldn't for the life of her figure out why. But it didn't matter. She was sick and tired of being the damned victim here, of playing the role of the poor, sickly, amnesic wife and mother.

Again . . . it was all just bullshit.

"What about Nick?" Marla asked Carmen as she lingered in the kitchen where the cook, Elsa, was already marinating a cut of meat. A big woman with heavy breasts, a thick waist, and merry eyes, she rubbed spices into a thick slab of beef.

"He's gone, too. Left early this morning and Mrs. Eugenia had Lars drive her to Cahill House for an early meeting." Carmen's dark eyes flashed. "Mrs. Eugenia wasn't too happy that she had to be downtown before eight."

"I don't blame her." Marla finished her coffee and made her way upstairs where Fiona was just picking up James from his crib.

"Let me handle this little guy," she said, and over Fiona's worried glances, fed and changed the baby. "You can take some time off this morning."

"But it's my job—"

"Mine, too. I might go out this afternoon, so I'd like to

spend a little time with him first,'' Marla said with a smile. "You don't mind, do you?''

"Of course not. You're his mum.''

"Precisely.''

"I'll be back in a bit then,'' the girl said, brightening at the opportunity for a little freedom.

"Thanks.''

Marla bathed her son and it felt so right to watch his eyes sparkle as she swished his legs and arms with the warm water. He kicked and gurgled and she thought him the most precious child in the universe. "Yes, you are,'' she said, poking his little belly with her finger, "even if your daddy's a first class jerk.'' The baby smiled and waved a fist, as if he understood and Marla's heart cracked. Why couldn't she just be happy with her children and her husband, why couldn't she accept that this was her life and it was a wonderful, enchanted, privileged existence that most women would envy?

Forget about Nick.

Forget about all the things that are bothering you.

Enjoy, Marla!

But she couldn't. Yes, she could revel in her baby and daughter, but she needed to know so much more. She wrapped her son in a towel, dried him, powdered him and dressed him in blue pajamas that he was already outgrowing. "You're such a big, big boy,'' she said and carried him downstairs into the den.

The house was relatively quiet. No one was about, so this was her opportunity to do a few things where she needed privacy. She put the baby in his playpen and reached for the phone.

In a matter of seconds she was connected to the San Francisco Police Department, but was informed that she'd have to leave a message for Detective Paterno as he was out. She asked that he call her back and then hung up to dial the University of California at Santa Cruz and ask about Pam's daughter.

"I'm sorry, there's no one enrolled at the university with

the last name of Delacroix,'' the woman at the registration office said, without a note of inflection.

Great. Marla tapped her fingers on the arm of the couch. James was lying on his back and cooing, happy with the world.

"Maybe the Delacroix girl is registered under another name,'' Marla suggested, thinking hard, trying to remember something, *any*thing about Pam or her daughter.

"Then I'd need that information, but even if she were a student here, I wouldn't be able to tell you. It's our privacy policy.''

No other questions helped locate the girl and eventually Marla had to hang up. She was getting nowhere. Fast. She glanced at her wrist to check the time, but wasn't wearing a watch.

That was odd. She was certain she'd always worn one . . . oh, for God's sake, in all that jewelry upstairs, she'd surely find some kind of timepiece. The clock on the VCR said it was nearly noon.

Carrying the baby, she hiked up the stairs to her room, dug through a jewelry box filled with earrings, bracelets, and, as expected, a watch with a linked metallic band. As she reached for it, she hesitated, for there, hidden beneath a pair of faux pearl earrings and a silver bracelet was a ring, a gorgeous ring, the facets of its blood-red stone winking brilliantly.

"No way,'' she whispered, picking up the ring and holding it in her palm. She wouldn't have missed it in an earlier search. She'd been through this box a half dozen times and the stone was too large to have been overlooked.

She slipped the ring onto her right hand. It felt awkward and heavy. It slid between her joints, the gold band loose. *Of course it is; you've lost weight since the accident, all of your clothes are almost a size too big. It makes sense that the ring and probably the watch don't fit.*

Either that, or they never belonged to you in the first place.

She glanced in the mirror over her bureau. A pale woman with short hair, green eyes and high cheekbones stared back at her. Her bruises had faded and aside from a little swelling from the cuts to the inside of her cheeks when Nick had ripped out the wires, she was herself. With her baby. That part seemed right, it fit. But the ruby ring didn't, though she had a niggling idea, just the hint that she'd seen this piece of jewelry somewhere before.

On someone else? Who?

She studied the contents of the jewelry box. Most of the earrings, pins and bracelets weren't valuable, could have been bought at any department store . . . but not so this ring. She knew intuitively that it was worth a small fortune.

Why would she keep it here?

It was planted, you dope. You mentioned it to someone who either put it back or told someone else and they returned it. Because someone's trying to drive you crazy or they don't want you to question who you are.

Why?

She dropped the ring unceremoniously into the box, then snapped the watchband over her wrist. Yep, it was too big, but she wore it anyway.

James yawned and began to fuss, so she kissed his head and carried him to his crib. She watched as his eyes closed and his thumb inched toward his mouth. Once he was settled, she walked into the hallway and paused at the guest room. The door was ajar and she spied a duffel bag that had been tossed into one corner, a shirt slung over the bedpost. A hint of Nick's aftershave wafted into the corridor and memories of the night before rained over her in a torrent of sweet, heady seduction. *Don't even go there,* she warned herself. *It was just lust. Sex. Two restless people who needed a release.*

But it hadn't been before.

Nick had stopped his truck, held her in his arms and comforted her on the night he'd driven her to the clinic.

Then dumped you off with Alex and left.

Because he's my husband, she thought angrily. *What else could he do?*

Wasn't he also the one who had dragged you bodily out of bed and was hell-bent to see that you got some decent medical care? Without his interference, you might still be loaded up on painkillers and Valium or whatever the hell it was. She nearly laughed aloud. Nick was right. He didn't fit the image of some sort of twenty-first-century hero.

No way. No how.

"Mrs. Cahill?" Tom's soft voice caught her off guard. He'd just come down from the servants' quarters. "I was about to get your medication."

"What medication?"

"The painkiller Dr. Robertson prescribed."

"What is it?" she asked, walking away from Nick's room.

"Acetaminophen."

"Tylenol?"

"Yes."

"Anything else?"

"Well, it's with codeine," he said.

"What was I on before?" she asked, stepping closer to him. "What did Dr. Robertson prescribe when I got out of the hospital?"

"Halcion."

"What's that?"

"Triazolam. It's a mild sedative."

"Great." Had she needed one? "Look, forget any pain pills. I think I'll just stick with Bayer, okay? I'll take it when I need it for the pain and if I can't sleep, too bad. I'll deal with it."

"But—"

"It's my body, Tom, and no matter what you've been told, I'm in control of it. If there's a problem with Dr. Robertson, I'll talk to him. The same goes for my husband. I'll deal with him."

"They only want what's best for you," he said, his face totally guileless.

"If you say so. In the meantime I'll handle the pain however I see fit."

"Mrs. Cahill, this is my job."

"And if you want to keep it, you won't push this issue, Tom. I don't need a nurse and both you and I know it. Somehow it makes my husband feel more secure but that's his problem, not mine. So, thank you for your concern, but I'm not taking any more bloody pills and that's that."

She left Tom standing in his tracks and didn't give a damn. Too many people were trying to tell her what to do, and it wasn't flying with her.

She walked back to the suite and closed the door behind her. As she did she heard Tom's footsteps pound down the stairs. She tried Alex's door. Of course, it was locked. Again. Why? She drummed her fingers on the doorknob, then on inspiration, walked outside the suite down the hallway and tried the door to the office that opened to the corridor. It didn't budge. But she'd seen Eugenia open it the other night when she'd been lying on the floor thinking she was going to choke to death.

Someone had taken the trouble to lock it again.

So you'll just have to devise a means to unlock it. By hook or by crook. Whatever it took.

Marla made her way around the railing to the spot where she'd vomited nearly a week earlier. Kneeling, she ran her fingers over the short pile of the carpet. It was bone dry; the stain had been washed away until it had disappeared.

Had someone—the intruder if he existed—poisoned her, caused her to lose the contents of her stomach? She rocked back on her heels. Tom had told her he'd given her triazolam, a drug she'd never heard of. She stood, leaning on the railing and glared at the locked door to Alex's office. Something important was hidden inside. Otherwise the damned thing wouldn't be locked.

So she had to get in.

On quiet footsteps, Marla took the stairs down to the second floor, heard the maid vacuuming in the library, then, cautiously she crept into her mother-in-law's suite. Nervously she closed the door behind her and didn't bother with any lights, letting the sunlight filtering through the curtains be her guide and telling herself that she really wasn't trespassing. This was her home. She had the right to know what went on within these hundred-year-old walls.

The other night Eugenia had extracted the key to Alex's office from her jacket pocket—a navy blue jacket. Maybe it was still there.

Fat chance. It's been five days, remember?

Carefully Marla eased the door to the closet open and stepped inside. She snapped on the light and quickly scanned the cedar-lined room. Each of her mother-in-law's outfits was neatly hung on double rails, arranged by color, jackets above, skirts below, matching shoes in cubbyholes near the floor. Marla worked quickly, her fingers damp with sweat as she reached inside the pocket of each jacket—navy blue to flaming orange—and came up with ticket stubs, hankies, a few coins, anything Eugenia had absently left.

But no keys.

"Damn," Marla grumbled, realizing the key to Alex's office was probably on the woman right now, somewhere down at Cahill House wherever the hell that was. Nonetheless she started searching the handbags. Furiously she unclasped each and every one and again she came up empty. The closet was hot, stuffy and she was about to leave when she heard the door to Eugenia's room open. Her heart froze. How could she explain herself if she was found out? She flipped off the light and slowly backed up, parting the clothes and stepping onto the top of the cubby before forcing the garments back together and pulling a plastic-encased gown in front of her. She nearly jumped when she heard the vacuum roar to life. Slowly, tediously, the maid cleaned Eugenia's room. Marla held her breath. Maybe the maid wouldn't come into the closet, maybe Marla would get lucky, maybe—oh damn.

There was a pause in the hum of the motor and the door opened, spilling in a shaft of light. Marla didn't move a muscle as the girl pushed the vacuum cleaner into the tight little room, the roar of the machine nearly deafening. The overhead light flashed on. Marla pressed back against the wall and realized that her cover, the plastic bag she'd found in the rear of the closet was yellowed, the gauzy, beaded white dress inside probably Eugenia's ancient wedding gown.

Closing her eyes, she waited as the machine bumped against the cubby on which she stood, jarring her bones. She didn't dare breathe. How long could it take to vacuum a damned closet? Suddenly the machine was switched off.

"What?" the maid called loudly.

Through the crack between a long dressing gown and the plastic cover Marla saw the maid turn her head toward the door. She was a small Hispanic girl by the name of Rosa, a tiny thing who didn't say a lot as her English was poor at best. Abandoning her idle machine, Rosa stepped into Eugenia's bedroom.

"Ah, Señora Cahill, *si, si.*"

Then Eugenia's voice. "Please, can't you do this later?"

Oh, God, what now? How could Marla explain what she was doing in her mother-in-law's private quarters? Sweat dotted her forehead and ran down her spine and her heart was thumping wildly.

"I need to lie down," Eugenia explained.

"*Si, si, I come back luego. Later.*"

"And Rosa, please, have Carmen call me when the guests arrive. The Reverend and Mrs. Favier will be here in a while."

The Reverend and . . . then Marla remembered. Alex's cousin Cherise and her husband had been scheduled to visit with her but Marla had been bedridden that day. Because of the damned drugs.

She strained to hear the rest of the conversation. When were Cherise and her husband scheduled to show up? Somehow Marla had to escape from the closet without anyone knowing she'd been inside. Before the guests arrived.

Sweat began to run down her arms.

Rosa retrieved the vacuum, then hurried away. Marla didn't

move, didn't dare step down and a few seconds later she saw her mother-in-law walk into the closet, remove her navy blue jacket and hang it on a rack on the opposite side from Marla's hiding spot. Eugenia kicked off her high heels and set them directly under the jacket, then shrugged out of her blouse and stepped out of her skirt, leaving her in a lacy slip and panty hose. Wearily Eugenia snapped off the light and closed the door behind her.

Marla let out her breath, hoping beyond hope that no one was looking for her, that she find a means of escape before she was missed.

Slow as death, the minutes ticked by and Marla waited, mentally counting off a quarter of an hour before finally easing her way out of her hiding spot, stepping carefully onto the carpet and edging through the dimness toward the small crack of light filtering under the door.

She reached for the light switch and ever so gently flipped it up. The closet was suddenly awash with bright, intense light. Squinting, she found the jacket Eugenia had recently shed and reached into the right-hand pocket. Her fingers touched cool, notched metal—keys. *Thank God.* Carefully, so that the metal wouldn't chink, she extracted a keyring.

So far, so good.

She stuffed her prize into the front pocket of her jeans.

Now . . . if she could make it past her mother-in-law without waking her.

If she's asleep and not sitting on a chair or her bed and flipping through a magazine or knitting.

But there was no sound of pages turning or needles clicking. Marla had to take a chance. Otherwise she was trapped.

After turning off the light, she wrapped her fingers around the doorknob and turned. The lock clicked softly.

It's now or never she thought and inched the door open. Eugenia's bedroom was semidark, the shades drawn, the soft sound of snoring coming from the bed where thick covers were drawn to the older woman's neck. Sending up a silent prayer that the stupid dog was nowhere about, Marla hurried across the room, reached for the door and quickly, silently opened it.

Her mother-in-law snorted and Marla slipped into the hallway where she closed the door and dashed up the stairs, nearly tripping over Coco in the process. With a yip, Coco scurried down the stairs, tail between her short legs, then darted into the family room. "Good riddance," Marla whispered. Eugenia's keyring was burning a hold in her pocket and she wanted to try the door to the office immediately, open it if she could, then replace the keys, but as she reached the landing on the next floor, the doorbell chimed loudly.

Damn. She checked her watch and waited as Carmen answered. A woman's voice echoed up the stairs.

"I'm Cherise Favier. I don't think I've met you before. I'm here to see Marla."

Marla's heart sank. By the time the visit was over, Eugenia would be up and searching for her keys. Her only hope was to get rid of Alex's cousin quickly, before anyone disturbed her mother-in-law, then hurry back upstairs. Turning quickly, Marla made her way down to the foyer where Cherise was unwrapping a leopard-trimmed cape and handing it to Carmen.

"Marla!" Cherise exclaimed, then her expression changed from delight to confusion. "You—you look fabulous!" A lie. Marla had seen her reflection less than an hour earlier. "I've been dying to see you." The blond woman clasped Marla's hand with both of hers and forced a smile that threatened to crack her perfect makeup. "We . . . Donald and I have been so-o-o worried about you." She glanced over her shoulder to the front door. "He'll be in shortly," she said slightly nervous. "He got a call—an emergency of some sort—on his cell phone just as we drove up."

At that moment a tall, strapping man appeared in the doorway. His brown hair was thick, curly and starting to show a few strands of gray. His shoulders were broad, stretching a black leather jacket that was tossed over a black shirt and at odds with a startling white clerical collar.

"Donald, you remember Marla," Cherise said.

"Of course I do." Donald flashed a thousand-watt smile that showed off white, fat teeth and a few gold crowns. His face was tanned, lined and warm. Half-glasses covered the bridge of a nose that had been broken more than once from the looks of it. In one hand he carried a well-worn Bible. With his free hand, he surrounded Marla's shoulders as he gave her a hug. "It's good to see you," he said, and dropped a kiss familiarly onto her forehead. "Thank the Lord that you're all right. My, that was nasty business that landed you back at the hospital the other night."

Cherise beamed up at her handsome husband. "Amen."

"I didn't go to the hospital."

"Oh, clinic, whatever," he said waving the hand with his Bible. Marla eased out of his embrace. It was too familiar, too intimate, too forced. "You gave us all quite a scare, you know. Well, a couple of them."

"The Lord moves in mysterious ways," Marla quipped back and Cherise's smile froze. The Reverend Donald's eyebrows quirked at her joke, but she didn't really care.

"Why don't you come into the sitting room where we can talk?" Marla began ushering them into the sitting room where they all settled into chairs and Carmen, as if on cue, carried in a tray with a coffee service, tea pot and basket of scones. "Mrs. Eugenia mentioned that you would be having guests," she explained, pouring three cups. "She'll be down in a few minutes."

Marla's heart dropped. If her mother-in-law was up, she couldn't very well unlock the office and start going through Alex's computer files and desk.

"You probably heard from Alex and Nick that I've been trying to reach you," Cherise said. Seated on a small sofa near her husband, she added sugar substitute to her cup, then adjusted the hem of her short black sweater. She was a pretty woman, beginning to age, with blond hair, pale skin and red-tinged lips that matched her fingernails.

"Nick mentioned that you called."

"I was crazy to know if you were okay and then Alex blocked us from the hospital—" Cherise caught a look from her husband and snapped her mouth shut.

Donald settled back on the cushions, as if he intended to stay. Maybe even read scripture. "How're you feeling?"

"Better."

"You've had a rough time of it," Donald said and though he was being kind, Marla felt as if there was a hint of condescension in his words.

"I'm okay," she said.

"But I've heard you have some kind of amnesia," Cherise said. "It's temporary, right?"

"I hope so."

Cherise said solemnly, "We'll pray for you."

Her husband nodded. "Perhaps we should join hands now and ask for the Father's forgiveness and guidance?"

Cherise set down her cup and reached for Marla's hand. Donald did the same, but before the prayer could get under way Eugenia clipped into the room, Coco at her heels. She'd donned a somber gray suit that matched her expression and suddenly the keyring in Marla's pocket seemed to weigh a ton. The dog growled low in her throat, then took up her position behind Eugenia's favorite chair.

"Cherise. Donald," Eugenia said without a smile.

"Aunt Genie!" Cherise shot to her feet and flung her arms around the smaller woman.

"How are you?" Eugenia said tonelessly as Cherise stepped back and beamed.

"Better now that I've seen Marla. We—Monty and I—were sick to death with worry. I was frantic to see her. I wish Monty would have come with me, but he was busy today and I didn't know when we'd have another opportunity," Cherise said, taking a seat again as Eugenia settled into her wingback and dropped one hand to scratch the little dog's ears.

Cherise opened her palms, fingers stretching wide in supplication. "Look, there's been a lot of bad blood in the family and it's gone back generations, we all know that, but it's time to put a stop to it. I mean, when I heard that Marla had almost lost her life . . . I just fell down and prayed. Something like this really puts things into perspective."

Donald clasped his hands and let them fall between his knees. On his left was a wide gold band proudly pronouncing he was a married man, on his right was a signet ring of some sort and another on his pinkie where a large diamond flashed. "Cherise and I think that this is an opportunity for the family to come together, that when tragedy strikes, or nearly strikes, it's important to put the past behind us and look forward. To take God's hand and walk with Him, thank Him for all the blessings he's bestowed upon us." Donald's smile was placidly serene and phony as hell.

Cherise reached over and squeezed Marla's hand. "You and I, we were always close. I thought of you more like a sister than a cousin, or an in-law. And I know Monty, he was always fond of you. Is fond of you." Her eyes were round, sincere, but there was just a hint of something more in their amber depths—something dark and sinful. "We're here to see that the rift that seems to have widened between us in the past couple of years is bridged."

What the devil was this all about? Marla wanted to escape from the saccharine and goodwill and idealistic, shopworn phrases that rang false in her ears.

The front door opened and Nick, wearing his scarred leather jacket, jeans and wary expression strode in. The corners of his mouth pinched at the sight of Cherise and her husband.

"Cherise," Nick said, nodding at his cousin. He stuffed his hands into the back pockets of his jeans. His gaze skated over his cousin's upturned face to land full force on Marla. Stormy blue eyes bored into hers. "So, how's it goin' today?"

"Better," Marla said, refusing to think about last night in the living room and how his body felt against hers. "Lots better. I think I'm starting to feel human again."

"Jaw still hurt?"

"A little."

"A lot, I'd wager," he said, unzipping his jacket.

"I'll deal with it."

"I imagine you will." One edge of his mouth lifted a fraction, then he turned to Donald. "You must be Cherise's husband."

"I'm sorry," Eugenia said and made quick introductions as the Reverend rose and extended a big hand over the coffee table. "I've heard a lot about you," he said to Nick.

"Not all bad, I hope."

Donald smiled. "Nah. Cherise thinks you're one of the good guys."

Nick snorted and sent Marla a look that could sear through stone. "Then she's a distinct minority."

Donald laughed, Cherise blushed and Eugenia's frown deepened. Nick grabbed a cup of coffee and settled one hip against the window ledge, his long, jean-clad legs stretched in front of him.

In the ensuing small talk, Marla learned that Donald had once been a pro football player, a running back, one of those Christian athletes who prayed before each game. But all that was before God had decided that a three-hundred-fifty-pound linebacker would tackle Donald, crack three of his ribs and break his ankle in two places, thus ending his short, though seemingly awe-inspiring, career.

". . . So the man upstairs thought I needed to lead a congregation rather than a team," he said with a smile, then set his cup on the table. "And that's one of the reasons we're here." He reached toward his wife and she, like a trained dog, linked her fingers through his. His other hand smoothed the worn leather binding of his Bible. "Cherise has been concerned that the family is splintering. Her parents are both gone now. Nick, you took off years ago and your father, too, has passed on."

Where was this leading? Marla wondered.

"Recently we've had so many problems within the family

that there have been ugly accusations slung in all directions. Words have been spoken in anger. Words that most of us regret.

"Cherise . . . well, I think I speak for Montgomery as well, has been very upset ever since the accident that nearly took her cousin's life. When she tried to contact Marla, she was treated as if she were an outsider." Donald's big shoulders slumped. "We were hoping that we could all start over, that the fractured parts of the family could come together and we could put our differences behind us. That Marla lived was a miracle, most certainly God's work. It wasn't time to call her home yet.

"Now let's use His example and heal the rifts in our family." Donald's somber eyes met Nick's. "Let's be a team again."

Nick studied the preacher with a jaundiced eye. "I don't remember being a part of any team."

"Certainly. The Cahill Family Team."

Marla thought she might get sick. Was this guy for real?

"You're serious?" Nick said. "The Cahill Family Team? Kind of like the Trapp Family Singers?"

"Don't be so snide." Cherise pursed her scarlet lips and managed to appear wounded. "Of course we were a team. Years ago. When we were kids."

"That was a long time ago," Eugenia pointed out.

"I know but I'm enough of an idealist to think we can get it back again," Cherise insisted as her husband stood and drew her to her feet. "No matter what has happened, we're all family."

Donald said, "We're inviting you to the church, for services this Sunday. Afterward we'd like to have all the family to dinner at our house."

"Please come," Cherise insisted and hugged first Nick, then Marla. She took Eugenia's hand in hers. "Bring Alex, Cissy and the baby."

I'd rather share a rat with a python, Marla though.

"Will Montgomery be there?" Nick asked, and Cherise's smile faltered a bit.

"I'll invite him of course. With Monty you sometimes don't know. I really wanted him to come today, but unfortunately he had other plans. I'll try to talk him into coming over to the house on Sunday, though."

"We'll see," Eugenia said frostily but Cherise didn't seem to notice.

They were about to take their leave when Nick asked, "Was Pamela Delacroix a member of Holy Trinity?"

Donald's spine stiffened slightly. His expression, beneath his calm exterior, shifted slightly. Warily. "Yes," he said, his eyebrows knotting. "It was a great loss for the congregation."

Marla couldn't believe her ears. "You *knew* her?" she asked. Finally, a connection.

"Not personally, no, I'm ashamed to say. She wasn't a regular, but she did attend services once in a while."

"What about you? Did you know her?" Marla demanded, her eyes fastened on Cherise.

"Not at all. I mean, I wouldn't even have known what she looked like," Cherise said quickly. "The Reverend was right, she came a couple of times a few months ago, but she didn't join any of the groups we have available. We offer Bible study several times a week, and a woman's focus group and even singles counseling, but she didn't join in."

"Then how did you know she attended?" Marla asked. "Did she tithe with a check?"

"No . . . after she died one of the women who teaches an adult Sunday school class mentioned it. She'd seen Pam's obituary in the paper and we started our prayer tree—that's a telephone chain within the congregation, so that everyone could pray for her and her family."

"Did you meet her family? Her daughter?" Marla asked.

"I didn't even meet Pam," Cherise reminded her, but she seemed uncomfortable, suddenly eager to leave, as if there was something about the conversation that made her nervous.

Nick cocked his head to one side. "You didn't mention that

you had any connection with her when you stopped by the hotel the other night.''

"It slipped my mind." Cherise shot back. "So sue me."

Her husband sent her a sharp look and she instantly softened. "Sorry. Yes, I should have said something when I came by the hotel," she admitted, avoiding the censure in her husband's gaze. "It just slipped my mind."

Donald made a point of checking his watch. "I hate to cut this short, but I've got an appointment with the church treasurer in half an hour."

Marla and Nick escorted the guests to the front door. Carmen, as if she'd been listening to the conversation, hurried to the closet to fetch Cherise's cape.

"It was good to see you again." Cherise gave Marla a hug as Donald shrugged into his jacket. A handshake or two later they were out the door, their arms linked, the picture of Christian fidelity and love.

"What the hell was that about?" Nick asked.

Eugenia lifted a tired hand. "Just another way to wheedle back into the family's graces. They're after money, Nick. They can whitewash it with all sorts of euphemisms and terms such as 'family solidarity' or 'God's work' or 'being a part of a team' or whatever, but the bottom line is, Cherise is trying to cozy up to the family fortune." Eugenia cast a quick glance at Marla. "Don't get me wrong, she probably was concerned about you. Cherise isn't a bad sort. Just self-involved. And that husband of hers . . . well, he can pray until he's blue in the face, he's still got his problems. Alexander hired him at Cahill House and it turned into a horrid scandal."

Wearily Eugenia picked up her tea cup and placed a raspberry scone on a small plate. "Couldn't keep his hands off one of the girls." Her lips tightened and she broke off part of the scone. "I wouldn't have been surprised if her condition wasn't because of him. She never did say who the father of her child was, and she'd attended services at Holy Trinity. It doesn't take a rocket scientist to put two and two together." Eugenia took a small bite of her scone. Coco, lying at her feet, watched her greedily. "Needless to say, Alex had to let him go. The scandal did so much damage. It's amazing that Donald's parish kept him on, but then he always swore that the girl was lying, that he hadn't touched her. In the end the girl dropped the charges."

"This just gets better and better, doesn't it?" Nick said sarcastically. "All part of the Cahill family history."

The phone jangled loudly. Nick strode into the front hall, snatching the receiver by the second ring and said, "Nick Cahill." He carried the receiver back to the sitting room, his eyes focused on Marla. "Yeah, she's right here. Just a sec."

"You're on," he said, handing her the phone. "Detective Paterno."

"What does he want?" Eugenia demanded.

"I called him earlier," Marla explained and took the police officer's call while her mother-in-law regarded her as if she'd gone mad. For privacy's sake, Marla headed up to the library, all the while telling Paterno about the night when she'd ended up in the clinic and what she could recall about the accident that killed Pamela. ". . . I don't remember all the details, but I know someone was in the middle of the road that night and he was lit up like a Christmas tree, the lights blinding. I swerved to miss him and the truck did the same. I can't say for sure what happened to him, but he jumped out of the way of the truck and ended up on the opposite side of the road from me," she said. Paterno had a few more questions for her then asked her to come to the station to make a statement.

She hung up promising to call him if she remembered anything else, then returned to the sitting room.

Eugenia appeared stunned. "Nick says you remember the accident."

"Yes." Marla nodded. "Most of it."

"But you don't recall why you were going to Santa Cruz?" Eugenia set her plate on the floor and Coco inched forward, sniffed and gobbled the tiny piece of scone that was left then licked the plate for extra measure.

"No," Marla said, rubbing the back of her neck. "Nor why I was with Pam, or how I knew her." *But I'm going to,* she thought. *One way or another.*

A door slammed in the back of the house and footsteps hurried along the corridor. Coco barked, then quieted as Fiona, her face so red her freckles were barely visible, hurried through the foyer and into the sitting room. "Sorry I'm late," she said, apologizing all over herself. "Little James, is he all right?"

"Sleeping," Marla said, and the girl didn't wait for any other instruction, just hurried up the stairs, her raincoat billowing behind her.

"Flighty thing," Eugenia observed, her gaze following Fiona's path. "I really don't know if she's right to look after James." She patted her jacket pocket and scowled. "Have either of you seen my keyring?"

"You've lost it?" Nick asked.

"Misplaced, I think." Eugenia's face folded in concentration and Marla felt like a criminal, the keys suddenly so heavy she was certain they would jangle as she moved. "Strange," Eugenia said. "I remember having them this morning."

"They'll turn up," Nick predicted.

"I suppose, but it's so unlike me to lose them." She whistled to Coco and headed toward the elevator, leaving Marla alone with her brother-in-law.

"Look, Nick, I think we should talk about what happened last night," she said, forcing the issue that hung like a cloud between them.

"I made a mistake."

"We both did." She rubbed the back of her neck and closed her eyes. "I'd like to say it shouldn't have happened, but I can't. I don't regret it."

Nick's jaw tightened. "You should."

"Do you?"

His shoulders hunched. "I don't think this is the time or place to discuss it."

"Maybe you're right," she admitted, "but it's something we can't just ignore."

"We have to," he said, and she saw the struggle in his eyes, the strain of his emotions in the tightness of his muscles. "Besides, I have something I want to discuss with you."

"Okay. Shoot."

"While you were high on painkillers, I've been busy."

"With what?"

"Trying to find out what the hell's going on around here." He withdrew a large envelope from his inside jacket pocket and handed it to Marla. "This is a start." She opened the flap and found herself staring at copies of snapshots of Pam Delacroix, if the heading on the paper was to be believed. Her insides twisted and she bit hard on her lip as she was finally able to put a face to the name.

So this was the woman.

And she was dead. Marla studied the laughing face, clear skin, arched eyebrows and green eyes.

"She looks a lot like you, don't you think?" Nick asked.

"I suppose," Marla whispered, her gaze moving from one shot to another, studying each photo that had been copied onto the paper. "There's kind of a resemblance." Her head twisted when she saw Pam with a fresh-faced girl of about eighteen. The girl, dressed in a graduation gown, was radiant, one arm linked with Pam's. "Her daughter?" Marla guessed.

"Yeah. Julie."

"She's in college now, right?"

"Was. She dropped out."

"Because of her mother's death," Marla said, feeling responsible. Dear God, would this nightmare never end?

"Nope. That's the strange part. Julie had already quit school a few weeks before you and Pam headed south."

"Is that right?" How odd. "Then why were we going to Santa Cruz?"

"That's the million-dollar question, isn't it?" he said, folding his arms over his chest and straining the seams of his jacket. "Maybe you had another destination," he prodded, recalling his conversation with Walt Haaga.

"Where?"

"I was hoping you'd remember."

"Not much chance of that," she said sarcastically. "At least not yet."

"But don't you think it's odd that you left your children and Alex without saying a word?"

"Very."

"Then you drove off to God-only-knows-where with a woman who looked enough like you to be your sister?"

"But I don't have a sister . . ." she began, then held her tongue. *Sister.* She felt something deep inside, the niggle of a memory that hadn't quite surfaced yet. "No one's mentioned a sister. Just a brother."

"Rory."

"Yes." Still holding the pages, she dropped into the chair she'd so recently vacated. "He's in a home of some sort because of an accident, right?"

"Yes."

"But there's more to the story. I have a feeling, because of the way everyone reacts whenever his name is brought up, that people are keeping something from me."

Nick's lips folded over his teeth. *He knew.* She could read it in his eyes.

"What is it?" she prodded. "Damn it, Nick . . . I think I deserve to know."

Walking to the window, he hesitated, raked his fingers through his hair and stared outside. "I suppose you have that right."

"Damned straight."

He glanced over his shoulder, his eyes serious, and Marla braced herself as he sat on the arm of an overstuffed chair. "There was an accident years ago. You were around four, I guess, Rory under two. Your mother had you both in the car, ready to go somewhere and I have no idea where it was, but she had you both buckled and strapped in when she had to run back into the house. Rory pitched a fit, you unbuckled him, and he got out of the car. You must've closed the door and when Victoria hurried back, she didn't notice that her son wasn't in his car seat but was outside the car, squatting near the rear wheel, probably looking at an insect or something on the driveway. She threw the car into reverse and ran over him.''

"No.'' Marla's hand flew to her mouth. Her insides twisted painfully.

"He wasn't killed, of course, but the brain damage was severe. Irreversible. The doctors were able to save his life, but that's about all.''

Marla's stomach turned over. She felt as cold as if a blue Norther had knifed through her bones. "I had no idea,'' she whispered, expecting something—some spark of a memory to flash behind her eyes. None came. Nothing at all and she decided that this time it might be a blessing.

"You were barely more than a toddler yourself at the time.''

"But they . . . my parents . . . did they blame me?''

He shrugged a shoulder. "You're the only one who knows that.''

"No. There are two of us. Me and my father.'' She stood and walked to the foyer. "Maybe it's time I found out just where I stand with dear old Dad,'' she suggested. "I think I should visit him.'' The idea gained strength and she thought of the keys in her pocket. Surely some of them would fit into the ignitions of the cars in the garage whether Eugenia drove or not. But Marla didn't dare let on that she had her mother-in-law's keyring. Not until she'd let herself into the office again.

Nick walked into the foyer. "Do you want me to take you?''

"Yes.'' Suddenly she was certain. Not only did she want to see her father, but she wanted Nick with her. She handed him the pictures of Pam Delacroix. "The sooner the better.''

"Then let's go.''

"Just let me grab a coat, and a purse and . . ." It occurred to her then she had no wallet, no driver's license, no credit cards, not even an insurance card. It was as if she had no identity, none whatsoever. "I'll be down in a minute." She hurried upstairs, found a leather purse with a shoulder strap, a pair of sunglasses in the top drawer and a tube of lipstick. She thought of the keys in her pocket and decided it would be best to hide them . . . but where? Somewhere where they couldn't be found. She glanced around the room and frowned. There were too many servants and relatives who had access to her private quarters. Nowhere was safe, especially since Eugenia was on a search for the keys. Marla started to put them in her handbag, thought better of it and slid the keyring back into her jeans pocket where she could feel their presence.

She'd have to use them and soon or have duplicates made, but then she didn't have so much as a dime on her and no checkbook or debit card . . . or anything. "Damn it all anyway," she muttered, hurrying down the stairs.

No ID. No money. No car. No damned memory.

It was as if she really didn't exist.

Chapter Fourteen

"They fished Santiago's lab coat out of the bay," Janet Quinn said as she stuck her head into Paterno's office. Behind her the click of fingers on keyboards, whir of fax machines and buzz of conversation drowned out some piped-in music that no one listened to anyway. "The ID tag was still intact, but it was a little hard to read. Someone had crushed a cigarette into it, marred up the picture pretty good. Then, of course, the water took its toll." She eased into the room and slid a couple pieces of typewritten paper across his desk. "Here's the report. Everything's down in Evidence if you want to take a look at it."

"Don't suppose there were any prints on the tag?" Paterno asked without much hope. He picked up the sheets of paper and gave them a cursory once-over. Whoever was behind this Cahill mess was too smart to be caught making so basic a mistake.

"Just Santiago's." She plopped herself into a chair.

"And the lab coat?"

"Nope."

"Figures." He shifted a tasteless wad of gum from one side of his mouth to the other. "I talked to Crane Delacroix this morning," Paterno said, remembering his short conversation with Pamela's ex-husband.

"Enlightening?"

"He didn't want to say too much. I think he's got a lawsuit pending against the Cahill family, though nothing's been filed as yet and the Cahills have a way of settling out of court. Anyway, he didn't have many kind words to say about his ex-wife. Said she'd filled their daughter's head with all sorts of nonsense and that was the reason the kid had quit school, also said that Pam had mentioned to him that she was about to come into a lot of money. When he asked her about it, she was evasive, said she was working on a book deal, but seemed to regret even bragging to him. The way he figured it, she was just blowing smoke."

"What do you think?" Janet asked.

"I know she was working on a book." When Janet seemed about to ask where he'd gotten the information, he said, "Don't ask."

"Damn, Paterno, what'd you do?"

He waved off the question. "Let's get a search warrant for her house, have a look at her files, maybe catch a clue that'll help us."

Janet, who, to Tony Paterno's knowledge, had never so much as bent the rules a hair in the name of justice, eyed him warily. "What did you do?"

"You don't want to know."

"Hell, Paterno, if you aren't careful, you're gonna screw this up."

"Not this one."

She reached into her pocket, pulled out a small notebook and, taking a pen from the cup holder on his desk, scribbled a note to herself. "I'll get on it right away. Did the ex-Mr. Pam have anything else to say?"

"Not a whole lot. When I asked him about his daughter, he

said they weren't speaking, that he'd seen her at Pam's funeral but nothing since. She's married and lives in the Valley somewhere—he thinks around Napa or Santa Rosa, but being the attentive father he is—he didn't have an address or phone number. Just a name. Julie Johnson. The husband is Robert, but he and his father-in-law haven't met." Paterno impaled Janet with his gaze. "As I said, not exactly a hands-on kinda father. Anyway, I think we should track her down, see what she has to say."

"Julie Johnson's a pretty common name."

"Yeah, but Julie Delacroix Johnson isn't and I've already got her social security number. Check DMV, the Internet, marriage records." Then he leaned back in his chair and dropped the bomb. "Julie Johnson was the name of the girl who made noises about filing charges against the Cahills."

"What?" Janet said, a smile crawling from one side of her mouth to the other.

"That's right. Same name. Now, at the time the girl went to Cahill House, she claimed she wasn't married. It could be a coincidence."

"My ass."

Paterno sniggered. "My guess is the Delacroix girl got herself knocked up, ended up at Cahill House, and the preacher couldn't keep his hands off her . . . or maybe she made up a story about the reverend. I want to know what happened to her next."

"I'll find out," Janet promised. "Anything else?"

"Yeah. Marla Cahill called and claimed that her memory is coming back. Not all of it, mind you, just bits and pieces, but enough that she remembers being in the car with Pam Delacroix. She doesn't know why or where they were going or even how close a friend she was with the other woman, but she says that she saw someone in the road, lit up like the Goddamned Fourth of July, the way she tells it. Both she and Biggs swerved to miss the bastard. She went to one side of the road, the trucker the other."

"Jesus, do you believe that?"

"Not yet. She's coming in later today to make a formal statement, then we'll see."

"What happened to the guy who ran into the road?"

"Since he wasn't flattened into a pancake and there was no trace of a body anywhere in the woods, I assumed he got away, but I'm checking with the hospitals in the area, see if anyone was admitted that night or the next morning. Maybe when Mrs. Cahill gets here she can give us a better description, but I doubt it."

His phone rang and he answered on the first ring with one hand while motioning Janet to stay seated with the other. The call was short, a report from the lab on a murder case he was working that had occurred off Lombard Street a couple of nights before. He hung up and leaned back so far his chair groaned in protest.

"Why would anyone be in the middle of the road up there in the mountains?" Janet asked.

"And why would he seem to glow?" Paterno's mind sifted through the possibilities.

"Maybe he didn't. Maybe Marla Cahill was blinded by the truck's headlights."

"She claims that this was different, that the light came from the guy in the road, that she saw the truck's beams a second or so later and by then it was too late."

Behind her glasses, Janet Quinn's eyes narrowed. "You don't think this has anything to do with the pieces of that mirror we found up there, do you?"

"Don't know." Paterno scratched his chin.

"What if the guy held up a mirror—like a hand mirror of some kind—so that it threw the beams of the Mercedes' headlights back into the driver's eyes?"

"Why not just take a huge flashlight? Wouldn't that be easier?"

"Too heavy and bulky, hard to dispose of if he was caught."

Paterno tented his hands under his chin. "Why would anyone jump in front of a car like that?"

"To make sure she saw him long enough to duck out of the way. It gives him more distance, right? Because the glass is so reflective. Otherwise he'd have to wait until she caught him in her beams. This gives him a couple more seconds and every second would have counted. He knew that she'd slam on her brakes and swerve to avoid him. The road was wet, she'd probably crank hard on the wheel, slam on her brakes, try to avoid hitting whatever was in the middle of the road, then smash into the guardrail," Janet said, thinking aloud, speaking faster and faster as she visualized the scene in her mind. "The guardrail was weak there, where she went through, remember, as if the metal had been welded? But the Highway Department had no records of any repair work."

"So you're thinking the weld was made to weaken the rail rather than patch it up or strengthen it."

"Precisely!" She thumped her fingers on the corner of his desk and grinned widely.

"I think we'd better slow down a minute here," Paterno said, refusing to be caught up in her enthusiasm. There were too many other possibilities to consider. "Don't you think you're jumping to conclusions? Who would want Marla Cahill dead? And why not kill her outright—push her down a flight of stairs, or slit her throat? Why all this trouble? Just to make it look like an accident? I'm not buying it. The plan's too risky. It would be too easy to get the wrong car."

"Like the semi driven by Biggs."

"Unless we've got all this wrong and Biggs was the intended victim," Paterno thought aloud. "Someone went to a lot of trouble to see that he never woke up, while Marla Cahill went home to her private estate. Maybe Biggs was the target all along."

"Except that he's clean as a whistle, remember? The Boy Scout."

"Unlike anyone related to the Cahill family." Paterno

gnawed on his stale gum. Shit, this case was driving him nuts. "I guess we'll just have to wait and see what Mrs. Cahill has to say."

In Nick's opinion, Conrad Amhurst may as well have been dead. Lying flat on his back, tubes running in and out of his body, a morphine patch keeping his pain at bay, the old man rolled one eye toward the doorway of his private room as Marla tapped on the doorjamb. "Dad?" she said, approaching the bed while Nick lagged behind. He didn't want to mess up the reunion, if that's what the hell it was, and this place, for all its modern conveniences and view of the bay, made him uncomfortable. He didn't like rest homes any better than he did hospitals.

A leather recliner occupied one corner of the private room, a door opened to a bath with one of those showers that were flush with the floor so that a wheelchair could be rolled under the spray, and the wheelchair itself was pushed into a corner. The room had industrial grade carpet, cheery wall paper and a view of Sausalito across this stretch of the Bay. But it still felt and smelled like an institution. Hot. Stuffy. And the man on the bed was as near death's door as any mortal could be.

Marla touched the back of one of Conrad's bony hands. "It's Marla."

Conrad lolled his head to one side and stared up at her through pain clouded eyes. "Marla?" he repeated, confusion evident in his features. Once a robust man who had carried himself with pride, he'd been ravaged by age and disease, reduced to a skeleton. His skin was pale and spotted, his gray hair so thin his scalp was visible, but deep in the sunken holes that held his eyes, there was a flare of distrust. "No." He jerked his hand from hers, reached to the bedside table and fumbled for his glasses. With some effort he managed to slide them up his nose, to stare at her through owlish lenses.

"Yes, yes, I know I look different, but it's because I've been in an accident . . ." she hurried to explain, "but I'm okay now."

His lips pulled into a scowl as he stared at her.

"I cut my hair, but—"

"You're not Marla." Conrad's gaze moved beyond her to land on Nick. In a flash of lucidity he added, "And you're not my son-in-law." Suspicious eyes glared up through his thick lenses. "Marla . . . She . . . was here the other day. With her husband."

"No, Dad, I wasn't here. I can't speak for Alex, but—"

"She was here, damn it. You weren't," he said thickly, his voice gruff and furious, his face turning red. "An imposter, that's what you are. You're both imposters." He motioned toward the window ledge where pictures of Marla, Alex and Cissy were propped. Next to the portraits was a framed snapshot of James at birth. "That's Marla and her family."

"Yes, Dad, I know, I just came with Nick because he could drive me and—"

"And you thought because I'm about to meet my maker you could come in here and pull the wool over my eyes." The look he sent her was filled with contempt and a shiver raced down her spine because she sensed he'd studied her with the same disdain in the past. "You never understood, did you?" he rasped, his old voice fading. "You're not my daughter."

"But—" she said, then stopped short, her skin paling, her lips trembling. For a second she clutched the rails of the hospital bed. Her eyes rounded as if she'd had an epiphany. "Oh, God—"

"Get out of here, Kylie," Conrad whispered once again, the malice in his eyes magnified by his glasses. Pure, raw hatred flared his nostrils. "And don't ever come back. You're never getting a dime from me, do you understand?" With all the effort he could muster he flung a hand toward the railing and fumbled for a swtich. "Get out. Now!"

She backed up a step.

Footsteps hurried down the hallway and Marla turned as a

big-bosomed nurse with a dour expression bustled through the doorway. ''Mr. Amhurst called the nurse's station,'' she explained as she reached Conrad's bedside. ''Is there something you wanted, Mr. Amhurst?''

''Yes,'' Conrad hissed so hard, spittle sprayed from his thin, pale lips. ''Get these people out of here and never let them back in!''

''But she's your daughter,'' the nurse said gently, trying to mollify her patient.

''Bah! She's not mine. No matter what that whore of a mother of hers says.''

''Mr. Amhurst!'' The nurse feigned shock, though, the way Nick figured it, she was probably used to the old man's foul language and tirades. The nurse sent Marla a look that quietly told her Conrad Amhurst wasn't completely in his right mind.

''Get them out and be quick about it,'' he ordered, and the nurse ushered them out of the room.

''It's the morphine,'' she said. ''Sometimes he's completely lucid, others . . . well, he can't distinguish reality from his dreams. Please understand, he's very ill.''

''Was my husband here?'' Marla asked, reeling from her father's violent rejection. It was as if he hated her. ''Alex Cahill, did he stop by . . . with someone?''

''Not on my shift, but you might check with the desk. Maybe someone there might remember. Guests are supposed to check in, to register, but not many do.''

''We didn't,'' Nick said as a bell dinged softly and the call light over the doorway of Conrad's room blinked on again. ''I see it's one of those days,'' the nurse apologized as she turned on her heel.

''We're going.'' Nick grabbed Marla by the elbow and half-pulled her down the long carpeted hallway. Smooth wooden rails were mounted along the walls of the corridor and wide windows opened to manicured lawns with neatly tended flower beds and an expansive view of the Bay. Every so often there was a sitting area, filled with couches and chairs, lamps and tables that, Nick suspected, were rarely used. The complex was plush. Elegant. But it was still a home. An institution. A place for rich people to come to die.

At the front desk, Nick checked the register. If Alex had appeared in the last few days, he hadn't bothered to sign in. "Let's get out of here," he said to Marla. A guard buzzed them through electronically locked French doors and Nick felt better. God, that place was a prison. No matter how it was dressed up.

Outside, a salt-laden breeze pushed a few clouds across the blue sky. Seagulls called and swooped at the glassy surface of the Bay and the air held an icy chill of winter. Crisp. Cold. Cutting.

"Conrad always was a miserable old bastard," Nick said as they walked along a sidewalk to the parking lot.

"He's ill."

"And he wasn't much better when he was healthy, believe me."

At the door of his truck, Marla finally glanced up at him. She'd regained her composure to some extent, but two points of color still stained her cheeks. "The next time I get a brilliant idea to meet my relatives without an invitation, just shoot me, okay?" she suggested.

"I'll try to remember." Nick opened the door and Marla hitched herself onto the old bench seat.

Nick climbed behind the wheel and fired the engine. "He didn't think you were Marla."

"I caught that." She snorted. "But then, can you blame him? Even I doubt it at times." Squinting against the sunlight piercing the windshield, she added, "And he called me Kylie." Her fingers drummed on the armrest as he pulled out of the parking lot. "Kylie." The name sounded familiar. But why? Was it hers? No . . . it couldn't be. Did she know someone with that name? She concentrated so hard, her eyebrows slammed together as she tried to recall a past that was beginning to appear to her. It was still shadowy and dark, as if veiled, the final curtain not yet lifted.

Nick sliced her a glance as he guided the truck toward the highway. "Does that name mean anything to you?"

"Yes—I mean, maybe." Blowing out a breath, she reached for the purse she'd taken from her closet, found the sunglasses and slid them onto her nose. "It seemed . . . oh, I don't know." She wiggled her fingers as if trying to grasp something elusive, then concentrated so hard trying to recall anything about her life before the accident that her head ached. "It's all a jumble in my mind, but I'm sure I've heard the name before . . . that . . . oh, this sounds crazy, but at some level, deep down, I felt that Conrad knew who I was more than I do. Isn't that weird?" She rolled her eyes and cracked her window, letting in the salty air. "It's so odd. Everything about my life seems out of kilter. Sometimes I don't know what's real and what's not, but the animosity he felt for me, the pure hatred on his face, that seemed more like the truth than all the other things I've heard."

"He wasn't too keen on seeing you."

"He hates me."

"At least he does today," Nick allowed.

Marla stared out the window, to the green hills. "So what's with all this talk about how close I was with my father, how he showered me with gifts, how I was basically the light of his life? As far as I'm concerned it's all fake and way overblown. Or maybe even downright wrong. Ever since I woke from the coma I've had this gut feeling, this intuition, that he and I didn't see eye to eye. That we really didn't like each other." She slid Nick a look. "I guess that's putting it mildly, huh?" She almost laughed at the absurdity of the situation. Except that it was too painful. The sorry truth was that she was related to so many people and felt connected to none. Except the baby and Nick. Not even her own daughter. Not her husband. "So much for fatherly affection," she muttered, then asked, "Why did he think I'd been there earlier with Alex?"

"The nurse said he's in and out of reality because of his

drugs.'' Nick shifted down as the truck took a sweeping corner where the road rimmed the Bay.

"Are you buying that?" She stared at him hard.

"I don't know, but something's not right."

"Amen."

"I guess we'll ask Alex."

"It should make interesting dinner conversation," she said, then lapsed into silence. Her father thought her a fake, an interloper, an imposter. He acted as if she was someone else, someone who a woman he referred to as a whore had tried to pass off as his daughter. Did he dream it? Or was it part of his past?

"Did you know that most of Conrad's estate will go to James when he dies?" Nick asked.

"The baby? My father's estate goes to my son?" That was crazy.

"Yep."

"Now, wait a minute," she said, holding up a hand in protest. "How do you know this?"

"I've been doing my homework."

"Prying, you mean."

He switched on the radio. A commercial for cellular phones blasted through the speakers. Nick found another station. Soft rock of some sort. An old Billy Joel tune. "Call it what you will, but I'm just trying to figure out what's going on down here."

"Me, too," she admitted though she was a little disconcerted to think that Nick might know more about her life than she did. "You're sure about the will?"

"As sure as I am about anything. I've got a private investigator working for me."

"So?"

"He's got connections, or so he says. The upshot of the will is that everyone else gets a pittance, but the baby is the primary beneficiary."

"For God's sake, why?"

"Seems your father always wanted a namesake. The will originally stated that a male heir would inherit most of everything and since Rory is severely handicapped, the onus was on you to produce a son."

"Even though his last name isn't Amhurst."

"Hence the James *Amhurst* Cahill."

"I can't believe that. It's . . . it's so archaic. So . . . so . . . sick." But then she remembered the man who was her father. Somehow, it fit.

"It's the old man's money, he can do with it what he wants," Nick pointed out as Marla watched a jet slice across the sky.

"But James is barely nine weeks old."

"And damned lucky to be a male."

"Or cursed." She didn't like the feeling that had been with her since seeing her father lying in his bed, a shell of the man he'd once been, a skeleton filled with hate and suspicion. So where was the doting father who gave out stock certificates and expensive rings like candy? Where was the man who raised her and nurtured her and looked forward to her bringing him grandchildren . . . ?

"Who is Kylie?" Nick asked suddenly.

"I wish I knew. But I know I've heard the name before . . . seen or heard it somewhere. I just can't remember where."

He tapped his fingers on the gearshift as he thought. His eyes narrowed on the road and he said, "Maybe you do have a sister after all. A half-sister."

"It's a possibility I suppose," she agreed as he'd echoed her own suspicions. "But why doesn't anyone know about her?"

"Because it was his nasty little secret. It could be that it's all twisted in his mind and he's confusing you with her."

"Maybe," she allowed though the idea seemed far-fetched and disjointed. But why else would he call her by another name? "Or maybe I am Kylie. How would I know?" She offered him a lift of one brow.

"Then where's Marla, and why does everyone think you're Conrad's princess of a daughter?"

"Not everyone does," she pointed out, watching as fence posts and grassy fields gave way to houses dotting the landscape, flying by in a blur as the truck roared down the narrow road. "Cissy doesn't. Conrad doesn't. I'm not even sure if I do. What about you?" She twisted her head to stare directly at him. "You knew her. Very well from the sounds of it." His fingers curled over the wheel. "Do you think I'm Marla?" she asked. His lips thinned. The skin stretched tight over his cheekbones.

"Yes."

"Why? My face has changed a lot. I've been through hell in that wreck, then had plastic surgery. You haven't seen me in what—over a dozen years?"

The veins in the back of his hands stood out. His knuckles turned white. "That's true."

"Then how would you know?"

When he didn't answer, she touched his arm. "How, Nick?"

"Because of my reaction to you, damn it!" He slid her a glance that cut right to the quick. "Let's start with last night," he suggested as the tires sang against the pavement. "You were there, you know what happened."

"Y—yes," she said, dropping her hand.

"I usually don't lose control, Marla," he said earnestly. "It's not my style." His gaze, so blue, so cutting, so damned intense drilled into hers and she wanted to shrink away. Instead she met it straight on. "It only happened once before. A long time ago." His smile twisted with self-loathing. "It's a pity you don't remember it."

Her stomach did a slow roll and she notched up her chin. "Damned right it's a pity," she said. "I don't care what happened between us, Nick, I just want to remember."

"Well I do, lady. I care and I remember and I'll be damned if I'm going through that hell all over again."

He shifted down and roared past a sedan that was slowing for a turn.

She flopped back against the seat, her emotions ripped and raw. There was so much of life that was disconnected, jagged little bits and pieces that just didn't fit. And her relationship with Nick was so volatile, so worrisome, so damned intense it scared the hell out of her. "Then I guess we'd better find this Kylie person."

"If she exists."

"Right."

Lapsing into silence, he rammed the truck into fourth and stepped on the gas. Marla folded her arms on her chest and wiggled her foot nervously. He was her only ally and sometimes her worst enemy. She felt as if she could trust him and reminded herself he was probably the last person she should have faith in. He had an old grudge against her, a personal axe to grind.

"I want to show you something," he said, taking the turn to Sausalito rather than connecting with the highway leading back to San Francisco. Tucked on the interior side of the peninsula at the northern end of the Golden Gate Bridge, the small community was spread upon the hillside, pastel houses, flowers and shrubs climbing the hills for views of the sparkling water.

"Show me what? Where are we going?"

"I thought we'd check out Pam Delacroix's address."

"Why?"

"To try to jog your memory," he said, some of his animosity fading. "Is that okay with you?"

"Anything's worth a try."

He pulled into a marina on Richardson Bay and parked in a lot designated for residents. "She lived in a houseboat?" Marla asked, eyeing the floating homes docked along wide wooden piers.

"Ever since her divorce." Nick pointed out a sun-bleached dock near a two-story floating home and Marla felt as if a ghost had slid through her soul. She tried to imagine the woman she'd seen in the snapshots living here day to day, carrying groceries, calling her daughter on the phone, making plans to sell houses . . . and yet she remembered nothing.

Determined to remember something, *any*thing about the woman who'd given up her life in the wreck, Marla hopped out of the truck and slammed the door. Though the day was bright, the sky clear aside from the clouds rolling in from the west, Marla felt as if she should be skulking in shadows, hiding from the eyes of neighbors if they chanced to peer through the blinds. The wind blew in chilly, November gusts as she approached the front door where a carved wooden heron with glassy eyes held a welcome sign in its long beak. Nick rapped hard. Waited. No one stirred within. No one answered. The blinds didn't move. Using his hand as a visor, Nick tried to peer inside.

"You really weren't expecting anyone to be here, were you?" she asked, shoving her hands deep into the pockets of her coat.

"No, but I thought seeing this might trigger something for you, ignite some memory."

"I wish." She studied the two-storied house, the pilings, the decking and the empty terra cotta pots positioned near the door. No flowers bloomed now, the pots empty aside from a few dried stems. Just like the house. A chill swept through Marla as she stepped across the deck where Pam had walked hundreds of times before, watering her plants, or painting the trim, or sunbathing in the patio chairs that had been stacked beneath the overhang of an upper deck. Climbing the staircase, she felt a deep sadness for the woman she couldn't remember.

On the second floor, too, the blinds were shut. "I feel like I'm treading on her grave," Marla said, wrapping her arms around herself and hearing the water lap at the pilings and shore. She stared across the bay toward Angel Island and thought of the woman who had been with her in the car, the woman whose face she'd seen in the photographs Nick had shown her. But there was nothing. Nothing but the questions that had tormented her since first waking from her coma.

Shaking her head, Marla squinted up at Nick. "I'm sorry. This isn't doing it for me. If you say it's Pam's house, I'll believe you, but you couldn't prove it by me."

"It was just an idea. A shot in the dark."

"Guess it was a blank," Marla teased. She was starting to trust Nick. Rely upon him. Confide in him. Which was just plain nuts.

Think about last night, Marla. You can't trust him and you damned sure can't trust yourself with him. At least not emotionally. He was leaning against the railing, staring across the water, his back to her, one hip thrust out. The wind caught in his black hair, his jacket had risen above his jeans, allowing her a glimpse of his leather belt and the faded denim of his low slung Levis stretched over firm, taut buttocks.

He glanced over his shoulder and she looked sharply away. "I think we should go," she said, and from the corner of her eye caught his sexy smile. Damn him. He'd known she was staring. Probably even posed on purpose. Sometimes he could be so cocky. So arrogant. Such a bastard. She started for the pickup and called herself a dozen kinds of fool. What the hell was there about him that caused her to forever wonder about making love to him—even while they were trying to unravel the mystery that was her life?

Damn. Damn. Damn.

She sat as far from him as she could when he got into the truck. "I need to see Paterno," she said as he threw the rig into gear. "I promised to make a statement."

He looked at his watch. "How about one more stop first?"

"Where?"

Slicing her a bad-boy smile, he said, "I think it's time you and I found a little religion." His eyes twinkled with wicked pleasure as he drove a few blocks toward the center of town then took a side street. Five blocks later, he shifted down, slowing to a crawl. "This is where Cherise and Donald hang out," he said, pointing to a modern-looking church. Painted slate gray, with a swooping roof that pinnacled in a copper spire, the church was the most imposing building on the block. A fluorescent sign near the street announced the times of the next week's services. The Reverend Donald Favier was going to speak on the wages of sin. Beneath the announcement a verse from Psalms was quoted. The asphalt parking lot looked new and was sparsely occupied with a couple of sedans, a shiny Volvo wagon and a dark Jeep.

As Nick slowed, Marla studied the wide front porch and carved double doors. "I think I've been here," she said, the hint of a memory teasing her brain. She bit her lip and tried to pierce the fog in her mind.

"Let's go inside. See what's up." He turned into the parking lot and Marla's feet were on the asphalt before he'd shut the door and pocketed his key. The closer they got to the church, the more certain she was that she'd been on these grounds, but not in the light of day singing hymns with a large congregation, or listening to the reverend spread the good word. No. The images that toyed with her mind were watery but dark and she had the feeling that she'd met someone here.

With Nick at her heels, she hurried up the few wide steps to the porch. He reached around her, intent on yanking open the door.

It remained firmly in place. Bolted shut.

"Shit," Nick growled.

"The story of my life," she said, and when he looked at her she waved off his questions. "I've been dealing with a lot of locked doors lately."

"I guess God doesn't work nine to five," he observed.

Marla rewarded him with a pained expression. "Or maybe He's just out to lunch."

"Very funny."

"I thought so."

She sent him a scathing look. "This isn't the place for your irreverence." But she couldn't maintain her stern expression and chuckled as they clambered down the stairs.

"Just trying to lighten the mood."

"Okay so you *are* funny."

They took a flagstone path to the rear of the building where an etched sign on the door indicated they'd found the office. Nick knocked, then twisted the knob. No luck. The door didn't so much as budge.

"So far we're batting a thousand," Nick observed as they heard the sound of an engine roaring to life. Tires screeched loudly from the other side of the church. "You don't suppose we scared someone off?" Nick asked taking off at a dead run.

Marla raced after him, struggling to keep up with his longer strides as he circled the church, then stopped short in the parking lot.

Nick's truck was where they'd left it and the two sedans and wagon were still parked in their spots. "There was a Jeep here a few minutes ago. Right?"

"I think so. Yes." She nodded, trying to catch her breath as the short sprint had winded her. "It was parked over there, by that bush." She flung a hand toward a scraggly forsythia, and took in deep breaths. Lord, she was out of shape.

"That's what I thought." Nick's eyes narrowed on the empty spot.

"It could just be coincidence that the driver decided to leave—"

"My ass." His lips compressed and he looked up and down the street, searching the slow-moving traffic. "Damn!" He kicked at a pebble and sent it careening into the tire of a Pontiac. "I saw a rig like that before. The night Cherise came to visit me at the hotel. Someone picked her up in a dark Jeep." Nick squinted down the road, as if willing the escaping vehicle into his field of vision.

"There are thousands of SUVs in the Bay area," Marla said, shading her eyes as she looked west, into the lowering sun. "It wouldn't be that much of a stretch for the same one to have picked up Cherise and then been parked here. Maybe it belongs to her husband, or the church or a friend."

"It could be. Even so, do you think it was a coincidence that whoever was driving it, took off after we showed up?"

"Perhaps."

"And perhaps not," Nick said, all trace of his earlier humor evaporating as the first clouds began to roll in from the Pacific. "I don't believe in coincidence."

"Neither do I," she admitted. "But why would anyone take off? Why not stay hidden?"

"Maybe he thought we'd come looking for him. Or had a key or would break the damned door down. Who knows?" Nick strode to the truck and flung open the passenger door. "Come on, let's go."

She didn't argue. Didn't like the cold feeling that crept up her spine.

Once inside the truck, Nick headed south. He didn't say much, his eyes narrowing on the traffic ahead, his brow furrowed, his fingers clamped around the steering wheel.

"You have an appointment with Paterno, right?"

"Yeah. I've got the address of the station in here." She opened her purse, withdrew the detective's business card from the empty bag. "You know, no one has found the purse I had with me on the night of the accident and so I don't have anything to prove I'm who I say I am. No ID, no money, nothing. I assume I had a driver's license, a social security card, credit cards and probably a set of keys and a garage door opener."

"Your purse wasn't with you?" He guided the truck into the narrow lanes of the Golden Gate Bridge and Marla stared west to the calming waters of the Pacific where fishing trawlers and tankers were visible on the horizon. The sky, once brilliant, had turned a darker hue as heavy clouds rolled steadily inland.

"That's what the police say, but I haven't found it in the house, either." She shoved her fingers through the short strands of her hair in frustration. "But the ring my father gave me, I found. In a jewelry box I'm sure I searched a dozen times before. It's almost as if someone planted it there."

"Who knew it was missing?"

"Just about everyone."

"Alex?"

"Yes. Why? Do you think *he* would take it?" Marla asked, though she'd considered the possibility herself. Her husband was so secretive, so overly protective, acted as if he were afraid of God-only-knew-what.

"I don't know," Nick admitted shifting down, "but he did leave in the middle of the night last night and he might have gone to see Conrad without telling anyone."

"Not that it's a sin to visit your ailing father-in-law," she reminded him.

"But it's secretive. He's always been that way, even as a kid. Right now, he's worse than ever." Nick stood on the brakes to avoid rear-ending a minivan that had stopped suddenly. "I wonder what the hell he's mixed up in." The traffic cleared and he stepped on the throttle. They drove through the Presidio and Nick turned south. "Before we meet the police, let's see your brother."

"Yes. I would like that," Marla said, though she steeled herself for another rejection. She didn't expect Rory to take to her any more kindly than her father had.

It was worse than she imagined. The building was old but had been renovated, the gold brick face clean and neat, the interior bright. "I'm sorry," she was told by the nurse at the reception desk after explaining her plight. "No one but family is allowed in. If you don't have any proof that you're Marla Cahill, then I can't allow you to pass."

"What about me? I'm Marla's brother-in-law." Nick whipped out his wallet and flashed his Oregon driver's license.

"Sorry." She shook her head, then she smiled benignly at Marla. "When you have some identification, you can visit your brother."

"But—"

"Hospital rules."

They got no further with an administrator and Marla left the brick building feeling discouraged. "So far we've been on a wild goose chase," she grumbled, pulling the collar of her coat closer to her neck as they walked along the sidewalk.

"Maybe things will improve." But Nick's voice didn't hold a lot of conviction.

They piled into the truck and Nick drove toward the police station. Skyscrapers cast shadows over the city streets and pedestrians clogged the sidewalks. Rickshaws and bicyclists vied with cars, trucks and vans. Somewhere a few streets over a siren screamed.

"Did Alex tell you where he went last night?" Nick asked.

"I haven't seen him today. I'm not even sure that he came back to the house," she admitted. "Carmen told me he had early meetings this morning."

"It's not the first time he left." Nick eyed the street signs, then turned left. "The other night, after he brought you back from your appointment with Dr. Robertson, he took off again. He didn't tell you about it?"

"No," she admitted, her fingers trailing on the armrest of the truck and a bad feeling settling in the pit of her stomach. "What my husband does is a mystery to me." She tried to find an excuse for Alex's actions and failed. "I know he's been in some big negotiations with some Japanese businessmen, investors, I think, but other than that I don't have a clue as to what it is he does."

"Don't you think that's odd?"

She chuckled humorlessly as he braked for a taxi that nosed into his lane. "I think my whole life is odd, Nick," she admitted. "A husband who doesn't confide in me, a daughter who rejects me, a mother-in-law who acts like I need a keeper, a baby whom I just remembered, a father who despises me and thinks I'm an imposter, and a brother-in-law who . . . who . . ."

"Who what?"

She couldn't admit it. Couldn't say the damning words— that she was attracted to him, that at his touch her knees went weak and her blood ran hot. "Who . . . bothers me," she said and his lips twisted at her understatement. "Anyway you cut it, it's not exactly *Ozzie and Harriet* or the all-American family and yeah, Nick, I do think it's all strange. Real strange. I just hope that I can figure it out soon before I go out of my mind.''

"Or before you get killed," he said solemnly.

"Killed?" she repeated, rolling her eyes. She wasn't going to be caught up in some melodramatic paranoia. She'd considered the fact that someone might be trying to murder her, but she'd always tossed off the idea, condemned it as her own brand of fear. To hear it from someone else made it so much more real. But she still wasn't buying it.

"Think about it," Nick insisted. "The night of the accident you saw someone on the road and he did something to flash a light into your eyes, right?"

"Well, maybe."

"It could have been planned." Nick cranked the wheel sharply for a corner.

"Now, wait a minute. That's a pretty big leap. How would he know where I was, that I was driving *Pam's* car at that particular time?"

"I have no idea, but it is possible. Then you thought you were threatened at your bedside, the next thing you know you're throwing up and nearly dying. Someone could have given you an injection or put something in your food."

She wanted to argue, but couldn't. He was only voicing her own fears, the ones that had been nagging at her, the ones she'd steadfastly pushed aside. "Who would want to kill me?"

"I thought you might know."

She closed her eyes and leaned her head against the headrest. "I don't even know who I am, much less who's at the top of my personal enemies list." Her jaw was beginning to ache again, a dull throb starting to pound. "Why go to all this trouble? Why not make it easy and just shoot me?"

"Because they're trying to make it look like an accident."

"They. Now it's more than one." She sighed and shook her head as she stared at the tall buildings stretching skyward. "No way. This is too far-fetched. I was in an accident. Period. I threw up because of a jittery stomach and a bad case of nerves. That's all. There wasn't anything sinister about it,'' she said, trying to convince herself. No one was really trying to kill her.

Or were they?

Nick found a high-rise parking lot and turned in. He plucked the ticket from an automatic machine and drove up the ramp, his eyes scouring the parked cars as he searched for a spot.

"Why would someone want me dead?" she asked.

"Because someone's afraid of you, of what you'll remember."

A chill as cold as the Pacific ran through her blood.

"Is that why you moved back to the house?" she asked with sudden insight. "To protect me?"

"One reason," he admitted easing the truck into a space between a BMW and a Honda on the third tier. Cutting the engine, he said, "Tough as you think you are, Marla, you need someone to watch your back."

"And you've volunteered for the job?"

He didn't crack a smile as he stripped his keys from the ignition. "You have someone else in mind?"

"I'd like to think I can take care of myself."

"You don't even remember who you are." He leaned closer to her and the smell of musk and leather reached her nostrils, the tip of his nose nearly touching hers. Taking her hand in his, he rubbed the back of her hand with his thumb. "Don't you think, given our history, that I would be the last person on earth to appoint himself your personal bodyguard?" His eyes were dark with the coming night, his fingers warm.

"I . . . I suppose," she said, trying hard not to look at the blade-thin line of his lips, nor feel the heat of his body, a heat so intense it fogged the windows. "But I do have a husband—"

"Whom you don't sleep with, who is always out of the house, who leaves in the middle of the night," he reminded her. "Whom you don't trust."

Marla swallowed hard as his gaze drifted to her throat. She reached for the handle of the door with her free hand, her fingers surrounding the cool metal. "Are you trying to tell me that I'm not safe anywhere, not even in my own home?"

His eyes were dead serious. "That's exactly what I'm saying."

"But this is all conjecture, just some crazy idea of yours."

"I hope so. God, I hope so," he said fervently. His breath was warm, his gaze seductive and deep inside Marla felt the first stirrings of desire heat her blood. Oh, she couldn't do this. Not again.

She pulled the handle and the door swung open. "Let's go see the detective."

"You blew it again! Jesus Christ, what kind of moron are you?" The voice on the other end of the wire was angry as hell. "How hard can it be to kill someone?"

He wanted to tell the bastard to go fuck himself. Standing in the phone booth, night starting to close around him, he wanted to reach through the damned wires and choke the fucker. "Listen, if you want Marla dead so bad, then just do it yourself," he growled, knowing the prick was too chicken to get blood on his lily-white hands. A coward of the lowest order.

"We have a deal."

"I know." He calmed a little, his eyes narrowing on the traffic light at the corner where a couple of teenagers were straining against the leash of a big dog who seemed determined to bound into traffic. "I'll take care of it."

"No. Not now. It's too risky. She's starting to remember. And we're running out of opportunities. Pretty soon everyone including the police will get suspicious."

"I'll do it tonight," he promised, smiling at the note of panic in the other man's voice. "I'll take care of it tonight."

"No . . . not at the house. Everyone's on edge as it is. I'll come up with a plan. We have to wait."

"You're the one who's in the big hurry to have her dead."

"And you're not?"

His fingers sweated around the receiver. "As a matter of

fact, I'd like to take my time. Stretch it out. Make her beg for mercy."

"Shit. You're sicker than I thought. But lay off for now. Until I work this out. We might have to wait until the old man kicks off. Then you can kill her. And I want you to make it neat. Don't . . . don't torture her."

"What the hell do you care?" The bastard at the other end of the line was suffering from a twinge of conscience. Didn't that beat all? He laughed and reached into the inner pocket of his jacket for his cigarettes. "And that's why you hired me, isn't it? Because I'm sick? And because I have the goods on you, my friend."

"Let's get one thing straight, okay? We're not friends. We never have been, we never will be. This is just . . . business."

He jabbed a filter tip between his lips. "What happened to blood is thicker than water?"

"It's bullshit. You know it and I know it. Now just wait until I contact you, then you can do your job and you'll get paid."

"I'd better. Because if I don't see the money, if you pull a fast one, I'll give the police and the newspapers the true story. About you and all the sins you try so hard to hide. Everything that you've done is documented, *amigo,* everything. Including all that shit at Cahill House a while back. Your ass is as good as nailed. So don't fuck with me."

He slammed the receiver down and turned his collar against the wind rushing off the ocean. *Sanctimonious prick.* Just wait. He hiked down the hill a couple of blocks, ducked across the street in front of a cable car and walked along the boardwalk of Fisherman's Wharf, blending in with the tourists who braved the chill of winter. His ankle still hurt on days like this, a painful reminder that he'd failed to kill Marla. He'd rectify that situation and soon.

Crab venders were hawking cold crab and hot chowder. Over the rush of traffic and the noise of tourists an occasional bark of a sea lion cut through the chill winter air.

Smoking, he slowed his steps as he walked behind an older Asian couple huddled against the wind. All the while he thought about Marla. The princess. Beautiful and rich. And the hottest cunt he'd ever had the pleasure to dip into.

He'd once fancied himself in love with her.

But then he'd always been a fool when it came to women. Right now she was spilling her guts to that stupid ass of a detective and she was with the brother. Was he the guy she was with last night? The guy whose face he couldn't see in the darkened window? The guy touching her naked body for Christ's sake? Or had it been her husband?

Either way, it got him horny.

He'd enjoy offing her, but he'd have to come up with another plan to kill her, one that was a little more personal. Yeah, that was it. Something . . . intimate and seductive and deadly. He didn't give a shit what the rich bastard who'd ordered the hit asked for. This was his game and he wanted her to see his face before she died—let her know that he'd gotten his revenge. He imagined her eyes rounding in recognition, her lips trembling in fear, the way she would plead for mercy.

One more time baby, he thought, his cock growing hard at the inward vision of her fear. He flicked his half-smoked ciga-rette into the gutter and veered into one of the bars advertising cold beer and fish and chips. Settling onto a nicked bar stool, he ordered a draft and as he sized up the tiny waitress with the big tits, he wondered if there was any way he could fuck Marla before he killed her.

Chapter Fifteen

"So you still don't remember why you were with Pamela Delacroix that night?" Paterno asked as he rocked back in his chair in his cramped, messy office. It was tight, stuffy and smelled of stale coffee.

"Not yet." Marla looked him steadily in the eye. Perched on a chair on the other side of his cluttered desk, she added, "I don't remember much about her, but I think it's only a matter of time before it all comes back to me, and when it does, I'll let you know." She was trying not to sound irritated but couldn't help herself. They'd been talking for over an hour, she'd signed a statement about the accident and was getting tired. Her mouth hurt like crazy and being grilled by the detective didn't help her mood. Nick had remained silent for most of the interview, sitting next to her in an identical beat-up chair on one side of a messy desk while Anthony Paterno observed them both. Half glasses were propped on the end of his nose and file folders, complete with rings from coffee cups, were stacked haphazardly, a computer was near his right shoulder and a bulletin board behind him was filled with pictures of several different crimes. Snapshots of Pam's wrecked Mercedes, Pam's bloody body, the charred remnants of a huge semi and the gaping hole in the guardrail were in one grouping. Marla had trouble dragging her eyes away from the macabre images of twisted metal and the dead woman. She shivered when she remembered that night and Pam's terrified screams.

"I heard someone at your number called 911 the other night requesting an ambulance, only to turn it away when it arrived."

"Bad news travels quick," Nick observed.

"Computers. Everything's linked these days." Paterno looked from Nick to Marla. "So what happened?"

There wasn't any reason to hide the truth, so Marla told him about getting sick and opting to go to the clinic to meet Phil Robertson. All the while she spoke, Tony Paterno leaned back in his chair, chewed gum as if it were the last piece on earth, and scratched notes to himself on a small yellow pad. When she finished, he looked at her over his glasses. "You were pretty lucky from the sounds of it."

"I guess."

"What made you sick?"

"I don't know."

Paterno slid a glance at Nick. "Good thing Mr. Cahill here is so handy with wire cutters. Real lucky that he was around."

"Very," Marla said lifting her chin a notch. She heard the insinuation in the cop's question, a silent accusation that she'd been with a man other than her husband, but she refused to rise to the bait.

"You've moved back into the house?" Paterno asked Nick, his dark, assessing eyes studying Marla's brother-in-law.

"As of that night, yeah."

"Why?"

Nick grinned, that wide, don't-try-to-bullshit-me smile that Marla had seen more often than not. "I guess I finally succumbed to family pressure."

"From whom?"

"My mother. My brother."

Paterno's eyebrows elevated. "You don't strike me as the kind of guy who lets himself be led around by the nose."

"Depends on whose doin' the leadin'," Nick drawled, his blue eyes sparkling in challenge and even Paterno's lips twitched. "I figured it was time. The other night convinced me."

"Because Mrs. Cahill got sick?"

"Because she nearly died." Nick's grin evaporated. "As you said, it was a good thing I was around."

Paterno nodded and scratched the back of his neck thoughtfully. "So where was your husband?" he asked Marla.

Good question. "Out. On business."

Paterno picked up a report, adjusted his glasses and said, "It says here the 911 call came in at 11:50 p.m."

"That's about right." Nick crossed his legs, propping one battered Nike on his other knee.

Paterno wasn't satisfied. "Pretty late for business, don't you think?"

She bristled a little, heat climbing up the back of her neck, though she, too, wondered about her husband's mysterious whereabouts. What was he up to? Why didn't she trust him? And why did she feel she had to defend him to this cop who was just doing his job? "Alex doesn't keep banker's hours."

"Neither do a lot of us." Anthony Paterno dropped the page onto his already overburdened desk, then folded his hands over the entire messy pile of papers. "Mrs. Cahill, can you think of any reason why anyone would want you dead?"

"You think someone is trying to kill me?" she asked, her heart pounding. It was the second time within a couple of hours that someone had suggested what she'd tried to shrug off as paranoia.

"If your story is accurate, then someone deliberately got in the path of your car. Now your thinking's still a little fuzzy, so I wouldn't jump to too many conclusions on that alone, but you did nearly die the other night and I was just wondering if anyone could have given you something to make you vomit, knowing you might suffocate?''

"No, I don't think so," she said. "I ate with my family downstairs. It was the first time I'd come down to take a meal with them and I had to have soup as my mouth was still wired shut. Later I had something to drink. I kept water or tea or juice near the bed and it was usually brought up by someone on the staff. But I wasn't given any different medication or anything." She decided to be as forthright as possible with the detective. Leaning forward, she placed her elbows on the edge of the desk. "I guess I'd better tell you that I thought there might have been an intruder in my room that night."

"Hell, yes, you'd better tell me." Paterno's head snapped up. His gaze narrowed. "Who?"

"I don't know. I was asleep and thought I heard someone, a man, whisper '*Die, bitch!*' as he hovered over my bed, but when I really woke up and turned on the lights, no one was there. I even checked the bedroom floor but the only thing I accomplished was to convince my daughter I'm certifiable and should be locked in some kind of lunatic asylum." She sighed. "The upshot was that no one was in the house who shouldn't have been."

"But you '*felt*' that someone was there?"

She shrugged. "I didn't bring it up before because I can't say for certain. I've got a serious memory problem, I've been having crazy, disjointed dreams and I might have imagined the whole thing. Maybe it was part of a nightmare."

"But you're not sure?"

"No," she admitted, her blood turning to ice when she thought of the feeling that someone was hovering over her bed. So close. So evil. So intent on doing her harm. "I—I'm not sure about anything. Even today when we visited my father. He was certain I was someone else, someone named Kylie and I . . . I can't remember enough to prove him wrong."

"He's pretty sick, isn't he?"

"Very," Nick answered. "The nurse thought it might have been his painkillers talking."

"But you don't know if he was rambling or there was some truth to his accusation." Again the hound-dog face was turned toward Marla as Paterno scratched a note to himself. "So, I'm asking again. Who do you think would want to harm you or kill you?"

"I don't know," she admitted.

Paterno's gaze swung to Nick. "You seem pretty close to all this. Have you got any ideas?"

Nick hesitated. "I haven't been down here long enough to figure it out. I know that my brother has been working odd hours, and he keeps to himself more than I remember in the past."

"And the corporation's got financial troubles."

"Its share."

"Why would Mrs. Cahill's husband want to kill her?"

"No one said he did," Marla cut in. "Alex wasn't hovering over my bed that night," she added indignantly. She would have recognized Alex's voice. *But he wasn't home, was he? He had to be called back to the house. Could he have snarled his threat, dashed out of the room and . . . what? Gotten into his Jag and driven to a late meeting . . .* "It wasn't Alex."

"Be that as it may, is there any reason he'd want you dead? Have you got a lot of life insurance? Does he have another woman? Does he think you're involved with someone else," he asked, and his gaze traveled pointedly to Nick again.

"I don't think so."

The chair creaked as Paterno pushed himself to his feet. "We don't have enough here, no concrete evidence that someone's out to kill you, to warrant police protection."

"I'm sure I don't need it," Marla insisted. "The house is a fortress."

Paterno didn't look convinced. He clicked his pen nervously. "No security system is foolproof. If your intruder was real, that proves it.'' Sifting through the pages on his desk, he pulled out a copy of a pencil drawing.

"This is a composite sketch of the man we think killed Charles Biggs. One of the nurses on staff got a look at him and talked to the police artist.'' He handed the sketch to Marla but the shaded drawing meant nothing to her, nor to Nick. "Now,'' Paterno turned on his computer and typed rapidly, "we took this, did a computer enhancement and came up with this.'' An image of a mustached man in squarish glasses and a thrusting jaw came into view. Paterno rotated the screen and Marla gazed at the face of a stranger.

She shook her head.

"How about now?'' Paterno clicked on a key and the mustache disappeared.

"No . . .''

"And now?'' The glasses came off.

He tried several different combinations, adding beards and changing hairlines and color, but each image was just another stranger to Marla. "You have to remember I don't even know my own family,'' she admitted.

"What about you?'' Paterno asked Nick.

Leaning forward, Nick studied the images as the detective flipped through them again. "I don't think so,'' he finally said and Paterno, a disheartened expression converging on his oversized features, snapped the computer off. "We're looking for Pamela Delacroix's daughter,'' he said. "She's married to a guy named Robert Johnson. Haven't found her yet.''

"I'd like to talk to her when you do,'' Marla said. "To offer my sympathy, if nothing else.''

"I'll see what I can do,'' the detective promised.

They talked for a few more minutes, then Paterno seemed satisfied that the interview was over. "Okay, that about covers it for today, but if anything else happens, I want to hear about it.''

"You will,'' Marla agreed as she and Nick stood. "I don't suppose you've located my purse?'' She hoisted the shoulder strap of the handbag she'd taken from her closet onto her shoulder. "I should have had it with me that night."

"It's still missing?" Paterno frowned, chewed, clicked his pen. "I'll have the scene checked again."

"Thanks."

The phone on his desk jangled. Detective Paterno snatched up the receiver and wedged it between his shoulder and chin as he answered. "Paterno . . . yeah . . . no, I'm just finishing up here. I'll be down in five." He hung up and reached for his jacket. "I'm serious about this. If anything happens out of the ordinary, give me a call."

"You got it," Nick promised.

By the time they walked out of the station, night was falling over the city. "I'll buy you a cup of coffee," Nick offered as they waited at the crosswalk and a crowd gathered on the corner. Rush hour traffic clogged the city. The smells of exhaust and rain were heavy in the air.

A chilly blast of air ripped through the streets, catching in the hem of Marla's raincoat and blowing the short strands of her hair from her face. Nick's hand was at her arm, his offer hanging in the wintry air.

"I don't know," she said, though she longed for more time with him, time alone, time to sort out her feelings.

"It's just coffee."

The light changed. They hurried across the street in a tide of pedestrians. "I should get back before dinner. I haven't seen Cissy since this morning and I put the baby down around noon." She smiled up at him wryly. "I am a mother, you know, and therefore have a few motherly duties."

"Then we'll get a cup to go," he said as they stepped into an elevator and rode to the third level. They didn't touch on the way to the pickup. Marla's jaw ached and her head pounded with a thousand nagging questions, none of which she could answer. Who was she? Why did her father think she was someone else? Why couldn't she remember? Would anyone really want her dead? Why, when she was married to one man, was she so perilously attracted to another?

She leaned against the seat and closed her eyes. The sounds of the city—the rumble of engines, whine of wheels, honk of horns—faded as Nick switched on the radio and some country song filled the interior. What was she doing even having coffee with Nick? It was sure to spell disaster. She had only to think about last night and remember how easy it was to fall victim to temptation. Even now, at the thought of his hands bunching in the satin, delving beneath it to skim her skin, her breath caught in the back of her throat.

What would be the sin?

Her marriage was a facade. She didn't even sleep with her husband.

Why not take a step on the wild side, discover the woman she sensed was hiding in Marla Cahill's life, in her house, in her skin?

Opening her lids a crack, she watched Nick from the corner of her eye. Rugged. Male. All honed features. Sinew and muscle. Tensile strength and quick mind. She bit her lip. As if he had somehow divined the turn of her thoughts, he slashed a look at her that cut right to her center. Blue eyes found hers and locked for a heartbeat. He felt it, too. Here in the confines of his damned truck with the city pulsing around them, oncoming headlights daring to breach the intimate darkness of the truck's interior, Nick felt the fire. The want.

In that split second, she responded—immediate and incendiary, hot as a devil's breath and far more dangerous.

Don't go there, she warned herself and hugged the passenger door. *You have too much to think about right now—someone might be trying to kill you. You don't really know who you are. Kissing Nick would only lead to more. Touching. Caressing. Pressing hot skin to hotter flesh. Just like last night, when you were nearly caught. You would be making the worst mistake of your life and you could lose everything: your husband, your children, your home, your own self-respect.*

She squeezed her eyes shut, tamping down the unwanted emotions.

"Don't worry," he said as he slowed the truck. When she opened her eyes, she found him hunting for a parking space. "You're safe with me."

Oh, yeah, right. About as safe as I would be with a lit match in a pool of gasoline!

She smiled at the thought. "Maybe you're not safe with me, brother-in-law."

"That, lady, is a given." He parked not far from the waterfront, half a block from Ghirardelli Square where the brick-faced buildings surrounded a courtyard and clock tower.

Nick zeroed in on a coffee shop that specialized in exotic flavors. They ordered to go, sampled from a tray of muffins and scones, then carried their steaming cups outside. Fog curled in gentle wisps through the streets that were guarded by old warehouses now housing shops and boutiques. Thousands of tiny white lights glimmered in the trees while lampposts gave off a bluer, more ethereal glow.

"Maybe you should tell me about us," she said as they walked together around a mermaid fountain in the square. "You know, where we met. What we did."

"That was a long time ago."

"Try to roll back the years, will you? One of us would like to catch up on her memories." Cradling her cup in her hands she took a sip of the warm latte and licked a bit of foam from her lips.

Nick caught the motion and glanced away. "I guess you've got a point." Sipping from his paper cup, he looked down at her. "It all really started about oh, sixteen, maybe seventeen years ago. We were in our twenties and we'd known each other all our lives because our parents ran in the same social circle.

"I was always getting into trouble—one thing or another. Usually booze or women or both were involved. I had trouble staying in school, and didn't like it, much to my mother's embarrassment and my father's disgust. He had to bail me out time and time again, but I just never quite fit into the Cahill mold.''

"The rebel.''

"Yeah, well, at the time, you seemed to like it.'' Together, in an ever-dwindling crowd, they walked along the sidewalks.

"It's seductive,'' she admitted, hating to think she was the kind of woman who liked to step onto the wild side, who found dangerous men who lived by their own rules attractive, but knowing there was a grain of truth to it.

"You changed your mind about me.''

"How?'' She took a long swallow of coffee, felt it warm her from the inside out as she studied the lines of his face, the hard angle of his jaw and the way his dark hair fell over his forehead.

He scowled into the night. "I guess you finally decided you wanted to settle down. You started making noises that way but I wasn't ready. About that time Alex decided you'd be the perfect wife. For him.''

"And I just went along with it?''

He snorted. "You never just went along with anything, Marla. But you were a flirt and got your kicks out of pitting the two of us against each other,'' he said, his words tainted with a never-forgotten disgust. "I got sick of it and you got married.''

"So you didn't come to the wedding.''

"Didn't see any reason to be a hypocrite.'' His nostrils flared slightly. "I couldn't envision myself toasting best wishes to the bride and groom, so I was a no-show.''

"And that was that?'' she asked.

"The short and abbreviated version. Didn't want to bother you with details. Besides, it's all water under the bridge now.''

"Is it?'' she asked, lifting a doubting eyebrow as she recalled the passion of the night before.

"It has to be.'' His eyes turned a darker shade of blue. He grabbed her left hand suddenly and lifted it up so that her wedding ring glimmered in the lamplight. She gasped and nearly sloshed her coffee onto her coat. "Last night aside, you're still a married woman, Marla."

That was the damned truth. "I know," she said. "Oh God, how I know." Wrestling her hand from his, she added, "We both agreed we made a mistake. But I still want to know everything, Nick. Everything about us."

"Jesus."

"I mean it," she insisted, turning her face upward, feeling the mist against her cheeks, daring to meet his angry gaze with her own.

He finished his coffee, then crumpled his cup in his fist. "There's no reason to dredge it all up again."

"Isn't there?"

"Nope." He tossed his cup in a trash basket and she linked her arm through his as they walked along the shop-lined street, dodging other pedestrians and cars, smelling the salt in the breeze.

"Don't you think I deserve to know the truth?"

"What good would it do, *Mrs.* Cahill?"

"Maybe none, but I keep getting mixed signals from you. One minute I feel like you want me, the next you're pushing me away."

"Let's get something straight, okay?" he said. "I always want you." Her pulse leaped at the admission, at the anguish she saw in his features. "And I'll always push you away." Her heart ached and guilt sliced through her soul, the same brutal guilt she saw reflected in his night-darkened eyes. So this is what it felt like to be star-crossed lovers, to be fated to never be with the one man she loved, to feel the intense heartache that would certainly follow her like a shadow for years to come.

At that thought she closed her eyes and tried to get a grip. She didn't love Nick. Couldn't. She didn't even know him. Or herself. What was wrong with her? And why in God's name did she feel such pain to think she threw away a future with him? "I understand what you're saying, believe me, and I'm not trying to be difficult or to open old wounds, old pain, but I think it's important that I know everything about myself,'' she said earnestly, studying the lines of his face, the ravage of emotions that pulled his skin tight over his bones and caused his mouth to curve downward. "Everything," she repeated, refusing to back down. "No matter how hard it is to take. No matter how painful. I want it all. The good, the bad, the ugly."

"You might not like what you see."

"It has to be better than imagining and fantasizing and fearing and just plain not knowing." Determined, she grabbed his elbow, her fingers locking over the rough leather of his jacket. "Tell me the truth, Nick. No matter what it is."

"Everything?" he asked, and she saw something shift in his gaze; noticed the change from stubborn refusal to something far more treacherous. The air between them seemed to sizzle as his gaze dropped from her eyes, to her mouth and then lower to the hollow of her throat where she felt her pulse pounding wildly. Erratically.

"Yes. Everything. I want it all."

"Christ, Marla. You always have."

"I figured that's what you'd say."

"Don't you remember what happened last night?"

Her fingers clenched around his sleeve. "Help me, Nick."

His jaw slid to one side as he studied her. His lips flattened in self-deprecation. "For the record, I think this is a big mistake, but what the hell, as you said, you want it." In an instant he stepped into the doorway of a closed shop and in that tiny alcove, he wrapped his arms around her, gathering her close to his body, squeezing her tight. Lowering his head, he slanted his hungry lips over hers in a kiss as brutal as it was desperate. Hard. Unyielding. Breathtaking. Firm and demanding, his mouth rubbed insistently against hers and she felt a second's pain where the wires in her teeth had been removed. She caught her breath and in that precise moment, his tongue slipped between her teeth, the tip intimately, forcefully probing. He tasted of coffee, his skin was warm, the stubble of his beard rough against her cheek.

Pain diffused into pleasure.

Deep inside she quivered. Her blood ran hot. The night disintegrated around them. She closed her eyes and ignored the warnings screaming through her mind. Her blood tingled, her heartbeat thundered and she was lost to him. Her arms wrapped around his neck and she held tight as his tongue touched and mated with hers.

She couldn't get enough of him, clung to him, to this moment on the crowded street.

Heat, wild and hot and anxious, began to run through her veins. Her skin flushed in the cool air. Images of lying naked with him flashed through her brain and she saw in her mind's eye his bare muscular body straining over hers, his tongue running deliciously down her throat, to her breasts and lower still, along the flat slope of her abdomen, to taste the most intimate regions of her, to plunder her body and soul. She moaned softly, imagining the feel of his body joining with hers, of him thrusting deep . . . so hot, so hard, so . . . He lifted his head from hers and she blinked back the erotic images to face the cold reality of the San Francisco night, the fog, the other pedestrians, the sounds of traffic zinging past on the wet streets.

"I knew it," he muttered, his eyes mirroring the guilt of her own despair. "I knew it would be like this with you." He dropped his arms and she was suddenly standing alone. Bereft. Her heated skin cooling with the breeze that tossed dried leaves into the gutter and brought the scent of rain. "Damn it all to hell, Marla, we just can't do this."

"Don't you think I know it?"

"Then don't push it." Angrily he grabbed her hand and started for the truck. She yanked her fingers from his and shoved her fists deep into her pockets as she half ran to keep up with his longer, swifter strides.

"Don't blame me, Nick," she said as they crossed the street and she had to duck past a woman with a huge umbrella.

He cast her a hot, unguarded look. "I don't."

"You sure as hell act like it."

"I just don't want things to get any more complicated than they are." He took her hand to help her sidestep a man in a wheelchair. Then Nick let go.

"You were as curious as I was," she insisted. "You wanted to know if the spark was still there. Admit it."

"No way. I already knew. Last night proved a lot."

She didn't believe him and was about to tell him so, when he looked over his shoulder and stopped short. "Hell!" She nearly ran into him.

"What?" Whirling, she searched through the mist to see what it was that had caught his attention. Nothing but the lamppost and the crowd on the sidewalk.

"Come on." He grabbed her wrist and this time there wasn't any warm familiarity in his touch. Now he was running fast, dragging her with him, dashing through pedestrians and bicyclists, nearly tripping over a young mother pushing a stroller in the opposite direction.

"What is it?" she yelled, nearly breathless.

"I think we were being followed."

Her blood was suddenly frigid, her heart a tattoo. "By whom?"

"I don't know, but I intend to find out. Come on. Let's see if we can catch him." He darted through the side streets and around corners of buildings, cutting across traffic and causing more than one driver to slam on his brakes or honk his horn.

"Hey, watch out," one man in a cap and overcoat reprimanded from the open window of a van.

"Where's the fire?" another one joked.

Marla raced to keep up with Nick, her lungs burning, her legs beginning to cramp. All the while Nick's eyes were trained ahead, focused on the back of a tall man in a black parka who cut in and out of the crowd. The stranger darted unevenly as if he favored one leg. "You're crazy," Marla wheezed as they sprinted past the Cannery to Jefferson Street and finally, just when she was certain her lungs would burst, around a final corner, across a street against the light, and into the throng milling along the piers of Fisherman's Wharf.

"Shit!" Nick spat, his eyes scouring the throng milling on the waterfront.

"He's gone?"

"Ducked into one of the shops or restaurants, I'd guess."

"Or into his car."

"Jeep. I'll bet he drives a Jeep."

Marla's heart stopped for a second. "Like the man you were looking for earlier."

"Exactly," Nick slowed to a brisk walk and Marla gasped to catch her breath, her mind racing frantically.

Sweeping his head side to side, his eyes trained on the faces of the people he passed, Nick's gaze raked over the crowd, all the while keeping Marla's smaller hand clasped tightly in his. Nervously, taking in deep breaths, Marla, too, scanned the faces of the people collected on the waterfront, but discovered nothing out of the ordinary in the tourists and locals who strolled around the docks and shops on the piers. Nothing sinister or evil was evident in the faces that she met.

"Who is it?" she asked.

"I don't know, but there was a man, a tall thin man, who was lingering at the coffee shop. I didn't think much about it, but I'm sure he came in a few minutes after us. Later, while we were walking, I caught a glimpse of him again about a block behind us when I'd looked over my shoulder to check a street sign. He disappeared around a corner and I thought I was imagining things. Then, right after I kissed you, I looked up and thought I saw his reflection in the windows of a shop. When I turned, he was taking off."

"That doesn't mean anything," she said, relieved. "Come on, Nick, now you're the one acting paranoid. You're trying to muscle in on my psychosis."

Nick didn't so much as crack a smile. "You don't get it. I think I saw him once before," he said, obviously bothered.

"At the hospital when you were still in a coma and there was something about him that was familiar. I felt like I should have known him." Nick squinted into the false illumination of the city lights. His gaze scoured the piers and street. "That same night, I caught a glimpse of him in the hospital parking lot. He drove off in a dark Jeep. Black or maybe navy blue. I'd bet it was the same as the one that was parked at the church today."

"You think that whoever was driving it followed us to the police station and then here?" she asked, the hairs on the back of her neck rising.

Nick's fingers tightened over hers and they began walking along the waterfront, through the gauzy layers of fog rolling inland. "I'd be willing to bet my life on it."

"But why?"

"That's what we need to figure out. I don't know the answer yet," he admitted, pulling her closer, "but I'm sure it has something to do with you." He looked down at her and his face was set in grim, uncompromising determination. "Paterno thought someone might be trying to kill you. I've thought the same thing. So have you. Whether you want to believe it or not, your life might be in danger. I think you should move out of the house. Tonight. If an intruder got in the other night, nothing's going to stop him again."

"But I can't leave," she said, fear squeezing her heart. "My children are there."

"Take them with you."

"They're Alex's, too," she pointed out. "I can't kidnap my own kids and I can't tell him because . . . oh, damn, it's so crazy."

"Because you don't trust him," he finished for her, and she fought a sudden urge to break down.

"I don't know whom to trust."

"Me, darlin'," he insisted, gathering her into his arms again and dropping a kiss on her upturned lips. "You'd damned well better trust me. I could be the only friend you have."

His lips were warm and insistent, the hands that pulled her

tight strong and yet, though she wanted to trust him with all her heart, wanted to lie naked with him, wanted to feel his hands on her body, she couldn't shake the sensation that she was being a traitor, that throwing in with Nick Cahill was as good as making a deal with the devil.

And that some day she would have to pay.

Chapter Sixteen

"So what did Mrs. Cahill have to say?" Janet Quinn asked as she stopped by Paterno's office. She was sliding her arms through the sleeves of her jacket and was on her way out the door.

"Nothing much more than she told me on the phone," he said, tapping a pencil on the edge of his desk. "Except that she thinks someone broke into her bedroom and threatened her. Maybe he poisoned her and she ended up nearly choking on her own puke because her teeth were wired together. That's why 911 was called."

Janet rolled her eyes. "You believe her?"

"To tell you the truth I don't know what to believe," he admitted. "But she showed up here with her brother-in-law, not her husband. She and he were an item before she married the older brother."

"The husband was probably working."

"Maybe." Paterno didn't like it. "But I got the sense that these two—Nick and Marla—they had something going again. I could feel it."

"Oh, yeah, you, the great romantic," Janet chided with a smile and rolled her eyes.

"I'm tellin' ya, those two have the hots for each other."

Janet shook her head, her short brown hair feathering around her face. "As if you'd know."

"I know plenty," he grumbled and she chuckled deep in her throat, the way she always did when she had managed to yank his chain—which happened far too much in Paterno's opinion. "And I'm gonna call the highway patrol, see if they'll send someone up there with a dog. Marla Cahill claims her purse is missing and the way that car hit, it could have been flung to hell and gone in the impact."

"Those boys are pretty thorough. I think they would've found it."

"Doesn't hurt to check," he said as she waved and headed out the door. Paterno reached for the phone. He wouldn't mind taking a peek inside the missing handbag himself. No telling what he might find.

"Did you have a chance to check out those files we found in Pam Delacroix's computer?" She and he had gotten a search warrant, looked through the house and come up with nothing but some notes and computer records.

"Looks like she was trying to put together a book. About adoption law. Using real cases. Some fact, some fiction, but I need to go over it in more detail." He fiddled with his pencil. "I think it might be a good idea to stake out Alex Cahill's house, too," he said frowning. "Just to see what we can see."

"Why?"

He scowled and spit his gum into the trash. "I think someone might be trying to kill off Marla Cahill."

"Jesus, Tony," Janet said, leaning a shoulder against his door frame. "Why?"

"I'm checkin' into that. Near as I can tell she has some life insurance on her, not a whole helluva lot by those people's standards, and if her old man was pissed because she was involved with someone, why the hell did he have his brother come running down here when he and the lady were an item way back when?" He sniffed in disgust. "Too bad she can't remember jack shit. That way maybe we'd be able to figure out who's after her, have a chance to save her."

"And now?"

Tony Paterno leaned back in his chair. "Right now, we don't have squat."

"Where the devil have you been?" Eugenia asked as Nick and Marla entered through the front door. Looking frazzled, the older woman was holding James to her shoulder and the baby was fussing. "It's been hours."

"I'm sorry, it's my fault," Marla said and took the baby from his grandmother's arms. "How are ya, big guy?" she asked, her heart melting when his crying stopped and he observed her with wide, curious eyes. "Isn't that better?" To her mother-in-law, she said, "I had a couple of errands to run and I stopped by and gave a statement to the police about what I remember about the accident. It took longer than I thought."

The older woman's lips pursed in prim, unspoken accusation, but Marla wouldn't give her the satisfaction of feeling guilty.

"Dinner will be ready soon."

"Good. I could eat a horse." Marla's stomach rumbled at the thought. This would be her first real meal since the wires had been ripped from her teeth. "Where's Cissy?"

"She had a riding lesson." Eugenia checked her watch. "Lars went to pick her up. They should be back any time now."

"Good, I want to talk to her. If anyone sees her first, let her know." The baby fussed and Marla carried him to the kitchen where she searched for a bottle and formula.

Standing over gas burners, Elsa the cook was stirring a cranberry-orange sauce with a wooden spoon while potatoes simmered in a kettle. The smell of roasting pork wafted through the cavernous room where copper pots, stainless steel utensils and baskets of herbs hung from the beams. It was all Marla could do not to ask for a taste.

Rosa was unloading a stainless steel dishwasher while Carmen, her usually smooth brow furrowed, her lips tight in a frown, was searching through drawers and muttering under her breath.

"Anything wrong?" Marla asked as she mixed the powdered formula and distilled water in a clean bottle.

"Mrs. Eugenia is missing her keys and thinks someone must have taken them from her," Carmen said.

"Someone?"

Rosa's eyes rounded as she stacked the plates in a cupboard. Her face was paler than normal and she nodded her head furiously. "*Si, Señora Cahill, she is . . .*"

"*Loco,*" Carmen said, then slammed a drawer shut and lifted a palm in surrender. "I didn't mean it that way. She's upset, though, about the stupid keys and I know they'll turn up."

"Of course they will," Marla said, balancing James in one arm while placing the bottle in the microwave with the other.

Carmen opened an unlikely cupboard where measuring cups were stacked. "She must have misplaced them. No one on the staff would ever steal from the family."

Marla wanted to melt through the floorboards at the thought that some of the servants were under suspicion. The keyring in her pocket felt as if it suddenly weighed a ton. The microwave bell chimed. Shifting James to one arm, she withdrew the bottle and tested the contents on her wrist. Satisfied with the temperature of the formula, she said, "I'm sure Eugenia will find the keys soon." Holding James and his bottle, she hurried upstairs while Carmen began pawing through yet another drawer.

Nick was already seated in a high-backed chair, a drink in his hand. Eugenia stood at the window, frowning into the night, her back to the room.

". . . I wish I knew," the older woman was saying, unaware

that her daughter-in-law had entered. "These days it's impossible to keep track of everyone. That's one of the reasons I wanted you back here, Nick. I thought . . . no, I hoped that you would be a stabilizing force. You were good at finding out what was wrong with a company—a troubleshooter, isn't that what they're called these days. In mine they were auditors."

"Auditors are a little different."

"Doesn't matter. When Alex confided in me that Cahill Limited was having financial troubles, I thought of you and what you'd done for other corporations." She rotated her neck, as if to relieve a stiffness in her shoulders, and continued to stare through the glass. "But, the truth of the matter is that the corporate finances weren't the only reasons I wanted you back home. I guess you can see by now that Alex and Marla aren't as close as they used to be. They've been having trouble for years and I prayed that the new baby would change things, but . . . oh, well, it's obvious they're drifting farther and farther apart. Even though I knew that you and Marla . . . well that you were involved a long time ago, I still thought that you being here might help."

"How?" Marla asked, unable to hold her tongue, her cheeks flaming, her mind screaming with questions.

Eugenia whirled on one high heel and blushed to the roots of her apricot-colored hair. One hand, fingers splayed, covered her heart. "Oh, my, I didn't hear you come up the stairs."

"Obviously," Marla said dryly. She sat on a sofa and held the baby in her arm, offering him the bottle. "But, please, go on. This is fascinating." She couldn't keep the bite from her words. "Why would Nick help?"

"Let me guess," Nick suggested. "Alex and I have always been rivals and you thought if I came back here and showed even the slightest bit of interest in Marla, Alex would realize what a prize she is."

"Now, I didn't say anything of the sort," his mother argued, but guilt chased across her eyes.

"Jesus, Mother, that's right, isn't it?" Nick's disgust showed in the tic over his temple. "What if your plan backfired? What if Marla and I ended up together? How would you feel then?"

Marla's heart pounded and Eugenia, paling, looked from Nick to Marla. "Of course . . . of course, that would never happen," she said, clearly not convinced. "Marla has the children and you . . . you have that warped code of ethics . . . You always swore that you'd never be involved with a married woman and so I thought . . ."

"Son of a bitch. Who're you to play God?" Nick drained his drink then crunched on an ice cube in frustration.

"What business is it of yours?" Marla demanded, of the older lady. So angry she was trembling, she demanded, "Who are you to interfere?"

"Someone who puts family solidarity before everything else," Eugenia said stiffly. "I've been accused by Alex of being cold and unbending, but I only want what is best for the Cahill name."

"You can't run my life," Nick said. "Nor Marla's, nor, for that matter, Alex's. Didn't you learn that lesson from Dad? You tried to tell him what to do and it didn't work, did it? A tight leash only made him want to pull further away. Telling him not to drink only served to make him pour more liquid down his throat. No one likes to be controlled, Mother. It's against human nature."

Eugenia's lips quivered and she blinked against tears, but she staunchly held them at bay. Standing, her back ramrod stiff, she said, "I'll see you both at dinner," then left the room with as much dignity as she could muster.

"I should have known," Nick grumbled and the look he sent Marla reminded her of a trapped animal. "Hell."

From the foyer downstairs Marla heard the front door fly open to bang against the wall only to slam shut. Seconds later, in a thunder of footsteps Cissy, dressed in boots, jeans and a sweatshirt, appeared on the stairway. Her hair was a mess, her eyes bright, her cheeks rosy and she didn't pause for a second at the living room level, but pounded up the stairs to the next floor.

"That's my cue," Marla said, and handed James to Nick. "Get to know your nephew."

"But I don't know how to do anything with him," he said, holding the baby awkwardly.

She held out the half-finished bottle and Nick grabbed it with two fingers while he clutched James as if he expected the baby to squirm out of his arms, fall to the floor and shatter into a thousand pieces. "You're a smart guy. You'll figure it out," she called over her shoulder as she took off after her daughter.

By the time she'd reached Cissy's room, the girl was nowhere to be seen. The bathroom door was shut, the shower spray hissing and Marla decided to wait. She sat at the vanity and eyed the tubes of lipstick and bottles of nail polish in colors that seemed only appropriate for vampires and ghouls. "Don't judge," she told herself. "Remember how Mom hated what you wore."

She froze. Stared into a mirror dulled by hair spray as she recalled a conversation of years past.

". . . if you weren't so wild, if you showed him just a little attention, then maybe your father would appreciate you." Her mother's voice rang in her ears and a faded image of a worn-out woman who smelled of perfume and cigarette smoke, who tried to disguise the disappointment in her eyes, came to mind. She was thin, nearly bony as she stood in the doorway, her face in shadows, daylight slanting in through the Venetian blinds, shadows striping her floral skirt. In one hand she held a cigarette, the glowing red tip visible, the other rested wearily on her hip. "He'd recognize you for what you are."

"I hate him," she'd spouted.

"No, you don't—"

"Yes," she'd replied anger burning through her stomach. How old had she been? Ten? Twelve? "And he hates me!"

"Maybe you should try a little harder. He doesn't hate you. That's not a nice word, honey."

She'd turned her eyes upward, caught a glimpse of desperation on her mother's worn features. "He hates you, too."

That woman had not been Victoria Amhurst. Marla would have bet her life on it.

"Mom?" Cissy's voice brought Marla up short.

"What? Oh, hi," she said, still shaken. She was certain she'd seen her mother in that inward vision, was convinced that she'd been raised by the thin woman in the shabby cotton skirt and sandals. "Cissy, I'm sorry, I—I guess I was daydreaming."

Her daughter's face was drawn in concern. Her hair was dripping wet and a huge yellow bath sheet was wrapped around her torso. She held it tight in one fist clutched to her chest. "About something awful."

"Just . . . just a memory, I think," she said, attempting to slough off the painful image. "From a long, long time ago. But it's gone now and I wanted to talk to you."

"Can't it wait until I'm dressed? Jeez, Mom, this is my room, don't I have any privacy?" She grabbed a pair of Capri pants and a long-sleeved T-shirt from a drawer, then turning on a bare heel, hiked in a huff back into the bathroom.

Marla waited. Carmen rapped gently on the door, announced dinner, and disappeared again. By the time Cissy emerged she was dressed, her hair combed, her face scrubbed. "What do you want to talk about?" she asked suspiciously.

"First I want to apologize for my actions that night I got sick. I didn't mean to scare you."

Cissy lifted a dismissive shoulder.

"And I'm really sorry that I've been so out of it. Dr. Robertson changed my medication and I feel a lot better."

"Great," Cissy mumbled.

"It is. I want to go riding with you."

"You said that before."

"I mean it." Somehow she had to connect with her daughter. "This weekend."

"Isn't that when the big party is?"

"Party?" Marla said, then remembered. "That's the next weekend, I think. I'll double check with Nana."

"I thought you were supposed to be planning it," Cissy said slyly, as if she had caught her mother in some sort of lie. The chasm between them was wider than Marla had imagined and she wondered if it would ever be spanned.

"I am. I mean, I will. I've been sick . . . well, you know."

"Yeah, Mom, I do," she said, rolling her eyes dramatically and scrunching up her features as if she was trying to figure out how she could possibly be related to this freak of a woman. "Okay, why not? But I'm gonna tell you, you're scared to death of horses."

"Maybe you'll be surprised," Marla said, and Cissy's long-suffering sigh indicated that nothing her weird mother did these days would amaze her.

"Listen, Cissy, I know everything around here has been hard. Really hard. Especially for you and I want you to know that if I can make things easier I will."

"Yeah, right."

"I mean it." Marla sighed and lifted her hands in the air. "I love you, honey."

"Well, that's a switch," the girl said angrily, but her chin wobbled slightly.

"I always have."

"You think so. But you can't remember squat, can you?" Cissy sniffed and looked away quickly. "You were always more interested in everything else, everything but me. I mean, sure you bought me tons of stuff, but big deal. Who cares?" She kicked at a CD that was lying on the floor, sending it flying toward the bookcase.

"Cissy, I—"

"You never cared, Mom. Never. But with James, it's different."

"Oh, God," Marla said, seeing the pain on her daughter's face. "I'm so sorry, if I've ever hurt you, ever slighted you, I didn't mean to, I mean . . ." She swallowed the lump forming in her throat, fought tears. "You have to trust me. I love you."

Cissy just stared at her. Her lips quivered. "I—I think we should go to dinner."

"Please, honey, give me a chance," Marla whispered. "Let me prove it, make it up to you."

"You don't have to do anything."

"I know. But I *want* to. Doesn't that make it all the better?" she asked, and saw some of the wariness in her daughter's eyes fade.

"I dunno . . ."

"Just give it time."

"You know," Cissy said, keeping some distance between them as she sat at the foot of her bed. "You've been weird ever since you woke up from your coma. Different. Not like Mom at all."

"I heard you say you didn't think I was your mother."

"I don't! I mean . . . Shit, Mom, er, I mean, you're acting way too nice."

Marla's heart bled. "Is that such a crime?"

"I just don't believe it." Cissy cocked her head. "Maybe you've had one of those near-death experiences," she said, her eyes rounding, "you know, those mind-altering things that make you a better person."

"Let's hope," Marla said, offering a smile. She opened her arms wide and Cissy rolled her eyes.

"You're kidding, right?"

"Nope. Come on."

"Oh, God!" With an exaggerated sigh, Cissy got to her feet and accepted a hug. Marla clung tight, as if she never would let go. "I'll make it up to you, honey, I promise."

"Mom, don't make promises you can't keep," she said, but her arms circled her mother and Marla felt her shake a little, as if she was fighting breaking down, as if she couldn't quite trust the woman who had brought her into this world.

"You'll see." Marla dropped a kiss onto Cissy's forehead. "And I will ride those damned horses, one way or another."

Cissy giggled despite herself. "Oh, God, Mom. I hope you bring a camera."

Dinner was tense at best. Nick watched Alex from the corner of his eye. Usually smooth and charming, with a quick wit and a quicker smile, Alex appeared anxious, the lines of irritation around the corners of his mouth more pronounced, worry etched in the wrinkles on his forehead. Something was eating at him. Something big. The finances? Worry over his wife's memory loss? Or something more?

For the first week of his stay in San Francisco, Nick had put Alex's stress on the failing business.

Nick had sorted through the company records and it was obvious that Cahill Limited would have to divest some of its assets, or the lines of credit and outstanding bank notes would be called by the lien holders. The bankers had been stalled as long as they could be and Alex's international investors hadn't, so far, offered up a dime. As far as Nick could determine, the company's assets still outweighed its debts but the ratio wasn't all that great and unless a helluva a lot more income was generated, Alex would have to start laying off people and selling off some of the real estate holdings, many of which were mortgaged to the hilt.

Despite all that, huge donations were made each month to charities. Cahill House and Bayview Hospital benefitted the most and, though no one in this family seemed to accept it, the sorry facts of the matter indicated that Cahill Limited was about to go bust.

But money was only one of Alex's problems, Nick guessed now.

"So you saw the police, gave Detective Paterno a statement," Alex said after the small talk was dispensed with and Cissy had asked to be excused to do homework, which, Nick suspected, meant hanging out on the telephone or in an Internet chat room. She clomped up the stairs in platform shoes, leaving Alex, Nick, Eugenia and Marla at the table.

Marla pushed her half-eaten food aside. Nick figured she wasn't used to having solid food and obviously chewing was still a strain.

"Anything new?" Alex asked, reaching into his pocket for a crumpled pack of cigarettes.

Nick decided to gamble. "Paterno thinks Marla's life might be in danger."

Eugenia dropped her fork. "For heaven's sake, why?"

"Because the accident in the mountains could have been staged. Marla remembers a man standing in the middle of the road, trying to make her swerve, and the night she started throwing up, she could have been poisoned. She thinks there might have been an intruder in her room."

"My Lord, is this true?" Eugenia asked, her mouth dropping open.

"Yes." Marla nodded.

"But you never said anything . . ."

"I couldn't remember the accident originally and I told Alex and Nick about the intruder, but I thought that I was dreaming, having a nightmare."

"This is horrid. We have gates and a security system and . . ." Eugenia reached for her wineglass. "Certainly no one could ever break in."

"It's possible," Alex allowed, though he frowned as he lit his cigarette and clicked his lighter shut. "But I hate to think so."

"Well, we have to do something. In over one hundred years no one has ever broken into this house!" Eugenia's spine stiffened at the affront. "Not once."

"It might not have happened the other night," Alex said guardedly to his wife. "You said yourself that you thought it all might be part of your confusion. That you might have been dreaming."

"I wasn't sure."

Nick was having none of it. He kicked back his chair. "There's a chance she was given something that made her throw up."

"No . . . how . . . who would do such a thing?" Eugenia demanded.

"Someone who got into this house," Nick insisted, leveling his gaze at his mother and realizing just how much she was aging. "I think we should have the carpet torn up where Marla vomited and have the fibers tested, see if there are any traces of drugs."

"But we cleaned the carpet, it was shampooed," Eugenia said.

Alex inhaled on his cigarette. Smoke drifted from his nostrils. "What good would that do? Either someone broke in or not. We'll increase security, hire a bodyguard," he sent Marla a pained expression, "if that's okay with you, of course. You didn't take too kindly to me hiring the nurse without asking you first."

"I think a bodyguard is a little drastic," Marla said quickly. She already felt housebound, trapped in this elegant cage. She wanted more freedom, more time to find out who she was. Someone watching over her would only stifle her every move. "I'm not going to live my life in fear. I'll just be more careful."

She caught the gleam in Nick's eyes, but looked away, afraid her gaze would reflect the emotions that raged in her chest. She was falling in love with a man who was her brother-in-law, a man she couldn't have.

"And I need new ID, credit cards, a checkbook. I stopped in to see Rory today and the nurse wouldn't let me pass because I can't prove who I am."

"As soon as you're well enough—" Alex began.

"I am well enough, damn it!" She slammed her fist on the table. "Stop treating me like a China doll or an imbecile or both!"

"Okay, okay. Relax. Of course you need everything from a

passport to a gold card from Neiman Marcus,'' Alex snapped.
"I'll put it at the top of my priority list."

"No, I'll put it at the top of mine. I can handle it, Alex."

"Please, no more squabbling," Eugenia said, flustered.
"This is all so unbelievable. To think that anyone would break
in and try to harm someone in the family—"

"Believe it. Something's rotten here," Nick insisted, "and
it's more than the company's damned finances."

Alex's face was grim. He took a final drag on his cigarette
and squashed the butt into a crystal ashtray. "I'll do whatever
it takes to keep my family safe. I'll call a security company
tomorrow and have cameras and a better alarm system installed.
I'll talk to Paterno, see if he can have a cruiser come up this
street more often. I don't want Cissy going out alone—Lars
can take her and pick her up when she goes to school or to her
riding lessons and someone is to be with James every minute.
Every minute." His face was ashen and a very real fear tightened his features. "No one's going to threaten my family."

"Amen." Eugenia said.

"I think I need a drink." Alex pushed away from the table
and left the room. "Mother?"

"Maybe I will have a brandy. This is so . . . so disturbing
. . . oh, Lord, my keys!" She swallowed hard and paled. "My
keys are missing. Do you think the intruder took them?"

"No," Marla said quickly, her heart a drum. "I saw them
that night. You let yourself into Alex's office."

"Oh, yes . . . and I had them the other days. I let myself
into Cahill House several times while you were recuperating."
Nervously she adjusted her scarf and reached into the pocket
of her lavender jacket, her fingers searching for the missing
keyring. "But now they're gone."

"We'll have all the locks changed," Alex said. "Make a
list of every key you had and what it opened."

Marla panicked. She'd have to work fast. She'd have to
break into Alex's office the first chance she got. "I'll need a

set,'' she said, forcing a calm smile. ''Mine were lost the night of the accident.''

''I'll ask about them when I call Paterno tomorrow,'' Alex said. ''Not that they'll do any good as we're going to change the locks.''

Marla didn't argue but knew that she'd call the detective herself. If the keys belonged to Marla Cahill, then they should open every existing lock in this house. If the keys didn't fit, then maybe she was, as Conrad Amhurst had insisted, an imposter after all.

Nick reached into his duffel and found his cell phone, then he headed down the back stairs and through a door off the kitchen. Taking a brick path leading through the trees, he made his way past the arbor and swing set, deeper into the estate to a sanctuary where he'd come often as a kid, a thicket of firs along the back fence, the place he'd climbed over whenever he was hell-bent on escaping the demands of being Samuel Cahill's son.

God, he'd hated the old man, despised how he'd ruled the family with an iron fist that was sure to bend the laws and break his wife's spirit. ''Bastard,'' Nick growled, flipping open the cell phone and retrieving his one message. It was from Walt Haaga, who only stated that he'd landed in San Francisco this afternoon. Nick called the Red Victorian, and asked to be connected to the room under his name.

''Yep,'' Walt answered on the second ring.

''It's Nick.''

''About time I heard from you,'' the PI said. ''I checked in at the hotel this afternoon and since then I've been busy.''

''You've found out something?''

''Quite a bit. Why don't you meet me at the bar around the corner—what's it called?''

''Ivan's.'' Nick checked his watch. ''I'll be there in about fifteen minutes.''

He made it in ten. By the time Walt sauntered in, Nick had already taken a seat in a booth near the back of the pub and ordered a couple of beers. A few regulars were hanging out at the bar and a middle-aged couple was eating fish and chips in a corner booth. The floor was covered with peanut shells, compliments of the earlier after-work crowd, and a couple of pool tables, now empty, stood in the back.

Walt slid onto the bench on the other side of the table. A short, compact man, he wore a trimmed beard that was more the result of being too busy to shave than from any sense of fashion. He was going bald, but didn't seem to mind, and his skin was tanned, from the hours he spent outside working on his sailboat. "It's been a while, Cahill," he said as he picked up the beer that was sweating on the table, waiting for him. He tapped his long-necked bottle to Nick's.

"A couple of years," Nick allowed.

"And now you're in San Francisco."

"Temporarily."

Walt snorted. "If you say so."

"I do. So, what've ya got?"

"Interesting stuff." Walt took a long drink from his bottle. "Let's start with your cousin."

"Cherise?"

"No, her brother. Montgomery." Walt scratched his beard and eyed the bowl of shelled peanuts on the table. "Now that one, he's a piece of work."

"What about him?" Nick asked, his muscles instantly tightening. In all the time he'd been in San Francisco, he hadn't once seen Cherise's brother.

"Your basic lowlife. Never worked a day in his life, that I can see. Tried the military but that didn't take. Sponged off his old man until he died, then a string of women, including his sister. One of his ex-girlfriends filed assault charges against him, but it never went to court. Either she changed her mind or was paid off. I haven't figured out which yet."

Nick frowned. "Swell guy."

"Yep. He's been in several scrapes with the law—drunk and disorderly, that kind of thing. Got himself into a barroom brawl one night about ten years ago. He and the other guy started taking punches and it turned pretty ugly. They ended up pounding the shit out of each other. Monty ended up with three cracked ribs, a rearranged nose and new dental work." Walt paused for effect, took another pull on his Coors. "The real kicker is this: At one time good old Monty was seeing Marla."

All of the muscles in Nick's shoulders bunched. His fingers tightened around his bottle. Something inside him snapped. "Seeing her? As in . . . ?"

"As in doing the horizontal bop."

Walt must've seen the disbelief in Nick's expression. "It was kept quiet, of course, but Marla, she's not one to put a lot of stock in her wedding vows. She and Alex, they've split up a couple of times. They both were involved with other people, but they always end up reconciling. Who the hell knows why? I figure either the money is keeping 'em together or they're one of those couples who can't live with each other any more than they can live without. So . . . one of those times they were split Marla and Montgomery got it on."

Nick's stomach turned sour at the thought. "I don't know what Marla would see in Montgomery," he growled, resisting the urge to reach across the table, bunch the front of Walt's shirt in his fist and call him a liar. But in all the years Nick had known Walt Haaga, the PI had always told the truth.

"He's got looks, supposedly, though that beating took its toll. When Fenton was alive, Montgomery spread money around like it was water. That's changed now, of course, but when he was seeing Marla, his side of the family still had their share of the family fortune." Walt took a long pull from his beer and motioned to a waitress for another. "To her credit, the fling didn't last long, a month or two at most. Then she and Alex reconciled. Again."

Fury, dark and dangerous, shot through Nick's bloodstream

and jealousy, an emotion he hadn't dealt with in years, surfaced. "Who else?" he asked, hating the fact that he had to know.

"Who else what?"

"Who else was Marla's lover?" he asked.

The waitress deposited another round of beers on the table and Walt, watching her saunter back to the bar, said, "I don't have a lot of names, but Marla wasn't as discreet as she could have been. She was involved with a married guy she met at that tennis club she goes to and then there were rumors that she was seeing her daughter's riding instructor. Seems as if your sister-in-law is a hot pants."

Nick's fist balled and he thought of how Marla had responded to him last night. He'd blamed it on the damned chemistry between them; now he wasn't so sure.

"Where's Montgomery living?" he asked, figuring he should have a talk with his cousin.

"Right now he's got a place in Oakland. There have been times when he's been down and out, had to mooch off his sister, but right now he seems flush, able to afford a nice place of his own. Snazzy apartment with a weight room, clubhouse, pool, the whole nine yards."

"What's he doing to support himself?"

"That, I haven't been able to determine. No visible means," he said as two men in their twenties ambled in, ordered "a couple of brewskies" and took positions around one of the pool tables.

"What about the Reverend?"

Walt plucked a peanut from the bowl on the table, cracked it and said, "Another charmer. Ex-football player who found God."

"I know. I had the pleasure of meeting him today."

Walt popped the peanut into his mouth. "He got himself into some hot water last year at Cahill House. Involved with one of the girls . . . but it's a little nebulous," Walt admitted. "The girl made some noise to her mother who just happens to be . . ."

"Pam Delacroix," Nick said. "I heard about it today from the detective in charge of the case. The police are looking for her."

Managing a cat-who-ate-the-canary grin, Walt said, "They're a step behind me." He cracked open another peanut shell.

"You found her?"

"Yep." Pleased with himself he tossed the nut into the air and caught it in his mouth.

"How?"

"I'm brilliant. And I have a great Internet source." He washed the nut down with a swig of beer. "She lives in Santa Rosa. I thought I'd go pay her a visit tonight. Want to come along?"

"Wouldn't miss it for the world," Nick said.

"Thought you'd want to be there. You know, this is starting to get interesting."

"Or dangerous," Nick thought out loud, trying to tamp down the jealousy that had consumed him from the minute Walt had brought up Montgomery. "There are a couple of things we need to check out," he said to Walt. "Marla and I went to see her father today and the old man, who's pretty much out of it, was convinced that she was an imposter, that the real Marla had been there just the other day and this woman was named Kylie. He rambled on about her being some whore's daughter and I figure there was a time when a woman tried to shake him down, claimed her daughter was his."

Walt's eyes narrowed. "I'll start with birth records. Don't suppose you have a last name?"

"That would be too easy." Nick finished his beer. "And it might be nothing. The old man's about to kick off. And is on a lot of pain medication. I'll be surprised if he lasts a week."

Walt nodded. "So what's our game plan?"

"Let's start with Alex. I want you to follow my brother. See where he goes. He claims he's in meetings but doesn't come home until after midnight."

"Sounds like a girlfriend."

"Could be. He and his wife don't sleep in the same room. He keeps his door locked."

Walt let out a quiet whistle. "Some marriage," he observed, taking a swallow. "A woman with a string of lovers and a husband who locks his doors and keeps strange hours. Have you ever asked him about his late night activities?"

"A couple of times. He's pretty vague."

"So you think he's hiding something?"

"I *know* he is. I just want to find out what."

Walt wiped a hand over his mouth. "I'd be glad to do the honors. Anything else?"

"Isn't that enough?"

"More than."

"I think it's time I paid a visit to Cousin Monty. You've got his address?"

"Yep. We can go there after we meet with Julie Johnson. But we'd better be careful," Walt advised, finishing his drink and slamming the bottle onto the scarred table top. "The guy's dangerous."

Nick dropped some bills onto the table. "No problem." His grin was pure evil. "So am I."

Chapter Seventeen

"What's in it for me?" Julie Delacroix Johnson asked as she sat in a tufted chair in her apartment in Santa Rosa. Dressed in a miniskirt and tight black sweater, she crossed one leg over the other and swung her foot nervously, her slip-on shoe in danger of falling off her toes. She'd allowed Nick and Walt into her home, but she was wary. Her husband, Robert, who looked all of eighteen, regarded the other men with wary dark eyes, pulled out a kitchen chair, swung it around and straddled it. His arms were folded over the back, biceps bulging as he cradled a beer between his hands. Trying to look tough. To Nick's way of thinking it wasn't working. The kid was a punk. And he was hiding something.

Walt had taken a seat on a velvet couch that looked new, sharing the tan cushions with a black cat that lifted its head disdainfully before scuttling off and hiding under a table that held a vase of silk flowers. Music was blaring from big speakers, the bass so loud that the floor shook. "If I tell you all about Mom, what do I get out of it?" Julie asked.

"Peace of mind," Nick said.

"She's talkin' cash here," the husband cut in, clarifying the situation. "Cold hard cash."

"And I'm talkin' freedom." Nick stood at the doorway. He wasn't going to be pushed around by some punk kid with a thin goatee and a know-it-all smirk. "She won't have to do any jail time for aiding and abetting a crime."

"She didn't do nothin' illegal," the punk said, his chest swelling as he jabbed a finger in the air over the back of the chair.

"If she has any information about a crime, then she could be charged," Nick said coolly. "If not aiding and abetting, then withholding information, or something. Believe me, the cops won't dick around. Charles Biggs was murdered and probably Pam Delacroix was, too." Nick turned his eyes back to the sultry girl. "I'd think you'd want to nail her killer."

"It was an accident," she said, her voice uncertain, her round eyes suspicious.

"I don't think so. Neither do the police. So don't try to shake me down. I'm not in the mood."

"Why not, dude?" the husband asked. "You said you're a Cahill, right. They got plenty of money."

"That's my brother," Nick explained. "Alex. *He's* the *dude* with the bucks." Sick of the situation he went to the stereo and snapped off the amp.

"Hey!" Robert protested.

"You can turn it back on after we leave."

"Shit."

Julie's face turned the color of chalk.

Walt picked up on it. "Do you know Alex Cahill?" he asked. "Did you meet him somewhere?"

"No," she said quickly. Too quickly.

Nick wasn't buying it. "All I have to do is ask my brother."

"He won't say nothin'. She don't know him!" Robert insisted.

"Okay, okay, but you know Donald Favier, right? The Reverend."

Julie's mascara-rimmed eyes slid away. She licked her lips nervously and looked as if she wanted to disappear. "I went to church there at Holy Trinity a couple of times. With my mom."

"And you ended up at Cahill House where he was the pastor."

She swallowed hard and blushed. Some of her hard-edged crust melted away and she looked like the kid she was. "Yeah. I was pregnant."

"Were you the father?" Nick asked Robert.

"Yeah, so what of it?" the boy shot back. "Jules, we don't got to say nothin' to these losers."

"What happened to the baby?" Nick asked.

Julie's eyes closed for a second and she looked as if she might be woozy, but she managed to lift her chin. "I had an abortion."

"Your idea?" Again Nick asked Robert.

He shrugged. "It was Julie's problem—er, decision. I went along with it. Whatever she wanted."

"So what about the charges against the Reverend? Did he touch you inappropriately while he was counseling you?" Nick asked gently, and Julie's eyes turned red, as if she were fighting tears. She bit at her thumbnail. "Julie?"

"He . . . he was nice to me," she said, and a tear drizzled down the side of her nose. She worked feverishly at the nail.

"Did he talk you into the abortion?"

She swallowed hard. Shook her head. "That . . . that was my idea. He wanted me to have the baby and give it up for adoption. I just couldn't do that. I couldn't stand knowing that someone else was raising my kid . . . I should have kept it, but . . . I just . . . didn't . . ." Tears were running down her face and Nick had to force himself to stay where he was.

"Hey—you don't have to answer none of these questions, Jules," her husband said. He swung out of his chair to stand next to her, placed a big hand on her shoulder. "You guys can just leave, okay? You're upsettin' her."

"No . . . it's okay. They're right. I need to talk to the police," she whispered.

"No way. Jules, remember, we've got a sweet deal goin'. We don't want to fuck with it."

"But I don't want to go to jail."

"You won't, babe. They're just blowin' smoke up your ass," he said, edgy, and Nick wondered if he was on crank. All hyped up. A meth addict?

"Try us," Walt said. "What kind of a deal do you have? Who'd you make it with?"

"She's not sayin'."

"She can talk for herself." Nick looked straight at the girl. "You don't need this kind of trouble. And think about your mom."

Julie swallowed hard, picked at some lint on the arm of her chair. "I don't know."

"Jules, please, this is a real good deal, don't blow it." Robert's hand rubbed her shoulder and if his look could kill, Walt and Nick should be six feet under and pushing up daisies.

Sniffing loudly Julie fought a losing battle with tears. Mascara ran down her cheeks. She slapped the tears angrily away. "I . . . I have to say something," she said. "It's eating me up inside."

"Oh, shit, no." Robert shook his head, squeezed her shoulder. "Think what this means to us, baby. This is our ticket—"

"Your ticket? What the hell did you do?" she demanded.

"Hey, whoa." He backed up a step and hooked a thumb at Nick. "These pricks are just messin' with yer mind, baby."

"Careful, punk, or we'll mess with something else," Nick warned, then turned back to the girl. "What is it, Julie?"

"My mom . . . I talked with her about a week before she died," she said, and Robert, in a dramatic show of exasperation meant to shut her up, rolled his eyes and muttering loudly, stormed into the kitchen where he kicked the cupboards so loudly, Julie jumped and the cat scrambled toward the bedroom for a better hiding spot. "Stop it, Robert!" she screamed. "Just stop it."

"Oh, yeah, I'll stop it, all right. Sure." Robert shot out of the kitchen, keys in hand. "I'm outta here. If you want to kill a good deal, fine, but count me out." He blew out the door in a cloud of self-righteous fury. His shoulder connected with Nick's as he shoved the door open and it was all Nick could do not to grab him by the scruff of his hot neck and knock some sense into him. Instead he let the kid pass and the door slammed shut behind him with a bang. A second later the sound of a motorcycle engine revving cut through the night. Tires screamed and the bike, gears grinding, shrieked out of the lot.

"Good riddance," Julie muttered, folding her arms over her chest. "I don't know why the hell I married him." Then, as if she realized she had an audience who'd overheard her unhappiness, she leaned back in the chair and began rocking. Her lip trembled and she stuck it out in anger. "Ungrateful prick."

"What about your mother," Nick said, trying to get Julie's mind back on track. "Do you know where she was going that night?"

"I think so. She called. Needed a place to hang out for a while, a place no one would find her, and there was an apartment down at school that my friends had rented, but they were gonna be out of town for the weekend. I fixed it so Mom could stay there."

"Why did she want a place to hide?"

"It was something to do with a book she was writing. A book about adoption and parents' rights or something. She was kinda into all that at one time. She called and said she needed a place pronto, that she had something to do first but then needed a place to crash. It was all real frantic. She said she had a friend who needed help because she wanted to leave her husband but he wouldn't let her have custody of her baby. I—I didn't know that it was Marla Cahill. I mean, I wouldn't have . . . oh, shit, it doesn't matter. Mom told me she was gonna do some research and work with the woman, try to help her find a way to keep the kid and instead of a retainer, she got the woman's story for her book.''

Marla. Marla had planned to take Alex's kids away from him.

"She was gonna use my story, too, as part of the plot, but I wasn't cool with it. Even though it was part fiction, I thought people would find out. I didn't want my friends to know about the baby . . .'' she shrugged. "Anyway it's not gonna happen now.'' More tears rained from her eyes. "Why . . . why do you think someone killed her? That woman that was driving, did she do it on purpose? Dad wants to sue her. She . . . she's Alexander's wife, isn't she?''

"We think someone caused the accident, made the driver swerve,'' Walt said, and Nick noted the girl referred to Alex familiarly. What the hell was this all about?

"Who made her swerve?''

"We don't know,'' Nick admitted, though the suspect list was narrowing and his brother was being elevated to the top. That thought made his blood congeal. Even now Marla could be with Alex.

"So what was the 'sweet deal' Robert was talking about?'' Walt persisted.

"Oh, God . . .'' she hesitated. Worked at her thumbnail until there wasn't much left. "It's weird now, when I figured out that everybody's related. I . . . I kinda got involved with an older man when I was at Cahill House. He, um, he liked me. Robert and I were broken up over the baby and this man . . . he was nice. Treated me good. Mom found out and nearly had a stroke. She contacted some lawyer she knew and started ranting and raving that she was going to sue whoever it was. All she knew was that he was older and married but she was ready to string him up by his balls.''

"So when did she find out the guy was the preacher?'' Walt asked.

Julie opened her mouth, started to say something, but snapped her teeth together and folded her lips together.

Walt said, "You don't remember?"

She blinked hard.

"Julie?" Nick prodded.

"He wasn't the guy who came on to me," she whispered, casting her eyes to the floor.

"Wait a minute." Walt rubbed the back of his neck. "I thought you and he—"

She shook her head. "Everyone did. That's what everyone's supposed to think. That's the deal Robert was talking about." She looked earnestly at Nick and her little face, streaked with black, crumpled. "It wasn't like everyone thought. He was just being nice and, well, Alex . . ." she whispered, her lips trembling.

"My brother?"

"Yes! He worked out a deal with me and Reverend Favier so that it seemed like he was the one, so that my Mom wouldn't insist that I press charges."

"Why would Donald Favier let his name be smeared?" Nick asked. "It could have cost him his congregation. I'm surprised they didn't string him up at the church and throw him out."

"It's *his* church. There's no other one like it," Julie said. "It's not like a franchise for McDonald's, it's not part of a bigger deal. There's no archbishop or pope or supreme pooh-bah or anything."

"Still, his reputation took a major hit," Nick said. "Why would he take the fall?"

Julie's lips twisted into a cynical smile that was far older than her years. "Well, duh, why do you think?" she asked, swiping at her nose with the back of her hand. "For the same reason I did. For the money."

The house was dark. Quiet. The only sound Marla heard came from outside her window, the rush of wind through the branches of the fir trees in the backyard. *It's now or never,* she thought, throwing back the covers of her bed and grabbing her robe. As she tossed the robe over her pajamas she heard the soft chink of keys—Eugenia's keys—in her pocket. And now it was time to use them. She had forced herself to stay awake until she was certain her mother-in-law, the servants and Cissy had gone to their rooms. Nick had disappeared earlier and Alex hadn't returned from wherever it was he went after dinner. At least she hadn't heard him come home.

She closed the door to her room and walked across the suite, one hand in her pocket holding the precious keys to keep them from clinking. She tried the door to Alex's room. Locked. No surprise there.

"What are you hiding?" she wondered aloud. She let herself into the hallway and, aided by one lamp left on all night, she padded stealthily to the office door. Her nerves were strung tight as piano wires, her hands clammy, nervous sweat beading between her shoulders. She tried to insert the first key. No go. She used the second. It slid into the lock but wouldn't turn. She withdrew it, put in the next. It, too, wouldn't budge. In the foyer downstairs the grandfather's clock struck one.

Come on, come on, she thought, trying two more keys before finally the lock gave way with a soft click. Heart in her throat, Marla stepped into a room that smelled faintly of cigarette smoke and Alex's aftershave. "Now, Marla, think," she whispered, closing the door softly and dropping the keys back into her pocket. She turned on the desk lamp and walked through the office to the exercise room, past the seldom used equipment and into Alex's closet. His scent was stronger here where his jackets and suits lined the wall. Quietly, she pushed the door of the closet open just a crack to peer into her husband's private sanctuary. Relief poured over her as she noticed that his bed was undisturbed, the covers as tight as if he expected a surprise military inspection.

Letting out her breath, she hurried back to the office and as quickly as her nervous fingers could move riffled through Alex's

Rolodex. Since the first time she'd looked, she'd remembered more and more of the names listed, as in the intervening few weeks, she'd met some people, heard conversations about others and recognized about a third of the names in the file.

Concentrating, she made mental notes of the friends, family and business associates of Marla and Alex Cahill, but stopped short as she flipped over a card and the name Kylie Paris caught her eye. *Kylie.* Again. Her heart stopped. So there really was a woman by the name Conrad Amhurst had called her.

Her throat went dry. She bit her lip. Dear God, was Kylie *her* name? She'd thought as much before, but that didn't make any sense. Why would everyone, her husband included, think she was Marla? Or did the name Kylie belong to someone else? Was it possible that she, Marla, did have a half sister, as her father had suggested, or was his anger just the ramblings of a sick, disoriented old man?

You never understood, did you? You're not my daughter. Get out of here, Kylie. And don't ever come back. You're never getting a dime from me!

Money? He was concerned about money? This man who was giving everything he'd amassed in his life to one tiny baby?

His raspy accusations still ringing in her ears, she pulled the card from its holder, reading the address and phone number listed under Kylie Paris's name. Telling herself that it didn't matter that it was the middle of the night, she licked her lips and picked up the receiver. "No guts, no glory," she whispered as the dial tone seemed to blare in her ear.

With trembling fingers she dialed. Waited. Crossed her fingers. Within seconds there was a click and then a woman's voice—playful, catty, mischievous. "Hi. Guess what? You blew it. I'm out. Sorry you missed me, but you know the routine. Leave your name and number and I'll call you back. *If* you're lucky. Ciao."

Then a beep. Marla hung up. Fast. Swallowed hard. Should she have left a message? Who was that woman? Her sister? A stranger? Or had she recorded that flippant message as Kylie Paris?

If she could only remember! She stared at the phone and considered calling back. What would it hurt to say that she was Marla Cahill and was looking for her sister . . . No, it would be better to meet the woman on the other end of the line in person. Face-to-face. Maybe seeing Kylie's face would jog her memory. As it was, Marla couldn't waste any more time, so she dropped the card into her pocket with Eugenia's keys, and searched through the remaining names in the Rolodex one more time, hoping that seeing a name or address or phone number would trigger her memory, but she was disappointed.

"Never give up," she told herself and turned her attention to the computer. She needed a password to get into the e-mail and used combinations of dates and names, information she'd learned over the past couple of weeks, but nothing opened the damned files. The clock in the foyer chimed the half hour. One-thirty. How long would Alex be out? All night? She tried to open the desk, but the drawers were locked. Of course. "Damn it all to hell . . ." she said, then reached in her pocket for Eugenia's keyring. There were three small keys on the ring. One was probably for the liquor cabinet, the other presumably for the secretary in Eugenia's room and the third . . . fit into the desk perfectly.

With a click the drawers opened.

Hallelujah!

Quickly she sorted through the files and found copies of tax statements and bills, mortgage and bank information, all neatly filed in manila folders. The bills were staggering, the loans against several properties, this house included, more than she could imagine—into the millions of dollars. Hadn't Alex inherited the house and ranch from his father? She scanned an investment portfolio, and noticed as the months had passed that withdrawals had been made, not just dividends and interest, but the principal balance as well until it had dwindled to less than a tenth of what it had been three years earlier.

Where had all the money gone?

If she could believe what she saw, Alex and Marla Cahill were in debt to their eyeballs. No wonder Alex worked late and was talking with foreign investors. She closed the drawer, opened another and found medical records, going back several years. She opened the file marked Marla and in the pool of light from the single lamp she perused each statement, learning that a few years earlier she had been treated for tendinitis in her elbow and had suffered from a sprained ankle four years ago. She shuffled through the bills, several for minor surgeries—facial work done in the past two years, plastic surgery to keep the years at bay.

What a waste, considering the accident. She was about to slip the billings back into their file when she saw a last itemized bill for surgery. She read the notes and frowned, her brow puckering. Surely she'd gotten something mixed up. But the bill stated very clearly that Marla Amhurst Cahill had undergone a hysterectomy three years earlier.

Nearly three years before her son James had been born—two before he'd been conceived.

"Oh, God," she whispered her mind spinning wildly, a thousand thoughts racing through her brain. She remembered the night at the clinic when Dr. Robertson had refused to let her see her own medical records, placating her, while Alex had insisted she go home, that she was too tired to be rational, but he'd wanted to hide her medical records from her.

Because of the hysterectomy.

Because it would prove that James couldn't possibly be her baby.

Her insides churned. She was sweaty all over. She leaned hard against the desk as her mind spun with questions. What the hell was going on? She *remembered* her son's birth. It was one of the few complete memories that she had. But then she'd found the empty bottle of premarin—female hormones—in the medicine cabinet, prescribed for people going through menopause or after having hysterectomies.

But the baby . . . the baby . . . Oh, God, had her anxious mind dreamed the birth? And why didn't she remember Cissy's?

Because you're not Marla Cahill, damn it! You've sensed it all along!

She was going out of her mind . . . this couldn't be happening. *Get hold of yourself, Marla. Now! Don't fall into a million pieces. Search. Hunt through Alex's things. Find out* why *he's keeping secrets from you!*

With fumbling fingers she folded the damning document into small sections, then stuffed it into the pocket of her robe with the keys and the Rolodex card with Kylie Paris's phone number and address. Was she James's mother? Or had she, in fact, had her female organs removed? She hadn't been out of the hospital long enough to have a complete menstrual cycle, only about three weeks, but she had no visible scars from an operation. *They don't cut you on the outside any more.* She wasn't taking estrogen and hadn't had any hot flashes, unless someone had slipped them into her meals . . . But you don't know, do you? You don't know if you're Alex's wife or the children's mother? You don't know if you've got your uterus and ovaries, you don't even know your damned name.

Panic took a stranglehold on her throat. It crossed her mind that someone—who, she wasn't sure—might be trying to drive her crazy. Make her look paranoid. Why? To take the children from her?

She took in a deep breath. Grabbed hold of the reins of her wildly galloping emotions and pulled hard. Somehow she would find out—figure out what was going on. Given the right amount of time, she would uncover all the dirty little secrets of the Cahill clan.

And of your own, Marla. What secrets are you hiding?

"Don't think that way," she scolded. She was running out of time and there was one last unexplored drawer in the desk. "Give me strength," she whispered.

She pulled on the handle, slid open the drawer and saw the gun.

A small, silver-plated pistol.

Her heart nearly stopped. As she ran her fingers over the smooth metal, her blood became ice. Why would Alex have a gun? To protect himself and his family—a family he rarely saw? Or to do bodily harm? Her throat went dry as she lifted the weapon, checked the chamber and saw the bullets. The damned thing was loaded. It felt awkward in her hand. Heavy. She flipped on the safety and considered putting it back in the drawer because she didn't want Alex to know that she'd been snooping, but . . . maybe she'd need it and maybe by taking it she'd prevent him from using it.

Oh, Lord, she couldn't trust him, she knew in her heart she couldn't. Who was this man who kept secrets, locked doors, and hid pistols in his desk—this man to whom she was married. She glanced down at her wedding ring as her fingers curled over the handle of the gun. Who was she who remembered a baby but had undergone a hysterectomy?

You're not Marla Cahill, her mind insisted again. *You've known it from the moment you woke from the coma and heard the name. Conrad Amhurst knows it. Cissy knows it. Little James fussed when you first held him and Coco, that skittery dog, acts like you're a witch. Your entire life is a lie, Marla, or Kylie, or whoever you are. A deadly lie.*

Her heart was thrumming loudly, her mind ringing with questions when she heard Coco give off a soft woof from the floor below. Marla went instantly still, her ears straining. She should leave. Now. But what about the gun? If she took the pistol from the drawer Alex would realize someone had taken it. If she left it, he could use it . . . against her . . . or the children. Carefully she put the pistol in her pocket as she heard the sound of footsteps. Coming up the stairs.

Alex!

Damn.

Her stomach knotted. There wasn't any time to go out to the hall and hurry to her room. He'd see her through the railing as he ascended the stairs. She had to hope that he would go in through the suite and while he was making his way to his room, she'd hurry out this door and creep down the hallway past the suite to James's door. From there she could sneak through the nursery to her own room.

With trembling fingers she tucked the files away, closed the drawers, locked them, then reached over and locked the door to the hallway. He was on the top step. She heard it squeak. Silently she rolled the desk chair back, slipped off the seat, and shoved it into its space in the desk.

With one motion, she snapped off the light and padded quickly into the exercise room, shutting the door behind her until it was open only a crack. Then she waited, sweat pouring off her, her heart racing a thousand beats a minute. His footsteps were heavier in the hall and he paused at the door to the suite.

Please don't let him find me.

He started walking again, his tread coming toward the office. Within seconds his key was rattling in the lock. Circumventing the NordicTrack, Marla retreated to Alex's closet. Barely daring to breathe, she paused again as she heard him enter the computer room.

"Son of a bitch," he said under his breath.

The hairs on Marla's arms stood on end.

"What the hell? Why's this screen saver on? Who's been in here?"

Her heart plummeted. Of course he'd realize someone was in the room because the monitor wasn't blank. A phone jangled softly and Marla jumped before she realized it was a different ring, a soft sputtery noise, not the regular ring of the house phone but Alex's cell.

"Hello?" he snapped and she heard the sound of the desk chair rolling back. *Get out now. This is your chance. Run through his room and the suite to yours.* On quiet footsteps, she made her way through the closet, crept across the wide expanse of carpet to his door and, with a sinking sensation realized that not only was his door locked but it was dead-bolted as well. She couldn't go out this way and lock the dead bolt behind her.

Damn. Her mind raced. She rubbed her clammy palms down

the front of her robe. What could she do? Could she risk him realizing that the dead bolt had been thrown? Her pulse galloping, she returned to the closet and exercise room, her eyes searching for a tiny alcove, some niche where she could hide until he went to bed and fell asleep. Then she could let herself out through the office.

His voice filtered through the door she'd left ajar.

"Yeah . . . I know . . . No, I didn't call . . . I said I didn't— Shit! You're sure? Yeah, I know about caller ID . . . Well, when? Within the last half hour? I wasn't home yet . . . Jesus H. Christ, someone's figured it out!"

Marla froze. She pieced together the conversation. Alex had to be talking to Kylie Paris and she was telling him about the phone call that Marla had impetuously made to her number. Oh, God, no! Somehow the woman was in cahoots with Alex, mixed up in this mess, but how? Why? Her head was pounding and she knew she had to get out. Fast.

"Well, hell, I don't know how! Probably Nick. I knew it was a mistake to drag him down here . . . okay, okay, calm down. Everything's going to be all right. But you have to leave . . . yes, now, damn it! They could be on their way, go to the carriage house . . . you'll be safe there for a day or two . . . lay low and I'll come for you . . . what? Of course I love you. If I didn't, would I have done everything I have for us?" His voice had taken on a desperate edge. He loved this woman, this Kylie. He'd done "everything" for her. Whatever that meant. "What? Yes. Okay. That's better."

Marla didn't wait another second. He was involved in something deadly. Something that may have cost Pam Delacroix and Charles Biggs their lives. Something that might have been behind her nearly dying the other night. Oh, God, no one was safe. She had to get away, grab the children and run. Then, once she knew Cissy and little James were secure, she could figure out what was going on. But one thing was certain: Alex was in love with another woman. Probably Kylie Paris, who could very well be her half sister.

Heart in her throat, she crept stealthily through Alex's closet, across his room and through the door to the suite. She triggered the lock in the knob and couldn't worry about the dead bolt. Tamping down her panic, she made her way across the thick carpet of the sitting room and through the door to her room. She couldn't do anything tonight. She had to play dumb, like nothing was out of the ordinary, lull Alex into thinking she didn't suspect him of anything.

Oh, God, if only Nick were here, she thought desperately, then chided herself on her need to depend upon a man. *You can do this, Marla, you have to. Your children are depending upon you.* She tucked the gun under the mattress, threw off her robe, tossed it on the end of the bed and, as she slid under the covers, she heard the door to Alex's room open, his heavy tred crossing the carpet in swift strides to hesitate on the other side of her door. She slammed her eyes shut and tried to breathe normally. Slow. Regular. *Relax. Let your muscles go slack.*

Her bedroom door creaked open and she feigned sleep, breathed deeply, forced her eyes to be still while her pulse raced.

He walked closer, his footsteps halting at the bed where, just as the intruder had last week, he leaned over her. She could feel his breath on her face and she wanted to scream. *Breathe slowly. Don't panic. This is your only chance.*

"Marla?" His voice whispered over her face. She nearly shot out of the bed but forced herself to lie still. "Honey?"

She smacked her lips a bit, let her mouth fall open on a sigh.

The seconds dragged by and she itched to open her eyes and stare into his lying face. Was he her husband? Her lover? Her enemy?

"Marla?" he called again. His voice was calm, soothing.

She didn't answer.

"Are you awake?" Damn it, he wasn't going to give up. She rolled over, her forehead knitting and she flung one arm out across her pillows as if she was disturbed in her sleep.

"Marla?" His voice was louder now, an angry tone edging it.

She had to respond. "Wh—what?" She blinked her eyes open and squinted up at him. "Oh, God, you scared me! Alex?" Acting confused, she glanced at the clock and yawned. "What time is it?"

"Late. I know. I just got home. I think someone was in my office tonight. Here, the office here in the house."

"Who?"

"I'm asking you."

"I don't know . . . oh, God!" she gasped as if a horrid thought had taken hold of her mind. "The intruder! Do you think he's back?" She sat up in the bed, pulled the covers to her chest and snapped on the light. "The children!"

"I don't think it was an intruder," he said, his gaze slicing through her facade.

"No? Then why are you waking me up?" she asked, allowing herself to let some of her fear into her voice. "We *have* to change the locks. I—I thought you were going to do that. The kids!" She flung off the coverlet.

"They're fine."

"You checked?" she demanded and made her way to the nursery, rushing to the crib as if she really thought someone had broken into the house. James was sleeping soundly. "Thank God," she whispered.

"I just think someone got into my office and—" He followed her to the hallway where she opened the door to Cissy's room and looked inside. Cissy was asleep, her television flickering in blue shadows across her face. "She knows she's not supposed to leave this on," Marla said as if irritated at her daughter, then marched across the room and snapped off the TV. Cissy didn't so much as flinch.

Back in the hallway, she stared up at him, "Are you going to check the other floors?"

"No . . . Marla . . . I don't think anyone broke in."

"But you said . . ."

"I thought maybe you were in the office."

"Me? How? Isn't it locked?"

"Yes."

"Then how . . . ?"

"I don't know," he said and his face in the shadowed hallway looked evil, his gray eyes cold as death. "But Mother's keys are missing."

"You think I found them and broke into your office?" She ran fingers through her hair as if she were weary to her bones. "Oh, Alex, don't be ridiculous."

"The screen saver was on in the office."

"What does that mean?"

"That someone had used the computer in the last ten minutes, it's programmed to stay on that long before going into sleep mode and the monitor turning black."

"Well, I can't explain it." She gave him a pained expression, then reached upward and ran her hand down the side of his face. "You're working too hard. Go to bed, Alex. We'll figure this out in the morning."

"Just tell me you're not lying," he said, his eyes hard and assessing.

"Okay, 'I'm not lying' and you're acting like a lunatic!" She turned, intent on making her way to her room when his arm snaked out, grabbed her by the elbow and spun her around.

His features had contorted into a barely controlled rage, his nostrils flaring, his lips barely moving. "Don't cross me," he warned, his fingers digging tight into the muscles on her forearm. "That would be a big mistake." He let go of her then and stormed off to the office. Probably to discover that his gun was missing. Marla's knees nearly gave way. She held on to the rail and told herself to buck up. She had to put up with only a few more hours in this house. And now she had a weapon.

Tomorrow she'd take the kids and leave.

And go where? With what? You don't have any money. You don't have any identification. You don't have a car.

But she'd find a way to leave this prison.

Even if it killed her.

Chapter Eighteen

"I swear to you if you try to take my son away from me, I'll kill you!" Alex's face loomed over hers as they stood in the foyer. Fury etched his features, hatred turned his gray eyes black.

"No! Oh, God, no!"

Marla's eyes flew open. Her heart pounded wildly. Sweat oozed on her body.

She was alone. In her bed. In the dark. Somewhere outside a tree branch banged against the window and in the foyer the old clock ticked off the minutes, but there was no one with her.

Slowly, as the horrid nightmare disappeared, she pushed herself upright, gathering the edge of the blanket in her fist and holding it to her chest. "It was a dream," she told herself. "Just a dream." She glanced at the clock. Four-thirty. Not yet light outside. She rubbed her arms, but the nightmare didn't fade. The image was too lasting and sharp. It seared deep into her brain, a replay of some other scene, one that came back with mind-numbing clarity.

"I won't let you get away with this," Alex had growled. "I won't let you take him away."

"Watch me, you bastard," she'd thrown back, advancing on him. "I'll take you to court, I'll do whatever it takes, but my baby isn't going to be raised in this . . . this travesty of a situation. Where is he?"

"Not here."

"Bull!"

"Look for yourself."

"If you've hurt him . . ." Her voice faded, strangled at the thought. "I swear—"

"Never. He's just hidden away."

"I don't believe you." She'd taken the stairs two at a time and he didn't follow. Oh, God, he was telling the truth. She raced to the bedroom floor and was only vaguely aware of the phone jangling over the beating of her heart. The nursery was empty. Cold. Austere. She swept through the other rooms, but knew in her heart that he was telling the truth and this house, one she'd often thought was a storybook mansion, was cold and heartless, no servants, no family, no . . . baby. She was breathless by now, her labor had been only a few days before. She made her way to the stairs and paused on the living room level, holding on to the rail and seeing Alex, his back to her on the phone. His voice was soft, yet distinct.

"Yes . . . yes, I said I'll be there. Just wait . . . I don't know . . . two hours, maybe three . . . I have a situation to take care of here . . . yes, I know . . . I do, too . . ." His lover, he was talking to his lover and . . . and this all had something to do with the baby. "Hang in there . . . look at the ocean, walk on the beach . . . just calm down . . . that's it."

"Who is that?" Marla demanded, hurrying down the rest of the stairs.

He hung up. Looked guilty as he whirled around.

"Where's my baby?" she demanded.

He'd grabbed her then. With lightning swiftness, he grabbed her upper arms in his big, viselike hands. She felt the blood drain from her face. His grip was so tight she'd been certain he would snap her bones as easily as matchsticks. His face had contorted with a hatred so intense, he'd actually sprayed her with spit as he'd shaken her. "Don't push me. This is the way we planned it."

"Like hell," she'd countered.

"We have a deal."

"Had. *Had* a deal. I want out! And I swear by God that I'm going to take my baby with me. Away from this horrid place and all the lies, all the treachery."

"Don't threaten me," he'd warned. " 'Cause you're in the big leagues now and I swear to you if you try to take my son away from me, I'll kill you!"

And then . . . and then what? Her memory eluded her once again as she sat and shivered on the bed. "Oh, God," she whispered, burying her face in her hands. What had she gotten herself into? Who was she? What kind of person would bargain with her husband about the fate of her child? *Don't cross me,* he'd warned just last night, *that would be a big mistake.*

She'd stumbled into the bedroom, lain in the dark and stared up at the lacy, spider weblike canopy and waited until she'd heard him leave. Just as he always did. Where had he gone? Whom did he meet? What was he doing? She'd finally dozed off without any answers, sleeping fitfully as in the waking moments that peppered her sleep, she'd tried and failed to come up with some kind of plan to wrest her children from their tyrant of a father, to save them.

From what?

From whom?

Alex and the woman he was involved with?

If only she could remember.

Damn it, somehow she would. She reached under the mattress. Alex's cold pistol was right where she'd put it. Close. So she had a weapon and Eugenia's keys—surely there was a key to the ignition of one of the cars, and with enough digging through documents, she might be able to access some of the bank accounts. She needed to find her checkbook statement and some kind of ID—then she could draw out some cash—maybe from one of those automated cash machines . . . if only she could come up with a password.

Her head pounded.

She had to do it. She had to find a way out of this mess.

This is the first day of the rest of your life. This is the day you escape and start living.

The door to the suite cracked open.

She jumped. Reached for the gun.

Her fingers surrounded the cold metal as the door to her room inched open. Her nerves stretched to the breaking point. Beads of sweat ran down her temples.

You won't take my kids from me, you son of a bitch, she thought, expecting Alex. Holding her breath, she narrowed her eyes as a man's head was thrust into the room.

"Marla?"

"Nick!" She sagged in relief. *Nick.* Thank God. She wanted to crumble into a million pieces.

Stepping into the room, he closed the door behind him. Stripped bare to the waist, he wore only a pair of disreputable jeans. "Are you all right?" His voice was a balm. Tears burned behind her eyes. "I thought I heard you cry out."

"I—I probably did. I mean, I'm sure of it." She slid her hand free from between the springs and mattress, leaving the gun. "I had a dream, a nightmare, but it seemed so real." Still sitting in the bed, she plowed both sets of fingers through her short hair. "I dreamt that Alex . . . he accused me of trying to take the baby away from him, he . . . he threatened to kill me. But it really happened. I *know* it did. We were standing in the foyer and he was . . . he was . . . so angry. Ruthless." Closing her eyes, she leaned back against the headboard. "God, it was horrible."

"But you're sure you're okay?" he asked again. *Gently. As if he really cared.* She heard him approach the bed and felt the mattress sag as he sat on the edge. He touched her shoulder and she fought the urge to tumble against him and sob like some stupid, weak female. No, that would never do, but a part of her melted as she felt his fingers, so strong, so warm, touching her shoulder through the thin fabric of her pajamas. "Are you okay?" he said again, and she opened her eyes.

"I think so." Her voice was lower than usual, raspy as she fought to control herself at his tender gesture. Deep in her heart she knew that no one in her life had ever been this concerned about her. This kind. Not her father, not her husband, no other man in her life . . . She swallowed hard, refused to fall apart.

"I was just checking on you. Why don't you go back to sleep?" he suggested, and in the darkness she saw the outline of his face, noticed how his eyebrows pulled together in concern, sensed the tension in his muscles.

"I can't. I have too much to do today." She cleared her throat and admitted, "I have a lot to tell you, Nick. A lot."

His fingers tightened over her arm. "What?"

"I, um, I need to get my thoughts together," she said, as deep inside she felt a yearning that she had to ignore. He was so close. Too close. She smelled his skin, felt his heat . . . oh, Lord, she couldn't be distracted. Wrapping her fingers around his wrist, she said, "Listen . . . just give me a few minutes to shower and look decent, then I want to tell you what I found out."

"Promise?" he asked, his teeth flashing white.

"Promise." Oh, God, she'd love to kiss that cocky smile off his face.

She scooted to the far side of the bed to break contact with him. This was much too intimate, too tempting, too erotic . . . too dangerous.

"You've got fifteen minutes."

"I only need ten," she shot back and winked at him as she dived for the bathroom.

Nick watched her leave and didn't follow, though he wanted to, damn it. Despite everything else, including the knowledge that they were in danger.

Gritting his teeth against the lust that burned through his body, Nick forced himself out of the room. He didn't like the turn of his thoughts. Seeing her lying there, feeling her warmth through her pajamas, smelling her perfume, knowing she was vulnerable made him want to hold her, to comfort her, to kiss her and touch her . . . "You miserable bastard," he growled under his breath as he made his way downstairs. This woman was so unlike the conniving Marla he'd known in the past and yet he was drawn to her, wanted her, felt the need to make love to her even more strongly than he had fifteen years ago. She was different, he sensed that. Mature. Self-reliant. Sexy without knowing it. This stronger woman appealed to him at a deeper level "Give it up," he muttered on his way to the kitchen. He'd nearly scared her out of her wits when he'd knocked on her door and she'd seemed so vulnerable and frail for a second that all he'd wanted to do was hold her. *And make love to her. Until they were both spent and gasping.* Hell, he was a fool. There was too much to do before he allowed erotic thoughts to enter his head, but his damned stiff cock wasn't taking the hint.

He needed to tell her about Pam, and about Monty, but it could wait. In the cavernous kitchen, he dug through the cupboards, scrounged up some coffee and made a pot in a machine that gurgled and sputtered. He glanced outside to the darkened garden where he'd spied Marla on the swing looking lost and frightened. As if Marla Cahill had ever been afraid of anything. He tapped his fingers nervously on the counter, his head crowded with thoughts of Alex, Julie, Monty . . . and, of course Marla. Alex was fast running out of money, he was bribing every one under the sun, lying between his teeth and all of it centered on his wife. Somehow . . . slowly the pieces were fitting together and the puzzle picture being created scared the hell out of Nick.

But Marla's involved. You know that. You still can't trust her.

The coffeemaker gurgled its last dying breath. Hooking two

cups on his fingers, he carried the pot upstairs to the suite, then poured them each a cup.

He told himself to wait for her in the sitting area, that she'd emerge in a few seconds, but curiosity and pure male lust argued against him and won. He pushed open the door to her room and, hearing the shower running, walked toward the bathroom where steam was fogging the mirrors and the smells of soap and water were heavy in the air.

Don't do this, the rational part of his brain screamed, *you're only begging for trouble.*

But he couldn't stop himself. He set her cup on the counter near the sink and, in the mirror, caught a glimpse of her body through the steamy glass doors. His gut tightened. Through the hot mist he saw a flash of long legs, and an impression of white breasts with dark nipples. She was bent over, rinsing her hair, and he noticed a flash of her rump, two firm cheeks that caused his manhood to swell, harder than before.

Get out now, before she sees you, he told himself, but she turned then, lolling her head back and the fleeting image of a dark triangle at the apex of her legs was visible through the wispy veil of steam.

God, she was beautiful, nearly ethereal looking with her thin waist and sleek, wet skin. His damned cock thickened painfully, pressing hard against his jeans. She was humming, slightly off-key, over the rush of water.

For Christ's sake, man, you don't *have time for this!*

Knowing that he was playing with fire, that he should just leave her cup near the sink and make tracks back to the suite, Nick didn't budge. Instead he waited, sipping his coffee, leaning his hips against the edge of the counter and staring at the foggy vision as he listened to the sound of her voice. She rotated under the spray, lifting her arms. He saw the slope of her shoulders, the curve of her spine and just a glimpse of two dimples over her buttocks.

Caught in her own world, she hadn't noticed him yet, which suited him just fine. A smile played upon his lips as she twisted off the faucets suddenly and opened the shower door. She reached for a towel as her eyes met his through the haze.

A glorious flush swept up her skin. "What're you doing?" she asked, startled and dripping, dark, damp ringlets framing her face.

"I brought coffee." He motioned to her steaming cup, took a sip of his own.

"And stayed for the show?" Her green eyes glimmered with naughty intrigue and her smile was downright wicked as she placed her hands on her wet hips in mock disgust.

"I only caught the final act."

"How did I do?"

"Pretty good."

"Just pretty good?" she teased, not bothering to reach for a towel. She stood dripping, water running down her face and neck, beads drizzling over her breasts and collecting in her hair.

"Actually," he said, setting his cup down, and knowing he should be doing anything, *anything* other than what he was planning. "I think you were good enough for an encore."

"Meaning?" she asked, her full lips twitching, one eyebrow arching coyly as her gaze lowered to the waistband of his jeans for just a second. That was it. To hell with everything else.

"Meaning this." With an evil grin, he reached forward, grabbed her around the waist and felt her tumble against him. She laughed and he captured her lips in his. Warm and wet, they molded to his as her giggle turned into a sigh. He didn't need any further encouragement, wouldn't think of the hundreds of reasons why he couldn't take the time, couldn't get involved with her, couldn't be with her. Now, for the moment, he just wanted to escape. To love her again. His hand slid down the curve of her spine as he pressed hard against her, forcing her to walk backward into the shower.

His tongue explored her lips and mouth, his fingers kneaded her slick skin and he wanted her with the same desperate ache that he'd always felt whenever she was near. He'd thought he'd killed his need for her years before, but realized now he'd played himself for a fool. He wanted this woman, needed her. Reaching behind him, he scrabbled for the handle of the glass door, pulled it closed, then turned on the spray.

"Oh!" she cried out and he kissed her harder, felt his pulse leap as he slid his hands over her soft flesh. Warm water splashed over them and she wrapped her arms around his neck, her breasts rising in open invitation. His blood was pounding through his brain, his cock straining against his suddenly wet jeans. He couldn't stop, wouldn't think, damned the consequences as he kissed the curve of her neck.

She gasped as the hot water streamed down. "Nick," she whispered. "Oh, God . . ."

Her fingers were in his wet hair and she let herself go, forgot for the moment all her doubts, all her fears, all the craziness that was her life. She felt the pulsing spray of hot water against her back, his hard body pressed against her breasts and abdomen, his long jean-covered legs spread and molded to hers. This was madness, ludicrous, and yet she couldn't stop. Liquid fire swept through her blood, desperate want pounded through her brain and she throbbed deep inside, aching, needing, hurting to feel his touch.

His arms surrounded her, one hand splayed against the small of her back, imprisoning her close to him, long fingers brushing the cleft of her buttocks. "God, I want you," he whispered, his voice ragged, his eyes haunted as dewdrops of spray caught on his lashes and ran down his nose.

"And . . . and I want you," she admitted as shame burned through her mind. *Don't do this Marla, you're making a horrible mistake, one you'll never be able to rectify.*

But his hands were persuasive, his lips demanding as he shifted, turning them so that her shoulders were pressed against the tiles at the back of the shower and the water cascaded over his shoulders. His hair was wet and curled over his forehead, his eyes were a dark, erotic blue and he stared up at her as he lowered himself slowly, cupping her breasts between his hands, pushing them together and kissing first one damp anxious nipple, then the next. She writhed as his breath scraped across the wet, dark buds and she trembled deep inside, burning with the need to feel more of him, all of him.

"You're so beautiful," he breathed, his thumbs rubbing the tips of her breasts before he pushed them together and buried his face between them. Her legs went weak as he turned his head and, as water tumbled over him, began to suckle. She arched against the tiles as one of his hands slid around her back and held her tight to his face. Cradling his head, holding him close in the hot water, she gave in to the desire that burned in the deepest part of her.

He kissed and teased and tasted, nipping and sucking at her breasts, the hand at the curve of her spine forcing her closer still.

"Nick, oh, God, Nick, oh, please . . ." she whispered, her mind spinning wildly, her body aching for even more of him. He breathed against her and moved lower, his tongue sliding over the skin of her abdomen, touching and tracing her belly button as she gasped for air. Then he slid lower, now on his knees, his mouth caressing her slick abdomen.

She gasped as his hands slid down her backside and he kissed the curls at the juncture of her legs. "Let go, darlin'," he said, his breath fanning her sensitive skin, her legs parting to allow him to touch her, kiss her, explore her.

She could barely breathe, couldn't think, could only feel. All of her senses tingled as he opened her, tasted her, his hands kneading her buttocks, his tongue playing sweet magic, his breath swirling hot within her, the water misting around them.

"That's my girl," he said as the first spasm hit and her mind shattered. She wanted to touch him, to hold him, to tell him she loved him, but she was forced against the wall of the shower, her hands flung outward, her fingers stiff as they scraped the wall, searching for something, anything to clutch.

He moved a shoulder, hooked her knee over it and gained deeper access. Her heel pressed into his back. Dear God. Sweet,

sweet torment and glorious torture were her companions. It was as if her whole being were centered deep inside her. "Come on, darlin'," he breathed into her as he maneuvered her other leg over his opposing shoulder and kissed her deep, touched her so intimately tears rolled down her cheeks and she couldn't find her breath.

A low, raspy, animal sound escaped from her throat. "Nick, o-o-o-oh, Nick . . ."

"Let go, darlin' . . ."

She bucked. Again. And again. Something deep inside broke and tears ran down her face, mingling with the shower's hot spray. "Oh, please . . ."

In one swift movement, he swung her legs over his head and straightened. "Nick, I—"

"Shh." He lifted her from her feet, turned off the water and dripping puddles on the carpet carried her into the bedroom where he placed her on the rumpled covers of her bed. "Now, Marla . . ." he said, determination edging his voice, the expression on his face serious, the need in his eyes naked. "Make love to me."

Swallowing hard, knowing she was about to cross a bridge that would surely crumble behind her, she reached up and found the buckle of his belt. With unsteady fingers she unhooked the sodden leather strap, let it fall free and caught the button at the waistband of his jeans. She tugged. His fly opened with a quick series of pops. Swallowing hard, with renewed determination, she pushed the heavy, sodden denim over his hips. He kicked the jeans onto the floor and she caught her first glimpse of his naked body.

Tough sinew.

Stringent muscles.

Coarse hair.

All male.

Strong muscles stretched as he gently pushed her back on the bed, kissed the dewy drops of moisture from her breasts, then stared deep into her eyes.

"Tell me you want me."

She licked her lips. "I . . . I want you." Oh, Nick, if you only knew, she thought, throbbing with a raw, hungry passion that burned through her.

"Tell me you'll never regret this."

"I won't." It was a lie. She'd regret it the moment it was over. But she didn't give a damn.

"Neither will I," he said, then covered her mouth with his.

Strong knees nudged her legs apart and she trembled. Ached. Yearned for the feel of him. His thick erection brushed over her abdomen and she tingled, her skin on fire, her breathing difficult. "I've wanted to do this from the moment I saw you again," he whispered, kissing the side of her cheek. "Even though you were bruised and hurting, I wanted you as badly as I ever did."

"And . . . and I wanted you," she admitted, guilt boring deep in her heart as she let her fingers explore the ridges and planes of his shoulders and arms.

Slowly, watching her reaction, he nudged at her between her legs and she gasped. Sweat beaded his brow, strain pulled at the muscles of his face as he settled over her, braced on his elbows. She ran her fingers down the smooth muscles of his back, traced the ridge of his spine and he kissed her again. Hard. He nudged again and she quivered, arching upward, wanting the feel of him inside her.

"Oh, lady." With one slow thrust, he delved deep.

Her breath caught somewhere between her lungs and mouth as he withdrew so slowly she thought she would die. Her fingers dug into the muscles of his back. Then he thrust again, covered her mouth with his and gave into the need deep in his soul.

Marla arched upward, catching his rhythm, moving with him, as each thrust was harder than the last, deeper, more forceful. She clung to him, barely able to breathe as the first light of dawn pierced the window, coloring the bed and canopy with shades of gold.

Nick held her close, his breathing raspy and shallow, matching her own gasps as he made love to her. Liquid heat swirled deep inside, her mind spun crazily, and she held fast to him, loved him, rose to meet each of his strokes, gave herself up to him, body and soul. Faster. Faster. Spinning wildly. She closed her eyes and couldn't find her breath as the first wondrous, mind-splintering spasm hit.

His hoarse cry came a heartbeat before her own. "Marla . . . oh, love . . . damn you, damn us, . . . damn it all . . ."

The world shattered behind her eyes. He threw back his head and held her as if he'd never let go, his body straining hard before he fell against her, his weight welcome, his face buried in the crook of her neck. "I knew . . ." he said, gasping, his fingers stroking her hair as his wet chest hair rubbed against her breasts. "I knew it would be like this with you."

"Like before?" she asked, barely able to force the question, for she wasn't sure that they'd been lovers long ago, that she really was Marla Amhurst Cahill.

"No, not like before." He raised himself on his elbows and stared down at her with those laser blue eyes. He drew in a long, deep breath and traced the curve of her jaw with one thumb. "Better. So much better."

"I bet you say that to all the girls," she teased, inwardly pleased, wishing she believed him.

He laughed. "Just to one."

"Liar."

"Not me." His eyes were intense and he kissed her again. "Now," he slapped her gently on the buttocks, and glanced around the room. "As much as I'd like to lie here all day with you, I think we'd better get up before the rest of the house does."

She groaned, but as her mind cleared, she knew he was right. They were pressing their luck and there was no time to waste. "I have so much to tell you," she admitted worrying her lip. "So much . . ."

"Well, darlin', that makes two of us. Come on."

* * *

"The old man's dead," he said from his favorite phone booth just down the hill from the rich bastard's house. The fog was peeling away, sun shining and the coffee shop across the street was just opening up.

"What? How do you know this?"

There was an edge of panic in the guy's voice. Good.

"I offed him. I got tired of waiting."

"Damn it, I told you to lay off."

"You said we had to wait until he kicked off. Well, the old fart kicked."

"The police will be all over us!"

"They'll never know. The Doc put Amhurst on oxygen last night. I took him off."

"Christ, this messes everything up." The rich bastard was panicking, his voice rising an octave.

"Speeds everything up you mean. And you should be glad. He changed his will once, didn't he, cut Marla out, then had second thoughts in order to get him a grandson? Why wouldn't he again? This way the kid inherits."

"He couldn't have changed it again, you moron! He wasn't in his right mind."

"Says who?" he threw back, seeing red at the insult.

"Look, if anyone suspects—"

"No one does. The way it stands now, the kid inherits, you get the bucks and you pay me. *Pronto.*" His eyes narrowed as he smelled the other guy trying to squirm out of their agreement.

"There's still the problem of Marla."

"I'll take care of it."

"Now wait a minute. I'm not sure—"

"She'll be dead by nightfall."

"No, it's too risky. Not on the same day her father dies."

"Don't worry about it. It'll look like an accident. That's what you wanted. Right? This was your fuckin' idea."

"No. Now listen. Wait a few days, okay. Until things calm

down. And don't call me back on this cell. Do you hear me? I hired you to do a job and you'll be paid, but I'm still calling the shots.''

"Like hell.''

"I'm warning you—''

He laughed and reached into his pocket for his cigarettes. "Relax, *amigo,* this is your lucky day.'' Then he hung up and started for his Jeep. His blood was on fire as he lit up. Killing Conrad Amhurst had been too easy and just a means to an end.

It was Marla he wanted. But then it always had been.

"... and so I pretended to be asleep and when he came in I tried to fake him out, act like I didn't know what was going on, that I hadn't been in his office,'' Marla said as she sat on the couch in the sitting room. Nick had lit the fire and stood with his back to the flames, his empty coffee cup in his hands, his eyes drilling into hers. They'd drained the coffeepot as the house began to stir. The cook was already rattling around in the kitchen and soon Cissy would wake for school. "I found several things in his desk. There was a gun. I took it and hid it under the mattress in my room. Then . . . then there was a Rolodex card with Kylie Paris's address and phone number. I've got it as well. And a statement from a hospital for Marla Cahill's hysterectomy. Full hysterectomy,'' she said, a million thoughts running through her mind as the caffeine jolted her bloodstream. "It was dated three years ago.''

Nick regarded her with wary eyes. "So either you're not Marla or the baby isn't yours.''

"James is mine,'' she stated without a waver of hesitation. No matter what else happened, she *knew unerringly* that she'd given birth to her baby. She took a sip from her tepid coffee, draining the cup before adding, "And somehow Dr. Robertson is in on this. He didn't want me to see Marla's medical records, though the operation was done in Los Angeles at a private hospital, not at Bayview. But there must be some note, or cross reference. For whatever reason he wouldn't let me have even a passing glance at the folder.''

"Get the address to Kylie's apartment and we'll go there," Nick said as he rubbed the stubble darkening his jaw and Marla remembered the feel of its scratchy texture against her own skin less than a half hour before.

"What about the gun?" She shivered as she thought of the cold, deadly weapon.

"Keep it hidden for now. Out of Alex's hands. Will the maid find it?"

"I don't think so, not even if she changes the sheets."

"Good." He started for the foyer.

"I won't leave without the baby, Nick. I can't take a chance that Alex will somehow try to kidnap his own son."

"From his house?"

"Anywhere." Marla was adamant. Firm. Above all else she'd protect her child. "And we have to see that Cissy's safe, too."

"From Alex?"

"And whoever else." Her stomach curdled when she thought of the man who was supposed to be her husband. Nick had already explained about the dwindling finances of Cahill Limited, Pam Delacroix's intention of writing a book, and Julie Delacroix Johnson's involvement with Alex. Marla had learned how Alex had let Donald Favier take the blame for the scandal, then paid everyone to keep their mouths shut. He could even be behind Charles Biggs' death and the attempts on her life.

She had every reason to feel fear. For herself. For her son. For Nick. "You don't know the hatred on his face. The way he threatened me."

"Then we'll take James with us," Nick agreed.

"And we'll wait until Cissy's at school. I think she'll be safe there," Marla said, thinking ahead. "For some reason I don't think she's a part of this. Whatever it is, it has to do with the baby. And me.''

Nick's eyes locked with hers. "Because of the will."

"What?" She didn't like where his thoughts were leading.

"The baby is at the center of all this because he's going to inherit the bulk of Conrad Amhurst's estate," Nick said, and she felt the knell of doom peal in her heart.

"This is worse than I thought." She set her empty cup on the table. "If you're right, then James is safe until Dad—Conrad dies. And after that . . ."

"He's as expendable as you are," Nick said, finishing her grisly thought.

"Let's get him up." She shot to her feet. She had to get out of this house. Now! She couldn't stand another minute in this elegant death trap. "We'll take Cissy with us and drop her off at school and we'll find a safe place to keep James until we can sort all this out."

"We can go to Oregon. I have a place there."

"Would it be safe?"

"Probably not," he admitted, frowning as somewhere on a floor above, footsteps could be heard. "I do have a watch dog of sorts, but I doubt if Tough Guy would deter too many people."

To Marla it sounded like heaven. Peaceful. Safe. At least within this horrid, complicated and terrifying nightmare, she'd found Nick. If nothing else, she knew what it was like to love someone. To care. "Someday," she said hoarsely, "I'd like to see it."

"Someday you will," he promised, but she didn't know if she could believe him.

Before she could answer, the phone rang sharply.

"Now what?" His expression sober, Nick checked his watch, strode into the foyer, and grabbed the receiver before the telephone jangled again. "Hello?" A pause. The lines around his mouth deepened. "Marla Cahill? Right here."

Marla's heart dropped.

"Just a minute." Nick carried the receiver into the sitting room and handed it to her. His eyes locked with hers. "It's the nursing home in Tiburon."

Her father. Doom settled in her heart. "This is Marla Cahill," she said, though she wasn't certain.

"Good morning, Mrs. Cahill," a strong, female voice greeted. "This is Kara Dunwoody, the administrator at Rolling Hills Care Center in Tiburon. I'm afraid I have some bad news. Your father passed away this morning . . ."

"You wanted a break in the Pamela Delacroix case?" Janet Quinn asked as she dropped into the chair opposite Paterno's desk. She was carrying her oversized briefcase and set it on the floor beside her.

"At least one. Two or three would be better." He reached into the drawer, discovered he was out of gum, and leaned back in his chair. "What've you got?"

Janet grinned. "We found Marla Cahill's purse. With the impact of the accident, it had been thrown about fifty feet and slid down an embankment. We would never have located it if she hadn't been so insistent that it was missing." Janet's eyes were bright behind her glasses, as if she was privy to an important secret. Paterno had seen the look before and recognized it. She was holding something back. Something important.

"And?" he prodded.

"And we found her wallet . . . well, actually more than her wallet. But there's an interesting little twist here. The credit cards, driver's license, and checkbook weren't issued to Marla Cahill. All of them, every piece of ID was in the name of Kylie Paris. She lives here in the city." Janet reached down, snapped her briefcase open and withdrew a small handbag, wrapped in plastic and tagged, then pulled out a larger plastic bag filled with other items, all tagged as well. Through the plastic, Paterno viewed the driver's license. "Notice anything?" Janet asked.

"Only that Marla Cahill and Kylie Paris could be twins." He stared at the image.

"Believe me, they're not."

"And I thought the resemblance between Marla Cahill and Pam Delacroix was close. It is nothing compared to this."

"Think what it could be, if, after she was in the car wreck, the surgeons altered her face a bit. You know, people would expect that after the accident and the plastic surgery, Marla Cahill just might look a little different from the way she did before Pam's Mercedes did a nose dive off the highway."

"Who is this woman?" Paterno asked, waving Kylie Paris's ID at the other detective.

Janet was only too happy to answer; she'd been waiting for that question. "According to state records, Kylie Paris was born a couple of years after Marla Cahill, to a woman named Dolly Paris, who, at one time, worked as a waitress at a men's club where Conrad Amhurst played cards and golf. She wasn't married at the time, had no permanent boyfriend, but managed to get pregnant. There were some rumors that the kid was fathered by a member of the club, but no father was listed on the birth certificate and Dolly died nearly five years ago. Heart disease. Kylie grew up with a series of . . . almost stepdads, for lack of a better term. Smart kid, did well in school, got herself some scholarships and worked her way through college. After graduation she talked her way into a job at an investment firm downtown. Very ambitious girl. Even had another offer at a competing firm."

"Had?"

"Yep. She quit. About a year and a half ago. Just out of the blue. Didn't give much of a reason, but it was out of character as she was determined to claw her way up the corporate ladder, no glass ceiling for this girl. She wanted the good life and how. But then, one day, just up and gives it up." Janet's eyes gleamed. "None of her friends have heard from her since. She just seemed to drop off the face of the earth."

"She died?"

"Nope. Don't think so. Otherwise the rent on her apartment and her utilities would be delinquent."

"And they're not?" Paterno said, his mind racing. Who the

hell was this woman—this potential half sister to Marla Cahill. What was the connection?

"Paid every month to the leasing company."

"Really?" he asked, feeling that tingle of exhilaration, that spurt of adrenalin that he always sensed when a case was about to be solved. "Why did she quit her job?"

"This is where it gets good. I think she quit to have a baby— a baby she didn't want anyone to know about. Marla Cahill's baby."

"Whoa. Wait a minute—"

"Marla Amhurst Cahill was sterile. It turns out that she had a hysterectomy a few years back, one her father didn't know about. It was all hush-hush, the hospital records where Dr. Robertson works sketchy, but I dug up an old insurance claim and bingo—there it was. A full hysterectomy. There is no way Marla Cahill is James Cahill's mother. So when her old man, Conrad, nutcase that he is, changes his will, cutting her out unless she comes up with a male heir, she manages to come up with one.

"A *Cahill* heir, not an Amhurst."

"The old man had always wanted a son. Even though he treated Marla like a damned princess, he wanted a boy."

"He had one," Paterno reminded her.

"Yes, but Rory was in an institution, would probably never father any children."

"So his daughter concocted a scam to give him a grandson?" Paterno was still skeptical. "Talked this half sister or whoever she was into having a kid for her . . . into stepping into her goddamned shoes?"

"That's the way I figure it. It was a good thing Kylie Paris was avaricious and would do just about anything for a buck, had the same blood type, O negative, and managed to produce a boy."

"That's beyond lucky if you ask me."

"They are half sisters—same blood type as their father.

That's where the negative comes in. It's a lot less common than positive.''

Paterno's eyes narrowed. ''What if the husband didn't go along?''

''Have you ever seen a Cahill turn down money?''

He snorted. ''Just the black sheep.''

''Nicholas Cahill's different.''

That much was true.

''I wouldn't put it past Alex Cahill to have masterminded this whole sick scheme. He and the missus weren't always tight, you know. They'd split before and rumors were that neither one held very fast to their marriage vows. She had a fling with the brother before she and Alex were married and I talked to a maid who had been fired a couple of years ago. She's the one who tipped me off about the hysterectomy. From there I searched through old records. The maid told me that Marla might have had a quickie affair with her cousin, Montgomery, just to piss Alex off at one time'' Janet tossed her bangs out of her eyes. ''But through it all Marla and Alex stayed together. Because of love? I don't think so.''

''You think it was the money?''

''I'd bet my life on it.''

That much Paterno wouldn't argue, but he still wasn't convinced that Janet was anywhere in the vicinity of the mark. ''How would Marla explain her pregnancy—the real Marla.''

''Either the two women would trade places, which would be tricky because there are so many people living in that mansion, or, she could have worn pregnancy pads, the kind actresses wear. The she'd have to make sure no one saw her without her clothes. Faking morning sickness and all the other symptoms would have been relatively easy—she could have even put on a few pounds just to round out her face. Remember, I think not only the husband but the family doctor—Robertson—was in on this.''

''Why would Robertson play along?'' Paterno argued. There just wasn't enough to go on here, and yet . . . maybe.

"The same as everyone else. Money. The Cahill's give a lot to his clinic and Bayside and probably Phil Robertson's private retirement account."

"You're sure about all this?" He rubbed the kinks from the back of his neck and gave Janet's idea some thought. She was never very far off the mark, but this time her theory seemed too far-fetched. "There are still a lot of holes to fill," he said.

"Ya think?"

"More than a damned sieve," he grumbled, but some of the story fit. His stomach was beginning to burn again and he opened his drawer, looking for his ever-present bottle of anti-acid.

"Well, it's just conjecture until we prove it."

"Jesus," Paterno whispered, staring at Janet with a jaundiced eye. "I don't know if I'm buying it. There are just too many gaps." He opened the bottle and popped four or five tablets into his mouth. "What if someone found out? How would Marla pull off the pregnancy scam? Wouldn't someone at the hospital or the house know and spill the beans? And what if Kylie balked, or had a girl . . . hell . . . this is just too damned unbelievable." He chewed the antacids. They tasted like crap, but did the trick.

Janet's grin widened. She was so goddamned sure of herself. "Let's go see, shall we?"

He swallowed the pills. "You think you've nailed this one, don't you?

She snorted a laugh. "That's why I get the big bucks."

"And the glory." Paterno chuckled without much humor. "Don't forget the glory."

"Never."

Paterno swung his gaze to his bulletin board where the photos of the accident scene and Pam Delacroix's mangled, bloodied Mercedes were posted. "So why the accident? Why try to kill off Marla?"

"That, I don't know," Janet admitted as Paterno turned his attention back to the pictures on Kylie Paris' drivers license.

They looked enough alike to pull it off, and yet, there were too damn many unanswered questions. He tossed the license back to Janet. "Well, I guess we'd better find out if your theory holds water." He felt a moment's satisfaction that at least they had something new to go on, thin as it was. "Let's go have a chat with Mrs. Cahill."

"If that's who she really is."

Chapter Nineteen

Clutching James as if she thought someone would snatch him from her arms, Marla leaned against the back of the elevator in the apartment building on Fulton Street. Over seventy years old, built of yellow brick, the apartment house was wedged between the University of San Francisco and Alamo Square, close enough to the house on Mount Sutro, the elegant old manor she'd called home ever since leaving the hospital. The elevator seemed eerily familiar, the smells and sounds of this tired building nipping at the worn edges of her memory.

Had she lived here? If so, how long, and how had she ended up as Alex Cahill's wife, or pretending to be his wife? She'd been in this elevator before. She knew it. At the thought, her legs turned to rubber and her throat went dry. Trepidation battled with curiosity. She needed to find out who she was, what was behind the door of Kylie Paris's apartment. Yet it scared her to death.

You have to find out. You have no choice.

Nick stood next to her. Gaze trained on the digital display of the floors, he waited as the elevator landed. His shoulders were tight, the cords in the back of his neck evident, the air thick.

James cooed softly against her neck and she closed her eyes. No matter what, she wouldn't give him up.

Never.

She'd die first.

The doors to the elevator car parted. Marla's heart jolted. She found herself staring into a long, oval mirror on the wall facing the elevator.

The woman in the reflection looked haunted. Tall and slender, gripping a baby as if she thought he might disappear into thin air, the image was a woman she didn't know. There were no more bruises on her skin, no visible stitches. Short mahogany-colored hair feathered around high, pronounced cheekbones, wary green eyes, arched brows and a straight nose dusted with freckles. A wide, sensual mouth trembled before her lower lip was caught between white, remarkably straight teeth.

Marla Cahill?

Kylie Paris?

Who?

She met Nick's eyes in the reflection, saw his iron will in the set of his jaw, the determination in the thin line of his mouth, the shadow of fear in his eyes. "Let's do this," he urged.

She nodded. Fought the urge to run.

Lies. Her life had all been lies, she thought as, by instinct, she turned right and entered a hallway that was eerily familiar. Her heart thudded, her chest was tight, nervous sweat broke out on her back. "I've been here before," she said to Nick, swallowing hard. "Damn it, I know it."

They stopped at the door of 3-B. The place Kylie Paris called home. Nick knocked, rapping hard.

Not a sound issued from inside. No murmur of the television set, no scuffling of feet, no gasp of surprise, no eye in the peephole, no greeting warning the visitors that an inhabitant was on her way to the door. Nothing but silence. Dead air.

"What now?" Marla asked, standing on worn gray carpeting in this narrow, poorly ventilated corridor. The lights were dim, the whole feeling dingy and colorless. "I don't have a key."

"Then we'll get one from the doorman."

"How?"

Nick scratched at the day's growth of beard on his cheek. "Let's see if he thinks you're Kylie. Give me the baby and go downstairs, insist that you lost your key. See if he lets you in."

"All right," she said, certain that his ploy wouldn't work.

She was wrong. The doorman, who hadn't been at his post when they arrived, offered her a patient smile showing off a gap in his teeth, and produced a key from a locked box in a closet. Pushing seventy, with thick silver hair and an amused expression, he said, "You know, Ms. Paris, you should make a duplicate and hide it somewhere. What would you do if old Pete wasn't here to bail you out?"

"I don't know," she admitted truthfully.

"Sorry to hear about your baby," he added and she froze. "Terrible thing to lose one after carrying it so long." Her insides turned to ice.

"Y—yes," she said, her skin crawling. Had she told this man that her baby had died?

"Well, yer young yet, they'll be more." He raised an eyebrow. "Next time maybe it would be better to get yourself a husband first."

"Would it?" she snapped sarcastically, as if she'd done it a hundred times before.

He didn't so much as flinch. "It's what the Good Book says."

"And doesn't it also say something about 'Judge not, lest ye be judged'?"

"That it does, but me and the missus we've been married nearly fifty years, had our kids all four of 'em afterwards. A baby needs a mother *and* a father, but then, you already know that, I s'pose. Anyway, sorry about the loss."

"Yes. Yes, of course, thank you," she said and knew the

blood had drained from her face. The doorman thought she was Kylie . . . and Kylie had been pregnant . . . oh, dear Lord.

Grasping the precious key, she backed away, then hurried up the shabby stairs rather than wait for the wheezing elevator. On the third floor she ran down the hallway to the door of 3-B where Nick, holding a sleeping James, was waiting.

"See what you can do if you put your mind to it," he said with a smile.

"You wouldn't believe," she whispered and told him her conversation with the doorman as she slid the key into the lock.

She stepped through the door and back in time.

With her first sweeping glance of the tidy apartment, a thousand memories assailed her. She froze, her heart thudding as piece by painful piece the memories of her life came into clear, sharp focus. Clutching the doorknob she saw a green corduroy couch—the couch she recognized that she'd bought at a yard sale. An afghan was thrown across it—knit by her mother, not wasp thin, dour faced Victoria Amhurst, but a warmer woman who smelled of cigarettes and perfume laced with vanilla. Dolly . . . her name had been Dolly. "Mom," she whispered, knowing the woman who had raised her was dead. Her knees threatened to buckle.

She wasn't Marla. Just as she'd suspected. Her name was Kylie Paris. And she'd been driving to Monterey the night of the accident, at the wheel of Pam's Mercedes, in an attempt to find her baby. Dear God, she knew, remembered why she'd been with Pam. Involuntarily she looked at James. Precious, precious child. It began and ended with James. After being released from the hospital, Kylie'd had the fight with Alex, figured out that he and Marla were keeping the baby hidden away in Monterey and asked Pam to help her.

But it had all gone wrong. Somehow the trip had been booby-trapped, as if it had been a setup! Alex had tried to kill her. He had to have been the one . . . and Marla . . . she'd been in on it, too. Kylie felt the blood drain from her face.

"Are you all right?" Tenderness and concern shone in Nick's eyes.

Kylie's stomach clenched and her throat worked. "This . . . this is my home," she said, her voice hoarse, tears filling her eyes. She walked through the rooms remembering the double bed she'd bought with her first paycheck, from the bank where she'd worked before joining the securities firm; the bureau was an antique, she'd refinished it with her own hands; a Tiffany lamp was her prize, she'd paid a small fortune for the colored glass. She ran her fingers over the bureau and stared into the bathroom, pink tile and matching floor mats.

On the frame of the mirror was a magnet.

Whether you think you can or think you can't, you're right.

That saying had become her mantra, the code she'd lived by. And she'd lived here, alone, though there had been men in her life, a succession of lovers who had come and gone . . . Good-time Charlies, the kind of men she would never settle down with, because she had no intention of settling . . . for anything less than the best.

Now, she leaned against the doorframe to the bedroom and saw their handsome, strong faces in her mind's eye. Ronnie. Sam. Benton . . . and there were others . . . but none had touched her as Nick had. None had been near the man, or the lover that he was.

"You'd better sit down," he suggested now, shifting James from one shoulder to the other. "And tell me what's going on."

"I was just remembering," she said, spying a window ledge where the one animal she'd owned, a stray tiger-striped cat with wide green eyes and the ability to destroy every pair of panty hose in her drawers, had often sat. She'd dubbed him Vagabond and he'd left two years after he'd shown up. Kylie had never known what had happened to him, though she'd searched for weeks, calling shelters and friends, neighbors and even the police. The SFPD hadn't been interested, of course, and she'd been left with the painful sensation that even her pet had abandoned her.

"Damn," she whispered, vaguely aware of Nick watching her as she moved through the apartment. She opened a closet door. An array of cleaning supplies and equipment met her eyes.

In that second, with amazing clarity, she recalled the concrete and steel elementary school where she'd shone academically, making up for the fact that she'd been branded a bastard, a girl who didn't know who her father was. She'd matured early, before anyone else in her class, and the older boys had teased her. One even, near the end of the school year, had lured her into a janitor's closet and offered her ten dollars for a peek at the most bodacious breasts in all of Ben Franklin Elementary. It had been a dare and she'd never been one to back down from a challenge.

The closet had been stuffy, lit by a single bulb, surrounded by shelves filled with cleaning supplies, toilet paper and boxes of plastic bags. Three boys and Kylie had been wedged among the mops, trash baskets and fading posters of Farrah Fawcett and Raquel Welch.

"Come on, Kylie, why not?" Ian Perth had asked, his breath stinking, sweat pouring down his fleshy, red face.

"I heard you'd do anything for money," Brent Mallory had added. He was sunburned, his teeth were way too big for his face, his blond hair stuck up at weird angles.

But it had been Lucas Yamhill, a tall, good-looking boy who had nearly convinced her. He was a freshman in high school but hung out with younger kids sometimes. His dad owned the local grocery store and another one in the next town south of San Leandro. "Come on, show us your titties. Ten bucks can buy a lot."

She'd wanted to do it. Just to show creepy Brent and Ian that she wasn't afraid and because she wanted to impress Lucas. She would have loved to have flashed Lucas. Why not? And it was worth ten dollars.

So she had. Right there in that hot, tight closet, she'd lifted her T-shirt, tugged it over her head and let it drop onto the painted cement floor.

Brent whistled through his teeth.

With a flourish, she'd tossed her hair like the models in those shampoo commercials did and it swung free to her shoulders, then didn't move. Her cleavage was visible. That was enough.

"Hey, no fair. You're wearing a bra!" Ian complained, feeling cheated.

"That's right," Brent agreed when he realized he'd been tricked. "I'm not payin' to see that. I've seen my sister parading around in her bra plenty of times."

Lucas's evil leer caused a tingle to race through her blood. "I'll make it twenty if you let me take that off you."

"Twenty-five," she said sassily, beginning to perspire. "And not with those two watching."

"For twenty-five and a private viewing, I want to touch." His eyes, when they looked at her, had darkened from light brown to nearly black and there was another signal in his murky gaze. "I want to touch all of you."

She felt a palpitation between her legs and a flutter of her heart. A billion butterflies took flight in her stomach. "Lose them," she said about Ian and Brent.

"No way. I paid three bucks!" Ian folded his beefy arms over his chest, but Lucas was older and had convinced the others to scram.

Lucas closed the door behind them. The lock clicked into place. Kylie could barely breathe. Slowly Lucas removed two ten dollar bills and a five and placed them on top of an over-turned bucket, smoothing the bills flat. He also pulled out a thin foil packet—one that held a condom—and set it on top. "I'll double it if you strip naked."

"I—I don't know."

"And I'll give you a hundred if you let me—you know. Touch you."

"Touch me?"

"Yeah." His voice lowered. "You know what I'm talking about."

She bit her lip. Shook her head. It was hard to breathe. But she was starting to understand . . . and it scared her.

"Have you ever seen a guy?"

"No."

"I could show you," he offered.

"Would I have to pay?"

His laugh had a dirty ring to it. "Nah. I'd like to touch you with it." He was a big boy, a year older than his classmates, nearly fifteen. Almost old enough to drive. She swallowed hard. She was curious and she liked Lucas. He was popular. Athletic. Rich. "We could . . . you know . . . get it on," he suggested silkily.

"No!"

"I thought you'd do anything for money." Lucas traced the slope of her jaw and went lower down her neck.

She batted his hand away. "Not that."

"I won't hurt you," he whispered.

She thought of the money and of Ian and Brent probably listening on the other side of the door, their ears and eyes pressed to the keyhole. A sick feeling swept over her.

There was something in Lucas's eyes that scared her. Something that tempted her. Something that caused her to breathe a little shallower and her blood to pound in her eardrums.

Her mother's warnings echoed through her brain. "Don't let any boy get into your pants, Kylie. They'll just use you," Dolly had told her. "You could catch something filthy or find yourself in big trouble. I'm way too young to be a grandma!"

When Lucas reached for the button of her jeans, she grabbed his hand. Stopped him short. "No . . . I don't think this would be such a great idea," she said, her voice unrecognizable. She *wanted* him to touch her. She was one of *those* kinds of girls, the kind who *liked* it.

"Oh, come on, Kylie. I want you so bad, baby." He was

touching her and kissing her and her mind was spinning crazily. "And no one will know."

Just the whole universe! Ian and Brent and their big mouths would spread it all over the school. Not to mention Lucas himself. He'd brag to everyone and anyone else who would listen that he'd scored in the janitor's closet!

Lucas kissed her. Hard. His hands opened her jeans. "Just feel good, baby." He shoved a finger between the denim and her skin, groped and touched, squirming to reach lower.

"Don't." She pushed him away and nearly fell into the stack of trash cans. Her heart was thudding, her breathing rapid and she felt a forbidden want deep in the most secret part of her. "No!"

"But—"

"No way." She shook her head and reached for the money, but he snatched it, and his stupid condom up in one fist.

"So you're just a tease," he snarled.

"I didn't say I'd do anything like that!"

"Cunt. Cock tease."

"Get out!" she cried, the horrid words echoing through her brain. Why had she agreed to come into this stupid closet anyway?

"Don't worry. I will."

He adjusted his fly and yanked open the door. Ian and Brent nearly toppled inside. Kylie turned around so they couldn't see her breasts and sweeping her T-shirt off the floor, scrambled into it. She yanked it over her head. Tears streamed down her face.

"Ya get any?" Brent asked Lucas.

"Plenty."

For the next three weeks, until school was out, Kylie's life had been pure hell. Lucas had taunted her. Brent had snickered every time he'd seen her and Ian had avoided her eyes. The rest of the class had found out about her stripping in the closet and the story had been exaggerated a thousand horrid ways. Kylie had somehow managed to walk tall and survive, but the incident had been burned into her memory. Until the crash. All those years ago she'd silently vowed that when she grew up she'd do anything, *anything* to escape the chains of poverty.

And she had. Even going so far as agreeing to give up her baby for the almighty buck.

"Oh, God," she whispered now, tears running down her face as she sat in this tiny apartment which she'd called home for over five years. She looked into Nick's worried eyes. "I'm . . . I'm Kylie Paris," she whispered. Nick had never loved her. They'd never shared any romantic trysts or rendezvous. She swallowed hard, stared into his blue eyes.

"And Marla?" he asked, and the way he said her name made Kylie want to die inside. He loved another woman. Not her. "How is she involved in all this?" He motioned to the small, cozy, lived-in living room with its magazines and crossword puzzle books stacked on the tables.

Kylie sank onto the cushions of her yard-sale couch. "She's my half sister. I—I found out about her about the time I started high school . . . my mother let it slip that Conrad Amhurst was my father, that there was a half brother who was retarded and an older sister who was . . . Conrad's darling." Her throat worked at the thought and remembered the day when tall glasses of iced tea had been sweltering on the small table in their apartment.

"You've known all along?" Kylie had challenged, glaring at her mother as Dolly sat at a small, scarred Formica table, casually leafing through the *Enquirer* while smoking a cigarette.

"I was sworn to secrecy," her mother had admitted.

"About me? About my dad?" Kylie had been outraged. "Why?"

"You were an embarrassment." Dolly, loose blond curls pulled away from her face by a headband, added, "He's rich. Socially prominent. I was an embarrassment too."

"But . . . but . . ." Kylie had leaned against a wheezing refrigerator. "Rich?"

"If you're thinking about getting any of his money, forget

it," Dolly said with acrimony, her husky voice filled with recriminations. "He paid me off a long time ago."

"That's not legal."

"Maybe not, but I signed some document—" She waved her long fingers in the air, disturbing the smoke curling toward the flickering fluorescent lights overhead in the tidy, spartan room. "I don't think I want to take him and his lawyers on. I don't have the time, or the money. It . . . it wouldn't work." She turned a page and tried to bury herself in an article on Princess Diana.

"Then you're a wimp," Kylie declared and snatched up her glass. The ice cubes clinked and she downed the tea in three long swallows.

"I know I'll lose." For the first time Kylie noticed the lines of strain around her mother's eyes, the tired slump of her thin shoulders.

"I wouldn't give up," Kylie declared brashly, condemning the woman who had borne her as weak. "Never."

"Then you're foolish. Or like your father."

"Who is?"

"Conrad Amhurst. He's married. Has a couple of kids with his wife."

"And doesn't want to be bothered with me," Kylie had added, wounded to her soul. She'd known she had a father of course, but hadn't realized he'd lived so close and that he never saw her, either by choice or circumstance. "What kind of a bastard is he?" she asked, then she cringed at the use of the very derogatory term she'd heard about herself.

"Powerful. Harsh. Unforgiving. Relentless."

"He sounds like a jerk."

"He is. But he did give me some money and then there were the hand-me-downs."

"Crap! You mean . . . you mean those dresses you said you got at the church . . . that they were from . . ."

"His daughter. Marla."

"His *real* daughter."

"You are his real daughter," her mother had said, a little of her old backbone resurfacing.

"No, Mom, I'm not. I'm just the bastard. As you said, an embarrassment." But she'd listened to every word as Dolly explained everything then, about being a waitress at an exclusive club and being swept off her feet by the dashing, rich and very married man who had eventually gotten her pregnant. Dolly had known of his children and of a wife who, he claimed, bled him dry and would never ever consider divorce. Dolly had also learned that she hadn't meant a whit to her lover. "He gave me a hundred thousand dollars," she admitted.

"And you blew it."

"We lived on it, damn it, Kylie." Dolly angrily jabbed her cigarette in the overflowing ashtray. "Someday you'll understand."

"Never. I'd never roll over and play dead like you did!" Kylie had gone to her bedroom, thrown open the closet door and hurled all her clothes on the bed, clothes with designer labels that, though a few years old, would rival and outdo any girls' in her school. Skirts and sweaters and blouses that Kylie had worn self-consciously as they were so different from the jeans and T-shirts that her mother had bought at the discount stores.

"You have to know that you mean everything to me," her mother had said, walking up behind her and wrapping her arms around Kylie's waist as outrage burned through Kylie's body, the sting of being unwanted biting deep. "I've always been proud of you and he should be, too. The odd thing is that you look so much like her, like Marla. The Amhurst genes run strong, I guess."

Kylie had refused to cry but had decided to get even. With her father and with that snot of a privileged half sister. But first she had to meet them and to that end she'd devised a plan.

The first of many.

It hadn't taken long. She was barely fifteen when she was able to sneak into the city. With the help of the telephone directory, Kylie had located the offices of Amhurst Limited and gained access as far as her father's offices where a fussy secretary had bluntly told her that Mr. Amhurst was in meetings all day and far too busy a man to see her.

"Then I'll wait," Kylie had insisted and plopped down in a wingback chair in a reception area, while pretending interest in the *Wall Street Journal.* Men in business suits occupied the leather couches and fiddled with the clasps of their briefcases, only to be called one by one through the cherrywood doors emblazoned with gold letters that read, Conrad Amhurst, President. Kylie had waited until her bladder had been ready to burst.

At five minutes after five in the afternoon, she'd been ushered outside by a no-nonsense janitor who had flatly told her to go home.

She hadn't. She'd parked herself on the bench across from the private parking lot. Chewing on red licorice and sipping a Coca-Cola, she watched as the expensive cars rolled away from their designated spaces and took off through the city. Finally, near dark, a sleek black town car with smoky windows purred out of the lot only to drive away. She'd known her father was in there, had seen a man's profile, had imagined him locking eyes with her, only to turn from her.

As if he hated the sight of her.

She'd visited his country club, only to be told by a snooty receptionist that "members only" were allowed in. She'd left messages that were never answered, telephoned his office and home only to have no call returned. It was as if, to Conrad Amhurst, she didn't exist.

Kylie didn't give up.

One Sunday she had the confrontation she'd waited for.

She knew the church he attended, had seen him from afar, with his family, walking into the cathedral-like building one fog-shrouded spring Sunday. Kylie had worn one of Marla's cast-off dresses, a deep green velvet that was too hot, but the nicest of the lot. She'd attended the service, sitting in a pew only a few rows back. Marla had seen her then, their eyes, so like each other's, had locked for a few seconds. Marla was older, but her hair was the same red-brown as Kylie's, her nose as straight, her chin a little sharper, her eyes the same green. It had been spooky, like looking into a mirror that was slightly off, the reflection not quite perfect. Victoria Amhurst had turned as if she'd sensed the intrusion into her perfect life, spied Kylie, whispered something to her husband and then quickly faced the altar, her back ramrod stiff, not so much as another glance being tossed over her shoulder as the organist started to play and the congregation launched into the first hymn. She nudged her daughter and Marla, taking the cue, never looked over her shoulder again. But she knew Kylie was there, staring at her, Kylie had *felt* the other girl's fascination, her curiosity.

After the service, on the church steps, she'd boldly walked up to the family as they were speaking with the minister. Conrad's eyes had cut Kylie to the quick. He'd turned scarlet, made a quick apology to the preacher and with a smile that looked like a grimace, he grabbed her elbow so hard it hurt. Propelling her away from his family, down the steps and into a private sanctuary where cherry blossoms littered the ground and the trees were beginning to leaf, he turned on her. A soft wind had tugged at the hem of Kylie's hand-me-down dress and ruffled the graying strands of Conrad's dark hair as the first drops of rain had begun to fall from the overcast sky.

"I think you'd better leave," he'd whispered in an angry, don't-even-think-about-arguing-with-me tone. His face had been flushed but his lips bloodless. "And never come back to this church again."

"It's a free country," she'd shot back.

The hard finger dug deeper into her arm. "But some people are freer than others. That's a lesson you'd better learn."

"I just want—"

"You get nothing. I've paid for you and paid dearly. Now leave or I'll make your life miserable, a living hell."

"You've done that already," she'd whispered.

"That's where you're wrong. If you think things are bad now, just you wait. You may as well know that if you cross me, you'll regret it for the rest of your life. Now." He reached into his pocket and pulled out his wallet. From within he extracted five one hundred dollar bills. "Take this and buy yourself something nice and never, do you hear me, *never* accost me, or my family again. I won't be bullied or blackmailed or compromised." He'd pushed the crisp bills into her fist and turned on his heel, plowing through the churchyard unaware that pink blossoms were falling on the shoulders of his crisp gray suit or that Kylie would never give up.

Throat tight at his rebuff, Kylie held fast to the money. She thought about going back and making a scene and tossing the bills at Conrad's feet. But she stopped herself. That would accomplish nothing.

She couldn't be so obvious.

To get what she wanted, she decided, she'd have to be sneaky.

And she had been.

Now, memory after memory washed over her, painful insights of her life coming into clear, sharp, and horrid focus. As an adolescent she'd felt cheated. And bitter. Hatred for Marla Cahill, her father's little darling, had burned bright in her chest. After the confrontation at the church, Kylie had seen Marla from afar and sensed that the girl who looked so much like her was as curious as she was about her half sibling. Marla traveled around the world, learned to sail in San Francisco Bay, attended cotillions, shopped in New York and Paris, spent Christmas vacations in Acapulco or the Bahamas or Aspen. She drove her own BMW and attended a prestigious private college her father had endowed with a library.

Kylie had been given cast-offs and icy stares. But once she'd gotten a little of her own back by managing, as she looked so much like her half sister, to dress up in one of Marla's cast-offs and charge an outrageously expensive dress at a small boutique to Conrad Amhurst. When she'd said breezily to the clerk, "Charge it to Daddy," the eager salesgirl, her head filled with the commission she would earn on the floor length, beaded black sheath, had nodded rapidly, telling her that the dress was made for her as she'd rung up the sale.

Somehow Marla had found out, though, to Kylie's knowledge, she'd never ratted on her half sister and had only brought it up again when they were adults, when she'd come to Kylie with her plan.

Now, as she sat on the edge of the worn couch and looked up at Nick holding her son, she felt as if the world had dropped from under her feet. Yes, she'd been a scrappy girl, a stubborn woman, a person who had clawed and fought for everything she'd ever earned. But it had come with a price.

She flopped back on the cushions and stared at the ceiling. "I don't think I was a very good person," she confessed to Nick. "In fact I know I wasn't." She let out a long, deep breath as she thought of all the years she'd been envious of her half sister, of all the nights she'd lain awake thinking *Why me? Why doesn't my father love me?* Or the nights when a harder and uglier emotion had burned in her blood, pure, hot hatred for a privileged half sister who had grown up knowing a father's love. Kylie had fed on that hatred, becoming competitive with a sibling who acted as if she didn't know Kylie was alive.

"The truth is that I hated Marla, wanted to get back at her," Kylie admitted, and remembered seeing Marla again here, in this very apartment.

"So what happened?" Nick asked. "How did you end up living as Alex's wife and pretending to be her?"

"That was a fluke, I think. It only happened because I didn't die in the wreck." Her mind spun backward. "Marla couldn't have children and she found out that our father had changed his will, that he was cutting her out unless she came up with an heir—a boy. Cissy wasn't good enough."

"That's unheard of today."

"Conrad Amhurst lived by his own rules, liked playing games with people," she said. "You said so yourself but he must not have known that Marla had the hysterectomy. Anyway,

Marla approached me about having the baby—*her* son. All I had to do was get pregnant, have the baby and give him up, to pretend that he was hers.'' As she said the horrid words she cringed inside, thought she might throw up. ''I know, I know, it's godawful. I was . . . very self-involved.'' Standing, she walked to Nick and pried James from his arms. Gazing on her baby's precious face, his fuzzy hair and his tiny fingers, Kylie couldn't believe she'd been so heartlessly cold and calculating.

''That was all you had to do?'' Nick said coldly.

''Yes. And keep my mouth shut.'' Holding James she couldn't believe it of herself, but remembered all too clearly the day Marla had suggested the plan. ''Marla had worked it all out, knew that she and I had the same blood type, had even talked a physician into falsifying the records.''

''Robertson.''

''Yeah, a family friend who wanted money funneled into his clinic and Bayview Hospital, as he owns a lot of stock in it.'' Kylie's stomach turned sour as she settled into her favorite recliner, the chair Marla had occupied that fateful evening. She remembered the encounter as vividly as if it had been yesterday.

''I have a proposition for you,'' she'd said as Kylie, surprised to find Marla in the hallway, had opened the door and Marla, in raincoat, umbrella, sunglasses and wide-brimmed hat, had breezed inside. If she found Kylie's habitat unappealing, she'd kept her opinion to herself.

''A proposition?''

''Yes.'' Marla had set her umbrella near the door and pulled off her hat. Hair, cut similarly to Kylie's, had billowed around her face. Marla had stared at her, sizing up her half sister. ''You've always gotten the shaft from Dad and I think I know a way to even the score.'' Her green eyes had narrowed thoughtfully, her finely arched brows knitting.

''Why would you even care?'' Kylie hadn't bought Marla's latent concern. Not for a minute.

''I really don't. Not a lot. But I need your help.''

Now that was something. The powerful and pampered daughter of Conrad Amhurst had *needed* her. For the first time in all of Kylie's pathetic life. Kylie had been wary, but hadn't been strong enough to tell the rich bitch to go to hell and leave her alone.

"She outlined this bizarre plan," Kylie admitted to Nick, shuddering inwardly as she remembered how easily she'd been seduced into going along with the scheme. "She wanted me to get pregnant—artificially inseminated—and, once I was certain I was carrying a son, hide out until she could take him off my hands." Oh, Lord, it sounded so awful now, so horrid. "Marla planned to wear padding for six or seven months, the kind TV actresses wear, first a tiny one, then larger as the pregnancy went on, until I was in labor and it was time to make the switch."

"What if you were carrying a girl?" Nick asked, clearly skeptical.

"That . . . it wasn't an option. She wanted me to terminate, to get an abortion and start again but I refused. I told her if I ended up with a girl, I'd keep her." Kylie turned tortured eyes to Nick. "But you have to understand I didn't want a baby, not even . . . not even this one." Her voice lowered. "And I was so anxious to get back at Marla for all those years she was the princess, I refused to go along with the artificial insemination and of course I upped the ante." Her lips twisted when she remembered how she'd demanded more money from her sister.

"Of course." Nick's face had turned hard as granite. "So you slept with her husband and bargained away your child."

"That's about the size of it," she admitted, her voice cracking. Tears flooded her eyes and throat. Guilt and recrimination tore at her soul. How could she have been so callous? So cold? So heartless? She brushed a kiss across James's downy crown. "I felt that I'd really gotten one over on Marla."

"By sleeping with her husband."

"And doing something she couldn't. I even . . . oh . . . I even think Alex looked forward to our time in bed together. There was something about him, an anger when he . . . well, when he kissed me. It was as if . . . as if he wanted to get back at her. We both had this vendetta against her, or at least that's what it seemed like.'' She shuddered when she thought of the nights she'd spent in Alex Cahill's bed, the satisfaction she'd felt that she was having sex with her spoiled half sister's husband, the pride Kylie had felt that she could give him and her father what Marla was incapable of. She'd finally bested her half sister.

''And you got pregnant,'' Nick said without inflection.

''Yes. Within two months.'' She blinked rapidly. ''We were lucky. As soon as possible, we had tests checking the sex of the fetus and *voilà,* Conrad Amhurst was assured of a grandson.''

''Son of a bitch,'' Nick muttered, his lips flat over his teeth. He walked to the window and peeked through the blinds. ''So you went along with everything.''

''I'd planned to. But then . . . I felt the baby kick and . . . the further into the pregnancy I got, the more I knew I couldn't go through with it. I couldn't give up my child. I couldn't abandon him the way my father abandoned me and . . .'' She frowned at the irony of it all. ''For the first time in my life, as soon as James was born I realized that there was something more valuable than money.''

''Come on Kylie, or Marla, or whoever the hell you are. Don't play this cornball reformed sinner role with me, okay? I'm not buying it. How much were you supposed to get once the old man kicked off?''

She winced.

Nick crossed the apartment and stood over her, his expression dark and filled with contempt. ''Tell me, darlin'. Just how much is Conrad Amhurst's baby worth?''

Closing her eyes as she held James, she said, ''A million. I agreed to do it for a million.''

''Jesus H. Christ.''

''But then—''

''Don't tell me, you wouldn't take a nickel for him,'' Nick sneered and Kylie wanted to die. The heater in the apartment clicked on, blowing hot air and she thought she heard the sound of a door opening in the hall.

"No," she admitted, shaking her head. "I won't lie. I upped the price."

"Holy shit."

"To three million."

"You're unbelievable," he snarled and she knew she was destroying everything they'd shared, every tiny dream of happiness she'd ever had with him.

"What happened? Did they agree to pay you?"

"Eventually." At the time, in Alex's Jaguar, Marla had laughed at her. Alex had been stricken. He'd smoked and driven past Golden Gate Park where Kylie had seen a mother pushing a stroller, the baby sucking on a pacifier and trying to pat a floppy-eared dog tugging at his leash. The mother looked frazzled, trying to deal with baby and dog, but at that moment Kylie had realized she was lying to Marla and Alex. No amount of money would replace the love she felt for this baby growing inside her, the desire to love and be loved back.

"You're worse than she is," Nick accused. "Worse than Marla."

Kylie felt as if he'd slapped her. "Probably," she admitted. "But when I went into labor, I knew. I'd convinced myself before I had the baby that it would be best for him to grow up with two parents, in a lifestyle that few people can have, that Marla and Alex weren't bad parents, lots of kids had worse . . . Oh, yeah, right." She snorted at her own naiveté. "Alex had pointed out that the baby, raised as a Cahill, wouldn't want for a thing, whereas if I were to keep James, he'd be raised in a single-parent household with a woman who was struggling to make ends meet and always working. I'd never see the baby anyway and he would suffer."

"What was your response?"

"I told him to go to hell," she said, remembering the horror on Alex's face as Dr. Robertson had walked into the private room where the labor pains were becoming so intense she couldn't think.

"Did you?"

"For all the good that it did. It was too late by then. I was already about to deliver. Alex told me that if I so much as breathed that I would fight him in court, he'd make my life torture. I wouldn't have a chance to win with the team of lawyers Cahill Limited has at its disposal. They'd take everything from my past, all the mistakes I'd made, twist the facts around and make my life look worse than it was, throw it all in front of the court and prove that I was unfit to be a mother. By that time Conrad would be dead anyway and the money would be gone. The baby would be the biggest loser." Kylie shook her head. "I can't believe that I bought Alex's bill of goods. You know, Alex even pointed out that this way, by giving my baby to Marla to raise, I would finally give my father something the old man had always wanted—a grandson. Is that convoluted thinking or what?" She felt the tears raining down her face. "I'd even convinced myself that I'd have other children, that I could give this baby up."

"But you changed your mind."

"Yes." She looked up at him through the sheen of tears. "Oh yes. The minute I saw James in the hospital, the first time I heard him cry, I realized there was no amount of money that would keep me from him. I would take on the Cahill family and every lawyer they threw my way. I'd go into debt, do anything to keep James." She saw the doubts in Nick's eyes and knew all they had was lost. "Look, Nick, I don't expect you to believe me."

"I don't."

"Fine. You can damned well think anything you want, but that's what happened." Kylie couldn't fight the tears of shame that washed down her face as she looked at her baby, her precious baby, sleeping, blissfully unaware of her pain as he cuddled in her arms. "I'm . . . I'm so . . . sorry," she whispered to him now. Blinking rapidly, dashing away the hated tears with the back of hand, she said, "People have died . . . because of what I've done." Her head ached as all the jagged little pieces of her life came together, reminding her of a time in her life she'd rather forget. She forced her chin upward and met the fury in Nick's eyes with her own angry gaze. "I'm not the woman you thought I was. I'm not Marla."

His smile curved cynically. "And that begs the question. Where the hell is she?"

"I don't know," she said, then rubbed her temple. "No . . . I heard Alex talking to her last night. I'm pretty sure it was her and he said something about her hiding out in the carriage house."

Nick's smile turned to ice. "At the ranch?"

"I don't know."

"I do." He pulled her to her feet. "Let's go."

She wanted to ask, *And what about us,* but didn't. It was over. She could see it in his eyes. "Yes. Let's." She crossed the floor and yanked open the door.

A man was waiting for her, a tall man with brown hair, sunglasses, a goatee and a gun with a silencer pointed straight at her heart.

She froze. "Who are—?"

"Marla," he said in that same horrid voice she recognized from the hospital and again in her room. *Die, bitch!* Those were his words. "What the hell are you doing slumming around these parts?" he asked with a cold, ruthless smile.

"Who are you?" Nick demanded, but in a second he recognized the face. It had altered from the time they were kids, but his heart nearly stopped as he realized he was facing Montgomery Cahill. In a heartbeat Nick knew this man was the killer.

"What's the matter, Cuz? See a ghost?" Monty asked.

Nick sprang.

"No!" Kylie cried, clutching her baby.

Monty pulled the trigger.

Chapter Twenty

Kylie screamed.

The baby wailed.

Nick went down in a heap.

Blood oozed from his stomach.

"You bastard!" Kylie fell down beside Nick, felt for a pulse. "Nick, Nick, please—"

"He's dead."

"No . . . I can't believe."

"Want me to put another slug in him just to make sure?"

Still holding the baby, she sprang to her feet and lunged at Monty. He sidestepped and leveled his gun at her child.

She froze. "You wouldn't."

"Like hell."

Oh, God, he'd kill the baby. Just as he killed Nick. "No, please, don't hurt the baby, but Nick, we can't just leave him."

"Let's go, Marla," Monty insisted, irritation tugging at the corners of his mouth.

"No . . . I'm not who you think I am."

"That's all right, sweetheart, 'cuz, neither am I. Now you

can come quietly with me or I'll kill the kid." His voice was flat. Toneless. He wouldn't hesitate to pull the trigger. She was sure of it.

Kylie had no choice. She looked back to see Nick lying in the hallway, his face white and drawn, his lifeblood spilling onto the shabby carpet. "But we have to call an ambulance, do something, I can't just leave him here . . . Nick . . . Oh, God, Nick . . . I love you."

"Save it, Marla. You don't know the meaning of the word." Montgomery grabbed her arm and yanked her, dragging her toward the service elevator.

"Nick," she cried, horror gripping her heart. She'd lost him just when she'd found him, when she'd discovered who she really was. Now he was dead. Killed. Gunned down. Because of her. "Why did you kill him?" she cried, dying inside. She couldn't lose Nick. Not when she'd just found him, discovered who she really was.

"He was expendable."

"Expendable?" she whispered, clutching her child, sick inside. "No one's—"

"Shut up, cunt," he growled in that same ghastly voice he'd used as he'd loomed over her bed at the house. "Lover boy bought it and now you and me, we're gonna get it on. Just like before. And you're gonna love it, baby." He ran the barrel of his gun down the side of her cheek and she reached for it, but he aimed it straight at her son's head. "Uh, uh, uh. Don't want to see baby's brains blown all over the elevator, do you?"

Kylie nearly threw up. She was shaking, her legs weak. Fear gripped her heart in icy talons. "You're out of your mind," she said as he pressed the button for the basement level and ripped the baby from her arms. She tried to grab James again, but Monty shoved her against the side of the car. The baby screamed.

"Either you come with me quietly, Marla, or I take this kid and I'll either kill him before your eyes or, better yet, I'll leave with him and you'll never know what happened to him, got it? You won't know if he's alive, dead, or if I spend my days torturing him. You'll spend the rest of your life in your own private hell.''

''I'll kill you first!'' she cried, eyeing the alarm on the panel of the car and knowing she'd never use it, never take the chance with her son's life.

Monty's grin was pure evil. ''Try it, bitch.''

She let her arms fall to her sides. ''What—what do you want?''

''Just what you do, Marla. Everything. Every fuckin' thing.'' His gaze raked down her body. ''I want what I deserve.''

Nausea roiled up her throat. ''You tried to kill me. You jumped in front of Pam's car on Highway 17 and then you were in the hospital and in my room. You put some kind of poison in my juice.''

''That was tricky. I had to sneak into your room, but I'd done it before. See, honey, you're smarter than you look.''

She remembered the figure she'd seen in her window. ''You failed,'' she threw back at him, refusing to be intimidated

''Not for long.'' He turned to the baby. ''Shut up, kid. Shut the fuck up!''

''He's just a baby!''

''Not just a baby. Conrad Amhurst's damned grandson. Shit.'' He spat out the words as the car jolted to a stop.

Kylie's head was spinning, her brain trying to come up with some means of escape as he prodded her out the door and into the basement parking garage that smelled of grease and exhaust. ''Here,'' he said, nudging her up a single, concrete flight of stairs and onto the street where the wind ripped around the buildings and the sky was dark as night. She thought of Marla and Alex, Eugenia and Phil Robertson, Cherise and Donald Favier. How many people were in on this deadly plot? How many people had died, all for the sake of Conrad Amhurst's money? Pam Delacroix. Charles Biggs. And now Nick. Precious Nick.

Because of her.

Because of greed.

Because she'd always wanted to be another woman.

Now, as she walked through the blustery morning, she had one eye on the gun Montgomery concealed in his parka, the other on her child. Could she risk screaming for help, snatching her baby away and damning the consequences? No . . . there wasn't enough time.

"Promise me you won't hurt the baby," she begged. "You can take him back to the apartment and leave him there or take a cab and offer to pay the driver to take him and—"

"Shut up!" Monty exploded, his eyes snapping fire. "The kid stays with me."

"But—"

"Get in," he growled as they reached a dark blue Jeep. The vehicle Nick had thought was following them, the one at the church where Donald Favier was a preacher. She had no options. With a sinking sensation, she climbed inside the dirty interior. The stale scent of cigarette smoke mingled with the odor of grease. Old taco wrappers and beer bottles were strewn across the floor of the back seat. "Put your seat belt on," he ordered as he settled behind the steering wheel, holding the squirming, crying baby on his lap. Kylie reached for her child and was rewarded with a smart crack on the wrist with the butt of his pistol.

"No tricks," Monty warned. "Don't try to pull a fast one." He twisted on the ignition with one hand, held the squirming baby in his other. "If I slam on the brakes, the kid is either killed by the air bag or goes through the windshield. Like Pam."

Terror drove a stake in Kylie's heart. She didn't dare move, did everything he said as the engine sparked and James started to cry in earnest. Monty pulled away from the curb and stepped on the gas. The Jeep roared up the hill. The baby wailed and Kylie was helpless to do anything. She thought of Nick. He was probably already dead and soon, soon, her baby would be too. Unless she complied. Or . . . Oh, God, could she go through with it—sleep with this vile killer? Could she pretend to be a woman she was not, just as she'd pretended confusion the night before with Alex? She nearly retched. Nausea roiled up her throat but she knew deep in her heart that she'd do anything to save her son.

Even if it meant seducing the bastard who held James's fate in his filthy, cruel hands.

"What the hell happened here?" Paterno yelled. "Call 911. Get an ambulance!" Paterno was on his knees, feeling for a pulse, sensing that Nick Cahill was about to die in the hallway outside Kylie Paris' apartment. "Hang in there," he said and the guy's eyes fluttered open. Doors opened to the corridor. Janet Quinn was already on her cell phone.

"Kylie," Nick said, reaching up with effort, grabbing Paterno's shirt front and tie in his fist.

"I know about her. Don't talk." The detective opened Cahill's jacket and shirt, saw the dark ring of the bullet hole and the blood still pouring out Cahill's wound. Gunshot. "Who did this to you?" He whipped out his handkerchief and ignoring all those warnings about gloves, tried to staunch the flow of blood.

"Marla . . . Kylie . . . Montgomery," Nick rasped.

"Hell, he's out of it."

"Monty," Nick repeated, his eyes glassing over. "He's got her."

"Who? Where are they? Where's Marla?"

"The ranch . . . Cahill . . . ranch . . . but Kylie . . . you've got to find . . ." Nick passed out.

"The ambulance is on its way," Janet said as she leaned down, felt for a pulse on the hand that had dropped away from Paterno's shirt.

"It had better get here fast." Paterno didn't think Nick would survive. Chalk one more up to the killer.

"Jesus," Janet whispered, more as a prayer than a curse as

she saw the wound and Paterno's blood-soaked handkerchief. "He's not gonna make it."

"You're never gonna get away with this," Kylie said as Montgomery reached into the glove box and pulled out an electronic garage door opener that not only opened the gate of the Cahill estate to swing open but also caused the garage door to crank up. "The house is filled with servants."

"Is it? Well, the old lady is down at Cahill House making plans for the annual holiday party, Lars has been deployed to drive her wherever she needs to go, the teenager's at school, Alex is making arrangements for your father's funeral and the servants that were left were given the day off—because the old man died."

Alone? She was going to be *alone* with him?

"This is how you got into the house," she said, eyeing the garage door opener. "Alex—did he give it to you?"

"Smart girl," Monty said, juggling James. "We'll go in."

"And do what?" she asked. "What is it you want?"

"Money."

"I don't have any."

"But you have access . . . through the computer. All you have to do is make a few transfers." He sent her a glance. "What's a few hundred grand for your kid's life?"

"I can't even log onto the damned thing," she argued. "I . . . I don't know the codes."

"Sure you do. You've done it hundreds of times. I've seen you."

"No, I can't. I'm not Marla."

"Yeah, right. I heard you the first time."

"But it's true. We switched places—"

"Shut up, bitch!"

Desperation tore at her soul. There was no way out of this mess. Monty was certain she was Marla. There was nothing she could do to dissuade him. He assumed she could give him

money from her accounts with Alex, but that was impossible.
Oh, Lord, what could she do? "But I can't remember," she
said.

His hard eyes slitted behind his sunglasses. "I know enough
of the code. You'll remember. Now," he said as he parked his
Jeep in the spot once reserved for Marla Cahill's Porsche, "let's
go." He forced her out of the rig and while he carried the baby,
he kept his gun in his pocket, but trained on Marla. She thought
of flinging herself at him, but that would accomplish nothing
and he would certainly kill her son. She looked for a weapon,
but other than a few old hubcaps on the wall, a vise mounted
on a workbench, and a tire iron that she had no chance of
reaching, there was nothing.

She was doomed. When she couldn't access the files, he'd
get angry and . . . and . . . oh, God, she couldn't think what
might happen to James. The elevator door opened and he half-
shoved her inside. James was fussing loudly now and Monty
was getting irritated. "Shut up," he growled at the baby.

"He's tired."

"Tough. Shut him up."

"Here, let me have him." She reached forward and Monty
slammed her back against the wall of the car, then punched
the bedroom floor with the muzzle of his silencer.

"Keep away."

Maybe a servant would be in the hallway. Maybe Monty
didn't know what was going on in the house, she thought
desperately, grasping at any little straw she could find. Fiona
might still be around and Rosa could be vacuuming or dusting.
Carmen . . . where was Carmen, surely she wouldn't have left
the premises . . . *oh, please God, let someone be here to help
me.* The elevator door opened into an empty hallway. "Let's
go," Montgomery growled as the baby quieted. The corridor
was empty. Lit by a few lamps. No sounds of rattling dishes,
muted conversation or footsteps disturbed the deathly silence.

Monty pushed her into the suite, then locked the door behind
him. "Well, well, well," he said, glancing around. "This place

hasn't changed much, has it?'' His smile was brutal. Dirty. Filled with horrifying promise. ''You and me, we spent some time here. A lot of it.''

Her stomach recoiled at the thought.

''I don't remember.''

''No?'' That stopped him. Beneath his thin moustache, his upper lip curled into a sneer. ''Well, that just won't do, now will it? Maybe I should find a way to remind you.''

Oh, God, this was her chance. If she could find the nerve. Dig deep. Remember the old Kylie, the one with brass balls, the woman who would stop at nothing to get what she wanted. ''And just how do you propose to do that?'' she asked with a lift of her eyebrow.

''I've got my ways.''

''All talk, Monty,'' she said, and he hesitated, obviously didn't believe her ploy.

''We'll see about that,'' he said. ''You just wait here.'' Slowly he placed James on the carpet.

''What are you doing?''

''You'll see.''

''Please, please don't hurt him.''

''I won't. Not if you do what I want.''

''Promise me you won't hurt him,'' she pleaded, terrified to her bones.

''Okay, I promise.'' His eyes glinted malevolently.

She didn't trust him. She was trembling inside, aching to be with her child who was lying by the coffee table. ''Now, you, in here.'' He waved his gun toward her bedroom. ''Come on, Marla.''

Just do what he says. James is safe in here. Maybe someone in the house will come by . . . if anyone was around. Heart in her throat, she walked through the open door and Monty followed inside, to Marla Cahill's bedroom with its perfectly coordinated drapes and bedspread. He glanced at the canopied bed and a slow smile curved over his lips. ''Okay, bitch, this is where it all started between you and me. Maybe it's time to end it here.''

She swallowed her fear and stared at him. "If you think it would be a good idea."

"I think it would be a helluva idea," he said, then, with the gun pointed at her temple, he grabbed her with his free hand, dragged her close and kissed her hard on the lips. He tasted of old smoke and coffee and she wanted to throw up but she closed her eyes and her mind, knowing that if she just got him into the bed, in a compromising situation, she could grab his gun or . . . or reach under the mattress and pull out Alex's pistol.

His hand was rough over her clothes, pawing at her breasts, groping lower. "Come on, baby," he said inching her toward the bed. The back of her knees hit the mattress. "Let's see what you can do. I remember you gave the best head I've ever had."

She moaned though her insides curdled and they tumbled on the bed together. In that moment, she flung one arm out and arched against him. He kissed her hard on the lips and she flipped on the control of the intercom, then held him tight, as if she couldn't get enough of him. Never releasing the gun, he ripped open her shirt with his free hand and rubbed her breasts, pinching her nipples through her bra. She pretended a fever she didn't feel and stripped him of his parka and sweatshirt, running her hands up his ribs to tangle in the springing hairs guarding a thin chest.

"Oh, yeah, baby," he murmured, his eyelids lowering to half-mast, his fingers still tight on the pistol, its nose digging into her throat.

She moved lower and her fingers slid his zipper down over a hard, anxious erection.

I can't do this, she thought wildly, but touched him with her fingers, stroking gently then harder as she heard him groan deep in his throat. *Dear God, help me.* With her free hand she reached over the edge of the mattress, her fingers searching between mattress and box springs, stretching to find the cold metal.

"That's it baby, now suck me," he said and she thought she'd puke all over him.

"Take off your pants," she ordered though her voice shook.

"You do it."

Forcing herself she complied, using both hands. The muzzle of his gun slipped a little. She wiggled, as if really getting into stripping him and as she lowered his jeans, let her fingers trail over the inside of his thigh.

"That's it, that's it," he growled. She slid one hand to the edge of the bed again, found the gun, and, sweating, certain he would figure out what she was doing, worked hard, inching it toward the edge of the mattress until she was able to pry it free. His fingers loosened over his own pistol, though he still held it. But no longer was it pressed to her throat. She said something dirty against his thigh. "You know I want it," she rasped. "No one was ever as good as you, Monty. I just didn't want to believe it."

"Prove it. Suck me."

Help me, she silently prayed, adjusting herself and using all the energy she could muster, drew her knee up swiftly. Hard. Connected with his testicles.

He bellowed in pain and curled into a ball. His gun fell off the bed. "You fucking bitch!" he gasped, scrabbling for his weapon.

Kylie yanked Alex's pistol free and clicked off the safety.

"You bitch! You're gonna pay!" he cried as he reached over the edge of the bed and his fingers curled over his gun.

Kylie didn't wait. At point blank range, she pulled the trigger. Crack!

The gun went off. Monty's arm exploded. He shrieked in pain. Blood and bits of bone sprayed over the bed, over Kylie, onto the wall and on the lacy canopy. Monty rolled away from her, blood pouring from the wound in his arm.

Somewhere nearby the baby screamed and there were footsteps racing, thundering through the house. Finally, help was on the way.

Sobbing, gasping, forcing herself from the horrid bed, Kylie trained her weapon on Monty. Naked, he managed to get to his feet, then as he took a step, the jeans bunching at his ankles, acting like shackles, held him fast. "Don't even think about it," she ordered, ready to fire again though the gun wobbled in her hand. He sank to the floor, dragging in breaths and moaning in pain.

"Don't move."

With a groan he passed out.

Her feet landed on the carpet as the door burst open.

Then all her bravado fled.

She was standing, half naked, face to face with her half sister, the woman she'd envied all her life. And Marla wasn't alone. In her arms, blinking and crying, was Kylie's son, James.

"Wha—what are you doing here?" she asked.

"This is my house."

"But—"

"I came for my son, Kylie."

"Don't take him away from me," she begged as Alex slipped through the door.

"Too late, Kylie." His smile was cold as ice, the shotgun in his hand deadly as he lifted it to his shoulder and sighted on Kylie. "The way I see this scenario is your lover, Montgomery over there, and you tried to steal our son, to kidnap and ransom him. Everything went wrong. Montgomery tried to double-cross you and you killed each other."

Kylie turned her gun toward Alex, who laughed.

"That's it, go ahead, try to shoot me or Marla . . . it'll only add credence to my story that I had to kill you to protect my home and family. And remember, the baby might get hurt with all the bullets flying. I don't think that's a chance you're willing to take."

"Why did you do all this?" she asked, anger and fear raging inside her.

"Did you ever really think I'd give this baby to you?" Marla asked.

"I figured you were in on this."

"From the start. You've always been a thorn in my side. It killed me to have to ask you to conceive my baby." Marla had cut her hair to the same length as Kylie's and they looked enough alike that few people could tell them apart. It was all so sick.

"How did you know where I was going that night . . . after we had the fight in the foyer?" Kylie asked, trying to stall, to come up with some plan to wrest her child from Marla and break free.

"Don't you think we knew you'd take the bait and drive down to Monterey?" Alex asked. "Jesus, we set that up, too. I made it look like Marla called me. I knew you'd figure it out, that you over heard the conversation—at least half of it—and that you'd call the automatic callback service and find out that the call had been from the bed and breakfast."

"But you weren't there, were you?" Kylie asked, her gaze turning to Marla, as she remembered the call.

"No. Montgomery did the honors. The minute you left Alex called him back and he took up his position on Highway 17." Marla's eyes gleamed as if she'd just won a very important game.

"But I could have taken another route," Kylie argued.

"But we followed," Marla said. "Alex, James and me. In a rental car. We followed you down to Haight Street and saw you get into Pam's Mercedes. From there it was easy—just call Monty and get him into position. Pam was a bonus. We were going to have to deal with her, too, since she was your attorney of choice and was not only going to help you in court but write the damned book. Even though you didn't die in the accident, at least we got her out of the way."

Kylie's fingers curled on the bloody bedspread. Was there no way out of this mess. Think, Kylie. Think! "Why would Monty want to kill me?"

"Not you," Alex said. "*Marla.* He wanted to kill Marla for

betraying him and he needed money. Monty had himself a pretty expensive cocaine habit.''

Kylie dropped her head in her hands, but again, she knew she couldn't give up, couldn't let them win. She was thinking fast, trying to come up with a way to snatch the gun from Alex and still save James. "And Cherise was in on this?''

"She had no idea," Marla said with a mirthless laugh. "But then she always was a fool. Just like her stupid brother. I used him, you know. When Alex wasn't interested in me, I used Monty to get back at him.''

"You really can be a bitch," Alex said, but there was a note of fondness and pride in his voice that Kylie found disgusting. They were all sick. Twisted. "Okay, now, we've got to use the .38." He kicked the gun toward Marla. "You do it. Go stand by Monty and shoot at her.''

Marla sucked in her breath. "I can't.''

"You have to.''

"No, Alex. I . . . I can't pull the trigger.''

"For Christ's sake!''

He stepped forward. A muffled shot reported. Alex's body jerked wildly and he fell to the floor, dropping the shotgun.

"No!" Marla screamed. Monty, one hand holding his gun, fell back again, his eyes closing.

Kylie lunged for the shotgun, grabbed it and rolled to her feet. She trained it on Monty but the man didn't move. She crossed the room and kicked the pistol into the bathroom, then with her weapon still trained on Monty, she backed up, nearly tripping over Marla, who had fallen to the floor and was huddled over her husband. "Give me my son," Kylie ordered.

"But Alex, he's wounded.''

"Let him bleed to death. Give me my son!" Kylie was standing over Marla and she reached down and yanked James from the other woman's arms. Marla was sobbing now, crying and cradling Alex's head on her lap while blood gurgled over his lips. The baby cried fitfully, but Kylie held him fast.

"This is all your fault!" Marla screamed up at her.

"That's where you're wrong," Kylie said. "It's all yours."

There were footsteps on the stairs, then running down the hallway. *Thank God!* The door to the suite banged open. Tom flew into the room. He stood horrified, eyeing the bloody, rumpled bed, Kylie's state of undress, Alex and Marla and the naked wounded man crumpled in the corner. "What the hell—"

"Call the police!" Kylie ordered as Monty moaned and Alex's breaths rattled wet and ragged in his lungs.

Tom didn't move.

"Oh, God, honey, don't die," Marla sobbed brokenly to Alex. "Not now. Not when it's all ours."

Monty rolled over, trying to struggle to his feet. "Take one step you son of a bitch and I swear, I'll blow you away!" Kylie warned sharply, then to Tom, "Call the damned police. Now!"

"They . . . They're on their way," Tom said, his face ashen. "I heard everything on the intercom when I walked into the kitchen and I called 911. I—I have medical supplies in my room."

"Then get them."

"You'll be okay?"

"Yes! Go!" The words sank in and Tom dashed out of the room. Somewhere in another part of the house Coco barked. An ambulance's siren wailed from far down the hill. Alex gave a final rasping breath. Marla sobbed brokenly, tears raining from her eyes. Montgomery groaned, the bones of his forearm shattered, all the fight seeming to have finally left him.

"What was it you told me? That you wanted everything? That you deserved it?" Kylie snarled at Monty, the gun shaking in her fingers as she kept it pointed at his pathetic naked body. "Well, it looks like you're going to finally get what you deserve, and its going to be hell." She glanced down at her half sister. Tears streamed down Marla's face, ruining her mascara and eyeliner as she tried to will life into her dying husband's body.

"Alex, please don't die"

Kylie, standing over her half sister, held James close. She almost felt sorry for Marla Amhurst Cahill.

Almost.

But not quite.

Nearly three hours later, Kylie sat at Nick's bedside in the intensive care unit at Bayside Hospital. He didn't move and the tubes running in and out of his body reminded her how frail life was.

"You can't die," she warned him, linking her fingers through his and battling hot tears that threatened her throat and eyes. "Do you hear me, you can't die!"

"Mrs. Cahill, there's someone to see you," the nurse said.

"I don't want to see anyone. And my name isn't Mrs. Cahill. It's Kylie. Kylie Paris." And she loved Nick. No matter what, she couldn't bear the thought of losing him. "You hang in there," she said, squeezing his hand.

"It's the police," the nurse clarified. "Detective Paterno."

Kylie looked up and through the glass she saw the detective's hound-dog face staring at her.

"I'll be right back," she told Nick, though she knew he couldn't hear her.

She hurried through the doorway and nearly ran into the policeman. "Can't I make a statement later?" she said, glancing back through the meshed glass to Nick.

"That's not why I'm here."

"Then what? Oh, God, it's not the baby." Panic stormed through her.

"No, no. As far as I know he's still with his grandmother and the nanny. He's fine. Eugenia had to be sedated, but the nanny, Fiona, she's a plucky thing. She and Carmen are holding down the fort." Paterno shoved a stick of Juicy Fruit into his mouth. "How's Nick doin'?" he asked, nodding toward the window.

"He's supposed to be okay," Kylie said, though she wasn't

convinced. "The bullet went through his spleen and they operated a couple of hours ago. The surgeon told me he would pull through, but . . ." She cast a worried glance over her shoulder. "He's not waking up."

"He'll make it. He's tough as old leather," Paterno predicted. "Now, I think you should come with me. There's someone I think you might want to talk to."

"Marla," she whispered, and a new, hot fury burned through her blood when she considered the sister who had suggested the baby scam in the first place, the woman Kylie had always wanted to best, the enemy who had tried to have her killed. Because of Marla and Alex's blind, self-centered ambition, Pam Delacroix and Charles Biggs had died unnecessarily, Alex himself had breathed his last, Conrad Amhurst had left this world a little earlier than he should have, and Nick was fighting for his life.

"Yeah. Now that her husband is dead she's talking, though she wants a lawyer. She admitted to the fake pregnancy scam and that they were lucky that you lost your memory, then they kept drugging you so that you wouldn't recall anything. They only tripped up a couple of times."

"The ruby ring."

"She mentioned that." Paterno nodded. "Alex put it back in your jewelry box the next day."

"And I thought I was going nuts."

"She didn't know how you broke into the office, though."

"I stole my mother-in-law's keys . . . was she in on this?"

"Nah! Clean as a whistle. Horrified by the whole mess. She knew Alex and Marla were having problems, and that the company was in trouble, but she had no idea how far it had all gone. I spoke with her and she was upset, but that nurse, Tom, he gave her a sedative and was seeing to her."

"Good. What about Dr. Robertson?"

"We're still talking to him, but he's a big part of this, probably end up losing his license and doing time. As for the man you thought was your husband, Alex had already stopped by the nursing home earlier today and made arrangements for Conrad Amhurst. He'd already called his attorney, was anxious to get the estate probated and fast. But I guess that's all water under the bridge now. The lawyers will have to battle it out.''

"I just wish it was over," she said.

"It will be. Someday." Paterno slanted her a look. "This was all about money, you know. The Cahills were nearly broke, Alexander had lost a bundle in the market and other investments, then his hush money—to Reverend Favier—"

"The Reverend Donald," Kylie muttered.

"Yes, to him and to Monty and to Phil Robertson all added up. The donations to this hospital and Cahill House were lavish, all hush money. Alex's only chance to pull out of it was for Marla to inherit. When you balked at letting him and Marla keep the baby, he faced financial ruin. He couldn't allow that and hired Monty to kill 'Marla,' as they'd had an affair a few years back and she'd tossed him over. Even Monty was duped. He didn't know that you weren't the woman he was trying to kill until he saw her walk into the bedroom earlier today.''

"Where is he?"

"Another hospital. Under guard. His right arm will never be the same, but it won't matter. The way I figure it, he'll be locked up for the rest of his life and maybe then some. His sister is with him. Shocked, of course, but praying for his soul.'' Paterno snorted. "She's gonna have to come up with a lotta Hail Marys and Our Fathers to get the guy upstairs to find forgiveness for Montgomery's black soul."

"I don't think the Holy Trinity of God church employs the rosary."

"Maybe they'd better start. It works for us Catholics."

They took the elevator to the basement parking garage and Paterno led her to a squad car. "This isn't normal procedure you understand."

"But then you're not exactly a 'by the book' kind of cop, right?"

"You got it." She looked through the window and found herself staring at her half sister.

"You two sure look alike," Paterno observed.

"A curse."

Marla's eyes thinned in a silent, horrid fury. Her makeup had long since faded and if looks could kill, Kylie would already be six feet under. "Got anything you want to say to her?" Paterno asked, and Kylie shook her head.

"It's all been said," Kylie thought aloud, and all the envy she'd once held for Marla turned to pity and disgust. "I need to be upstairs with Nick."

"Just thought you'd like a chance to tell her what you think."

"Later. In court."

Marla glared through the glass, her pretty mouth pulled into a sneer of disapproval, and though Kylie couldn't hear the words she spouted, the one she recognized was "bastard." The barb used to hurt. Now she didn't care.

"Take her away," Paterno said to the officer in charge.

He couldn't see, couldn't speak, couldn't . . . oh, God, he couldn't move his hand. He tried to pry open his eyes but his eyelids wouldn't budge. They weighed a ton and seemed glued shut over eyes that burned with a blinding, hideous pain.

"Nick?"

There was a touch, someone's cool fingers on the back of his hand. "Nick, can you hear me?" The voice, kind and female, sounded as if it carried from a great distance . . . far away, from a spot on the other side of the pain.

It was Marla's voice, no, not Marla, Kylie's.

He forced his eyes open and stared into eyes as green as a forest at sunrise. Pain blasted through his abdomen but he managed a thin smile as her tears rained on him. "Where ya been?" he croaked.

"I was just wondering that about you." She sniffed loudly. "You had me scared, Cahill, real scared."

"Are you okay?"

"Are you?" She eyed his face. "You look like hell, you know."

"I feel worse."

She laughed and linked her fingers through his. "Thank God, you're tough as nails."

"I'm just glad to be back, Marla," he said and saw the smile fall from her face. Then, when her eyes found his again, they narrowed.

"That's not funny."

"Sure it is, Kylie."

"I don't know where you get your sense of humor," she grumbled, and he reached upward, surrounded her nape with his fingers and drew her face down to within inches of his.

"Well, darlin'," he drawled, smelling her perfume. "Don't worry about it. I'm the outlaw, remember?"

"How could I forget?"

"You can't," he said with a crooked, wicked smile. "Because as soon as I get out of this place, you and me, we're gonna take the baby and Cissy up to Oregon to live and leave all this mess behind. Mother can come if she wants to, but it's my bet she won't."

"I thought you were mad at me," she said, trying to hold on to her soaring emotions.

"I was. But I've done a lot of thinking. We can have a good, no, make that great, life together."

"You've been in surgery and recovery. You didn't have much time to think."

"Didn't need it." He winked at her and she melted. "I hate to admit it, but I was wrong when I said you were worse than Marla, Kylie. I knew you were different from the get-go and I've seen you with the baby and with Cissy and . . . with me . . ."

"Oh, did you?" She wasn't convinced, though she wanted desperately to be so.

He managed a smile. "Oh, yeah, I did and I fought it, told myself that you were playing me for a fool."

She rolled her eyes. "Is that possible?"

"Unfortunately, it's been done before. Anyway, I guess I'm trying to tell you that I love you, Kylie Paris, and I know you did a lot of rotten things and feel guilty as hell for them, but I think, from the moment you had that baby, you changed."

Her throat was thick and she blinked hard. "You do, do you?"

"Absolutely. You evolved into the woman you are today, the woman I fell in love with."

"What do you know?"

"Just that you're not Marla, you're Kylie and I've never felt like this before. Not with any other woman. I would never have fallen in love with Marla again, Kylie. You're gentler, more caring and yet you have a tough side . . . you're not the woman I thought you were and that's why I love you," he said again, his blue eyes sincere, his gaze scraping against her heart.

This time she believed him. "And I love you," she whispered.

"I know you do, darlin'. And that's something I'm never going to let you forget."

Dear Reader,

I've got some great news! You just read IF SHE ONLY KNEW and I hope you liked it. ALMOST DEAD, the sequel to IF SHE ONLY KNEW, is now available.

You already met rebellious teenager Cissy Cahill. Well, she's back in ALMOST DEAD. The story starts ten years after IF SHE ONLY KNEW. In the intervening years, Cissy has grown up, dropped her bad attitude, and gained a handsome, irreverent husband. On top of that, she has a brand new baby who is her pride and joy. She should be blissfully happy, right? The trouble is that her past is back to haunt her. If it isn't hard enough to be a new mother, her marriage to Jack Holt is in a major crisis. Worse yet, another killer is stalking the Cahill family! Cissy's scared out of her mind. Everything she believed in is falling apart. She also has to deal with Anthony Paterno of the San Francisco Police Department, the same man who investigated her family in IF SHE ONLY KNEW.

ALMOST DEAD was such a fun story to write! Not only did I get to bring back Cissy and Paterno (who also appeared in FATAL BURN), but I was able to set the book in one of my favorite cities, San Francisco. In fact, the Cahill House on Mount Sutro is patterned after a friend's four-story home on that very hill. I've actually stayed in the upper story with its old, watery glass, and incredible view of the bay!

I think you'll like ALMOST DEAD. To read an excerpt, just turn the page or log onto *www.lisajackson.com*. My Web site also features a new contest and information about both books.

Thanks for reading IF SHE ONLY KNEW, and please pick up a copy of ALMOST DEAD. You won't be disappointed!

Keep reading,
Lisa Jackson

A WOMAN WHO WANTS TO GET EVEN . . .
The first victim is pushed to her death. The second suffers a
fatal overdose. The third takes a bullet to the heart. Three
down, more to go. They're people who deserve to die. People
who are in the way. And when she's finished, there will be no
one left . . .

WILL DO WHATEVER IT TAKES FOR REVENGE . . .
Cissy Cahill's world is unraveling fast. One by one, members
of her family are dying. Cissy's certain she's being watched.
Or is she losing her mind? Lately she's heard footsteps when
there's no one around, smelled a woman's perfume, and
noticed small, personal items missing from her house. Cissy's
right to be afraid—but not for the reason she thinks. The truth
is much more terrifying . . .

INCLUDING MURDER . . .
Hidden in the shadows of the Cahill family's twisted past is a
shocking secret—a secret that will only be satisfied by blood.
And Cissy must uncover the deadly truth before it's too late,
because fear is coming home . . . with a vengeance . . .

Look for ALMOST DEAD
in bookstores
everywhere!

Prologue

Bayside Hospital, San Francisco, CA, Room 316
Friday, February 13
NOW

They think I'm going to die.

I heard it in their whispered words.

They think I can't hear them, but I can and I'm listening to every single syllable they utter.

"No!" I want to scream. "I'm alive. I'm not giving up. I will fight back."

But I can't speak.

Can't utter one damned word.

My voice is stilled, just as my eyes won't open. Try as I might, I can't lift the lids.

All I know is that I'm lying in a hospital bed and I know that I'm barely alive. I hear the whispers, the comments, the soft-soled shoes on the floor. Everyone thinks I'm in a coma, unable to hear them, to respond—but I know what's going on. I just *can't move; can't communicate. Somehow, I have to let them know. My condition is bad, they claim. I understand the terms 'ruptured spleen,' 'broken pelvis,' 'concussion,' 'brain trauma,' but, damn it, I can hear them. I feel the stretch of skin at the back of my hand where the IV pulls, smell the scents of perfume, medicine, and resignation. The stethoscope is ice cold, the blood-pressure cuff too tight, and I try like hell to show some sign that I'm aware, that I can feel. I try to move, just lift a finger, or let out a long moan, but I can't.*

It scares me to death.

I'm hooked up to machines that monitor my heartbeats and breathing and God-Only-Knows what else. Not that it does any good. All the high-tech machines that are tracking body functions aren't providing the hospital staff with any hope or clue that I know what's going on.

I'm trapped in my body, and it's a living hell!

Once again I strain . . . concentrating to raise the index finger of my right hand to point at whomever enters the room. Up, I think, raise the tip up off the bedsheets. The effort is painful . . . so hard.

Isn't anyone watching the damned monitor? I must *be registering an elevated pulse, an accelerated heartbeat, some-damn-thing!*

But no.

All that effort. Wasted.

Worse yet, I've heard the gossip; some of the nurses think I would be better off dead . . . but they don't know the truth.

I hear footsteps. Heavier than the usual. And the vague scent of lingering cigar smoke. The doctor! He's been in before.

"Let's take a look, shall we?" *he says to whoever it is who's accompanied him, probably the nurse with the cold hands and cheery, irritating voice.*

"Oh, she's still not responsive." *Sure enough, the chipper one.* "I haven't seen any positive change in her vitals. In fact . . . well, see for yourself."

What! What does she mean? And why does her voice sound so resigned? Where's the fake peppy inspiration in her tone?

"Hmmm," *the doctor says in his baritone voice. then his hands are on me. Gently touching and lifting, poking, Then lifting my eyelid and shining a harsh beam directly into my lens. It's blinding and surely my body will show some response. A blink or flinch or . . .*

"Looks like you're right," *he says turning off the light and backing away from the bed.* "She's declining rapidly."

What? No! That's wrong! I'm here. I'm alive. I'm going to get better!

I can't believe what I'm hearing and should be hyperventilating, should be going into cardiac arrest at the words. Can't you see that I'm stressing? Don't the damned monitors show that I'm alive and aware and that I want to live? Oh, God, how I want to live!

"The family's been asking," *the nurse prods.* "About how long she has."

No! My family? They've already put me in the grave? That can't be right! I don't believe it. I'm still alive, for God's sake. How did I come to this? But I know. All too vividly I can remember every moment of my life and the events leading up to this very second.

"Doctor?" *the nurse whispers.*

"Tell them twenty-four hours," *he says solemnly.* "Maybe less."

Chapter One

Four Weeks Earlier

Click!

The soft noise was enough to wake Eugenia Cahill. From her favorite chair in the sitting room on the second floor of her manor, she blinked her eyes open. Surprised that she'd dozed off, she called out for her granddaughter. "Cissy?" Adjusting her glasses, she glanced at the antique clock mounted over the mantle as gas flames quietly hissed against the blackened ceramic logs. "Cissy, is that you?"

Of course it was. Cissy had called earlier and told Eugenia that she'd be by for her usual weekly visit. She was to bring the baby with her . . . but the call had been hours ago. Cissy had promised to be by at seven, and now . . . well, the grandfather clock in the foyer was just pealing off the hour of eight in soft, assuring tones. "Coco," Eugenia said, eyeing the basket where her little white scruff of a dog was snoozing, not so much as lifting her head. The poor thing was getting old, too, already losing teeth and suffering from arthritis. "Old age is a bitch," Eugenia said, and smiled at her own little joke.

Why hadn't Cissy climbed the stairs to this, the living area, where Eugenia spent most of her days? "I'm up here," she said loudly; and when there was no response, she felt the first tiny niggle of fear, which she quickly dismissed. An old woman's worries, nothing more. Yet, she heard no footsteps rushing up the stairs, no rumble of the old elevator as it ground its way upward from the garage. Pushing herself from her Queen Anne recliner, she grabbed her cane and walked stiffly to the window, where through the watery glass she could view the street and the city below. Even with a bank of fog slowly drifting across the city, the vista was breathtaking from most of the windows. This old home had been built on the highest slopes of Mount Sutro in San Francisco at the turn of the century; well, the turn of the *last* century. The old brick, mortar, and shake Craftsman-style house rose three full stories above a garage tucked into the hillside. From this room on the second story, she was, on a clear day, able to see the bay and had spent more than her share of hours watching sailboats out across the green-gray waters.

But sometimes this old house seemed so empty. An ancient fortress with its electronic gates and overgrown gardens of rhododendron and ferns.

Oh, she had servants, of course, but the family had, it seemed, to have abandoned her.

Oh, for God's sake, Eugenia, buck up. You are not some sorry old woman. You choose to live here, as a Cahill, as you always have.

Maybe she'd just imagined the click of a lock downstairs. Dreamed it, perhaps. These days, though she was loathe to admit it, her dreams often permeated her waking consciousness and she had a deep, unmentioned fear that she might be in the early stages of dementia. Dear Lord, she hoped not! There had been no trace of Alzheimer's in all of her lineage; her own mother had died at ninety-six and had still been "sharp as a tack" before falling victim to a massive stroke. Eugenia's gaze wandered to the street outside the electronic gates, to the area where the unmarked police car had spent the better part of twenty-four hours. Now the Chevy was missing from its parking spot just out of range of the streetlight's bluish glow.

How odd.

Why leave so soon after practically accusing her of helping her daughter-in-law escape from prison? After all the fuss—rude detectives showing up at her doorstep and practically insisting that she was a harboring a criminal or some such rot—they'd camped out at her doorstep watching the house and (she suspected) discreetly following her when Lars drove her to her hairdresser, bridge game, or Cahill House. At the last, she offered her time by administering sanctuary for unmarried pregnant teens and twentysomethings.

Of course the police had discovered nothing.

Because she was totally innocent. Still, she'd been irritated.

Staring into the night, Eugenia was suddenly cold. She saw her own reflection, a ghostly image of a tiny woman backlit by the soft illumination of antique lamps, and was surprised how old she looked. Her eyes appeared owlish behind her glasses with the magnifying lenses that had aided her since the cataract surgery a few years back. Her once-vital red hair was a neatly coiffed 'do closer in color to apricot than strawberry blond. She seemed to have shrunk two inches and now appeared barely five feet tall, if that. Her face, though remarkably unlined, had begun to sag—and she hated it. Hated this growing old. It was just such a pain! She'd considered having her eyes "done" or her face "tightened"; had even thought about Botox, but really, why?

Vanity?

After all she'd been through, it seemed trivial.

And so she was over eighty. Big deal. She knew she was no longer young—her arthritic knees could attest to that—but she wasn't yet ready for any kind of assisted living or retirement community. Not yet.

Creeeeaaaak!

A sound of a door opening?

Her heartbeat quickened.

The last noise was *not* a figment of her imagination. "Cissy?" she called again and glanced over at Coco, barely lifting her groggy little head at the noise, offering up no warning bark. "Dear, is that you?"

Who else?

Sunday and Monday nights she was usually alone, her "companion" Elsa usually leaving the city to stay with her sister and the day maid leaving at five. Lars was off every night at seven unless she requested his services, and she didn't mind being alone, usually enjoying the peace and quiet. But tonight . . .

Using her cane, she walked into the halllway that separated the living quarters from her bedroom. "Cissy?" she called down the stairs, feeling like a ninny. For God's sake, was she getting paranoid in her advancing years?

But a cold finger of doubt slid down her spine, convincing her otherwise; and though the furnace was humming, she felt a chill icy as the deep waters of the bay settle into her bones. She reached the railing, held onto the smooth rosewood banister, and peered down to the first floor. She saw, in the dimmed evening lights, the polished tile floor of the foyer, the Louis XVI inlaid table, and the Ficus tree and jade plants positioned near the beveled glass by the front door.

Just as they always were.

But no Cissy.

"Odd," Eugenia thought and rubbed her arms. Odder yet that her dog was so passive. Coco, though old and arthritic, still had excellent hearing and was usually energetic enough to growl and bark her adorable little head off at the least little sound. Now she lay listlessly in her bed near Eugenia's knitting bag, her eyes open but dull. Almost as if she'd been drugged . . .

Oh, for heaven's sake! She was getting away from herself and letting her fertile imagination run wild. She gave herself a swift

mental kick. That's what she got for indulging in an Alfred
Hitchcock movie marathon for the past five nights!

So where the hell was Cissy?

Reaching into the pocket of her jacket for her cell phone, she
realized the damned thing was missing, probably left on the
table near her knitting needles.

Turning toward the sitting room, she heard the gentle scrape
of a footstep, leather upon wood.

Close by.

The scent of a perfume she'd nearly forgotten wafted to her
nostrils and made the hairs on the back of her neck rise.

Her heart nearly stopped as she looked over her shoulder and
saw movement in the shadows of the unlit hallway near her bedroom. "Cissy?" she said again, but her voice was the barest of
whispers, and fear caused her pulse to pound. "Is that you,
dear? This isn't funny—"

Her words died in her throat.

A woman, half-hidden in the shadows, emerged.

Eugenia froze, suspended in time.

"You!" she cried as panic swarmed up her spine. The woman
before her smiled a grin as cold and evil as Satan's heart.

Eugenia tried to run, to flee; but before she could take a step,
the younger woman was upon her, strong hands clutching, athletic arms pulling her off her feet.

"No!" Eugenia cried. "No!" She tried to fend off her attacker
with her cane, but the damned walking stick fell from her hands
and clattered uselessly down the stairs! Nearby, Coco began to
bark wildly.

Oh, God.

"Don't do this!" Eugenia cried.

But it was too late.

In a heartbeat, she was hoisted over the railing, pushed into the
open space where the crystal chandelier hung. Screaming, flail-
ing pathetically, her dog still snarling loudly, Eugenia hurled
downward.

The Louis XVI table and tile floor of the foyer rushed up at her.

Sheer terror caused her heart to seize as she hit the floor with a dull, sickening thud. *Crack!* Pain exploded in her head. For half a second she stared upward at her assailant standing victoriously on the landing, holding Coco and stroking the dog's furry coat; and then there was only darkness . . .